ROB BENVIE

MAINTENANCE

Coach House Books, Toronto

first edition

  Canadä

Published with the generous assistance of the Canada Council for the Arts and the Ontario Arts Council. Coach House Books also acknowledges the support of the Government of Canada through the Canada Book Fund and the Government of Ontario through the Ontario Book Publishing Tax Credit.

This is a work of fiction. Any resemblance to any persons living or dead is purely coincidental.

LIBRARY AND ARCHIVES CANADA CATALOGUING IN PUBLICATION

Benvie, Rob, 1975-
    Maintenance / Rob Benvie.

ISBN 978-1-55245-251-6

    I. Title.

PS8603.E58M35 2011   C813'.6   C2011-904943-0

Maintenance is also available in ebook format: ISBN 978 1 77056 295 0

For a book-club guide to this and other Coach House titles, please visit www.chbooks.com/bookclubs

For my mother

'Don't be fooled,
By flowers and waves:
They're your family.'

       – Arthur Rimbaud, 'Golden Age'

'Not long ago when things were slow
We all got by with what we know
The end is near
Hearts filled with fear
Don't want to listen to what they hear.'

       – Bad Brains, 'Pay to Cum'

'Even when I was little, I was big.'

       – William 'Refrigerator' Perry

THE SPIRIT THAT PLAGUED US SO

Five storeys below, the Senegalese girls grow sweatier with each stroke. In midday's swelter their heels dance over green clay, crossing baselines to backcourt, Reeboked soles bouncing and pivoting. As one of the girls flubs a return, her opponent seizes the opportunity to angle a purple squeeze bottle over her head and, arching her back at a greedy angle, drenches her face in water. The runoff from her chin soaks the second skin of her Lycra sport top, which, while also purple, is not precisely colour-coordinated with the purple of the bottle.

From his distant perch on the Atlanta Smithson International's south balcony, surveying not just the expansive tennis courts but also the crowded cabana lounge and concrete poolside deck beyond, Parker Sweltham can't actually feel the moisture trickling down the girl's jutting collarbone, or detect the sweaty warmth of her underarms or her buttocks' cleavage, or inhale the reek he imagines in her damp ankle socks, or listen to her carbureted breath while she readies her next serve. From here, high above, the squeaks of her sneakers are mere blips. But he can somehow imagine these surfaces and scents as interchangeable with, or part of, the crush of sun-slaked Atlanta's heat, its taxis and the subdued tones of its offices' decor, the eagerness of its profit motives and its voices filling his phone with brusque messages, squawking logistics and demands. The girl in the purple sport top plucks a fresh Wilson from a plastic bucket and bounces it against the court. At the other end, her foe, markedly more wiry and stylistically inelegant in her play, yaps something with a wave of her Head Liquidmetal racquet. This too is unheard from a distance.

Sheltered in the cool protection of the balcony of his Smithson Matchless for Business Class™ Single Suite, Parker hears nothing, not even the chatter of television or the revving air conditioner. He is there but not there: he is smushing his nose into the cavity of the girl's belly, the exposed stripe of flesh at the lycra hem, jamming his face so deeply into her body he enters her muscles and tissues and internal fibres, face first into her heat, dissolving into nothing but some by-product of her thighs' stretch and sweat glazed on the peach fuzz he imagines lining her lower back.

The girl hoists her racquet back and squints up into the sky. Parker rests the glass bottle of chilled lime Perrier he has been semi-nervously sipping from on the narrow ledge before him and adjusts his fingers into fists. His stomach twists with dread over the looming reality of today's lunch sit-down with Smithson International Senior Athletics and Recreation Administrator Deryk Cheung and Cheung's humourless assistant, Michaela. Quarterlies hang on Parker's landing the contract, ensuring DynaFlex meets quotas and reaping him and his team a bountiful harvest of commissions. Michaela has been emailing Parker almost hourly in preparation for this information session slash product demo slash cost estimate.

The serve comes like spat lightning, its velocity highlighted by the sun; barely brushing the net, it glances neatly past the shorter girl. Triumphant, the server turns and jogs backcourt, switching her racquet from right hand to left, reaching with freed fingers to pinch a stuck section of fabric from between her buttocks, then with the same hand scratching her upper ear. Her opponent grunts and whacks her racquet against the clay.

Sightlines beyond the tennis court find asphalt segueing into a slotted mesa of parked minivans, then a decline into an unseen but possible horizon obscured by office towers and freeway ramps and clogs of traffic. Triangulating these points between land and sky is Parker. And there seems to be something in this, this idea of distance and its presentation: lines on clay delineating zones, speed generating revenue, proximity, ambition – something.

An unfamiliar sensation, an unwelcome thought, leaps forward from somewhere in Parker's core. Something is happening: an iciness and a sense of loss. He tries to resist it, fighting to focus and regrasp his surroundings. All that is distant – the horizon and the heavens, the time and trials that have delivered him here – is horribly close, yet remains distant. Like a dossier to which he has never been privy, tossed on his desk. His knees threaten to give way. He sniffs hard sniffs.

A nonsensical refrain – *grandfather clock grandfather clock* – sings inexplicably in his head.

The next serve is less commanding, coming at a flunked angle and met with a lunge and hurried volley crossing the court's span as the tall girl bounds back to root herself. The interval between one girl's *ungh* and the other's *hngh* is a flash; Parker's awareness of the perspiring Perrier bottle's wobble on the ledge is too late, the sight of its downward pitch a sharp boot stomp to his chest.

A moment passes. Then a youngish wail is heard below. Parker inhales and looks: glass glitters on the pool's ceramic deck. A child falls into a mother's arms, her scalp showing a stringy wad of blood. The faces of bathers turn upward and fingers point. Someone shouts *there*.

Parker backs into the room's air-conditioned vacuum, where CNN dominates: *Three killed twenty wounded after NATO aircraft mistakenly bomb Chinese embassy in Belgrade.* He lurches to the bathroom and grips the valves, staring at himself in the mirror, silently mouthing a sequence of panicked expletives. He fears he might vomit, but does not. Staggering back into the bedroom, he clicks to life a pen bearing Smithson's distinctive crest and searches for a suitable writing surface, finding only the laminated service guide. The pen digs futile trenches into the plastic; by the time he manages a few pen strokes he's already forgotten what he'd meant to get down, and why.

The hallway is empty. Parker hurries toward the elevator. His leather loafers make no sound on the thick carpet; the only sound is the change he jangles in his pockets.

Then: the recognizable whoosh and lurch of an elevator's arrival. He halts, then slides into a nearby alcove containing the floor's ice dispenser and a garbage bin. The elevator dings, then the doors part with a sigh. Parker crams himself behind the large machine, feeling his blood pressure pounding in his temples as a reedy man leads two uniformed security lunks into the hall, passing so close Parker can smell on them the same complimentary aloe toner with which he'd splashed his own cheeks only minutes before.

The reedy man, by appearances some sort of managerial lackey, begins briskly knocking on doors, moving room by room down the hallway, calling to guests in this heralding whinny. The first two rooms he tries are empty, but at the third – only one away from Parker's in the row – a woman answers. Parker can't see her, but she sounds drunk.

Parker's throat is a block of putty. Shame or something indigestibly worse burns in his chest. The lackey asks the woman if they could possibly take a quick look inside her room. She groans, but then agrees. Parker cautiously slides from behind the machine and chances a look as the guards and lackey disappear into the room, the door shutting hard behind them. Breathing deeply, Parker hurries to the elevator and hits the down button. Placing a fist against his jackhammering chest, he tries to remember if idle elevators in the Smithson remain on their present floors until called or automatically return to the lobby. Five floors, a long ascent. But then there is that funereal ding, somehow louder than before. He hops inside, spins, thumbs L and waits, jangling change. A century passes; a system grinds. Then, just as the doors ease shut, he can hear the distinctive clunk of a door opening down the hall.

The lobby is a hubbub of queues and ringing pay phones and baggage-laden guests mobbing kiosks and couches. Parker whisks through the crowd, making for the doors to the lower concourse, still unsure of what he is actually doing, or why. There are distant sirens, or the perception of sirens.

Then he hears a name being called, shrill through the noise; he shudders, recognizing it as his own. His already sinking spirits plummet further as he sights Michaela hurrying toward him. Parker continues aiming for those doors, hoping to vanish from the busy scene.

But Michaela heads him off at the entrance, a football-sized coffee pinned in her elbow's crook, a leaf of memoranda weighing down her arms. And yes: a pace behind is the man himself, Deryk Cheung, he of powers to forge season-defining accounts, followed by a pair of junior attendees in identically crested blazers. Parker looks back to see the lackey and lunks aimed roughly in his direction. He tries to explain to

Michaela that he needs a sec to check in, but he can't imagine with whom he should be checking, and she is already prefacing her restructuring of the April memo. Cheung observes, wordless.

Bystanders turn and hush as a trio of young lifeguards barge across the lobby, blowing whistles and humping a gurney toward the west stairs. Cheung looks to Michaela, who looks to Parker, who offers nothing. The managerial lackey passes, lunks close behind, issuing commands into a walkie-talkie with a volume and metre that seethes insistence: *I have police on the way,* he says.

The Senegalese tennis players enter via the entrance's revolving door, caught in the middle of a shared laugh as they almost collide with the gurneyed brigade. Sidestepping onlookers, the taller of the two girls wipes her forehead with a sweatbanded wrist and takes one of Cheung's junior attendees by his sleeve; they seem to know one another. Parker notices this girl too smells of aloe toner.

'What the fuck is happening here?' she says.

2

Late afternoon: the fenced backyard of the Swelthams' Mississauga detached split-level becomes its own shady pergola of seclusion. A slatted deck descends to a footpath flanked by beds of rhododendrons, boxwood, peonies and shrubbery, cascading to a trellis of trickling vines barricading against the Figueiredos next door and their yapping Finnish Spitz. Here one can lounge unhassled: far-off honks and woofs and jet takeoffs are filtered by the insulation of concrete planters. Weeping cherry trees and sunflowers drowse like flags, dead in no breeze.

Trixie opens her eyes. Unmown blades of a week's overgrown grass tickle her neck, earlobes, elbows. Somewhere a telephone rings, oddly in tune with a mosquito hovering at her ear. Yet she remains still. Corpse pose, *savasana*. Palms to the sky.

It's happened again: a gap of time outside inventory. The buckling of knees, the world's upending, emptiness – then, eventually, a tough return. Trixie sits up to a lazy *siddhasana* and scrapes a fingernail across her right temple. The summer light shifts; a power line creates a shadowed cable across the path's ruddy brick, the angle loosely reminding her of cigarettes.

Then, again: the phone, reminding her of the toaster strudel and a world beyond the backyard. It is June 1999 in North America. She is a mother and a wife, an editor, an amateur searcher of the cosmos. And: the envelope, that envelope.

'Stars and damnation.'

She actually says it aloud, this strange curse of her father's. *Stars and damnation.* She shouldn't echo Lloyd this way. But something has changed; there is an urgency brewing in this coming summer she hadn't anticipated. And so, with a bothered head, she rises and goes.

The toaster oven chuffs greyish smoke, but no flames. Trixie opens its front panel and dials down the heat. The Pillsbury Wildberry Toaster Strudel inside is a ruin of black crust and blood-hued filling. She plucks this desiccated pastry from the tray, almost burning her fingers, and tosses it into the sink to land beside a Kikkoman-crusted saucer. Running the faucet over the crusted husk, she listens closely to the clarity of the water's gush. Then she starts the dishwasher and cracks one of the two tallboys of Grolsch she finds left in the fridge. There is so much care and no care at all in these spaces – the sink, the unruly garden, the garage's storage units direly needing reformatting, the ailing furnace, the concrete below foundationing it all. It lives around her and because of her.

Trixie spatulas the destroyed strudel into the trash.

The living room television is paused on a video menu reading *Turok 2: Seeds of Evil*. This room is a mayhem of incompatible objects: a Ruffles bag spills yellowish dust next to a Nintendo controller and an empty bottle of Wild Cherry Pepsi staining rings into the coffee table; her own Gourevitch paperback lies fanned on the coffee table. The Sky-Watcher f/8 telescope sits in the corner, aimed at the Figueiredos' side deck. Trixie clicks off the remote and kills the screen.

Returning to the kitchen, Trixie locates the cordless phone and retrieves messages. She hopes for hang-ups, but there is a jerky sequence: Allie, her mother, describing the horrors of a frothy tidal pool in her basement that may or may not be a breeding ground for small frog-like creatures. A rep from the gas company about their last statement's error. Parker, phoning in from Hartsfield-Jackson; an airport PA squawks in the background. She returns the phone to its cradle, then thumbs through a drawer of papers and warranties. All this archaeology, but no envelope.

No luck in the first-floor bathroom. Same with the vestibule, among notepads and key rings, a wad of windowed envelopes bound in an elastic. She thinks: it was, to her best recollection, last seen in her purse yesterday afternoon. But after unsealing it and scrutinizing its contents, she'd strategically opted to stash it where it would not be found. Mission accomplished.

She is again unsuccessful in the spare bedroom, a room once intended for guests who never arrived, now used for storage and the tired IKEA desk she regretfully calls her home office. Atop a stack of cardboard boxes housing Parker's old Bauer skates and trophies and other junk, someone has left half a sandwich: Kraft Singles and pastrami, atop a paper towel. She inwardly curses Owen, then forces herself to reel back, recalling Dr. Fultz's professional edict to judge her son less sternly, to assert a *gentle but vigilant* parental presence – emphasis on *gentle*. Pick up the dirty socks, excuse the after-school dilly-dally, if only for a month. Six weeks, regular check-ins. Trust: the entryway to a new level of understanding, she is told.

The house hums with absence. Oak flooring costumed in Osaka hand-knotted rugs, half-dialled dimmers, calming lamps, a small pantry smelling of turmeric – all quiet. Only the dishwasher's chug as soundtrack.

Work at her PowerBook proves fruitless. Fact checking for the next issue of *Record of Truth* is tedious, and the tribunal report history is not a gripping read. *Co-accused in the second indictment had been arrested in Yamoussoukro on 29 October 1996; subsequently transferred to the Tribunal on 30 November 1996. Prosecutor filed motion before Trial Chamber 1 on 17 February re: all three accused, i.e., Kayishema, Ruzindana and Ntakirutimana, maintaining Kibuye violations in sequence.* Rooting through procedure notes weighs her eyes, and she finds herself fiddling restlessly with her screen's display contrast. Faxes, transcripts, Polaroids of blood-splashed bodies – the records are clinical in their horror.

She's cross-referencing recent testimony from Abuja when the telephone rings again. The cordless is in the kitchen.

'Hello?'

'Hi. I tried you like an hour ago.'

'I was working. You're where now?'

'Houston.'

'Houston. Is it *Astro*nomical?'

A lame joke. No laugh.

Parker: 'Did the pavers call?'

'Nyet. Did you … I haven't looked at the estimate.'

'Did Heath bring back the glue gun?'

Parker would be reclined on a hotel queen-size, loosening his tie, catalogues and sales sheets fanned around him. Her husband lives in day planners and coil-bound calendars and notepads; for last Christmas Owen suggested they give him a hand-held gizmo to replace the accumulating stacks, but the thing now sits in a kitchen drawer, still in its plastic with warranty and manual, awaiting return to Best Buy.

'Heath was by,' Trixie says. 'But no gun. He was really sweaty.'

'Mm. Well, that's how he is.'

'I took O back downtown yesterday.'

'Right. I was going to ask.'

'Afterwards Fultz said O was asking strange questions. He said young men rarely exhibit such destructive behaviours without some sort of, he said, *libidinal motivation*. His words, not mine.'

'Really.'

'He suggested in this roundabout way that he might be having doubts about his, um, sexuality.'

'O suggested this?'

'No no no. Fultz wondered if Owen might have a tendency or something.'

'God. And we're looking forward to a bill for how much?'

She sighs. 'Look … I know. But we obviously have a situation where not everything's understood. Honestly, I kind of think he secretly *enjoys* therapy.'

Silence.

'Something wrong?' she asks.

Nothing, he says. He tells her to take care, and he'll see her on Monday.

But something *is* wrong. It's in his tone: a warble of doubt. But surely her husband of seventeen years is thinking only of heart-rate meters and treadmill pad static and slide-show product demos, tromping convention lobbies free of concern over the rotten crumbs crushed into these old carpets and the groan of this house's ailing pipes and the assholes who insist on jamming their mail slot with those World Vision flyers that look like Consumers Distributing catalogues. He's not here to see it.

The bedroom is the cleanest and cruellest of these rooms. Bedsheets tucked firm, Parker's freshly laundered cotton boxers folded next to her own skivvies: the boys and the girls. One could see this straightened room as sanitized following juicy indiscretions, or primed for yet-to-be committed sins. Neither is the case.

In the closet's wicker hamper designated for off-season shoes, Parker has dumped a load of grungy workout sweats. There have been humidity issues, leaving many winter clothes dank and musty; coupled with the crusty sweats, the closet smells bad. Indulging a long shot, Trixie kneels and rifles through blankets, turtlenecks, wadded mittens. No envelope, of course. Digging behind the hamper she finds a lidless plastic storage box of rumpled papers, thin file folders, scraps. Photographs: vacationing mopeds in Nassau, DynaFlex seasonal bashes, Owen Halloweened in an ornate foam duck costume. Trixie flips through the first few strata of this box, knowing the dig will prove fruitless.

But here, unanticipated, is the recognizable black vinyl of an old journal's jacket, atop a brief stack of similar volumes. She extracts the book from the box and pries it apart. Pages crinkle with moisture, overused with scrawlings. She knows it well, but has forgotten so much.

10/17/79. Does it ever end? Everyone so assured. Think of Mercy, moaning every pitiful emotion. I look at my face, freckles look like syphilis. My neck looks like a turtle.

These were dreamy seasons, so long ago. Montreal at a decade's slumbering dawn. Days both soothing and devastating, like an afternoon bottle of depanneur wine or three. Trixie sits cross-legged on the floor, leafing through pages of these fevered scratchings crammed in during miserable metro hauls or library catatonia or over ciders on sunburned *terrasses*, to-do lists in margins, the quotations, doodles, phone numbers driven into pages. Years have passed since rereading these complaints and codes, long lost to her now.

Owen appears at the doorway. He has very little hair.

Trixie: 'What happened to the curls we knew and loved?'

'Buzzed it.'

Every day he looks different. Taller, thinner. He is only a boy. He leans against the door's frame. 'Can I take an advance on next week's? I Windexed, I swear.'

'Oh brother. Ten.'

'Come on. That's lunch.'

'Ten dollars isn't *my* lunch. Is it yours?'

He weasels. 'Fifteen?'

'This is for … ?'

'What? Crack cocaine and ammo. What.'

Again, he is only a boy. *Gentle but vigilant.* 'Take the card, get out twenty. *Twenty.* I will check.'

'In your purse?'

'Mm hm. And did you feed Satan?'

But he's already gone.

Up and down the hallway she retraces with mounting frustration, running her knuckles along the wall. Fruit flies circling the kitchen wastebin remind her of past days, old apartments. Sipping the Grolsch, she drifts to the stairs, swiping the balustrade and struggling to remain focused on the hunt at hand. Recall: it came from the purse, then the unsealing. Then the consideration and reconsideration and consideration of reconsideration, then the impulse to have it not be found by those who should not see it. Up and down the hallways, she levitates, teleports, phases through dimensions.

The writing switches to red ink, rotates ninety degrees into landscaped margins: *Sacred drunken night! Sacred if only for the mask you grant us* something illegible *We put faith in poison. We know how to live completely every day. Behold an age of assassins.* Copied from one of many paperbacks shoplifted from Argo Bookshop on Ste-Catherine, torn through while laid out on the rug in her Outremont three-and-a-half, gulping drugstore Italian wine and evading sleep – her brick-thick Penguin edition of Rimbaud's *Collected Poems*. The gaunt prodigy, with whom she grew semi-erotically obsessed in those undergraduate years, whose allure lay in the slender purity and crude passions of youth, somehow even more raw in translation. Her wispy Comparative Lit class prof darted across a sunken lecture floor, slapping the dog-eared paperback, and she was enrapt – Rimbaud did that to the young. But youth is now a mystery; she reads quotations in her own handwriting, a script she doesn't recognize: *My betrayal of the world is too brief a torture.* Through such eternities they time-travelled and flirted with celestial grace, arguing over bar tabs and attempting to live ferociously. Meanwhile the city groaned with settling foundations, woozing in decline after separation politics and an Olympic post-coital drift.

10/21/79. 3am. Sickening silence. Mice scrambling in the walls like fingernails clawing out of tombs. Called Victorio about it but that fat fuck never shows his pocked face anymore. So sick of this lack of control. Can't focus on anything. Dizzy and cardiac crossing Maisonneuve. So many choices and no way to choose. Seldom do people discern eloquence under a threadbare cloak. Confirmed Dean's List this aft. Reminder: send notice to Allie, she'll waggle a fist in joy. Things have to change.

At the kitchen table now, Trixie closes this ancient volume and bites her cheek, remembering a just-about-finished pack of Matinée Extra Milds in a raincoat pocket upstairs. She clears material from her eyes and stands. Muffled thumps come from upstairs – Owen's new barbells touching carpet. She smiles.

Twilight introduces a cooling of shadows. With head aching, Trixie again retreats to the backyard to droop into a wooden deck chair with the last Grolsch. The fraying eaves at the roof's northeast corner remind her of all the work that should be done that won't be done, or at least the remorse she should be feeling over it not being done, but does not. So many hours still ahead, so many messes to mop up.

Overhead loafs a hint of a waning moon, a librating ribbon of its influence. This same moon, she thinks, has bored a thousand generations with its loom. She takes comfort in knowing so many despairing humans have gazed up to the same sight. And none received the confirmation hoped for.

She braces herself, worried another blackout is coming. Her neck loosens in a way that has become frighteningly familiar.

Then: in the unmown grass by where she'd conked out, she sights a recognizable corner of envelope that snaps her back. With a rooster-ish blurt she fires herself across the yard and retrieves the envelope. On the face, no address, no addressee. She opens it and withdraws its contents: an index card, unlined, monogramless, of stock rigid enough to imply an aura of formality yet free of ornament. Businesslike, but not of business.

She rereads.

Hi Trixie! Great to run into you the other day at yoga! Be great to get together sometime! How about lunch or drinks next week maybe! Throw me a dingle when you get a chance … it'd be great to hear from you! Ernie.

Three different numbers, plus an email address and a fax number. Fax? The inclusion of this detail should mean something, but what that is remains unclear. A lot of *greats*. And: *dingle?*

Turning the note over, she discovers a blemish under the third sentence. Held to the light, the card reveals a deft application of white-out, annihilating a word or two. Trixie squints, angling the page, finding a slight twist of blue ink behind the white, pen-strokes that look like the lower section of a Y, with what seems an *o* adjoined. *You.* Or, possibly, *Yours. Yo* seems out of Ernie's character. *You* – you what? Some commentary on her character, presumably from the impression made after last week's Svastha class, with an awkwardness held between them like a vat of some unstable element. In this line, something compelled him to reconsider and withhold. He went for whiteout rather than starting anew. Again, this should indicate something, but Trixie comes up empty as to what. She folds the card and pockets it.

But this isn't the envelope she seeks, the one from the neurology clinic, filling her with dread beyond dread. That document and its results remain hidden somewhere, lost in the house's beleaguered floorboards, its veining cracks and caulking. She breathes deeply of evening air, then finishes the beer and heads inside. There's still so much left to do.

3

Against everything, you have to keep pushing. They will try to knock you down, defeat you, make you less. Odds are against you, always. So you have to tough it out solo. You have to persevere and believe, even when no one else does, because all you have is yourself and nothing else. Even those closest to you will be of no help in battles ahead. So you have to set guidelines. You have to establish a regimen and stick to it every fucking day. You have to look hard at what is real and keep going, even when the body and the brain scream no. You have to see the challenge as a thing that it is real and true and not something imaginary or dumb. You have to know what's what. Never weaken. Never show weakness. Never be weak.

Legs at shoulder width, wearing only Umbro shorts, Owen Sweltham stares into the weight-room mirror. The results of weeks' rigours – the curls and lifts, toning, bearing weight, fighting weight – are still barely manifest. To take this puny thing in the mirror and reshape it into its ideal version – this takes weight. Struggling to achieve mass, to occupy more space – this takes sweat. It requires a steady vision. You aim, focus, target. Shoot. Look at these shitty delts and these scrawny biceps. Look at this nothing chest. Look at these zits crusting this forehead and this neck, the greasy clefts of these nostrils. Everything is oozing and swollen and broken.

He drops and initiates crunches. Down on the mat, lowered under everything, the rattle of gymnastics horses jostling in the adjacent gymnasium, he fights to concentrate. Here, in the weight room dank with unlaundered towels and the stink of teenaged bodies, the work of flexing and leveraging of pressure takes place. With enough persistence and pain, any muscle, no matter how shrivelled, can be persuaded to harden and swell. You can conquer. You can solidify softness into steel – just like the steel-like material of the seven-pound jar of Xyience XGainer in his locker. And down on the floor, with pelvis pulled toward shoulders and breath heavy in his nostrils, Owen understands that if you are going to conquer your foes, you just have to get through this pain.

Against everything. You have to push against everything.

Lunchtime. Persian Pizza and Seafood is stuffy, crowded with bashed booths and wrecked video consoles and gunk-glazed trash bins, sunlight squared through windows imprinted with remnants of masking tape. Someone dings up triumphant scores on an ancient 1943 console, pixelated choppers pitilessly bombing aircraft carriers.

They wait in line for pizza, four of them.

'I'd destroy that ass,' Lucky says. 'She's got this sort of attitude. Nasty.'

'Hundred percent,' The Bying says.

Gwen Huang is the subject, in the context of tonight's Year-End Sokk Hopp.

The Calch: 'And you saw her this morning. With the boots.'

Lucky snorts.

Owen is last in line, feeling as fucked up as one can feel without crumbling into dust. This new hash is much wetter and more serious than Sad Tony's old hash; on top of the half-bottle of Triaminic after his workout, things are getting pretty wacky. His thoughts are pornographically pizza-fixated; there is no earthly or heavenly desire greater than his anticipation for this slice, Persian's specialty of extra-spiced sausage customized with sweet donair sauce, a.k.a. the Bubbafied Slice. Yet so much noise surrounds: the clanging of pans and revving of ovens, the barks of the Lebanese cooks, the digitalized bombing of Japanese harbours, Lucky and The Bying and The Calch flapping lips. And now Deanerz enters, burdened with a massive backpack and a hockey stick straggling loose tape. This talk of Gwen Huang rekindles an image haunting Owen since yesterday's morning's B Math: two rows over she sat with her earlobes and coloured contact lenses, her suede skirt and her veinless calves, and in leaning over to retrieve something from her bag her small tank top was hiked to expose a glimpse of lower back, the sheer gooseflesh there, and the floral hem of a Hanes waistband. Owen had sat paralyzed by this sight for the entire period, scarcely even noticing when the terminating bell rang. Thoughts regarding Gwen taint his tongue with a bitter taste that is most definitely not pizza, and all he wants to do is ride out this clammy smoke-out and sit and eat eat eat pizza pizza *pizza*.

One of the cooks, the one with the moustache and glass eye, sloshes a strainer of frozen fries into the deep fryer.

The Calch says, 'O.'

Owen nods, hearing him. 'Uh.'

'You're back on team now?'

Deanerz: 'Wait. O's still kicked off soccer?'

They are speaking to him, but he is unable to answer. The combo of dextromethorphan and hash is really setting up shop in his head, sending the possibility of uttering actual words adrift. Words are only sick echoes. And if these people can't see or *feel* the limitlessness of his thoughts, words will remain useless. He's elsewhere: from the coil-bound reader of photocopied pages from *The Norton Anthology of English Literature*, sixth edition, the class read Samuel Coleridge: *Nine fathom deep he has followed us From the land of mist and snow. And every tongue, through utter drought, was withered at the root.* There Owen lives, in a land of mist and snow and mozzarella clinging to a tear of dough, like tissue from a bone.

'I'll be back in,' Owen manages.

No one responds.

The line edges forward as The Bying receives his slice and moves to the register. Money is borrowed and lent throughout. Only The Calch and Lucky boast any real income, both shelving sneakers at Coastal Athletics on weekends. Deanerz has started on the fryer at Swiss Chalet, but The Calch is now hooking him up with an interview at Coastal; there you get discounts and don't wear hairnets. O is short as always, his only income those dollars wrenched from the Maternal Unit or by hawking CDs pinched from Sam's downtown – at the CD Plus near Kipling station they pay three to four-fifty for almost any unscuffed disc. And the scant amounts he does make usually end up in Sad Tony's clutches. Money remains an abstraction.

The small Lebanese guy behind the counter waggles a finger to fetch Owen's attention. O nods back.

The afternoon is the morning. He forgets what's next. Biology Three – the one about procedures, observation hypothesis conclusion and its chapter on genetics, where your father becomes your son and your grandmother is inside you, where you are molecules in stacks and nothing else. Or World History, the one with pictures of bodies in trees. But dead people are not bunches of bananas. Grade 11 is a nightmare.

The distance between where he currently stands in this greasy galaxy and the seat he will occupy through this next class, forty-five minutes of hostaged attention, is incalculable. The imprisonment of Owen Sweltham will not be relived. He remembers the clang of barred doors sliding shut, then long silences, sobs down hallways. All these impulses become hard to filter – it's impossible to strip the layers into something workable. The shit is heavy or it's nothing.

The Calch takes his steaming slice and buries its glisten in chili flakes. He nods at Owen. 'Seriously, O. You're playing with us this summer or what?'

Owen moves forward to accept his pizza. 'I'm destroying it,' he says.

At St. Dismas it was lineups too. Lineups for everything: water fountain, breakfast, showers, pills, phone privileges, pills, bathroom, laundry, pills. Waiting for disposable razors, towels, Right Guard. For fresh bedsheets, after tearing his own to ribbons. In those yellowed halls of linoleum and clanging lock bolts, any expression was so closely monitored and reined there was nothing one could do but just *exist*, waiting to be institutionally reformed. Nothing remained but to try and avoid others and wile away hours in a sedated stupor that led only to further stupor; he slumped through the hallways in standard-issue jammies and smoked weeks of cigarettes in the back foyer and avoided speaking with anyone. Periodic visits from the Paternal and Maternal Units went without incident. February faded into March; March faded into April. He idly half-memorized a battered *Funk & Wagnalls*, vols. A through M. He attended sessions in C Wing, where a jury of counsellors reminded him of his crimes. He scrubbed his ball sack with dispenser soap and rubbed his chin with towels that reeked of something vinegary. He lived a filtered life. And yet the promise beckoned: all would be reinstated in proper time, in due course.

During his third week of incarceration he was in the West Common Room, alone except for a guy named Barney dozing in a chair. Owen was scanning *Funk & Wagnalls*, reading about the Crimean War, smoking the last cigarette from his pack, when Fat Brian plopped next to him on the couch.

'Can we talk about this morning?'

December 1852: Sultan Abdülmecid I decided in favour of the Catholics, while Nicholas, protector of Orthodoxy, dispatched a mission to Constantinople, aiming at a treaty guaranteeing the rights of the Orthodox population of the Ottoman Empire.

Owen edged away. 'Reading.'

'You said some pretty serious stuff in session.'

'Read. *Ing*.'

'I'd like to open up. Like Susan was saying.'

'Susan's a Nazi.'

'Susan's not a Nazi.'

Siege of Sevastopol. Battle of Inkerman. Battle of Eupatoria. Campaign in the Sea of Azov. Siege of Kars.

'She said communication is your most serious obstacle. Do unto others. Be the change you wish to see. Behave as you'd have the world behave.'

The Russians refused the terms.

'I'm trying to help you. What don't you understand?'

Owen turned and faced Fat Brian. You have to learn to machete these distractions from your path and forge ahead. You have to push harder against everything.

He put out his cigarette on Fat Brian's eyelid.

In the Quiet Room you could be as loud as you wanted. You could holler and complain forever. No one cared.

'*Wink Martindale!*'

Or: '*Chuck Fuck Barris Barky Bob Barker Farker Fuck!*'

Or: '*Dick Van Dick Dickybird Dick Dyke Cockfuckingsucker!*'

Nothing changed the fact that you were there, captive. But you could grow accustomed to torments, learning to handle persecution. They locked up Nelson Rolihlahla Mandela and gave him a really ugly shirt when he got out. They threw the Godfather of Soul into lockdown in South Carolina. The world tries to beat you down, and you can only find freedom in fighting your way through. You have to just sit and let every minute squash you and dare you to submit, to strangle your soul and twist you into submission. But Owen knew no one could control him – but him. And no one could destroy him. But him.

Lying on his bunk, his intestines afire, he would stare up at buzzing fluorescent grids, their radiative glares engineered to enfeeble him. Horrible patterns emerged: refractions like butterfly eye-spots, raccoon claws, roses laid at gravesides. Cycles of the past. Tissue and bone.

Then, at the conclusion of millennia of drought and decay, a door opened.

Noel from Second Ward loped in and led Owen back upstairs. Then his captors listened intently with stethoscope to torso while a procedural world massacred all hope. They dared to explain to him, the incarcerated, how it was not the world, meaning *this* world, that did the actual killing. Or, in this case, violations and regulations. It was his fault, his and Ike's violence, that brought him here and kept him behind locked doors – and they were correct. They audited his behaviour in sickening detail, mincing Owen just as he'd minced his bedsheets. They jabbed and ballpointed. They waged queries and analyses.

And after it all he ended up in the same place he always did: across a desk from Fultz, his court-appointed counsellor's antennae perked and ballpoint pen readied for the coming litany. Clinician and prisoner, probe and project. Both sank into their opposing chairs.

'You reported sluggishness,' Fultz said, running a thumb down a clipboard. 'Dr. Stickings had you on … chlorpromazine and risperidone.'

'I survived.'

In Owen's every movement, his every tremble, the smothering weight of his own awesomeness has been what wracks him most deeply. Not easy, sustaining the heights demanded of ultimate greatness. These meds were almost successful in their efforts to wear down the People's

Champ. You falter in aisles and talk to your fist. You don't know when and where you are. Things are heavy like rubberized hex dumbbells and light like Librium. Owen once fought to balance his lunch plate of potato salad and lemonade while trying to visualize the flames of Hamburg's 1810 annexation as described in *Funk & Wagnalls* vol. C; he fell to lunar dust and was lifted to his feet by a slo-mo cosmonaut who ESPed his mind in the Sea of Tranquillity. Then the Paternal Unit was eyeing him over the neck of a light beer, telling him *every passing second* means a new future: apparently something the Paternal Unit's own mother would say.

Yes, superiority hounded him.

Fultz scanned his clipboard. A photocopied bulletin on his desk bore the headline *Restorative Justice in Youth Corrections*.

'Do you find yourself disoriented, or confused?'

Owen scoffed at this. When one's mental faculties operate at levels entirely beyond the scope of these technologies and treatments, as Owen's do, all these showers of glitter simply fail. Owen goes for the sharp, Ginsu-sharp. Slice and dice, Julienne-style. Like *ninjutsu*.

'Nope.'

'Nightmares? Bad dreams, you said.'

Dreams? The true hero defies the chokehold of such drowsy prisons, the assassins twisting *shuko* claws, slithering into bedchambers in deadest night. He trained himself to sleep with one eye cocked, ready for any opponent.

'Nope.'

Fultz returned pen to desk, removing his glasses to thumb eyes ridged in weary pouches. His skin appeared sunken and sore, an overshaved pink.

'So tell me something,' he said. 'Anything.'

To the wincing, pitying Parental Units, Fultz had expressed confidence that all waywardness could be quelled; we did not see here the beginning of a life of delinquency and malice, he said, but we certainly had a case. He reported that, while incarcerated, Owen was in tears every day. *Unable on some days to even properly dress himself,* Fultz slandered. But how could Owen possibly be expected to comply? His enemies lurked everywhere: steak knives like enemies and mascots, vials of poison singing to him like cartoons. He had to resist; like Mr. T put it: *Quit yo' jibba jabba*. Anger forked Owen's brain while he innocently consumed trays of Eggos. He died and lived, and he was launched upon the beach at Damascus as his Robitussin-poisoned blood ran into the surf. Meanwhile he fought to hold steady, letting his frown be his umbrella.

So he could tell Fultz nothing. And as the weary man fingered his intercom's keypad to inquire about the afternoon's scheduling, Owen reached and swiped the clipboard from the desk. To Fultz's horror, Owen began cramming the pages sheet by sheet into his mouth, stealing back his case notes, reclaiming his past as his own.

But that was months ago. Tonight spotlights scatter and flare, blemishes strobing across the loose crowd. The school gymnasium, navigable by day, is tonight recreated as a torture chamber of unrecognizable faces and flung shadows. Sweaty smells intermingle: hair mousse, contraband wine coolers tucked into sleeves, cologne-filtered sweat. Gummy slowness washes over Owen as he raises his face, letting the speakers' thump peel layers from his cranium. A girl in a Red Sox cap staggers into him; Owen rebounds her back and she is immediately forgotten.

Earlier hours pre-gymnasium are fuzzy. In the woods behind the school he'd joined Dean 'Deanerz' Prendergast and Lucky Chartrand and Chuck 'The Bying' Byng and Corrina Squelce – who'd arrived with Chuck – in huddling around bottles of Golden Glow and Schooner and a baggie of crumbling brownish crud that The Bying described as genetically enhanced shrooms. Prospects for the night's Sokk Hopp were discussed. The Bying predicted it would be a *final blowout*, which sounded completely retarded. With Cardinals cap in reverse, one Schooner in hand and another tucked in his belt, Owen wobbled uncertainly, the afternoon's cough syrup now a half-digested red mess painting the Shoppers Drug Mart's wheelchair access ramp. And when the shrooms eventually kicked in he'd been stricken with a vision, there in the darkened forest. Sunken in night's trickery, his friends became corpses, their faces teethy skulls, the muscles clinging to their bones atrophying, their fleshless frames and enamelled grins like marionettes on self-dangled strings.

In the forest's mausoleum he'd seen something new: a confirmation and a reminder that made him want to crack apart his own ribs. Even when they told him to chill the frig out, he felt on the brink of something important. He kept touching the knife in his boot; he'd found the groove-handled thing with the worn blade in the woods a week ago, glinting in the sun like a trophy. The weapon, tucked at his ankle, provided reassurance.

But now, inside the gym's fortress, everything goes haywire. The rent-a-cops and girls aligned on bleachers, the snarl of whoops, the hypnosis of enormous video screens, speakers blasting TLC. Despite it all, he hears a reassuring voice, perfectly clear, speaking only to him: 'Don't worry – all's all right in the end.'

Then someone takes Owen by the shoulders. He spins one-eighty and seizes his attacker's throat.

'What, O ... '

Eyewitness accounts of the ensuing scuffle would flow free-form throughout next week's rumour channels. One account saw Owen launching Chuck back into the surrounding fray, Chuck then flailing into exchange student Luther Wang, who then executed some serious Qwan Ki Do on them both. In another, the two stripped to bare torsos and squared off Mike Tyson Punch-Out!!–style before hired police busted in and sent them both downtown for punitive annihilation. Another version saw Owen morphing into a wild creature swearing to devour The Bying's heart as a supreme sacrifice to the unholy – with whispers that O's time out of school last term was to undergo some unspeakable demonic transformation. Everyone saw it happen, but no one knew what happened.

But the truth is, as he is being dragged full nelsoned by security toward the exit, all Owen senses is the violent clenching of his body's every tendon. He is granite, impervious under Par 56s and epileptic video monitors, his mind full of puke. But as the opening strains of K-Ci and JoJo's slow jam on the PA sends the dance's awkward and unmatched to the hallways, the swarm makes for an effective cover, allowing Owen to shake his captors' grip and make for the exit. Before anyone understands what has occurred, Owen bursts through the school's front entrance and is out in the night, free.

He can do nothing; he can do anything. He can strike back against the noise, fighting an unending battle. Against everything, you have to keep pushing. They try to knock you down. Everything is on their side; the thing is weighted. Odds are against you, always. So you have to go it solo. No one else will be there to help you. In the end, all you can do is fight.

The earth revolves, parrying a sluggish moon. Loafing dust joins the puzzle of Saturn's ring – his mother would refocus her telescope. Everything is united, crude in particles and scuzz, the cigarette-butt-stuffed beer bottles, the crumpled gum wrappers.

Owen sits immobile on the grassy slope beyond the vacant basketball courts, riding out this stone. Music from the gym has died, and Sokk Hopp attendees now spill into the parking lot below through jousting headlights, their faces flushed with contact, with giddiness, with humiliation. Potential violence sparks between two guys next to an Integra blasting Silkk the Shocker, but to onlookers' disappointment it turns out to be only a playfight, a joke.

Owen briefly wonders if this entire night has all just been part of some elaborate trick. He feels sick and his temples ache. He touches his head, now bare; he's lost his Cardinals cap.

Then The Bying is there, as if helidropped in.

'Puff?' he says, offering his cigarette.

Owen accepts. Toward the lot's front fencing he sights Gwen Huang, hanging with her usuals, Melissa Sachs and Moira Llewellyn and that girl Kath Kough. Gwen's windbreaker is zipped to her chin, sleeves pulled over fists. From here Owen can still see that lip gloss shining: it's a post-storm moon, barely there, but there.

Owen hands back the cigarette. They all smoke Belvedere Milds, except for Lucky, who goes for Export A's.

'Back there,' Owen says to Chuck.

'Yeah, cock.'

'I was fucked. I thought you ...'

He stops. The Bying nods, smoking. 'Let's get out of here,' he says. 'Things are getting hoary.'

They rise and head up the hill, back toward the forested path and the bus stop beyond. Everything is wearing off, wearing down, and they are tired. The only thing Owen feels is that never-fading want, a recurring dream never understood.

Gwen and her glistening ponytail. Gwen and her open-toe flats. Gwen and her lip gloss.

4

Teenagers play two-on-two, their enormous sneakers squeaking and strafing across the glossy floor, their sinewy arms forming ambitious Kareem skyhooks. Outside, Heath Sweltham sets his bag of Labatt Maximum Ice and Popeye's New Orleans Spicy Chicken on the sidewalk and crouches, wincing at his knees' creak, to look down through the window's tinted glass into the bright sub-level court and adjacent Nautilus gym. Down there humans heave in exercise's throes amid towel bins and contraptions of vinyl padding, their muscles engaged in affirmation, in yoga, Tae Bo, strength conditioning. Heath inevitably thinks of Nicole, her salty armpits and her big ass wobbling around a frayed thong as she flopped facedown on a plastic exercise ball. Just a month ago he was securely chauffeuring himself home in the Hyundai, brimming with humanity and drive-thru tacos and the security of a two-bedroom Annex walk-up. Now Nicole is somewhere toasting Heath's expurgation with a bendy-strawed Corona pinned between her knees while he sweats the commute back to a half-furnished sublet with bum cable and trickling water pressure. Fair enough, the Sonata was technically rightfully half hers since she footed the insurance, but still – as if she can even *drive* it. Yet somewhere she laughs her braying psycho laugh while he's cataloguing the poses of these days, his interminable routines, his futurelessness.

Patterns form. Omens of the end are everywhere and in everything. Reports of London nail bombs prompt extended sighing jags. Belgrade explosions and Colorado school shootings are drowned in twelve-packs and spliffs. The end of the twentieth century is manifest in Heath's scalp, which is now, unexpectedly and rapidly, recast into strange matter clogging his shower's drain. Rituals of shaving and flossing bring shocks of blood against white ceramic. He is increasingly aware of his body's downshift, already prepping for decomposition. Not even thirty-six years old. For his cholesterol he was prescribed Norvasc. For his acned jawline he's been taking Accutane. His shoulders' deepening crick, a new worry of wrack from tapping and mousing, is relieved only with Extra Strength Advil and weed. A tenderness behind the flap of his left ear has evolved into a strange scabby break; to this he has been applying a careful swab of rubbing alcohol in the mornings. Sometimes in the late afternoons he feels a distinct and unsettling detachment from his body, particularly a numbness in his extremities that might be from sleeplessness or poor circulation, or the first tinglings of some sort of impending internal rupture, cerebral or pulmonary, or nothing at all. For this, he self-medicates.

Patterns form. Every day, sixish, he passes this YMCA and its windowed athletics on his way to the TTC station, loping home from another ten-hour slog at the Clicon Office Solutions Junior Tech Support desk, where he fields near-hourly complaints from the fourth floor. All day he takes calls from people who resent speaking with him.

It says 'Print job now printing,' but the printer isn't doing anything.
It keeps saying connection failure. I gotta get this off by three or I'm screwed.
Is it all gonna blow on New Year's when the clocks roll over or what?
If anyone asks, just pass it off to tech support.
Oh wait. You're tech support – right?
Who are you again?

And nine times out of ten all he does is a quick restart and presto: situation resolved, back to the basement and semi-conscious monitoring of the internal network. Heath's desk features none of the typical ornaments found at his co-workers': no family photos or newsy clippings or Dilbert strips. Aside from the beige PC monitor, Heath's cubicle contains only a system-maintenance calendar and a stack of manuals for the six workstations for which he's been mandated supervision, manuals he unfailingly consults when tackling actual tech issues. Heath is perpetually torn between fear of others discovering his reliance on these manuals – thereby revealing his own dispensability – and the urge to throw these fat tomes in their faces and tell them to just fix the fucking problem themselves. But he doesn't; he answers the phone when it rings, and he tucks in his shirt and scurries upstairs when summoned.

I keep pushing Option-P like you told me, but I keep getting this weird annoying beep. Like this – listen – here it comes, wait. Okay, here it comes.
Beep.

Patterns form. And as usual at 6:30 he passes Delahaye's Star Variety, the Jamaican grocer where the girl with the red glasses and the strange rash scarfing her throat works. He glances in passing: yes, there she is, chomping gum and keying an ancient register. Two weeks ago he stopped in to pick up a Ting and she'd met him with a sympathetic gaze. After a brief but cordial exchange about Scotch bonnet pepper sauce, she'd unexpectedly suggested, rubbing her nose, that Heath might 'pop by sometime and we'll go pick up an ice cream or something.' Psyched out by the forward gesture, he'd agreed, though truthfully he'd left the store frightened and unable to swallow the palmful of stemmy naseberries she'd given him. Those too-wide eyes, that rash.

Nicole: *You think you're trying to be all polite, when you're really just being a schlep.*

6:35. At a stoplight a sun-blinded cyclist is nearly downed by a Lamborghini Diablo; shouts follow. At 6:41 a Korean woman tosses shreds of lottery tickets into the waning sun, into the street. Then all descend into subterranean arteries to hip-check turnstiles and squeeze onto platforms with all the other slurping slime. For the duration of the northward ride he forces himself to remain unconscious of what is happening, his entire body feeling wrung out and sopped up; he sees his face reflected in a security mirror and is alarmed by the density of his forehead's sweat. By 7:15 he is descending into this one-bedroom basement apartment in North York and casting his key ring on the counter next to the microwave.

He has one message.

'Hi. It's me. Just calling again about the loveseat. Think I'll get Lukey to come pick it up. So call my cell when it's cool to come by. All right. Um. Take care. Bye.'

Lukey. This name means nothing to him.

Moments later he is digesting the Popeye's and cracking the first of several cans of high-content ale while thumbing the universal remote. By eleven o'clock he is rolling a weary joint and longing, as he does every day, to drowse in oceans and orgies, not the menacing mountains of his nightmares.

Nicole: *I would say navel-gazing, if you could even see your navel.*

Patterns form. With the recognition of patterns comes the potential for forecasting future results. In bright televised worlds, Heath knows already how the defendants on *Law & Order* will confess to their sins, how the cheerful violence of *America's Funniest Home Videos* will entertain. How Montel Williams will perch in his chair. How modern civilization will meet its end.

Tscha: another can, another channel.

A Hilroy scribbler sits on top of the fridge, containing notes for his screenplay, title still TBD. There is a plan: thirty days at six, seven pages a day – the daily goal recommended in *Shear the Chaff: A Hollywood Veteran's Perspective on Screenwriting for the 21st Century* by Zach Weisgrau, also on top of the fridge. That's a first draft plus rewrites. Discipline is the key. Once you pump out the overarching concepts, the rest is filling in the blanks, setting it all in Courier. No one frets about details; the big ideas are what count. And discipline is a function of self-honour, which he lacks. But he'll wipe the slate clean. Once he gets his shit together, this thing will practically write itself. Those dinks on the fourth floor, razored and tanned – they'll choke on their frigging shawarmas when they see Heath's name drift across the screen.

Nicole said she required a *dynamic lifestyle*, a life more *energetic* and *driven by purpose*. When Heath asked what exactly this so-called purpose was that was going to drive her, she was unresponsive, only dangling her stubbed elbows in a vertical plea and saying, *There has to be more than this.* She was jogging again, spending stupid amounts on her hair at that salon with those Greek gum-snapping harpies: seventy bucks every week on her hair, plus tip. Her purpose-driven hair. Her stumped arms.

At 1:30 regular programming dwindles and infomercials begin. Late in the cheapness of the 1-900 night, only hot-tub blondes and multi-function slicers and golf highlights remain to woo and delay. He could haul out some *X-Files* tapes or smoke some more of that cheap weed. But he decides to shut it all down. After a hasty jack-off with muddled imaginings in which the girl with the red glasses achieves semi-symbiosis with the impossibly sheened thighs of the bikinied NightLine girl, then a hasty floss and flush, he hits the pit in desperate hopes of a solid six and a half.

But he does not sleep. Less than a month ago he was burying his face in the folds of Nicole's stomach, lapping up her sweat. Mere weeks ago he wasn't so alone in this bed, battling these feather-spilling Martha Stewart pillows he'd picked up at the Bay to replace the ones Nicole nabbed. Mere months ago he wasn't so achingly aware of this depressing pudge, these folds dropping toward his hips, this dimpled excess on his ass. He felt at least recognizably male-like then; these days he looks in the mirror and sees Kathy Bates.

She left him for a better life. Now he lies in decay.

This miserable apartment is both torment and refuge against the sad truth of it all. The refrigerator whines like a dying hyena through the night. Silence is an impossible dream, and sleep comes hard every weary night.

And when sleep comes, dreams are always of 'Brother' Bo Sweltham – alternately, 'Bo the Bro' – host of Friday-night cable's *Rockin' Sockin' Jock Talk* on cable access back in Halifax, where he and his brother grew up. The dream is of his slender mic perennially held at distance, his polyester suits and the stunning thickness of his shellacked hair foregrounding footage: bodychecks, dunks, second-base sliders. Heath dreams of his father, Bo, slamming doors: not entering or exiting rooms, simply stomping through the house, slamming every door he can find. Dreams are of his whispered growls and the choked smell of stale coffee: his coffee consumption was titanic, upwards of twenty mugs daily.

In the recurring dream, a cartoonish Bo comes leering over snow-peaked mountains, his fangy grin widening as he delivers his signature send-off – *See ya next week! Till then, keep on rockin'!* – as his mouth gushes a thick foam tinted a repugnant Pepto-Bismol pink, flooding canyons below with this gastric spew. And then Heath wakes with his heart once again racing and his guts in flames, punching the pillow until, exhausted, he falls back into rough sleep.

But soon everything will change. Everything will click into place. He has to change, or what's the point.

5

Parker Sweltham is nowhere, yet here he is. Thirty thousand feet above sea spray and cornfield, skyscraper and canyon. Six in the morning across Nashville to check in with Southwest Distro. Connect to Fort Lauderdale for lunch at Olive Garden with Dale at Dale Breckinridge Athletics. Taxi crosstown to Bricklayerz/Gymworks in Broward for a 2:30 sit-down with Shirley Hanias and team. Taxi to the Hyatt for room check-in with local reps Brad and Sumir, hurry uptown for product demo at SportsSpot Depot on 13th. Then back to Hyatt for room-service rigatoni and three hours of catatonic channel surfing before six hours of shallow sleep. Checkout at seven, direct flight to George Bush Intercontinental for rental pickup at Thrifty and on to morning demos at Tech City and Sugar Land Sport Depot. Drive-thru lunch en route to Sport Depot IV Jacinto City and drop-in at Verve! Weight Loss & Athletics HQ, then back west to San Jacinto College by four to meet with the guy with the glasses and the palsied forearms – business-card file confirms name Terry Driscoll – at the newly renovated Athletics Centre. Up top in time for that ten o'clock conference call with Santa Monica, prep for next morning's demo, registration by 7:30 latest.

He's everywhere.

But he's nowhere. He's cruising thousands of feet above the world in the attack of mid-morning light, filtered by a parfait of strange clouds over a grid of prairies hacked into right angles. To his right a teenage girl snoozes with earphones blasting, her perfume inducing a light headache. Parker loosens his tie, then suddenly a streakless grey ocean opens into thunderstorm turbulence – it's the next day and he's wearing a McGill sweatshirt and spilling salt packets on his lap. His itinerary is like a military campaign, hurrying with temporary settlements. Days flow together and borders intermingle, dissipating. He tries to calculate Air Miles, fails. Each city greets with taxis and shuttles, afternoons of vacuum-packed salads and heartburn sandwiches, evenings of cardboard takeout. Sleep means the fiercely laundered sheets of hotels. Dime-sized soaps, continental-breakfast English muffins, automatic wake-up calls. One night, somewhere, he pay-per-views a Ben Stiller movie he knows he will never remember seeing. Between transit points he is both displayer and display. In conference booths and in meeting rooms, in warehouse client demos, he shakes hands, coordinates distributor pickups, ensures the smooth and timely running of sample exhibits. Signing claims, calling warehouses, wrangling sales assistants. His smile is wide; it can be no other way. He's walking a pedway as spring showers pummel runways, then broiling in summer, his shirt pasted to his chest with sweat. And always, he carts collapsible signage, tucked under arm. The Do It Dynamic! literature, the sales sheets and rebate vouchers, the DynaFlex logo waved as a flag. He no longer possesses the ability to taste coffee in any form.

'You just toss it in the mail and it's 10 percent back,' he says, over and over. 'No questions asked.'

And then there is Deavers, the first and last thing every client mentions. Pittsburgh Steelers running back, Super Bowl XIII Champs 1978–79, Hal '(The) Granite' Deavers, now omnipresent in all DynaFlex Exercise Lifestyle campaigns since last season's contracting, beaming from the catalogue's cover. Page 3: Deavers bares an airbrushed rack of pearly whites while pumping free-motion pulleys. Page 9: Deavers, in an aquamarine sports top and a bandana emblazoned with a logo reading *Rock 'n' Roll Forever*, laughs alongside his attractive co-spokesperson, Lynn Goel. Page 11: Endorsing ten-pound free weights, Deavers's arms underlit to highlight muscular contours beside his personal testimonial: *Today more than ever: a comprehensive system to meet all of today's unique challenges.* Deavers will customize our salvation.

At seven o'clock the clock radio cackles Mariah Carey. Parker resituates himself with a long shower, the vibrating toothbrush head, a cursory glance at Fox News to remind him where he is. Chicago.

His cellphone rings.

Parker: 'Sweltham.'

It's Glen Mucks from DynaFlex Western Distro. 'Just needed to do a confirm on tomorrow with Kinestatix.'

'Right,' Parker says.

'So we're confirmed.'

'You bet.'

'You don't sound so sure.'

'Glen. I'm sure. Rest assured.'

So many calls to make, so many requests to process. But this is what he does best. His binder sits on the sterile hotel desk, its looseleaf squarely stacked and refreshed, waiting for annotations to today's schedule. Another morning begins.

Breakfast is a spinach pastry and decaf at the Sheraton coffee shop. Finding a corner booth honoured with cast sun, he spreads his project binder and tries to concentrate. Here are the lists, the specs and memoranda. Another day, another kick at the can. Yet his mind grieves with something more than jet lag, like some buried idea is fighting to claw its way to the fore of his consciousness.

A woman in a blue pantsuit heaves herself into the booth, dropping a stuffed Fendi bag on the table.

'Saul of Tarsus,' she says, 'I need *coffee.*'

She is frizzy, tanned. Sort of resembling a gawkier Nicole, Heath's girl. Ex-girl. Though of course with arms. She extends a hand. Parker accepts.

'Patricia Vierney.'

Then she reads his confusion. 'Dougald?'

'Sorry to disappoint,' Parker says.

Patricia squeezes the bridge of her nose. 'Here's me. Supposed to meet this Dougald character here about this xenoestrogen info session. And he keeps flaking on me. Which you don't need to know. Yoych.'

'The Empowerment Expo.'

'The frigging Expo. '

A waitress arrives. 'Coffee?'

Patricia: 'God, yes. Thanks. And grapefruit juice. Big. And I could look at a menu.'

They both look to Parker. He says maybe a refill on the decaf.

He still needs to sort inventory schedules and get through a slew of confirmation calls, but this Patricia is already settling in, wiping something from her sleeve. He closes the binder and pushes it aside.

'I'm at Gopal & Dodd in Biochemical Marketing,' she says. 'Cosmetics.'

'Sounds interesting.'

'It's terrible. It's atrocious. I hate my life.'

Parker understands that when talkative individuals say such things, showily withholding, it represents an invitation to ask. So Parker does.

'Unbeknownst to most, it's a cutthroat industry,' she says. 'All the posturing of eco-ethics, the vacuity of haute couture. Ruthless, like the tech sectors. For every moment of triumph I savour, there are twice as many I anticipate with total sickening dread. But I guess that's the way things roll. Of course, I'm paid a grotesque amount to do very little.'

Mugs of coffee arrive. Patricia orders an egg-white-and-asparagus omelette. Parker hands the waitress his plate, now littered with pastry flakes.

'Senior sales representative for DynaFlex International,' he says. 'You know it?'

She picks at her PalmPilot's sleeve. Parker continues the rehearsed line.

'We're one of North America's leading exercise recreation equipment manufacturers slash dealers. Our core competency lies mostly in servicing hotels and multi-location private athletics facilities. Universities, gyms. Lately we've moved into cruise liners.'

Patricia nods and takes a quick swallow of coffee, then flinches at its heat, drooling it onto the table and swearing: *fug*. Parker grabs a serviette to mop up the spill, rescuing his project binder from the spreading puddle. He looks for his phone, worrying for its peril. To his relief he finds it safe, in his breast pocket, close to his heart.

The Chicago Empowerment Expo teems with systemized longing: glossy cut-outs, elaborate leaflet dispensers, deodorization.

'Of all the top commercial events,' Expo Coordinator Todd Fenwick is saying through a mouthful of pita, 'we *rule*. Our participant ratings are leagues beyond Golden Years Convention, Dreamers Annual, Wellness 3000, all those guys. Attendee rates at least thirty percentage up annually. We're ruling it. You get laminates for all your guys?'

'Just me today,' Parker says.

'With all this hardware?' Pointing at the LiteReacher, the CycleBike, the Vision EnduroTrainer.

Parker: 'I had some muscle.'

Fenwick nods his admiration at the booth: a fierce logo overhead, fanned literature, Hal Deavers' chesty stature in a life-sized cut-out, plastic base assembled and locked. 'That Deavers from the Steelers?'

'Super Bowl Ex Aye Aye Aye. He does our stuff.'

'Christ Almighty, I'm old.'

Finishing a Dixie cup of orange drink, Parker spots some advance attendees in the lobby being cast away by ushers in blazers.

'What sets those who get something out of it versus those who don't,' Fenwick says, 'is their whole spiel. But we clearly have nothing to worry about here. The Granite. Man. How about that.'

Fenwick is dressed sort of referee-like: he wields a whistle and at least three laminated passes clipped to his belt, plus a squiggly cord leading under his shirt to some sort of communications device. Parker, like most booth personnel, adheres to *executive impassioned*: jacketlessness; tie, if worn, loosened to approachability; sleeves hiked mid-forearm; hair trim but boyishly mussed. Like a candidate on the campaign trail. Despite Fenwick's boasts, booth positioning at the Empowerment Expo – the E-Ex, informally – is uncommonly disordered. Parker manages a quick appraisal of DynaFlex's market competitors on premises. Some are local; others, like Parker, will have seen the conference program all the way from Pasadena to Toronto. There are the musclebound reps pumping one-armed push-ups and pitching protein powders, toned women in headsets and bodysuits blasting C&C Music Factory; dour men in lab coats claiming revolutionary nutrition breakthroughs. There are the junior execs waggling coupons, the wives before woks, the meditation gurus, the envoys with box cutters assembling boothing. All employ an infinite range of dubious contrivances, scoping in for mailing-list signatures and credit cards yearning to be swiped. But these adages and charts and pithy wisdoms all churn out the same claim: *There is a better version of you hiding inside – and I know how to bring it out.*

None of these wonders threaten Parker as the first attendees now stream in, badges strung around necks, cupping complimentary coffees carted from the lobby. He has the confidence of preparation on his side, reeling in curious browsers with buddyish amiability, embracing their desire to sculpt buttery backsides or kickstart lazy tickers, leaving them with reams of pamphlets and unwavering confidence in the DynaFlex brand. 'Hey,' Parker says over and over. 'Check out our website, try our free online self-diagnosis – you might be surprised. It's fun, it's accurate and it's fast. Five minutes and you'll be like … wow.' In his honed pitch, Parker remains, above all tumult and scrap, capable. Geniality is his scimitar.

Todd Fenwick jogs past with a gigantic inflatable palm tree held to his chest, trunk side up. He races down the line, past True Dreams Residential Communities and ErgoPeutic Custom Furnishings and You Too Can Rule the Roost, past an armada of therapeutic encasements, past a custodian in headphones running a humming industrial vacuum cleaner.

'Is there …' Fenwick begins, then trips over the cleaner's cord and flies face first toward the carpet. But the inflated tree swings under him, not only rescuing him from possible rug burn, but also improbably and amazingly leveraging and bouncing him back upright, so he ends up back on his feet – jarred, astonished, but uninjured. The tree, however, begins to deflate with a loud, slow fart.

Someone from another aisle shouts: 'Cellulite warfare today!'

All his life Parker has been unafraid. He has never even understood how to be afraid. And *yet*. And yet. Something has changed. Something to do with the landscape unfurling from that fifth-floor Atlanta balcony, something to do with where he is, or isn't: here and nowhere. Something of trajectory and ambition, like baselines on clay, like the movement of time diced into calendared days. Things in motion move differently now. There is a failing of focus. Distances widen and contract, subtly, almost imperceptibly.

Something has changed. Between points distant and close, a shift has occurred, but he can't pin it down. Parker Sweltham is nowhere. Yet here he is: a street-level cocktail lounge a block from the hotel, a place awash in sickish violet light, tables of darkened figures, spacey beats as background. Patricia the Biochemical Marketing Specialist sits across the table from him.

'Cosmetics is a dirty business,' she says. 'All this racket about SLS and parabens. And this Butyrospermum parkii controversy you've heard about.'

He hasn't. Parker inspects his fingertips, trying to grasp how his mind's signals trigger motion in these strange strips of meat and ribbons of bone. Distances, again: skull to nerves, pupil to horizon. But, it seems, these distances must eventually shrink.

'Suddenly every plant under the sun's a miracle, if you swallow the marketing. Hell-*ooo*. These avocado experts and jojoba whatever with, like, pineapples, and the biodermic this and that … Do they think we're total chumps?'

She pauses, completing her third SKYY and soda while Parker thumbs another Amstel Light. Patricia seems acutely conscious of the light around her, conspicuously positioning herself at deliberate angles to the tea candle flickering on the table between them, working its jittery light to highlight some feature Parker can't determine. Her sheened hair, her eyebrows' plucked arch, maybe.

'I wouldn't know,' he says, wondering how he ended up in this situation.

'We kill our skin over and over. It requires upkeep, you know. Decay is its natural state. So our technology should wage war against it. Your skin says everything about you. Ugly clean to the bone, like what's-her-face said.'

The bartender passes by. Patricia requests two Jägermeisters, *s'il vous plaît*. Parker worries where this is going.

Patricia: 'Bet you were a *total* jock.'

'Well. Volleyball. And track and field. Actually, I still hold the provincial high-jump record.'

'How do you know it still stands?'

Pause. 'It's not like I check. But I've checked.'

'The young champ,' she says. 'And now, exercise robots.'

'We've got some pretty impressive new models this year. Fourteen.'

'Do they really change that much, year by year?'

'It's a competitive field. Really.'

Patricia leans back, biting her straw.

'It's like the automotive industry. The guys in engineering, their work is all about updates. Truth is, even when they aren't updated, we say they are. I guess it's a way of making things more interesting.'

'Because, as we know, everything's boring. Life is generally pretty lifeless.'

'I suppose it can become a bit of a drag,' he says. 'The day-to-day, everything.'

'Not everything.'

She taps the straw against the glass's rim, poking his thigh with a toe; at some point she has apparently removed her shoes.

'Not you. You're an exciting son of a bitch.'

The shots arrive.

Well past midnight, and Parker is lying fully dressed on his bed in his room, worried about the Jäger's gastric creep and a difficult morning ahead. In the bathroom, Patricia Vierney has been vomiting for the last ten minutes, but is now silent. He is almost certain he has not done or proposed anything inappropriate, but can't be completely certain. The last time he was this sloshed was at the bachelor party of one of his college buddies, an ill-advised night out his counterparts took as free licence to down buckets of rye and holler like horny coyotes at young waitresses, a night that ended in a hellish peeler club in East York, a situation that would have been utterly humiliating if Parker's awareness of it had been even remotely close to lucid. But that was a different thing with different expectations, and lesser degrees of shame, than what is happening now. He has an 8:30 sharp for muffins and Americanos with Roger from Central GigaSport at the coffee klatch by their warehouse, a twenty-minute cab ride if gifted with light traffic. To be sloppy, reeking of liquor, would be to demonstrate unprofessionalism and thus untrustworthiness. And if Parker presented such a dishevelled mien, then all efforts of promoting 1-800-FLEX-TEC, the new DynaFlex Advantage twenty-four-hour tech support resource that headlines the agenda for tomorrow's client programming meeting, will be compromised. And if that happens, all will be lost. He can practically hear Glen Mucks grinding his teeth.

'Dougald,' Patricia moans from the bathroom.

Parker toes off his oxfords and tries not to think. He stares at the ceiling fan, unsure whether he or it is spinning. The lights remain on as he slips into sleep.

6

Evening spectres gather under hazy lamps, teenagers floating with cigarettes, parking-lot factions splintering and remerging. The shopping plaza is a circuit of neon and glass, lit by lottery logos and headlights. And below the play of constellations, a dark trio of boys in hooded sweatshirts gathers by the liquor store entrance, lighting matches and flinging them into a trash bin.

Trixie sits parked in her Volvo, finishing a Whopper Jr. and looking alternately at these boys and the sky. It is an eerie night, both in the celestial sphere and here in the plaza. Everything has happened on automatic: the drive-in order, Blockbuster to return the Tom Hanks tape Parker left a week overdue, hitting Mac's for paper towels and Playtex. Registers ring, turnstiles rotate; she considers a pack of menthols, but resists. The Korean clerk beams good wishes.

Now Trixie dabs her chin with a napkin and squashes the burger's wrapper back into its bag, then crosses the parking lot toward the liquor store. Approaching, she slows. The boys form an impassable zone: black apparel, downcast postures, voices at reckless volume.

Here she is a found species, a *Mrs.* In younger years she watched her mother Allie break down in tears when a Boy Scout came to the door one Saturday morning, soliciting Trees for Canada sponsorship, and in consulting an outdated list mistakenly addressed Allie as *Mrs. Grace*, a long-shucked maiden name. This threw Allie into a pillow-thumping jag that lasted an entire afternoon. This particular woe is one she is starting to understand.

'Excuse me, miss,' one of the boys says.

She attempts to sidestep this kid: hood-headed and twitchy, scratching sneakered heels against unsocked ankles, cheeks dusted with newborn stubble and fissures of pulsing acne.

'Miss.'

She stops. 'Yes?'

'We were just … ' the kid says, then pauses. He presents pleading hands, a slight bow toward the store. 'You're heading in?'

Another boy bows similarly. 'We'd really appreciate.'

Before she knows what she's saying: 'You guys want what?'

The first kid grows an inch. 'Two bottles of Golden Glow and a twelve of Alpine.'

'You're kidding me.'

'We'll be behind the ridge.'

'The *ridge*?'

He points to the lot's closest guardrail, a slope and a treed patch beyond.

Trixie considers these kids. 'Golden Glow? The big green bottle?'

'Actually, three would be sweet. We'll throw in another ten.'

Shoppers pass. They pass her two twenties and a crumple of fives, a conspiracy of allowances.

Trixie's pulse rises. 'Can I even carry all that?'

Another sweatshirted crony leaps forward. 'You are our goddess.'

The first kid: 'We'll be waiting just over there. Behind the ridge.'

'Thank you thank you thank you.'

11/09/79. Avec posse on St. Denis last night. Already drunk by eleven, dancing to Earth Wind & Fire, wore that fluffy blue dress. Chris said it'd be a terrible night. Saw Mona with that music columnist boyf. She looked clowny and pale, starving herself. Back from Hong Kong working as a hostess for millionaires. Licking up the spit of rich creeps in velour jackets. I admit I'm jealous. We hit the dance floor then into the muck of the night. Times not so hot but heated. None of this matters. Never does. And now I pay for it. They say you can never drink too much champagne. I can now confirm that yes, you can. Barf.

It's science fiction, time travel – timeless tropes exhort how fudging with past happenings inevitably sends the present swirling into chaos, how fiddling with the time flow invites certain ruin. Dominoes fall in a row in only one direction. She knows this.

And yet she continues, despite the twist of Whopper destabilizing her guts. Stepping over the guardrail at the lot's border, ferrying the clinking bags and box of beer, she becomes a wastrel in time's order. The kids are clustered at the foot of the grassy ridge, smoking and laughing in its semi-shelter. With her approach they take notice; the first kid, Hood Head, vaults up the hill, accepting the bags and box.

'We. Have. Boo-*ooze*,' the kid announces to his friends, bounding down the ridge.

Trixie follows him down the slope. 'Hang on, hoss,' she says. 'I have my thing of Tanqueray in there.'

One of the kids, skinny with a long pink nose, emits a wet burp. The girl next to him giggles: slouchy, with straightened blue-gold hair, her eyes transformed by eyeshadow into bruises. Here they are: kids in defiance, free in the night. All huff cigarettes. A year older than Owen, if that. This would be his life, just like her own, way back when. Undissuaded from a night's fun, they barely even balk at her presence – a mom in their midst, a *Mrs*. One guy cartwheels on the dewy grass with a joint gnashed in teeth. Long futures yawn before them.

To walk past paths already taken is to invite disaster. She knows this.

'Maybe I'll hang out and enjoy a tipple with you cool guys,' Trixie says.

Pause. Hood Head looks at her, frozen with an unlit cigarillo behind his ear, a Zippo poised – its emblem reads *Too Tough to Die*.

'*Tipple?*'

She cracks the gin's seal, gliding through time.

There would be nights now known only in nostalgic meanderings, nights in swirling snow, wandering with beer cans stuffed in their mitts. They smoked in bus shelters and waited for people who never arrived. Moments of escape that now seem so squandered; just like these kids, they thrived in curfewless, adultless bliss. Winter 1979: she broke from her family in lower Westmount to independence in a walk-up on St. Zotique with Mona and Sara, twins from POL 201 International Relations. Their *December to Remember*, they declared. On their third night, as deadening storms engulfed the city, they hosted a housewarming mulled-wine party with a mélange of classmates and French anarchists from the bakery where Mona part-timed. Amid unpacked boxes and bottles coated in candlewax, turntable noise and drunkenness filled the rooms; this would be the last time she and her roommates would agree on anything.

The party had laid roots in the living room, around a Ouija board and a salad bowl for an ashtray, but Trixie moved to the kitchen in search of a rumoured half-bottle of Gilbey's. As she scoured still-unpacked boxes, there was a clunk, a screw-top wine bottle on the dish-crowded counter, and then this shaky person, lighting a cigarette off the gas stove, almost igniting his beard. His eyes, uncertain in the cheap light, spoke defiance, everything she sought and missed. He looked over, grinning with dingy teeth like worn dimes, and said, 'You do what you can, right.' She said, 'Right-o.' She looked for this guy later while everyone danced to a Sam Cooke record, but he was nowhere to be found.

The next day the three were shopping at Jean-Talon Market, Trixie feeling like shit with her greasy hair back in an iffy ponytail and sweating gin. There he was: poring over a cheese counter, wearing black Ray-Bans and a beat-up duffle coat. Mona knew Rory through an ex-boyfriend; when he saw them, he smacked two brie wheels together like concert cymbals. Trixie told him she liked his scarf, a tattered red and green thing. He asked her why she bothered being so polite. These were freezing days, full of stupid problems they inflated to galactic catastrophes. You did what you could; one does what one can.

Darkness happens quickly. The gin happens more quickly. The kids are getting rowdy; one boy threatens to kick another in the kidneys. Trixie sits at the crest of the ridge, trying to match her sinkage rate with the blue-gold girl's. Hood Head is trying to articulate something to her about the fluidity of time; the point is unclear.

'Like this idea how it's not this straight-ahead thing,' he says. 'It's not left to right, like fucking *Garfield*. It's all happening at once, but the way we see it is because our brains are limited to this thing. And all the stuff is happening at once, and this thing you consider your life is only one slice. Or like a micro-slice. Know what I mean.'

'Well, Parmenides, a classical thinker ...'

'That's Greek, right?'

'Right. He saw time as a system constructed in the human mind, and what we think is time is really just a sequence of infinities. The only thing that's real is what doesn't change. But everything changes.'

Hood Head: 'That's fucked.'

'And I guess you could say that's how it was, initially: a compacted point of matter that exploded – *boof* – into all the cosmos. One initial burst became everything. Everything that's nothing.'

Indicating the sky, the kids, the constellations. She drinks from the bottle.

Hood Head's eyes show motors whizzing behind. 'The Big Bang. We did it in physics.'

'The inflation, into this galactic production out of a singular primary force. Nucleosynthesis ... to go from this tiny core of matter to us sitting here talking about it. It amazes me. I spend hours some evenings, just me and my telescope, staring up.'

'Wow. Everything goes so fast.'

His lips are creaseless and his jaw is lean. He lights cigarette after cigarette, guiltless. He could be Arthur Rimbaud at seventeen, that grainy December 1871 photo of a gaunt, sharp face, eyes already world-weary. But no: he doesn't possess that face.

There was a coffee shop by the hospital where, after repeated visits, they got to know you – where you were going, what maybe awaited you there. They knew your order, medium half-and-half. An old hippie mastectomied woman baked low-fat banana loaf. The pitying way this woman regarded them made Trixie want to strangle her.

'You remind me of my son,' Trixie says.

'What's his name?'

Pause. 'Billy.'

'*Billy.*'

A rumpled joint is passed to Hood Head. He looks at Trixie, still unsure. Then he puffs, extends. Trixie accepts. Why not.

'He does soccer.'

'I *hate* jocks,' he says. 'Meatheads.'

The smoke's ripe stink reminds her again of drowsy apartments, unvacuumed carpets, absence. She has years on these kids, decades of mistakes – but in the scope of the stars all are identical. They bellow punk rock lyrics and crush emptied cans, surely tittering at her shoulder pads and bangles. But they are restrained, still unsure – not yet desperate enough to be fully wild.

'He's not what you'd call a jock. He's a fully imagined human being.'

'Good ol' Billy.'

The blue-gold girl is now making out with the pink-nosed boy. Trixie is incredibly stoned.

Hood Head inches closer to Trixie. 'Wanna take a walk in the woods?'

Trixie stuffs the half-spent Tanqueray bottle back in its bag and moves to rise.

'Actually, you know,' she says, 'they say the universe is slowing down.'

Driving home, she cranks the radio and fights her desire to yell. The radio says, *Billions of people are deceived – should they die before coming to the truth, they will spend eternity in hell.* Only when rounding the final bend does she realize she's run two red lights. In a panic she pulls to the curb, bringing a gale of honks from a cab swerving past. She breathes with great concentration, then continues home.

The house appears at the base of the lane's tree-sheltered bend, filtered light burning behind its curtains. This experience – braking, decelerating, triggering the automatic garage door – is so familiar, it almost becomes a non-experience. But as the car's trajectory swivels, headlights training across the chunky mortar of the wall that borders the driveway's flank and the yawn of garage swinging into her vision, Trixie feels coldness rushing upward. The iris of her perception narrows and her head drifts back as the connection between consciousness and location is severed. She is young, hydraulic. The radio says, *We are living in a momentous time in history, the end of days and a technological whore of Babylon.* The Volvo's right door scrapes against the driveway wall with a metal shriek. Something loosened rattles across the hood.

11/17/79. Nightmares again last night: weird ribbony cords and sky of yellow nitrogen and a greedy mouth licking its lips. Woke up calling for Dad, smoked two cigarettes on the cold balcony to calm down. Rory says all orifices mean something about lost time. Time totalizes everything. He never showed tonight at Marie-Claude's vernissage, so of course afterward I hike up to St. Viateur to rattle his windows. I see the glow of his bedside lamp but no sound inside. Even put ear to glass for the shame of no one but me myself. But again he's out somewhere boozing and complaining. After a while I give up and head back to the front doorstep. Starts to snow and I'm ready to slit my wrists. Then this chick with these dudes sniffing behind comes up the sidewalk, laughing. She sees me and comes over and then the sympathy. Why are you crying, are you okay, that sickening damsel-in-distress-I'm-with-you routine. Cunt. Finally I hurry back to Parc to hail a taxi with nine dollars I don't have to waste. Somewhere R hugs his pillows and growls. But my boyfriend can be beautiful in the right light, and even if in the next morning's forensics you can barely put two syllables together, you can't just dismiss that.

An instant or an age later: she opens her eyes and instinctively shifts the stick into P. The hood's right corner is now a crumpled fold, its metal grated against the wall's sandstone.

This is not just the Tanqueray and weed at work. This is total failure. With an unsteady hand she withdraws the key from the ignition. The seat belt hugs her chest and her extremities feel absent. She sits, waiting for something to happen. Nothing happens.

She staggers away from the car and over the unruly lawn, key still in hand. Total failure, yes – she thinks of her father, and his own decline into lack. In his median days, post-diagnosis but pre-advanced, Lloyd suffered eternities of unresponsiveness, gaping all morning at their old beagle Echo Jr. snoozing on his ratty quilt. Total failure, increment by increment. Endings in explosions or in erosions.

Instead of going to the front door, she heads around the north side of the house, glancing into the lessened light behind the living room's diaphanous curtains, then continuing on to the shelter of the backyard. It is dark back here. She reminds herself to call Dr. Bokeria tomorrow, already disappointed in herself for things not yet done, or done too often. Drinking with teenagers – ridiculous. This yearning for escape is the desire of a child, not a woman. She goes to her knees, then lies still in the cool, overgrown grass.

7

Despite his howls and a deluge of cold night rain, the officers had little trouble hauling him down from the bridge-side railing. They cuffed him and pressed his squirming body against the cruiser hood; the engine tremored through his bones. Within minutes an ambulance was on the way. *To confirm: teenage kid, Caucasian, about sixteenish. Looks like a real live wire. Yep. Says another one was with him but no current visual.* One of the EMTs tried to calm him down, demanding he explain the ifs and thens of his crimes, the rationale behind such horrors. They asked what happened to the other guy, what happened to Ike. But he couldn't speak; he could only howl.

Below was darkness. *I had it all.* Darkness is infinite; Owen is not.

In their sessions Owen often tries to pry personal info out of Fultz, but the counsellor persists in remaining mum. Here lies an unbreachable gulf, an impossible floe of berg, Owen chopping at Arctic ice; it is 1911, maybe 1910, and he is claiming unmapped land for Norway with Legendary Explorer Roald Amundsen (July 16, 1872–c. June 18, 1928) and a crew in beards and pelts – this is from *Funk & Wagnalls*, a water-coloured archipelago in , vol. 1. And as their flag is staked in foot-thick ice, it is again, dismally, the beginning of summer 1999 and he is back on *terra cognita*. After hopeful rises of dawn come inevitable sundowns.

'Let's talk about the bridge,' Fultz says. 'You were up there.'

Yes. Affirmative, now and then. Fultz's sterile offices are reigned over by the reek of burned coffee and overworked radiators. Outside: rain and traffic oscillating in a steady gush. Inside: utility carpet and recessed ceilings and networks that routinely malfunction during peak hours. EZ-FM plays Enrique Iglesias, Shania Twain, Matchbox Twenty.

'I hate to replay the past.'

Fultz: his blackheaded nose for dilemmas, his hands always clammy.

Owen: 'Me too.'

While in custody, Owen possessed no shoelaces, no dignity. His only possessions were cheap reference materials, donated paperbacks, tattered comics. The dates and maps in his encyclopedia were the only things to get him through those afternoons; otherwise he'd watch *Seinfeld* with the other asswipes.

A classic Fultzian lift of brow. 'Perhaps you'll tell me what you guys were hoping to accomplish that night.'

'I don't know. Maybe get our faces on the Live at 5.'

A sniff. 'You sought attention.'

'Rock and Roll Hall of Fame.'

Fultz almost laughs, more with familiarity and disappointment than amusement. 'And Ike?'

Up there at the bridge's summit, teetering in the wind, Ike laughed at everything, alive and full of Jose Cuervo. Why? Why not. To walk in the morning of the dead earth, drunk and free – this is the stake of proud wolves, the glory of heroics. There they went, and there the course of history was shaped.

Fultz: 'You don't want to talk about Ike?'

'Nope.'

Another long moment passes. Voices murmur in the hallway. Finally, Fultz shakes his head.

'Tell me,' he says, 'what *do* you want?'

This is where it leads: into the mucky shit. Owen should be down there, cold and veiny, bobbing lifelessly on the harbour floor, weird weeds coiling his ankles like braces, staring wide into the deep. And then there's Coleridge from English class again: *Yea, slimy things did crawl with legs Upon the slimy sea. About, about, in reel and rout, The death-fires danced at night; The water, like a witch's oils, Burnt green, and blue, and white. And some in dreams assured were Of the Spirit that plagued us so.* At the bottom one meets these awful things, the death things. Whatever a witch's oils were, and how they burned, fuck knows. But that spirit that plagues us through the murk, through the slime – in drowning he would triumph over it all.

Owen picks a fleck of dryness from his lower lip. 'I'm fine.'

Fultz pens his clipboard. 'Still taking those ... weight-gain supplements?'

'No,' Owen lies.

'No side effects from your medication.'

'No, sir.'

This is true: he stopped taking them weeks ago.

'So everything's fine.'

'Yep.'

'All the problems of this world have been miraculously resolved.'

'I don't know.'

Fultz: 'Ask yourself, whose time are you actually wasting?'

Time: Owen could waste it all day. Whether a fifty-five-minute block or a generation – neither affects anything. It is the year 2210 and humanity has conquered its rival, death. Nations happily breathe methane and chomp magma like turkey burgers. There is nothing to fear. It is 3000 BCE and he is humping limestone up a seven-foot tract of sand, over and over every day in the Euphrates' glaze until finally perishing in a bout of plague. He files book reports printed on the inkjet Epson, words in twelve-point faded Caslon: *Why* Lord of the Flies *Sucked by O. Sweltham*. In between there was only waiting: lines for pizza, for doses, for GO trains.

'It's not like I want to be here, Hiram.'

'Hm.'

Back to his clipboard. 'I'm recommending we not increase your meds. Both professionally, because as a physician I don't think you need it, and personally, because as a friend, I don't think you need it.'

'That makes three of us.'

Fultz leans forward in his seat. 'Consider yourself fortunate. Typically you would either have been placed on general probation or instated into in-patient care. Happily, we've been able to avoid either. For now, your parents and I have agreed to pursue a less … aggressive route.'

So the prisoner dissolves and twists through time. Once there was brief unity; since then has been constant bedlam. He's been everywhere and every-when, all at once. Reincarnated a thousand times to rule it all, over and over again.

Only five months ago, he was still imprisoned. As noon displaced morning, the outside world was doused in rainfall, the windows of the West Common Room misted with greyish streaks.

Owen sat watching others smoking cigarettes under the shelter of Dismas's south entrance. His secobarbital dosage had been reduced from 300 to 200 mg; his hands had ceased trembling and he felt vaguely himself. For the first time in days he was able to sit comfortably, neither half-asleep nor restlessly pacing hallways. Having left his *Funk & Wagnalls* upstairs, he thumbed a well-worn comic book found in a communal stack of donations – *Archie's Mad House* no. 26, dated June 1963 – reading of googly-eyed aliens and steaming hamburgers and adolescent tumult. At the other end of the room others watched *The Price Is Right* on a tiny wall-mounted Hitachi. One of the group kept yelping *Showcase Showdown Showcase Showdown*.

Call this place Owen's Madhouse.

He'd moved down the stack to *Everything's Archie* no. 21 when he sensed an approaching presence, huffing and smelling of milk. But he refused to divert attention from the story: Dilton Doiley, Riverdale's lovable and industrious nerd, had devised another zany invention, some sort of hot-rodded pogo stick. Owen's eyes targeted frames, inked text, an ad for the Charles Atlas Dynamic Tension System: a kick of sand to the face, the worst of humiliations.

'Owen.'

They want to ruin him. They don't know him, even if they know his name and blood type. Even if he lowers himself as they compute his dosages and legislate his future, even if they subject him to the ordeals of *How Stella Got Her Groove Back* on Movie Night, which, despite the alluring sheen of Angela Bassett's skin – skin O imagines smells like a pleasing combo of pricey eau de toilette and sweaty buttocks – sucked so hard even the staff took it as an opportunity to catch up on paperwork. Even if he submits to all their demands, they still want more. They want him to surrender everything. An auburn-haired counsellor with a muskrat face requested he *let down the defences for a sec – we're not here to judge* as his fellow prisoners nodded, thumbs wringing and pens *skrtch*ing across notepads. He may be ruined, but he will never be owned.

'Owen,' this person said. 'I need to speak with you.'

Riverdale: an eternal springtime of luminous teens and stodgy but unpathological adults, bliss interrupted only by a rained-in afternoon or ski-slope weekend or heat wave, anxieties flaring only in dark exclamatory squiggles from the forehead of Big Moose or Pop Tate, where all concerns are resolved in just desserts for opportunists like Reggie Mantle, or punning reminders, or unambiguous morals – like that one where Archie joins the wrestling squad, persevering against odds to learn the valuable lesson that *a quitter never wins and a winner never quits.* Archie Andrews suffered in panelled torments, only to live again in a turned page, a new *Double Digest.* In Riverdale no one aged or died.

'Will you please just *look* at me.'

Owen looked. Fat Brian stood over him, Fat as ever, sweating, a patchy recede for a hairline. A wad of gauze and tape padded the left side of his face.

'Can we talk?'

Owen closed his book. Fat Brian remained standing, keeping a distance.

'FYI,' he said. 'Laceration and canalicular injury. But the ophthalmologist, she's optimistic.'

Over Fat Brian's shoulder Owen saw Daley, the limping Belizean janitor, at the hallway's entrance with a package of light bulbs in hand, the only staff present.

Cyclopean Fat Brian continued. 'I just want to … In sessions we discussed motivation, how we're motivated to do things. I just wanted to. We talk a lot about forgiveness … '

Owen leapt to his feet. Fat Brian flinched.

'You're fat,' Owen said.

Gently but solidly, he kicked Fat Brian in the balls.

Time passed. For weeks, centuries, he barely spoke. He was reminded incessantly of the terms of his sentence, warned of defying those requirements, assessed and processed by a carousel of dour analysts. The radiators heaved and failed over a record-cold winter. Jamaican guys on his floor promised to slice his face, but didn't.

During his incarceration they met in Fultz's office, assuming positions established during previous sessions: the prisoner in a sturdy utilitarian seater, his interrogator's stronghold his desk and vinyl-backed swivel. In plastic chairs sat Units both Paternal and Maternal; the Maternal dabbed a nostril with a wad of crunched Kleenex. There had been *active dialogue*, Fultz explained, as to how the future should and would play out on release. Emphasis on The Future, cleaving it from the ruins of the past. Flying hoverbots, the prisoner imagined. Teleportation backpacks, Venusian colonies, wormhole transit. But he kept mum. The prisoner traipsed through fields of cottony joy, cliff-diving into the earth's core to lounge in consuming furnaces, dunked into the most blistering Hell of Hells to suffer piercing pitchforks and chambers engorged blood-red with lacrimal drainage and asphyxiation.

The Paternal Unit uncrossed and recrossed his legs, looking sleek: new slip-ons, hair trim, jawline razored of any errant bristle, clutching stapled photocopies. In this face the prisoner's eye saw the conviction of a guy who could view every moment of his life as interconnected to the next, but never found anything in these connections. Living, as they say, one day at a time.

'In the past we've been pretty *lightweight* about looking the other way,' the Paternal Unit told Fultz.

'And we appreciate that,' the prisoner said.

The Paternal Unit brapped at him to cut the sarcasm.

They told him he had a choice.

The prisoner dropped forehead to knees, wanting nothing more than one solid bowl of Sad Tony's hash, washed down with a cool 1.5L of Labatt Max Ice. Oh, to waltz through the garbage fields and ice pastures and cyclones of Ragnarok or Rwanda or Riverdale, the killing fields and chocolate factories of this world. Everything is there, never expecting you to decide – it's all done for you.

They spoke his name again and again.

Fultz voiced conditions. Regular and lengthy counselling sessions. A system of restrictions, as any violation might prompt reassessment. Terms were struck: the final countdown to Armageddon would take place outside these walls. Fultz would serve as primary contact. Counsel this child. Admire this child. Validate and rescue him. Cage him not in wards and doses. Tarnish not these hopeful visions. Let him live.

Below the bridge was darkness. Darkness is infinite; Owen is not. He had it all. Below the bridge was dark. They asked him Yes or No. His gurgling gut did the talking. Son of the Cosmos. Rock and Roll Kicker of Ass. Leader of the Free World. They wanted him to say, *Yeah*. And even when *Yeah* was his answer he could barely even say it: *Yeah*.

But then he was freed, his debt to society paid. The Trespass to Property Act, RSO 1990, Ch. T.21, invasion of premises, plus linked charges of underage drinking and theft and forcible resistance to law officers, court dates, damages costed and restitution beseeched, graver charges of assault and battery contested and dropped based on video evidence, a fierce pen stroke for a whacked gavel – all this was behind him now, the Young Offender. He was reformed, remade in queasy morning light, led to his father's car like a useless feeb with a hockey bag full of dirty laundry. His mother, tanging of afternoon sake, embraced him not by the shoulders but strangely circling one arm around his head and the other around his neck. They'd brought him a Harvey's combo, still warm, and he sat in the shotgun seat eating slowly, his father at the wheel and his mother in the back seat detailing visions for upcoming gardening: tomatoes, basil, bay laurel, revivals from winter's damage, articles she'd clipped on phototoxicity. Then a diatribe about voter enumeration and her irritation with this current Unite the Right or whatever; she sounded tired. Then they were pulling into the driveway he knew so well, the house where he'd lived since the Dawn of Time when Man waged war against pterodactyls and lava rained over streetless plains, its windows like dull eyes and its garage a twisted smirk and its eaves a shitty hairdo for all eternity.

He'd been corrected through corrections. Everything was going to be all right, freed from the spectres of past days. Everything was going to be totally fine.

8

Freight supervisor Josef introduces the loaders assigned to today's DynaFlex inventory at the new Duracell Toronto Convention Centre as Cody and Creck: cousins, teenaged, with identical fops of brick-red hair. Soon into the load it comes to light they attend the non-denominational Boulder Church on Eglinton; Parker's seen their kaleidoscopic spots on TVO, starring an urn-jawed guy striding a daffodil-garlanded stage, a choir in gold-fringed gowns clapping to a band of sparkling Zildjians and banks of synthesizers. Cody and Creck argue in almost incomprehensible honks about the previous night's performance by the church's Senior Band, Project Luke 24:5. Cody and Creck play bass guitar and rhythm guitar, respectively, in the Junior Band, X-alted. Junior Band apparently hates Senior Band. Parker politely asks the guys for less talk and more action.

The parking lot sloping behind the centre is glazed with mid-morning mist as cars whoosh in for spots. Today is the final installment of the touring North American Empowerment Expo, nineteenth of nineteen, and the end of Parker's seasonal sweep. Before this his schedule had demanded weeks of meet-and-greets and regional daytrips: Nashville. Cedar Rapids. Milwaukee. Detroit. Hamilton. Then the Expo, the schedule of which Parker would have to consult his crumbling itinerary to recall in full.

But now: home. Just as his bag thumped down the carousel at Pearson airport this morning he'd rung Guus Goorts, interim Vice-President Sales, assuring he'd come drop off paperwork before heading down to the convention centre. Goorts said all was cool, and no one expected Parker back until Monday. Parker said he'd just like to unload some cargo. Just to pop by.

DynaFlex's Mississauga office at the fifteenth floor of Brunson Towers 100 hadn't changed. The kitchenette near Parker's office was still stocked with the same two lowly cartons of Wheat Thins and that untouched tin of Flemish candy donated by Kinestatix clients last quarter. Shelley's replacement during her maternity leave, the new Administrative Assistant Raekwona, eyed Parker with a strange glance he couldn't quite decipher, but seemed to imply suspicion. But it was only a matter of minutes before he gave up pretending to examine his desk and made his exit, almost leaving his car keys behind in his haste. Before he reached the door, Raekwona called after him, dangling his San Antonio Spurs key chain. 'Left your keys.' Parker smacked his forehead: 'Been on the road too long.' Oh absentminded he.

Cody and Creck have a knack for handling every piece of inventory off the truck with complete bewilderment. The job at hand is to get the boxed gear set in cardboard slats onto waiting dollies, then on to assigned floor locations, all clearly marked by colour-coded decals affixed to each piece. And these pieces are not heavy; it's work befitting toddlers with enough upper-body strength to lift a large jar of pickles. The gruff loading-bay supervisors are not exactly happy.

Parker observes this conflict brewing from alongside the truck, but takes little notice. He watches only the mist, the chain-link fences spread at the end of the lot. Every meeting during his son's time at St. Dismas meant a similar mist on grey paving, another conversationless ride and a robotic rail introducing the visitor parking lot. All throughout the process – arguing with legal, chauffeuring him to analysis, pencilling forms – everything seemed designed as an intricate experience of punishment for everyone involved. The lights, that parkade, waiting.

A thick-goateed man wearing a fleece Beer Store vest slaps gloves together. 'Your load's last in,' he says to Parker. 'We're a half-hour past doors.'

Parker looks at his watch, then at Cody and Creck, both gawking vacantly at a stack of pallets. Parker hauls himself up into the loading bay.

'Should we take in that next one?' Creck asks.

Parker jangles change in his pockets. 'It all goes in, guys. You don't need to ask. We'll sort it after. Just step it up. Our guy Hal will be here any second.'

Parker had asked Owen if he wanted this job. Decent bucks for a kid, make a couple hundred over the weekend. And, always, obeying Fultz's directives: to be *gentle but vigilant*. Parker emailed from Dallas: *hey bud! if you need a few bucks we need some guys lifting boxes on Sunday. $12/hr plus lunch and end bonus. write back or call my cell let me know. thanks dad.* But no reply came.

A behemothian coach rolls in, followed by a squad of rented vans. Moments later the lot is packed with elderly convention-goers. A daunting heap of unsorted DynaFlex hardware still remains strewn throughout the upper bay. Beer Store Vest Guy comes over, his rage levels rising.

'Yeah, I know,' Parker says, anticipating his complaint. 'It's all in now. Look, tell me ... Mel, is it?'

Parker extends a hand, initiating a process that is patently Parker's own, yet beyond his understanding. Something ruggedly human, the competence with which he negotiates assurance, laying unease to rest. Parker has been told by Guus Goorts that his instincts for equanimity and basic conciliation are almost paranormally acute. Parker knows that dedication alone can provide ample ammo in salesmanship. Effort in means reward out: a tenet he has always believed. He has earned the life he leads. Maybe it was Bo the Bro who pushed this: good fortune comes to those who seek it, not to those who slack off or gratuitously squander opportunities. Bo as patriarch spoke plainly – with hustle, with discipline, *no shitting around* – his was a results-oriented world view. Tanned, lantern-jawed, broadcaster and divorcé, he suffered no fools. He leaned toward gradual, steady accomplishment, and was forever uneasy for it. Such influence, muted if present at all, was always overshadowed by his wife's. And yet there was something there, a mantra in Parker's mind telling him to get his *ass in gear or reap the consequences* – a sentiment Bo advised the Leafs' defending lineup every week. And when, almost twenty years ago, Parker successfully transformed a background in athletics and a McGill B.Com. into a promising sales position with a golf equipment retailer-distributor in Pointe-Claire, he sat alone with a congratulatory pint and Cajun frites at a downtown pub and stewed over the numerous forces that had led to that triumph, understanding even then how much work had yet to be done. And yet, in hindsight, it had been so easy. All this, the chronicle of his life, happened practically on automatic. All it took was perseverance, a graceful manner and an unsweaty handshake.

Now Parker stands in Section A-6 of the main convention hall, scented in carpet disinfectant and overbrewed hazelnut coffee. Tensions with the loading crew have been averted and the hardware laid out enough to complete at least bare-bones boothing, so Parker should be free to breathe easy.

But since Atlanta there has been this change. At first he thought it might be something digestive or respiratory stopping up his chest. He has navigated tough situations before: the transgressions and trials of his son, the company's price-to-earnings ratio crisis during last year's NASDAQ swell, the imbroglio over his father Bo's gravestone at St. Andrew's, which in confusion between two clients had almost been placed in the earth reading, *Dearest sister and mother, she passed through glory's gate to walk in paradise.* Now he is troubled by questions he's never known and can't articulate. And questions demand answers. Glimmers appear in sudden advances: in the tiling over store queues, in channels flipped in a single suite, in runway beacons at dusk. Strange blood on pool-deck tiles. Explosions of glass. *Grandfather clock.* This is no forking-path choice he is simply unequipped to parse – like the poem Trixie included in a note early in their courtship, soon after first meeting at that girl Marie-Claude's art opening, something in Spanish, *Tu voz regó la duna de mi pecho en la dulce cabina de madera,* that seemed to imply some sort of meaningful desire but truthfully left him stumped, and the way she asked him about it the next day as they sipped shandy-gaffs on the fire escape only confirmed his failure to understand.

No, this new thing wells up in vague, shapeless symptoms, emptying his lungs and unsettling his balance. It is partnered with euphoria equally mystifying, exhausting. Unhelpful in wrapping up a solid day of purchase orders.

And yet nothing has changed. With this round of travels complete, today's booth will be the last he'll man until the next jaunt in the new year, sometime in the twenty-first century. He removes his jacket, rolls up his sleeves and assists Creck in assembling an UltraTraction Magna6 station, a complex task even for one as familiar with the gear as Parker. Streamlining shipping from the Bangalore plants to the warehouse in Georgetown, DynaFlex designers have opted for optimal packaging compaction over accessibility, the result being that each item tumbles out as a puzzle of incongruent bolts and metal workings. Parker has put a thousand of these things together, and every time it's an awful, sweaty chore.

Cody appears with an armful of Cokes. 'They were up for grabs,' he says. 'Plus I got that tape.'

The tape is to fix up a Hal Deavers cut-out torn in the dudes' brusque load-in. Parker and Cody and Creck take five to crack cans – which Parker suspects were not actually free – and regather their efforts. They are ridiculously behind schedule, and the spokesperson himself has yet to emerge: Deavers's commitment to his contract, Parker knows, has been erratic of late. But strangely, Parker doesn't feel anxious or pressured; normally he would be corralling passersby to Do It Dynamic! But instead he tabs his cola with these kids and listens with genuine interest to their complaints of Youth Group dramas, feeling zero fret.

Cody and Creck are arguing.

'It was Tuesday, fucko.'

'She said *Wednesday*, you vaginal bloodfart.'

Parker clears his throat. 'Fellas, maybe tone it down a hair. For the moms.'

Just as Parker realizes he's been mishearing Creck's name, and that it is actually *Craig*, he spots an instantly recognizable head from across the exhibition floor. Unmistakable: it's H-Bomb, moving down the line. Even in distant recognition, his brother's discomfort is clear. Movement, tentative; inspections, timid. The barely sipped cola slips from Parker's fingers and spills onto the carpet, fizzing.

'And if he was a homosexual he would've already sexually assaulted your poop chute, which is crusty with gay-guy drool,' Creck is telling Cody.

Parker asks Creck/Craig and Cody if they could please cut out the trash talk and fetch a cloth for the spill, then finally get the cardboard Deavers fit for display. At the rate at which Heath is ambling from booth to booth, he will round the southern quadrant and be at the DynaFlex corner in mere minutes.

'Just need to go out for a … yeah,' Parker tells Creck/Craig, who doesn't hear him. Neither does his cousin.

The stairwell rings with echoes: the buzz of utility lights, clangs of pipes, his own shallow breath. For a moment Parker hides behind the door in a kittenish hunch, unsure, gripping the door's latch. Then he realizes he is not alone.

'Service access only.'

Parker straightens and backs away from the door. A man stands a few steps above: uniformed, black, thin, a cuff of keys rattling in his fist. A thick slash scars his lip.

'Should I get on the intercom?' the man says.

Parker looks up into an infinity of harsh lights and stairs like shelves. Below is the same scene but darker: a growling descent. Understanding the question being asked, his salesman's aplomb is restored.

'Yes. No. Of course. Thanks.'

There is a prolonged moment in which neither man moves.

'So,' the uniformed man says. 'I'll escort you back.'

'No no no. Let's …'

Parker pries the door open, peeking back into the crowding hall. Heath is just passing Exfoliation Escapade and ETA Circa: NOW, a stack of bumper stickers in hand, moseying down the line toward where Cody and Craig/Creck still bicker. Cardboard versions of Deavers lie in severed hunks across the floor amid twists of packing tape.

Parker eases back into the stairwell.

'Trying to make a clean getaway?' the man says, nodding at the door.

'Skirting a conversation best avoided,' Parker says.

'Ah.'

This man, apparently a member of the custodial staff, steps down and introduces himself. His name is Adam Abot. Parker does the same in response. They shake.

'Busy afternoon?' Parker tries.

Adam waggles keys. 'They spill coffee, I'm there with the ReadiVac.'

Parker knows his present tactic makes no sense. Why dread an impromptu encounter with his brother, or anyone? Because something has changed. Where before he saw opportunities, he now sees silhouettes. His knees feel weak. Parker wonders if Heath will recognize the DynaFlex logo and make the connection. Chances are slim.

Parker: 'Is there another way back out from here?'

'Follow me.'

Adam Abot leads him down the stairwell, a stifling, metallic space. Parker notes a security camera in an upper corner, and in a moment of accelerated panic he imagines its lens as the probing eye of so many individuals and entities, a faceless mush of humans that includes even his son, whom he certainly does not fear yet often thinks about in a fearful way. And when, on the next level down, still another camera appears similarly positioned, he finds himself trembling, shielding his face from its view with his jacket's collar.

They pause on the P2 landing at a service door marked No Exit. Adam Abot unleashes his arsenal of keys and opens the door, holding it wide.

'Follow to the end, then take the last door,' he says. 'Service elevator should be operational. Punch, you know, M.'

The door opens to a low-ceilinged hallway emitting a weird reddish glow and a webwork of shivering piping overhead.

Parker balks. 'Am I supposed to be back there?'

'No one's supposed to be back there. This is for maintenance staff. But if you want to not be seen … Have trust.'

Parker looks around. No cameras here on this lowest level, only furnaces grinding and pipes working. 'If you say so. And thanks.'

'Consider it Christian charity. And if you're ever in need … ' He produces a card: *ProFix Reno & Removal: Fast, Professional, Hassle-Free.* And a phone number. The ink-jet-printed card is on weak cardstock, text in fourteen-point Arial. 'But if you ever want the service.' Adam flips the card. Another number is handwritten in marker on the reverse. 'Myself and some fellows have another thing on the go. All papers clear. We can cut a rate. Cash only. You see what I insinuate. As far as taxes, records, that.'

'Right. Okay.'

Adam Abot eases off, a twist in his face. Parker doesn't really follow.

'I assure you everything's legitimate. But if you need accreditation, I have multiple numbers. I'm talking top-notch, no funny business. Again, we have papers.'

Parker doesn't know what to think. 'Papers?'

'The Immigration. We're all landed, African. You know. Once upon a time.'

'Oh.'

Parker is finding it difficult to formulate any coherent train of thought.

Adam sniffs. 'If you want to pay some fool for your renovations, hire your slovenly neighbourhood contractor. Otherwise, call the number on the back. That's my personal number.'

Voices echo in the stairwell above, someone saying, 'Prosciutto or no prosciutto, if it's on the list we still have to have antipasto on the cart.'

Parker thanks Adam, still not sure about the nature of their transaction, then steps forward into this foreboding chamber of cement and steel. Strange roars surround; he chances a look back as the door closes. Passing the humming pipes and rounding a brief bend, he feels every step, every passing second, lurching through some oblique choreography. Steps. Goorts forwarded him an email this morning, marked *Urgent* in his Outlook, subject Re: *May Reports_PS, impressive results as always. Denise.* The drive to the boy's hospital would take just over an hour up Highway 15 in clear traffic; Trixie would always insist on stopping for coffee and pastries on the way, even though Parker, seething in silence, would have sawed off his arm to just get there and hurry back, he always complied. Forty-three years old, he has fewer years ahead than he does behind. The tissue rots off his endoskeleton and gutty fluids fill his chest and the discs of his vertebral column disintegrate to powder. He is laid to rest and eternal forgottenness. Steps: toward, not forward.

Arriving at the hallway's end, he pauses before the door, present coordinates escaping him. He is in the grip of something worming through his mind he can't quite identify. Here in the convention centre's bowel, in the patterns and itineraries, something frightening threatens, mere steps, or moments, away.

Elevator doors part. Parker passes through the third-floor lobby and into the convention hall: a formless roar indicates the Expo is in full swing. Someone shouts, 'Sixty days to self-confirmation,' and a moderately enthused chorus echoes back, 'Sixty days!'

And in the convergent dappling of halogens overhead and the wash of crowd and the stuttering flashbulbs of DynaFlex's Zero-G Life Trajectory, Parker sees something that freezes him to the core: The Granite himself, buttoned in a slimming tan sportcoat, his pink face erupting with sweaty joy, only an hour late. Before a skimpy but captive audience, Deavers speaks into a mic, eliciting titters and nods. These quips are inaudible from where Parker watches. There is an individual at Deavers's side, locked now in a tight squeeze signifying camaraderie and warmth. As a fan comes forward waving a Polaroid JoyCam, Deavers gives a thumbs-up, as does the sheepish man clutched in his embrace. United in the flash, Hal Deavers and Heath Sweltham could be taken for the best of pals.

9

Owen wakes. A thick seep of purple flows from his lower lip, drying against his T-shirt's Angry Samoans logo. He shudders, cold sweat on his forehead. He feels almost supernaturally nauseated, and the grossness striping his shirt shows something's already happened in that department.

He stands, then reels. After a second of reorientation, awareness returns: he is in the Byngs' basement rec room, low-ceilinged and close, stuffy and stenched with last night's cigarettes. The TV plays *The Bold and the Beautiful* with the sound low. On the grubby carpet, a bowl-like ashtray is upturned, a collage of spent smokables scattered alongside miniaturized artillery and weaponry from an unfinished bout of Risk. Lying among this wreckage is The Bying himself, face down in his briefs and a hiked Roots sweatshirt. Pale lamplight frowns upon the scene.

Owen climbs the stairs and pauses in the kitchen, still unsteady and toxic. He listens to a noiseless house, silence disrupted only by the syncopation of morning rainfall. The microwave reads 2:55, which makes no sense until he presses Clock and with a beep it re-establishes time as just before eight in the morning. Chuck's mom has assembled a basket of poppyseed bagels and single-serve Kellogg's pouches on the island bisecting the kitchen, along with a jug of pink grapefruit juice. Owen swigs a mouthful, then turns and horks into the sink. Demolishing most of this yuck with the faucet's sprayer, he goes for the fridge. On its bright shelves he finds a jar of Bick's Polskie Ogórkis; he sits in the chill of the open fridge, his head halfway into the light, back against the crisper drawer. The pickle is crisp and cool. He almost laughs out loud at how bad he feels.

The trudge home is a chore of slosh and headache. Early summer clouds howl with impending storms, the atmospheric electricity practically tickling the hairs of his neck. There is a flash in the sky – he counts, and five seconds later, thunder barks. One point five kilometres away, he calculates by a system taught to him by his grandfather Bo.

Rounding a corner, he sees his house at the end of the street. Sleepy in its brick and shrubs, a newly painted front door: his mother's Heavenly Blue. He has lived in this house his entire life. Others have been places: The Bying was born in a Munich army base and lived all over Eastern Europe until shipped to Canada at eight; The Calch came from Bangor and once hiked the semi-live Mauna Loa volcano; Lucky visits his mother in Mexico City twice a year. Even dumb-ass Deanerz drives to Sugarloaf every March break with his stepfather to hang at the family chalet. And Ike, he'd been *everywhere*. But Owen's been nowhere, seen nothing but the comatose walls of locked rooms in juvenile detention. And that was barely even an actual place – it seems more like a time.

Two driveways from his own, he stops. The morning sky is a graph, crackled with lightning. He could just not go home. He could run, leave, be something else. He could do anything – as much as he wants to do nothing.

Then the roof of his house explodes.

She is deep within a troubling, slow dream – a slightly younger, more feral version of herself enters a previously overlooked portal in the kitchen's north corner, discovering an eerie solarium-like room inserted in an architecturally impossible location contiguous to or below the house, the place populated by tremendous blossoming plants that are almost but not quite people, plus they have slavering fangs, and they glower down at her, the invader – when Trixie is startled by the crash.

She casts aside bedcovers to discover a view of sky where there should be no sky: grey overcast occupies the bedroom's upper east corner. The meeting of wall and ceiling is split with blackish finger-like protrusions tearing the eggshell paint, with wet fibres of material split at the apparent point of impact.

Trixie sits up, trying to determine if this is really happening, or still the boggling work of dreams. Cool air wafts into the room; she hears bird calls and traffic whooshes. A puddle of briny mess gathers on the hardwood under this gaping hole; raindrops gather on her bureau.

She pokes the body buried next to her in the bed.

Parker rolls over. 'What. No.'

'The ceiling.'

Again: 'What.'

He sits up. Then, seeing what she's seeing, he bounds out of bed while Trixie groggily looks for her slippers. Tobacco-hued water drools down the walls near where the tree lies cradled by the remaining wall. Chips of bark and plaster shards lie at the base of the break. Parker assesses this disaster in disbelief, a prominent morning boner still poking from his underwear.

'What happened?' he says, incredulous.

Trixie can't answer. She asks if they should be calling the insurance people. He says maybe, probably, still waking up. They look at one another, dumbfounded, then both at the door; fake artillery fire can be heard from downstairs.

Owen thumbs a controller, supine on the carpet, feet pointed away from the screen, and looking back overhead as digitized soldiers wage combat. His eyes are open, yet he seems unaware of his parents' hurry downstairs. Parker finds the remote and lowers the volume from ten to two-ish. Owen seems not to notice.

As Trixie goes to the kitchen and begins feeding the coffee maker, Parker dithers in the hallway, frustration split between son and wife. The boy's T-shirt is saturated with a dark stain; in an alarmed instant Parker sees this as blood, but then assumes it must be a spill of milkshake or something. Simultaneous to this reckoning is the awareness of how ridiculously unauthoritative, how unpatriarchal, he must now appear, clad only in sport socks, boxers and a Fruit of the Loom T-shirt.

Trixie returns to the hallway as the emphysemic coffee maker wheezes behind her.

'I'm at a loss for worlds,' Trixie says.

Parker looks down at his socks. These floors, once flawless, are now scuffed and stained with years of dragging soles. Trixie reaches to his face, picks a large clot of sleep from an eyelash, then flicks it away.

'I mean words.'

Parker calls: 'Hey, O.'

The screen turns bloody: a killer, killed. Ominous symphonic tones are triggered.

Owen looks. 'Yeah.'

Trixie moves into the living room, pulling her bathrobe tight around her to sit on an armchair's arm.

'You were awake when this went down?'

Owen seems confused. 'What time is it?'

Parker: 'Nine.'

Owen smiles. 'Still time to hit Smitty's for the Hay Stack Special.'

Parker looks to Trixie, who is openly reading her son's mind. A heavy stink of alcohol and odd smoke is present, and the mess on O's shirt, they now see, is clearly not chocolate. Parker consciously forbids his heart to sink, but knows his wife's won't be so easily prevented. So much effort, so many strained silences. So many months of her twisting her wrists. Right now is the first time in weeks these three have shared such close proximity. And the boy is licking too-pink teeth, saying stupid things.

'Between this and the front wall, it's like we're under siege here,' Parker says.

Trixie flares a nostril. 'Hardly the same.'

'Let's just sort this out and make some calls.'

'Who do we call?'

Pause.

'Fire Department?' Owen says.

Trixie: 'It's not like anyone's in actual danger.'

'It's an insurance issue,' Parker says. 'We have to report it.'

Parker heads to the kitchen and begins rummaging through drawers, looking for something.

Trixie points at her son. 'You really didn't hear anything?'

He slithers across the carpet, then flips in reversal to lie chest-down and grip the game controller. Shootouts continue. His heavy lids indicate he has not slept well, or slept at all. And his slurry voice tells he's not been being a good guy.

'Is this what you're doing all summer?' Trixie asks. 'Just … this?'

No response.

'O? At least react.'

'What.'

'Because I have to take off for the morning. If you need a ride or anything, let me know now.'

'Where are you going?'

'I have a doctor's appointment.'

'What doctor?' Before she can respond, Owen says, 'Is this because of that envelope?'

'Envelope?'

'On the CD tower thing. Neuro something.'

Trixie looks across the room. There it is, resting under a Joan Armatrading disc case. She folds it in her palms, both triumphant and defeated.

'What is it?' Owen asks.

'Nothing. Have you done your English paper?'

No response.

'Have you *started* your English paper?'

No response.

This is certain: the decrepit Fairmont boasted only a crackly AM radio, and as they cautiously crept toward the rubbled lot, the car's dying speakers offered 'Never My Love' by the 5th Dimension on CHUM 1050. Also certain: violating a barricade of plastic and signage, they exited the car to tour this patchy landscape of bulldozed mounds and untamed earth awaiting conduits and foundations laid. And there certainly was an imagined gravity to the moment that ensured its cataloguing for future days: the radio's squawking orchestral strains, the coupe's stuffy interior, the tarry smell of the site, the unmoulded land – all of this would surely live in memory.

Trixie had convinced Parker to drive up to the build site after dusk, to sneak inside and explore these foundations they would soon claim as their own. They peeled away paper sheeting and snuck into the beginnings of their life together. Everything seemed so skeletal and fragile in the throw of utility lights, the staked frames and half-laid footings and earth not yet flattened, sections of tarpaulin laid across skeletal chalkings. They strode together, gas-station coffees in hand, through unmade rooms with shared delight and unease, *probably shouldn't touch that huh*, shadows heavier than footfall on the earth. Beyond imagination there was little to see. Here a future welcome mat, a hot-water tank, a sliding patio door. Here were the coordinates of their future. Much was certain, but so much was not.

As they pulled away from the site, they stopped to take a long look back at the tiling row of nearly identical half-accomplished frames neighbouring theirs. The piles of boards laid out in such calculation meant all these plans were really happening; everything in the future looked busy and full. But a day becomes a dream, and a dream spills into years, and images go vacuumed into temporariness: teeth tearing earth in matrices of neighbouring plots, excavator booms rising and descending. Walls are raised. Things are built. This was 1983.

Parker looks up at the wounded ceiling and wall below. Tree branches drip dirty tears, stalky, gunked with sap. Fortunately, only a ceramic floor lamp and an inherited bedside table have been affected in the blow, and these things have been moved aside. But the tree might still shift; the wall itself likely won't sustain the tree's weight. Action needs to be taken, and soon. Storming clouds have moved on, and afternoon forecasts predict record highs. A small, strange part of him wants to wait, to see what carnage might ensue. But he shakes his head: no.

'O,' he calls.

Nothing. Knobs turn in the bathroom, clunking valves. Then the whine of Trixie's hairdryer. Parker heads back downstairs and checks the living room: Owen lies with his face buried in the carpet, snoring into the rug. Battles rage unabated, unmanned soldiers ravaged into oblivion. Missiles squeal, heralding failed missions.

When Brother Bo would direct his eldest son to perform endless menial household tasks, hosing down the driveway or raking lawnmower clippings every third summer evening, such requests were never met with objection. Now the son is the father, directing son, working together in silence, X-actoing back the carpet and edging the mahogany dresser away from the baseboards. The damage to flooring underneath is not as ruinous as expected, at least not yet.

Parker stands, wiping his forehead, again considering the mess before him.

'We could probably just give it the heave-ho,' Owen says.

He mimes a shove.

'Way too heavy,' Parker says. 'Plus look at that angle.'

Owen moves forward. 'If I get up there and push it up, we can nudge it over the wall and guaranteed it falls over by the bushes. Those bushes.'

Parker looks at his son, thinking about rope.

They head together to the rear of the house for another angle. Owen points: if they can manage a proper tug, then budge the tree right-wise, it should fall uneventfully onto grass. Parker wipes his face with his forearm, nodding. Minutes later he is knotting a length of polypropylene line around the felled tree's trunk and praying his son is wearing footwear with capable treads. Parker shouts to his son, telling him to please get down on his knees and not be so iffy up there. This plan seems so improbable. The tree is still wet with morning storms, its bark charred with contact.

Owen peeks back over the eaves. Thumbs up.

Often Parker tries to imagine himself up there on the bridge instead, climbing the cold metal ledge with darkness below, bracing against punishing winds. The water, the police. Owen's shirtless torso was drenched in rain and sweat. Reports said he was *howling* – not with tears, or with laughter, but emitting genuine howls, like some undomesticated creature.

Everything has changed and nothing has changed. It seems Parker has brushed by years like passing a stranger in an aisle, like drowsy transit across time zones, unaware of the true bearing of time's course. Now everything is remote, yet frighteningly close. His valves pump overtime, his brain works through its circuits. Food slows him; sleep eludes him. And decades or heartbeats from now, it will all cease. Nothing swerves this.

He looks up to the roof's eastern corner, where Owen kneels at a treacherous angle over a juncture of drainpipe, rubber gloves hiked up his freckled forearms as he cracks away stuck branches. Parker sees something he's never quite before registered: his son's intimacy with death. And for this, for reasons unknown, Parker envies him.

Trixie gathers her purse and sunglasses and key ring from the basket next to the fridge. Eight minutes behind schedule for her 1:30 with Dr. Bokeria, and with the thing with Ernie looming after, she is now an entire slot behind her projected itinerary. She pops a Nicorette in her mouth and rinses a tumbler in the sink. There is a thump against the roof, then a dull tearing sound and Parker's muffled voice saying, 'Watch it watch it.'

Staring into the stars, you envision the untold possibility of other worlds. Neptune basks in methane showers and Pluto grumbles in a life-less sub-zero clime. This morning's inbox brought her the latest bulletin from her astronomy newsgroup, a Reuters item about catastrophic collision between orbiting bodies, cloaking an adolescent star in trans-formative dust, and latest evidence of the Milky Way's progressive cannibalization of the Sagittarius Dwarf Elliptical Galaxy. And yet here is mould and alyssum and hawkweed, and still so many proofs to scour for *Record of Truth*, and something clogging the kitchen sink: last night's takeout noodles, stuffed in the drain, stinking of rot.

Nine minutes late now, she slides on her Vuarnets and makes for the door, mentally composing her traffic route in advance. Zapping open the garage door and backing out, she takes a last look at the house. Backlit by midday sun as it pushes through morning clouds, her son casts an elongated shadow across the ratty lawn.

SEVEN OF SWORDS

1

The lion seemed almost as tired as they were. It sprawled blinking in the dust, motionless, its paws caked with mud, soil thickening its mane. As the boy with the scarred lip sunk his teeth into the thumb-sized mango he'd found that morning, he sensed the lion's thirst directed at him, even from far across recessed earth. The boy's stomach clenched anew, not just with gnawing hunger but with the burn of fear. He'd already asked a soldier yesterday to shoot an antelope that had thumped down another boy and almost crushed his head. The soldier refused, saying ammunition was scarce and bullets would be only more vital in days to come. And there would definitely be days. It was best to keep moving.

Ajakageer loomed ahead; long nights sleeping in bushes lay behind. Lice squirmed in the boy's shorts. His mouth was numb with thirst and his left eye throbbed steadily in a way he didn't recognize. A whistle blew, and dozens who were sitting stood, and those unconscious woke. Again they moved forward together, slowly. The boy looked back, watching the lion. It remained motionless as the line of boys sank past the next incline. Not licking its paws, not twitching its ears, only watching, the lion kept its eyes fixed on the boy even as it disappeared into the distance.

The day previous some younger boys had cried and been scolded by soldiers. One boy was rapped on the temple by an uncocked rifle. They were reprimanded not for their fear – everyone, even the soldiers, just a few years older, was afraid – but for the energy wasted in such effort. Crying was tiring, and every calorie of one's energies would be required for walking. So no one cried, or at least not outwardly. There were miles yet to go.

They walked in clusters like constellations, brothers clinging to cousins, former neighbours in tandem. They were used to forming teams in village commons and fields, but now absent authority clouded their direction. The soldiers often lost track of the group's numbers, finding boys sobbing in the dust, others running off, delirious with thirst and grief. Boys ate dried leaves pasted together with mud or sucked on twigs. Some lay down in the brush, fell asleep and did not wake. In the afternoon the boy with the scarred lip felt something – a smaller boy tugging on his forearm, begging to know where they were going – and realized he'd been asleep, probably just for minutes, yet had never lost pace with the group.

At dusk they reached another village that had been laid to waste. In these strange cinders the boy almost recognized his own home, his own family. Except here nothing remained: no corpses or hacked limbs, no evidence, only a few charred huts remaining, walls without posture, paths of blown rubble and tufts of fires still at work. After the soldiers quickly scoured it for any useful spoils, they led the boys through the ruined village in silence. Reaching its outskirts, some turned and walked in reverse to remain facing its smoking depths, fearful at leaving those ruins, reminding them of their homes, at their backs.

As night fell they came upon an unexpected sight: a pair of idling trucks, headlights aimed at the waiting road. The soldiers leading the boys went first and spoke to the drivers, who stood leaning against the trucks' grilles, sharing a bottle of whisky. The drivers wanted the boys frisked, so all were lined up to show they bore no weapons – a ridiculous exercise, as most wore only rags. Their pockets were turned inside out, and anything to be had was taken: coins, keys, scraps. The drivers muttered to one another, drunk and bored.

The boys were ordered to hop in the truck's bed or ride atop the roof. Even with his sunken stomach and thinning biceps, the scarred-lipped boy was bigger than most, and so pushed ahead to a position atop the first truck, slumped over the vibrating cab. Boys fought to take hold before the truck geared up, and as it rolled out he heard protests and tears from those weaker souls left behind.

The wind of velocity bit their skin as the truck bounced along the rough road. The boy with the scarred lip lowered his head and held on, trying to forget everything that had happened and was happening. He worked hard to not think.

The boy only raised his head when, an hour or a year later, the truck began to slow. He squinted through dust held in headlights. Eleven boys had been clinging to this roof when the convoy left; as his eyes adjusted to the dark, the boy with the scarred lip counted only nine.

The truck grinded to a halt. Over the roaring engine the boys could hear the driver swearing inside the cab. The road ahead was a sculpted rise, at one side the sinking valley, a thick barrier of acacias at the other. Overhead was a starless black.

The driver honked and swore. Dust swelled in the lights and ribbons of heat rose off the truck's grille. Other boys began to talk in hurried whispers – one kid said this was where they would be getting off. Others disagreed. The boy remained silent, trying to discern the source of the disruption ahead.

Then they saw: a family of lions lay in the middle of the road, two adults and a cluster of cubs. They blinked back at the truck, their dirty fur golden in the headlights.

The soldier in the passenger seat hopped out and drew his pistol. He jammed a cartridge into its slot and shook it at the lions, but there was little confidence in his gesture. The cubs nestled deeper into their parents' shelter. The elders made no movement.

Another honk. The soldier said something back to the driver, with no response from the cab. A tall boy – recognizable to the scarred-lipped boy as from a village to the south – complained he had to piss, and moved to slide down from the truck. Another boy whispered sharply at him: 'Don't move.' But he moved, sliding down the right side of the truck to the ground and scurrying for the dark roadside.

The soldier advanced, again shouting and waving his gun. The lions' tails flicked against mosquitoes. The driver pressed on the horn, then reached out the window and tossed an empty liquor bottle at the lions. It struck the dirt in front of one of the cubs, raising dust but not shattering.

A shot was fired. With this, the lions flinched. The boys flinched. The valley quaked with sound. The soldier was drunk, now fearless. Then the boys heard the driver shout something from inside the cab as he revved the engine, urging. Several boys on the roof rose to their knees to look. The soldier's gun was pointed to the sky. The engine laboured. Some boys looked up, wondering where the fired bullet would end up; others hid their faces in their hands.

Another shot, and again all buckled with its announcement. This time the lions rose, the cubs hiding behind their parents. They were familiar with this sound, and knew to be wary. One lurched forward with a growl, and someone at the rear of the roof said, 'Didn't like that.' The soldier swore again at the lions, his drunken voice now wild. The lions rose and began to retreat, pacing single file toward the road's eastern ditch, the adults bookending their young. The soldier swore at them in victory.

The truck began to move. But the boy with the scarred lip kept his eyes on the lions. Before it disappeared into the roadside, the last adult lion paused. It turned back and gave these trespassers a final perusal. In that instant, the boy almost swore he and the lion locked sight, the creature's expressionless eyes seemingly identifying him, knowing him, everything of which he was capable. Then the lion turned and disappeared into the dark. They drove on.

2

Video footage: the garish set and backdrop montage of silhouetted athletics – slapshots raised, pitchers in windup, quarterbacks rushing – behind furnishings and swivel chairs of stoic mauves and hickory carpets. The square-jawed host manning the desk is Brother Bo Sweltham, Bo the Bro, host of *Rockin' Sockin' Jock Talk*, airing weekly on Cablevision Channel 10 COMM-TV. Returning from commercial break, the camera begins on a headshot of Bo delivering a characteristic intro: 'Gonna talk the talk and sit pretty with the nitty gritty,' then cuts to the guests, curling champ Sandi Hartlen, broom in hand, and former Canadiens defenceman Lyle Pinkett, sweating in a checkered blazer, and a discussion already underway.

Lyle is spazzing out. 'I have to say that is the biggest crock of BS I've ever heard in my frigging life,' he says. 'We're talking basic issues of sportsmanship here. We're almost in the twenty-first century. I'd have hoped we've moved beyond this horsepucky. Back when we were gunning for Lord Stanley's Cup we never worried about this kind of crap because you knew the damn rules. You knew when you put your stick on the ice you were there to play the game and none of this pansy bullpucky. None of these 50-50s sulking around. There's rules and then there's rules, and I say if the rules don't make any sense, then you gotta make your own rules.'

Bo looks at the camera, then turns to his other guest, who appears aghast. 'Sandi? Thoughts?'

'Well. If we all made our own rules …'

Lyle cuts in. 'We'd be a heck of a lot better off. We need some spine in our sportsmen. And sports females too, don't get me wrong. Some of you girls out there show a lot of pluck. I'll never forget something told to me by the great Gump Worsley in the '65 playoffs, Game 6 against the Blackhawks …'

Cut to Bo. His eyes drifting strangely, then someone offstage apparently signals him to wrap up.

'Sorry, Lyle, buddy,' he interjects. 'Going to have to stop you right there, 'cause we're out of time. Thanks to my guests Sandi Hartlen, skip for the Nova Scotia Regional Curling Champs, and of course NHL great Lyle Pinkett. This is Brother Bo, hoping we'll see you same time next week for *Jock Talk*. Till then, keep on rockin'.'

The camera dollies back and stage lights dim as the *Rockin' Sockin' Jock Talk* titles come to life with a rush of hyperactive guitar shredding. In the screen's upper right in the second before the stage blackens, Bo can be seen hopping nimbly over his desk, exiting stage left. Credits roll. Fade to black. Station ID.

In Tape 2 of Do It Dynamic!, titled *Blood, Sweat and No Fears* and Component A in the comprehensive DynaFlex Total LifeSystem 2000, a hefty package delivered by Xpresspost to Heath's doorstep last week, host Hal Deavers draws a correlation between the atrophying physicality of the modern male and the accreting glut of our *zombifying* information age. *Zombifying*: a term Deavers takes obvious pride in popularizing, and he returns to it repeatedly. In the Deavers paradigm, the merit of a man's spirit is in his self-propulsion, not caution and/or namby-pambying, like the programmers and bean counters who usurped past epochs' warrior kings. The torso and spine, the pivot of joints, the cardiac drive – these are the true components of action, and the way they circumscribe one's success is not imaginary but excruciatingly real. Deavers, headset mic at chin, promises self-improvement is not only possible but inevitable, if supported by a fighter's drive. This approach can be applied to anything: accumulation of wealth, conquering of phobias, remodelling of one's physique and, even, as Deavers puts it with a knowing grin, the *timeless game of seduction*.

They walk side by side, and quickly, both cupping football-sized coffees. The dull noise of Yonge Street's passing traffic and afternoon shoppers effectively Polyfils the conversationless gap between them. This day lives in wettened sidewalk and morning rain, coolness as relief from this summer's suffocation. Brunhilde says she is *staaarved* and demands they hit the Taco Bell at the next corner or she'll commit mass murder. Heath winces, thinking of his program, his checklists.

But then she is scarfing down her chalupa with a disturbing concentration, sour cream exploding through her knuckles. Heath tries to not to look too deeply into her weird peering pupils behind those red glasses, or at that Gorbachevish stain on her neck, focusing instead on unpackaging his own 7-Layer Burrito. But the place's lardy smell induces flashbacks of too many weed-addled pig-out sessions, too many proverbial Runs for the Border, too much guilt. Sweating, he pushes the burrito away.

Brunhilde takes a break from the excavation of her steak quesadilla, dabbing at her mouth with her pinkie.

'You know … '

'Hm?'

'I'm not crazy about how you're staring at me while I eat.'

He thinks she's kidding. She's not. 'Sorry. I didn't realize.'

'And you're not eating. Explain.'

He feels his face pulse with perspiration. 'I'm on a regimen. Some of this is sort of off my list. Mostly this guacamole.'

'A *diet*? That's pretty weak.'

He wipes his forehead and re-unwraps his burrito.

Believe me, Deavers pleads, I oath it to you. There is no greater confirmation of individual purpose, no clearer evidence of that burning inner desire that makes the motivated human being exactly what it is, than triumphing over that short-term instant gratification.

Despite the clamour of its squeaking consoles, the arcade down the block is mostly vacant, except for a group of Japanese kids crowded around a *Tekken 2* console near the entrance. As Heath unsuccessfully searches for a washroom, increasingly concerned by the sudden effect the lardy burrito and non-diet root beer are having on his guts, Brunhilde cackles with glee at finding a banged-up Double Dragon machine at the arcade's rear; for an entire teenage summer of lifeguard camp, this was her daily afternoon routine, she says, administering elbow punches to onscreen goons in the staff common mess.

'Come on,' she says. 'Back-alley beatdown.'

The years have not quelled her fighting fury. The game opens, dispatching brothers Billy and Jimmy Lee to the streets. While Heath struggles to figure out which button is punch and which is kick, Brunhilde's Jimmy Lee is already wading through oncoming spiky mohawked goons. When Heath-as-Billy quickly gets iced, Brunhilde barks at him to get Player 1 back in the fray. He digs out another quarter and joins back in. Then he dies again. And again. When Brunhilde, successful at dethroning a level boss, punches him lightly in the abdomen, he almost loses command of his sphincter.

After they both finally get their asses served by Jeff, the daunting boss at the end of Mission 2: Industrial Area, Heath's armpits are sopping and something seismic is happening in his bowels: the Taco Bell is not sitting well. But Brunhilde appears happier than she's seemed all day. Exiting the arcade and moving back out to the sidewalk and the grey of afternoon, she takes his arm and pulls him close.

Folks, Deavers says, *let's wake up. Whether we're waddling over for our second trip to the buffet, or spending that extra hour vegging out on the couch watching* Will & Grace, *we're not living. We're only digesting.*

Further down the street, Brunhilde lights a cinnamon bidi cigarette. She offers Heath one.

He passes. 'I'm on a regimen,' he says again.

'Right. This *regimen*.'

He tries to explain as simply as he can. Time now to regain control: to rule and not be ruled, cut out the cloudiness and recalibrate the radars. Reposition and apply the research. Despite his best efforts to frame it, this rundown sounds sad and weak.

'Maybe you need to think less about the physical model,' Brunhilde says, 'and more about the internal.'

'I'm on milk thistle and fibre.'

'I mean in a spiritual sense, as far as your relationship with God. This is our time of reckoning. The millennium.'

'Oh.'

They pause for a moment so Brunhilde, leaning on his shoulder, can dump out a pebble or something from her sneaker. Heath spots large letters pasted to a nearby storefront: UPSTAIR MISS DODONA PYSCHIC CONSEL LOVE CAREERE $$$ FUTUR PREDICTION NO APTT NECCESARY.

'Hey,' he says. 'Let's do it.'

She scowls. 'I don't think so.'

'Come on,' he says. 'Don't you want to know the future?'

'I know the future.'

'Come on. I'll pay.'

When we talk about driven, this is the true edge that makes the result-oriented person so much more – well, so much more alive than those who simply aren't courageous enough to make that leap toward. Getting what you desire and deserve. There is no greater confirmation of one's character than this true dignity – this wholeness and satisfaction.

Miss Dodona seems to be having trouble sitting upright. Muttering quietly to herself and wearing a purple sateen scarf over a stained Labatt Blue sweatshirt, she deals out a battered tarot deck. Seated across a decrepit card table draped in a similarly stained tablecloth, Brunhilde watches the cards flip with obvious unease.

The room is carpeted, not only wall-to-wall but floor-to-ceiling, with a coarse Astroturf-like dark green material. Posters and cut-outs are tacked to all walls: a UNICEF calendar, a Vedic astrology chart, a magazine photograph of the moon in waning crescent, some sort of long-faded diploma or certificate. Along with the juniper incense Miss Dodona has lit – missing contact between Zippo flame and stick on several attempts before successful ignition – the room reeks of cooking oil and cat piss.

Miss Dodona coughs and lays her palms flat on the table; Brunhilde, sensing a cue in this, leans in correspondingly. When requested, she lays her hands in Miss Dodona's. Compared to gawky, freckled Brunhilde, Miss Dodona – alarmingly obese, barely conscious – could almost be of another species.

'Look at this,' Miss Dodona slowly slurs. 'Dead and the ... *nzúmbe.*'

'And that's what,' Brunhilde asks.

'The, the ... undead.'

Miss Dodona lowers her voice, coaxing Brunhilde closer. Soon they are almost nose to nose and communicating in whispers inaudible from across the room where Heath sits anxiously eyeing the toilet in a back nook, cordoned off from the room by a beaded curtain.

Tarot cards are drawn, one by one. The Knight of Disks.

'Human harvest,' Miss Dodona says. 'Tremors in the sea.'

Two more: Seven of Disks, Seven of Swords.

'Betrayal. No ... '

She wipes her nose on her wrist.

'... failure.'

A small boy enters the room from behind the curtain and places a plastic tumbler of something resembling antifreeze by Miss Dodona's ankles. She shoos him away, then quickly downs half the liquid. Her eyes widen.

The next card is the Four of Cups. 'Luxury. Boredom.'

Next: the Moon. 'The illusion.' For the first time, Miss Dodona looks at Brunhilde squarely in the eyes. 'Everything is wrong. False. Pisces and Qoph.'

Miss Dodona cocks her head, spreading her jaws in such a way that Heath, fighting to calm the tempest stirring in his guts, can perceive the mania of her molars' metalwork. Backing away, Brunhilde's chin line pulsates with punctuated swallows – she's what Bo the Bro would have called *a timberwolf with its tail tucked between its balls.*

Heath bolts for the toilet.

Back outside, things have changed. The street gushes as clouds spread. But by year's end all this might be barren anyway, and the chambers of all dreams will close. No more tomorrows, and in the world's fits there will only be justice and regret. Two thousand years: a dubious accomplishment, for sure.

As soon as they reach the sidewalk, Brunhilde hurries away, folding her suede jacket tightly around her. Heath calls out, then catches up at the corner. She turns, eyes on her shoes, a blob of rain on her nose.

'What's wrong?'

She won't meet his eyes. 'I don't want to talk about it. It's sorcery and it's evil.'

They stand unmoving at the busy curb. Heath pinches the elbows of her sleeves. She responds with a deflective move that could be a flinch or an invitation.

'You're getting cold,' he says. 'Let's call it a day.'

Brunhilde exhales deeply through pursed lips: a gush like streetcar brakes. She throws her arms around Heath's shoulders and squeezes. 'You'll need me,' she says. 'You'll need me.'

In the introductory chapters of *Shear the Chaff*, screenwriting authority Zach Weisgrau considers so-called speculative genres such as science fiction part of Narrative Zone 5: *one of the most treacherous yet ultimately rewarding storytelling modes*. His No. 1 piece of advice for success in this zone is *compression of exposition*. The hallmark of an acute storyteller is the ability to engineer forward movement, keeping action moving with a stark thrust, working in lean, refined scenes: saying what needs to be said, never what does not. Allowing background info to flow naturally alongside brewing conflict, like pouring cement underneath a house on fire. No clunky voice-overs or framing devices – you look at *when* more than *what*. Give the audience credit, but never *too* much credit.

So what happens in this story is that there is a strange and unprecedented cosmic occurrence, due to some sort of comet residue or solar flare or gaseous cloud that envelops the entire earth, an unexplainable phenomenon – the details will require research, or maybe it could all be glossed over and left ambiguous. That could be interesting. But the point is not about the particles and formulae. It's the thing, the event, its effect on people. Maybe other species too, but who knows. Probably best to leave that whole area untackled. It's the story that counts, as they say.

Opening details come via a frantic succession of news broadcasts, possibly over or interspersed with opening credits. Newscasters spew the basic details of this thing, and it should seem funny at first, but then get scary. What happens is that in an instant – maybe it happens overnight, but come to think of it, night obviously falls sequentially over different longitudes, so maybe it's actually a rolling effect as this thing suffuses the atmosphere – another plot detail to be ironed out – every human being on earth is granted explicit awareness of the exact moment and circumstances of his or her own death. It's injected into the mind and just dwells there, as real as a memory: a total, first-hand understanding of how and when and where one dies. Blinding and real, with all the terror and remorse, the whole bouillabaisse of feelings such a moment would entail. All super-compressed and quick.

Between the twenty-eighth and twenty-ninth reps of his new nightly AbDestroyer routine, following an unproductive hour gaping at index cards representing pivotal screenplay plot points, a sharp pain strikes the left side of Heath's lower chest: a vacuum occupies the space that was, only moments before, held by breath. He immediately regrets smoking that last crumb of weed found in a grungy Quality Street tin – Tape 1 of Do It Dynamic!, as narrated by Hal Deavers' occasional foil/accomplice Lynn Goel, explicitly scorns the consumption of so-called *leisure toxics* – but after an especially shit afternoon fighting to get the new WPA configuration rocking while Bev from Communications barked at him about the necessity of *precision scheduling*, Heath had caved and sparked one for old time's sake, just a toot of this dry-ass B.C. weed a long-forgotten office temp had advanced him back in

April. This had clearly been a bad move. Wiping his brow with his forearm, he lies back on the mat and waits for the pain to subside. It doesn't. Hot stabs thrust upward from his abdomen. His heartbeat fills his ears. His hands go numb.

Hal Deavers had leaned in so close Heath could hear the dryness of his Dentyne. 'Man, you've got a snake biting you in the ankles, day after day. That's a snake you gotta just kick back into the darkness, just bap it back to where it came from.' Hal's teeth explained everything: squarely uniform and perfectly unyellowed, his teeth made dreamy promises. Dixie cup in fist, he waxed nostalgic about his rookie years with the Dolphins, a story about a manic-depressive coach with an axe to grind against club ownership who almost sabotaged his chances of upping to the pros, and the eventual triumphs of his career – *more average yards rushed per season than Larry Csonka* – a story of opportunity and dedication he relayed to the audience gathered at the Empowerment Expo booth with sheer delight. The crowd was suitably moved. Heath purchased the entire set.

And now he could see Nicole sharpening her expression for the mirror, sucking in her cheeks, saying *mwah*, concerned how her left eye was asymmetrically positioned to her right – which it wasn't. She'd be lounging at her parents' beach house near Lake Placid, slathered in cocoa butter, grinning through those Dolce & Gabbana sunglasses, preparing for this *life of meaning*. Nothing could keep her from this life.

The only other visitors to the emergency room at North York General tonight are a young Korean couple, near-hysterical over their toddler's phlegmy hack. The mother scratches her child's back and appeals to the attending desk nurse to *please see*.

Doors swing apart and a woman in a lab coat and plastic tiara bursts forth, tapping a highlighter on her thumb. Moments later Heath is seated on a cushioned examination bed, partitioned behind a plastic curtain.

'We took blood pressure and ran the ECG,' the woman says.

'Right.'

'You describe it as accelerated heart-rate response. This was during a workout or something?'

'The AbDestroyer. I'm on StrenuMethod. It's a lifestyle regimen.'

'Mm.'

Pause. Heath doesn't want to, but he does. 'Can I ask, what's with the … ?' Indicating the tiara.

She adjusts it. 'Tonight was my stagette. Got called in. Mr. Sweltham, how old are you?'

Okay. He is thirty-six, and yes, not exactly Jet Li here. No need for a medical professional to point that out. But you hear stories: *he was experiencing mysterious chest pains* – and the guy was barely forty, never realized a worthwhile dream, like parachuting over Shishapangma or whatever; instead he frittered away decades sourly filling in time sheets, his only day's joy a two-bag Doritos lunch. Hardly a life worth living, let alone wasting.

'Have you experienced any of these sort of … *sensations* in the past?'

In the past: needing a fifth teammate, cronies from the copy shop where he'd then worked had persuaded Heath to join their Tuesday-night Trivia Takedown league; Heath had offhandedly demonstrated ample general knowledge – knowing who Spiro Agnew was and citing a good chunk of the periodic table – to ably prop up their team, The Brainframe, fourth-ranked in the league. Against better judgement Heath allowed himself to be bullied into it; he was new in Toronto and keen to befriend, but waiting solo at the stuffy pub's uninhabited bar that first Thursday, he realized he'd made a terrible mistake. And as The Brainframe and their rivals poured in – yelly assholes filling bellies with cheap pale ales and shooters, hassling waitresses and pledging inter-team humiliations, all filling tables with pint glasses and gravy boats and wadded napkins – Heath's revulsion only rose. When the Takedown booklets were distributed, he braced to leave.

But Nicole's bare shoulder stopped him. This shoulder: poking through the hueless light of a Boddingtons sign at the edge of the bar.

Something caught him as she looked back over this shoulder, not at her forearm's abbreviated extension, but, it seemed, to her own posterior, not quite cartographable in a gingham skirt. That certain focused viciousness she held was evident even from across the bar. It was there in her lips and oily chin line, how she wore those matching pvc prosthetics, her self-containment – she knew how to not freak out skittish patrons. She did the bar's paperwork back with the cooks, a ballpoint pen in her teeth.

Though he was already drafting cvs toward leaving the copy shop's hell, Heath agreed to stick it out with The Brainframe for the season, which meant a return to the pub every Tuesday. And she was there. On Week 3 he got her name. A rapport developed; she predicted his teriyaki wings order. On Week 5 she told him the story of her injury, which he'd avoided mentioning so deliberately it had become kind of obvious and uncomfortable: four years ago Nicole lost both of her arms, or at least her forearms at equal points from elbows down, while serving in her first tour in the Balkans. Somewhere near Drvar the Land Rover manned by Ammunition Technician Nicole Chaisson and an attending officer from A Company supply section tripped an improvised incendiary device embedded in the tire-worn mud. By her account, as relayed to Heath after a second round of tequila shots, equipped with cocktail straws, she'd caught sight of the explosive at the last minute, but her reaction, reaching out in warning, was too late; the moment of ignition killed the officer instantly, but took only her outstretched arms. Nicole said the pain was so severe, so unbearable, and the response team took so long to get her medical attention, that she'd permanently damaged her vocal cords from hours of screaming; this was why her voice remained so husky – not from smoking, as Heath had assumed.

On the final week The BrainFrame placed a miserable sixth of seven in the league, so his soused teammates, fuelled by tequila slammers, organized a doleful van-taxi run to Kennedy's for a consolatory eyeful of boob. Heath hid in the men's room as they staggered out, strategizing and summoning his strength. A hazy conversation followed at last call, and though it meant an apocalyptic hangover best blamed on the pub's sticky taps, his crusade had been rewarded: a matchbook with a name and number. So he called. A reply came: a gratis pint if he'd walk her home after her humdrum Thursday-afternoon shift. He would, and did. He offered to carry her bags; she laughed and told him to worry about carrying his own shit.

From inauspicious beginnings miraculous possibilities are bred. Now Nicole is undergoing training with her cousin Elysia for her Global Adventure Challenge, preparing to pitch tents on Mt. Kilimanjaro and search scuba wrecks in the Egyptian Red Sea and feed HIV-positive orphans in Mauritania. All is possible, nothing restrains. For her, the future lies wide open, like a deep, stony chasm to be rappelled. Yet for the rest of the world, the coming fate is sadly clear.

In *Shear the Chaff*, Zach Weisgrau anecdotalizes his first experiences in learning to appreciate the worth of subtlety, of understatedness, of allowing smaller moments to steep before a combustive reveal: years back, when still a smoker, he'd accidentally set fire to three typewritten middle pages for ABC's action hit *Street Hawk* the night before deadline. Despite the burn, he'd reluctantly delivered it as it was, sans pages, and the script was approved and nodded forward. The episode was never shot, due to what Weisgrau terms *controversies and taboos given geopolitical norms of the day*, obliquely describing how friction over a Khomeini reference flared a Baha'i show runner's ire. But the experience was a formative lesson: anything and all can go. The writer's purpose is to wring solemn drama from nonsense, the scenes and situations etching together this cacophony, where true love doesn't always prevail, where a guy might be crushed under boot heel for no reason – where a damaged girl can demolish all to carve out a *life of purpose*. To perform demolitions on a world where nothing matters.

Despite what she may say, Heath does possess a purpose. He's just less of an asshole about it – he doesn't, and will not, fake it. Deavers, ranked eleventh all-time for yards per carry, told him outright to his face: 'I have never looked an honest man square in the eyes and not witnessed at least a glimmer of greatness.'

Instructed to wait, all he can do is slump into a seat in the empty post-examination waiting area. A TV mounted in the corner shows a Jays–Orioles game, its sound muted. He waits for someone to come. No one comes.

At the examination desk he finds a hawk-beaked kid in a doctor's coat wielding that same clipboard. Heath asks if he can go. The kid asks who conducted his examination. Heath says the woman with the tiara. The kid looks at him like he has just shat the floor, then disappears behind a thick curtain. Seconds later he returns, clipboard still in hand. He advises a nicotine patch. Heath says he doesn't smoke. The kid nods and hands him a packet of Ativan. 'Get a good night's sleep,' he says. 'Nothing to worry about. It's all in your head.'

On the first night in her bed he was disconcerted by the absence of groping. At first he was hopelessly limp; he felt like a pile climbing a pile. But then she felt her way with her mouth and her thighs did their work, guiding him with legs newly waxed – how she managed this grooming would be one of a thousand things he'd never understand about her. Like how her eyebrows stayed trimly plucked, or how she inserted a tampon. All that was her remained a puzzle. *You see a world of restriction. But me – I can do so much more than any of you could ever imagine.* A life as a list of stratospheric ambitions. Befriending the Daju. Conquering K2. Breathing the dust of the dingiest *favela*. Skysurfing over the French Alps. Living life beyond boundaries, armwrestling without arms. She loved him and humiliated him like no other could.

So now he dies, alone in his bed. His apartment is a world of ice, as incontestable and severe as a prison. Past scenes intersect and deteriorate into a craze of revenges and flubs, shaking him awake. His stomach churns; his heart rails. The Do It Dynamic! program equates cardiac vitality with mortal truth, its key messaging highlighted in purple all-caps titles. The premise is that, above all, having a life to live is in itself living a life worth living. This simple pillar should be enough to comfort him. But for Heath, squirming in his bedsheets, it just isn't.

Greatness. Touchdowns. Love. Humiliation. It's all in your head.

3

11/30/79. Am I authentic. Am I genuine. What am I doing? And I thought I could be a poet. The one who curates the actual thing. R says I have no core, no consciousness, no id. Just aspirations and nothing else. More wine and I am again a life-loving fool. And once again I say nothing.

The faxes from Simone, the designer, this morning present serious setbacks. The 'Spielberg at Dachau' scans for Figs. 2-7 – trenched heaps of what appear to be bodies but could be anything really, muddy mattresses or uprooted stumps or driftwood – are too low-res for print, meaning Trixie and her interns are back hunting down digital or hard copies. The author, Dr. Ruth Roth-Urquhart, is in Cologne for the biannual tribunal archive conference and has thus far been unreachable, but claims in her submitting query to have diced the photos from the web anyway, so not much hope for permissions clearance there. It's a provocative piece, the trenches in horrific blobs, squinting nothings signifying catastrophe and brutality – but the only catastrophe at present is these last pages holding up delivery of *Record of Truth* to the printers, laying it down into its own trenches, in its own sort of way.

Re-forwarding her email to Roth-Urquart, Trixie reminds herself for the umpteenth time to not pun in the light of atrocity. *Don't confuse history with the past,* Clementine would insist, raising a maimed hand; Trixie would just nod, feeling it would demonstrate ignorance to appear unable to parse this puzzling directive. Her occupation drowns in history, kingdoms and shifts, binding bloodbaths in matte pages that should catch fire with outrage: Armenian beaches, hate-radio broadcast scripts, Kagera River sunsets as bodies float in the haze. And yet every single day is a grind.

Under the editorial vision of Clementine DuPres, *Record of Truth* has found its reputation diminishing as the quarterly of record in genocide studies. But Clementine, who was robbed of three fingers in a Tonton

Macoute raid on her family's home in the late sixties – she will talk about it only after a few vodka sodas, and even then guardedly – had in May absconded back to Haiti under auspices of helping her brother Dickie launch a record label, though there have been whispers of immigration issues and drugs. Until a replacement hire can be found, which could take months, it's only Trixie and the interns to fulfill the editorial mandate. Times are tight.

Phones chirrup. Eleven hundred hours, another gulp from the cooler and three of her chalky pills. Weeks ago she'd been strategizing ways to target assumption of Clementine's post, preparing her plea to the board; now there seems little point. Trixie swivels and peers out the window at the rear of her smallish office. Set in another dreary overcast morning, the city is a patchwork of traffic and blacktop, a L'Oréal billboard with golden sheets of flesh as tall and long as a yacht.

12/05/79. New solo apartment is incredible. No more Mona and Sara and their cereal bowls on the floor. Dear R humped the futon frame and duvet splattered with menses and chocolate up the rusty curvy stairs all by himself. Like Lou Ferrigno w/pipsqueak arms. Then he steered the U-Haul fearlessly back up to the place on Coloniale, me riding shotgun, and at that moment we were a dear couple true. After, we sat sunburned on the rear fire escape flicking butts at the old Chevy frame in the neighbours' backyard, both w/nothing to say. Later glugged dépanneur wine then fucked for a while on the cushion in a mess of stringy packing tape, no acknowledgement of indebtedness because that seemed to be the way it had to be. Self-delusion. Fading and drunk, neither of us achieved blast-off and we fell asleep uncovered, no blankets or curtains. These windows are so wide, how to keep them covered? And then he leaves before coffee and I'm left here with so much to do. With the boxes and everything.

Lunch. Trixie is in the office kitchenette waiting for the electric kettle when she is struck with a distinct and intense wave of panic. She reels to the left and flails for balance, knees almost caving, finding an anchor in the countertop's edge. The iris of her mind's perception narrows and a vertiginous downward pull seizes the back of her skull. Fluorescent bulbs above splinter into watery shards. She inhales deeply but feels no air in her lungs.

Then the new intern Debbie is there, saying *howdy* while rinsing a mug in the sink. Trixie doesn't answer. Debbie asks if she's all right. Trixie nods and says something about another migraine. These lights, murderous on the eyes. Debbie dries her mug with a paper towel and recommends a particular brand of headache medication. Bufferin, maybe.

12/08/79. Last night R comes banging at the door. Four a.m. and I'm still up watching Tallulah Bankhead in Lifeboat *on TV4. Buzzer goes and of course I instantly forgive him for everything. Mostly disappointed in myself. In the bedroom he doesn't even take off his coat, just plops on the bed staring at his hands saying this shit about childhood and his father howling at him for not wearing sheepskin gloves. Pretty incomprehensible and he's frustrated at not being able to articulate. Then he's not even talking, just sobbing. And I'm lying there trying to sleep, looking at my nail polish and thinking about Tallulah, a bull out of a chute, and her doomed life, the life we all wish we could lead. Can't help but hate myself for not sympathizing. Eventually he's halfway under covers and after shuddering for a while conks out, still in his boots. All night we don't even touch. I should've offered an arm or something. But my sympathies aren't automatic. I'm not an android, despite how I seem.*

The new nurse, named either Rosie or Rosa, helps Trixie back to the examination room, leaving her to change out of the loose paper gown and back into her day clothes, folded neatly on the bed. As she refastens her bra, Trixie stares at a postered diagram of the human anatomy taped on the wall. The figure depicted is female, medium-built, wideish hips and just-sinking breasts, but stripped transparent to reveal all the coiling systems inside. Arrows and tabs delineate a respiratory system, endoskeleton, purplish arteries, womby passages, the strange crawl from spine to skull, the brain housed inside. Trixie knows this is her body too, but she could never feel it as such: a map, so dissectible. Hers is just too uncertain and unknowable. Even here, under this scrutiny.

'Knock knock.'

Bokeria enters, eyes lowered to his wristwatch as Trixie finishes buttoning her blouse. His deadpan demeanour is evidently intended to deflate tension. But Trixie feels indeflatable.

'Okay,' he says. 'Let's go through the latest with what we're dealing with here.'

It comes down to this. Maybe it is simply her desire to shrink from cruel possibilities. But somehow this whole experience – these weeks of gloomy waiting rooms and stark examination sites, all this probing and testing, printouts, all of it by herself – seems distant, unfelt and cold, at the end of a fork. Even though the subject is her own chemistry and her own skull and all that connects A to B: these prions and plaque formations and ataxic malfunctions. To separate her so-called consciousness from the actual chemistry requires only a leap of the imagination. That's all.

Bokeria folds a page between his thumb and index: last month's tomographic reading. He asks her her age, which he certainly should know by now: forty-one. A moment ticks by. Then he returns to his chart, combing its graphs like scanning items on a menu. In his thick accent, he explains the test results have come back with a fairly significant *whoa*. A lot of unknown integers. Cataloguing her symptoms – the dizziness, suggestions of hallucination, twitches, unaccountable gaps – it doesn't add up to anything too wonderful. Bokeria asks, not for the first time, if she has been overseas lately, or visited any non-domestic ranches. No and no. Variant Creutzfeldt-Jakob was his first guess, but that theory didn't jibe.

The message being this is serious business. A heck of a thing. A curveball.

He taps his finger twice on his desk. 'This … is …'

Trixie sighs.

Bokeria pauses to restart. 'What it is *is* just the intro of an ongoing treatment program. It will require,' he says, 'fastidiousness and diligence and, possibly, faith. From here on will be regular appointments and the expectation of in-patient treatment. A wellness regimen, as in diet and light cardio, daily medication. Lab visits. And no more drinking.'

'Can I smoke?'

'In here? Of course not.'

'No,' Trixie says. 'I mean, from now on.'

Bokeria snorts. 'I'll get Rosetta to dig out some literature on the, what's it called ... Butt Out Just Because. It's government-subsidized. She'll get you the literature.'

Trixie feels there is something she is supposed to be saying, but stays quiet.

'I imagine this all sounds rather dire, Mrs. Sweltham,' Bokeria says, 'but it doesn't have to be. I recently read a paper by a researcher in Arizona who's been publishing some interesting work relating recent revelations in cognitive processes to the worldwide ecosystem, how they might be mutually influential. It's really a beautiful analogy, even if the data is a bit dodgy. Geologists argue over a uniformitarian view of history versus catastrophic leaps, as in are these shifts lengthy, lumbering processes, or violent blips propelling the earth through its phases. This idea then becomes whether one's time on this planet should be regarded as a day-to-day sequential evolution or a chain of cataclysms. How should, or could, we allow ourselves to seek *meaning*?"

He catches himself, embarrassed.

'But I'm a physician, not a ... I appreciate how ...'

The chart is set to the side.

'Look. I recently had another patient, a younger woman diagnosed with a glioblastoma multiforme. Her family rallied around her through chemotherapy and dexamethasone, the entire process. Afterwards the family was tighter than ever. It was inspiring. One can use tragedy as an opportunity to reach out.'

'How is she now?'

Bokeria takes off his glasses. 'It's not the sort of thing one survives.'

Trixie looks again to that wall-mounted diagram, those hips and veins and, disconcertingly, no hairdo. But this is a caricature, fixed in time. It will never weaken and fade.

She can't help now but weep: quiet, tepid tears.

12/11/79. We go for breakfast at that new place by Wilensky's and run into all the usual scum. Again R becomes the clown prince, doling jabs, waving cigarettes. Doesn't even deign to acknowledge moi except to borrow a pen to take down a phone number. Robitaille asked me if I was still thinking about the book about Arabic numerology, which was weird since the idea had only arisen at Sabine's party last autumn destroyed on Chardonnay and I was babbling about Al-Masjid al-Haram this and the hajj and all that. I need to shut up and just stay shut up. Blind boredom like Beckett, imagination at wit's end spreading its sad wings. R slurps up a mushroom omelette and half of my bagel and hides in the bathroom when the bill arrives. Nothing changes. But I'm an easy mark. Afterwards at the corner as the crowd breaks up he grabs my mittens and actually kisses me on the lips. His lips are so cold. He knows I'm waiting for it. He reads me like a book – like a book he wrote.

'Still eleven kilos before I'm optimal,' Ernie says. 'See, what happens is induction kick-starts the process into a state of lipolysis, getting your metabolism burning off fat. What most don't get is the process by which these processes are activated. It's revolutionary, in terms of dietary science.'

He pronounces it *pro cess eez*, as if having spent time preparing it. His cologne, something like English Leather but less musky, mingles with the restaurant's sizzling garlic and candlewicks. Across the table Trixie fidgets, unsure of where her eyes should go: the mosaic tiling under her feet, the stucco roof overhead, the wineglasses' glint.

'Regulated cardio, free weights, some work on the conditioning. Heavy emphasis on core strengthening and tissue flexivity, which you only get from certain areas of concentration. But most importantly it's diet and intake. No sugar, no refined flours. Ascorbic acid. Magnesium.'

'I used to watch what I ate,' Trixie says, 'but it was too much work. I'm a salt freak.'

'God. That's so off my radar. The blood pressure.'

'It started when I got pregnant. I was so thin before. Then, you know.'

He picks at the remainder of his salmon with a fork. 'For what it's worth, you look great. Now. But you haven't been at classes lately?'

Trixie doesn't answer. The demolished plate of oversauced pancetta and spaghetti before her looks like an autopsy. She finishes her wine. 'You're really that concerned about your blood pressure?'

'What else should I be concerned about?'

'As they say, it's a temple,' she jokes.

He doesn't laugh.

Later they are driving. Seated shotgun, she runs a knuckle along the window's cool glass, watching the streak left there. Like the body's wetness: anatomy, again. She should be able to penetrate such images, distill their meaning. But she doesn't know how anymore, if she ever did. Skies are only skies, and rain-streaked streets are just rain-streaked streets, here in Ernie Baxter's Ford Focus, sloshing through the night.

Ernie's Introductory Molecular Biology seminar convenes early; he says he's finding the lectures increasingly exhausting. The lecture hall at York is so spacious, he says, vertigo claims him during lectures, projecting out and up into the endless rows of kids.

'They're all just sitting there, in these rows, wearing their sweatshirts. So young. Terrifying.'

The house lies ahead, dim within, no one waiting up. Ernie slows, shifts into Park and clicks off the radio.

'Which brings us to,' he says.

She notices, not for the first time, how perfect his posture is, how plank-like. 'Dinner was great,' she says. 'Not too heavy. Not too light.'

'That salmon was holy cow.'

'Surely.'

Perhaps it's the lonesomeness of an empty home that leads her to stall so, its damage still unmended. Perhaps it's perverse curiosity, wondering what could occur. She can sense her eyelids' heaviness. Yet she stalls.

'I don't even know anything about you,' she says.

He smiles, revealing his face's cragged contours. Both of them seem terribly old, here in their raincoats.

'Well,' he says. 'Never too late.'

It's a bare statement, so simply put she almost laughs. 'No,' she says, 'it's really not all that late.'

On the fateful day, Allie came storming into the Jack Astor's with her face pink and her hands shaking and her breath lightspeeding. At first she refused to sit with the family, pacing the aisle semi-hysterically, so wound up a server in a cardigan and pinned sash came to check if she wasn't experiencing some sort of seizure. Even when Allie caught her breath, sliding into the booth next to Bethany and tossing her handbag on the table next to Lloyd's jumbo Busch Light, Allie looked manic in silence. Lloyd took Allie's hand and stroked her palm with his thumb, cooling her as Trixie and Bethany took turns asking their mother what the hell. But Allie couldn't get it out. Then a waitress plonked a sizzling platter of chicken fajitas in front of Trixie, plus a teriyaki stir-fry for Bethany, and seeing the food somehow jolted Allie out of her catatonia; she asked the waitress if they served steak, which they did – Mongolian Beef and Butter-Brushed Sirloin and Pepper-Crusted New York. Allie nodded and requested *the biggest piece of cow you've got back there*, plus a crantini. As the waitress left, Lloyd asked everyone to get serious. Allie sighed and requested a minute, just until she got her drink, then. So they sat in pained silence until the waitress returned bearing a huge frosted glass that glimmered like Hollywood blood. Allie thanked the girl, took the glass's stalk in her fingers, tasted the crantini, then rested it back on the table. She looked both of her daughters square in the eye, one at a time, smiling. Finally, she patted the handbag and said, 'They talk about those moments when a life changes forever.' Lloyd sighed and begged his wife please, she was killing them. Allie laughed, took his hand in hers and with the other began to dig in the handbag. 'You know how Jan and Sapna and I go splits on the Pik 4 every week?' Lloyd said sure. Allie continued to dig through the bag, finally producing her leather wallet. 'Yeah,' she said. 'Well.'

Balmy winds sweep the marina. The lake's surface by night is a splayed nothingness, broken only by the intermittent sparks of buoys and reflected lights snapping from adjacent condos. Following the shoreline, they arrive at a brief pier, a rail overlooking a lower wharf where a trio of catamarans are tied. Ernie appraises the scene, the lapping water, night's skyline beyond, with a gaze that could be wistful, or just sleepy. He leans over the rail and makes an odd sound with his lips: a shiver or a curse.

Though it's only twenty, twenty-five minutes from this Port Credit harbourfront to her driveway, Trixie allows herself to feel fully transported. In one of O's first post-release consultations, Fultz told Trixie her son exhibited a tendency to psychologically disassociate himself from, as the doctor quaintly put it, his *whereabouts and whenabouts* – either a defence mechanism against the more difficult and perhaps painful aspects of his recent experiences, or a genuine neurological failure to process the essential order of things. While relaying this information, Fultz casually removed his white medical overcoat to reveal an Eagles reunion tour T-shirt reading *Hell Freezes Over*. Trixie's blood rose: this is her son's sickness. Is it not our basic condition to long to embark, to be elsewhere when things are not so good? Aren't we always doing this in varying degrees, day in day out? If there is only this, this reckless yearning, we are goldfish. Meanwhile, she couldn't help but think how Don Henley made thirty-five bucks from that hideous shirt.

Leaning against the rail with all this unconditioned air throwing her hair into a frizzed mess, she indulges the thought that she could be anywhere other than where she is. They could be any two idiots dangling at the end of any possible rope, here in full susceptibility to the satellites and systems of stars. Unshackled, if only momentarily.

'Anywhere but where we are,' she unexpectedly says aloud.

Ernie looks at her, that smile in full crinkle. He is handsome; this she can admit. But he hasn't asked about, or even mentioned, her marriage, leaving his intentions suspect. Just as much as hers.

From fibrous grey-violet clouds a helicopter comes chugging, sinking toward an unseen landing pad across the water. She'd flown in a helicopter once, with her parents in Kauai, when Allie's lottery windfall was still plump with possibilities; all she remembered was unfathomable nausea and her father's insistence on using the word *whirlybird*.

'The clouds block out the stars,' he says. 'Could be an omen.'

'I don't think so.'

'You asked me before where I grew up,' Ernie says.

She doesn't remember asking, but says nothing.

'Upstate New York, near Canastota. Until I went to Calgary for school. My parents were very intense individuals. Very … I guess I'll say *intense*.'

'Mm.'

'My father wrote painting-technique manuals, selling them to bored housewives. You know, the ones who take up macramé or crochet or watercolours to keep from going crazy. He actually had a show on TV in the afternoon, for a little while. But it didn't last. Obviously he came north as a draft dodger.'

'My father-in-law used to be on TV too. Sports.'

'Mom had loftier aspirations. She toiled forever at this book that was about I think the Korean War. Operation Ripper or Killer or something. She never finished it.'

Trixie sniffs. 'She must have been frustrated.'

Ernie looks at her, and for a held moment does not speak.

Barely even registering she's doing it, or knowing why, Trixie places her hand on Ernie's lower back. This contact feels stranger than expected, and when he flinches at her touch she almost withdraws, but doesn't.

4

Guus Goorts exhales deeply, playing with the wrists of his bicycle gloves; the synthetic leather *swacks* sharply with each pull, a gesture clearly meant to indicate a vexed assembly of thought at work. Goorts is the interim Regional Vice-President of Sales for DynaFlex International Athletics and Recreation Equipment Division, having been shuffled over last spring from head office in Windsor, an appointment announced as only interim, as Goorts is spearheading prep for the soon-to-be-launched DynaFlex sportswear line, and will be visiting factories in China for most of next year. His time so far has been pained; the winter saw conflicts with several distributors over discrepancies in accounts, a genuine clusterfuck it fell upon him to remedy. Interim profits were down, resulting in the necessity of aggressive marketing and expansion of client base – thus Parker's extensive road schedule.

'I would imagine it gets a bit lonely out there,' Goorts says, easing into the chair behind his desk. 'Drinking that rancid airplane shiraz, especially in the summer.'

Parker: 'Between you and me, if I never have to take another Wet-Nap bath again, you won't hear me complain.'

They both laugh, Goorts longer than Parker. Parker isn't certain, but he thinks he hears Goorts say *land sakes* to himself while wiping a teary eye. Then Goorts gets down to business.

'So. I went through everything you handed over last week, and I have to say on behalf of everyone that we are completely blown away.'

'All right. Well.'

'We seriously could not be more pleased. Calls pouring in from the U.S. contacts. Everyone gushing how effing fantastic it is to connect with Parker Sweltham. Kenny McBride from …'

'Providence.'

'… he said something like *Parker made not snapping up half a dozen StepMasters totally unthinkable.* Now he's ordering the entire suite for all six EFG locations. It's a bit of a coup.'

'He's a sweet guy. Kept wanting to talk about his granddaughter.'

To a bleeping notification, Goorts glances at his laptop screen, then turns back to Parker. 'So you know I'm out of here come the fall.'

'Didn't know it was so soon.'

'I'm in Chengdu over winter, then likely back to Windsor.'

'Right.'

'And I've had questions from the highers-up. Denise and others have been asking specifically about you.'

Parker raises his eyebrows.

'Obviously I've been posting only positive reports. About you, I mean. Some of the juniors in your department, let's not get into that, spank you very much. The extent of the incompetence stretching below us ... '

He trails off, gazing at his gloved palms. There is a lull in which neither speaks. From the copy room next door Parker hears the dull sound of something crashing or imploding.

'Can I ask you a question?' Guus Goorts says, still looking at his hands.

'Sure.'

'What do you want?'

Parker: 'Are we talking employee reviews?'

Goorts leans in. 'Forget that. We're generally groovy, you and me?'

'As far as I know.'

'I think we are.'

'Then I agree.'

'Parker. What do you *want*?'

The certain leer in the way Guus Goorts poses this question makes Parker uneasy. The question is posed almost antagonistically.

'Honestly not certain what you're driving at, Guus,' Parker says.

Guus edges further forward, lowering volume. 'What I'm saying is things are shifting. You know it. I, of course, know it. And as a result, opportunities are arising. Don't be demure and tell me you're not the type of man to seize opportunities. Because anyone with an eyeball socketed in their skull can tell you're a conquering soul.'

Guus sits back in his chair, looking again at his email.

'Parker,' he says, 'DynaFlex is posting its worst quarter in a decade. As I say, I've been talking with Denise and the others, and we are at the cusp of a huge overhaul. We're thinking you are key. We want to bump you and a few from the Whitby office up a notch, plus those underutilized guys from Calgary. So we need to ask where you stand. Both with the company and, if I can ask, personally. So. What do you want?'

Parker sits in the Camry, eating cold the Ziploc container of leftover penne he'd intended to have at his desk. He chews slowly, joylessly, listening to a radio report: with a soaring Dow Jones surpassing 11,000, prospects run wild. Under the first clear skies in weeks, the parking lot outside Brunson Towers sits empty of humans – a world of cars. Yet his teeth chop food and his tongue sends it back into his throat, where muscles contract to force it down into the complex tubing beyond, and from there somehow the chewed matter will travel many metres and undergo many transformations before ejection. It's like magic.

Last year Trixie took them through a phase of dietary regulation with an almost pathological furor. Hydrogenated oils, processed meats and refined flours were sworn enemies; everything was certified organic and in bulk recyclable containers. Mealtimes became drab affairs, drained of butter and ranch dressings. At one point O snapped at her: 'It's like you actually want us to starve.' One evening, with brown rice and unseasoned tempeh and steamed kale for supper, Owen fled to his buddy Chuck Byng's for Manwiches. Parker and Trixie cleaned their plates in silence. Then, leaving Trixie scrubbing dishes, he drove at an imprudent speed to the LCBO, picked up a sixer of ice beer, raced back and viciously downed all six, one after another, in the garage. The following night Trixie came home brandishing an extra-large Meat Lover's Pizza with Mozza Sticks and a 2L of Mug from Pizza Hut. No explanation was provided; none was sought. Each nabbed his or her own portion and retreated to separate rooms. The house, the family, is a body, a system of digestion and circulation, all that tubing and gunk and history.

He already feels the penne heavy in his gut; something is happening there. Because things have changed. The Perrier bottle, the spill of blood: an alteration occurred in this. And the question posed by Goorts – *What do you want?* – emphasizes something perverse. All his life, Parker has not known fear. As a provider, a fixer, a not-fucking-arounder, a team lead, fear has never entered his repertoire. But something has changed. His understanding of everything has been drained, leaving only some scummy remainder.

He checks himself in the rear-view mirror: dark veiny pits have replaced his eyes and his cheeks are engorged puffs. And all he can think is still *grandfather clock grandfather clock grandfather clock*, that nonsensical refrain looping into eternity.

Parker opens the driver's-side door and vomits the pasta onto the asphalt. It comes quickly, effortlessly.

Heath: 'Did you see her on that show? I think it was the Discovery Channel?'

Parker: 'We don't get that.'

'Yes you do. Channel 59.'

'Yeah, well.'

Heath and Parker stand at opposite sides of the counter island bisecting the Swelthams' kitchen. It's a muggy afternoon; the ceiling fan toils. Heath leans over the mahogany backgammon set, rattling dice in their leather cup. Parker has an Amstel Light he has yet to uncap; Heath has refused the offer of a beverage. This is unlike him.

They always stand when they play. Even as children they'd set out the board atop the hood of Valerica's olive-green Aires station wagon, or the Rubbermaid garbage can on the back deck. To sit while backgammoning was simply unimaginable, inhuman.

'Right there on the screen. I called her after, told her it was pretty impressive. To congratulate her. I left a message, but she didn't call back. You know Mom.'

'Mm.'

'Reminded me of watching *Jock Talk*. Which led me to dig out the tapes.'

'You have tapes of that?'

'There's a box. No idea how I ended up with it.'

Heath's jacket doesn't quite reach his belt line, and every few seconds he tugs its hem down in a gesture that seems to indicate more than just an ill fit.

'Montana,' he says. 'Big Sky country. Looks nice.'

Parker concentrates on the board. 'I've passed through, for work. It's big and empty. Your go, H-Bomb.'

The dice come up one and five. Heath scans the board, counts spaces, then moves the fruitwood checkers accordingly.

Bogged down with client scheduling while at the Econo Lodge Windsor, Parker hadn't remembered to tune in last week for his mother's televised moment. This particular instalment of *Terrestrial Adventures* featured segments shot at the Misery Gulch geological dig sprawling across Montana and the Dakotas, including a brief interview with one of the site's head coordinators, geoarchaeologist Valerica Kogalniceanu. Parker hadn't seen it, but Heath had: a flattering frame, relaxed at her desk in a homey office near the site, long whitening hair swept behind her ears, the creases of her pale eyes christened in prolonged UV radiation and thrown dust.

'Maybe we could pop down for a few days at Christmas,' Parker says.

Heath rattles dice, rolls a one and a one. 'Her letter implied a certain urgency. She specified those dates. Specifically.'

For a moment this hangs heavy between them. The house is quiet. Trixie has been out all day, a weekend conference or something. O could be anywhere.

'Is she sick?' Parker says.

Heath does a shrug-like move and bears off a checker. 'Don't know. Think it's a case where it's best to hope for the best, but buckle for the worst. You blink, and years have passed you by. One minute you're saying *heck no* to that risky opportunity, the next thing you know you're staring at yourself in the mirror asking where everything went wrong.'

Parker almost jumps; he all too well recognizes this hackneyed phrasing, so forced. This is Deavers's opening to Tape. 1, *Burn the Couch!* Verbatim.

He moves toward the refrigerator, away from what he knows comes next.

'Look, H-Bomb...'

Heath stiffens, tugging at his jacket. 'Can you not call me that?'

'Fine. But I'm not going to Montana. I'm needed here. It's employee evaluations. Your head would cave in if you knew. Plus the roof repairs. I'm needed.'

Silence. Heath sniffs and looks at the board. 'I saw the roof. You sic Berringer on that?'

'Berringer retired after his daughter's cancer. I have these refugee guys on it. You sure you're good?' Meaning a drink. Heath shakes his head no.

'Refugee guys?'

'I met a guy who has some guys. Anyway. All she wants is for us to tromp all the way down there just so we can tell her what she wants to hear. You know that.'

'I don't see what's wrong with that.'

Parker drains his beer and looks at the ceiling.

'It's just. People are dying all over the world. Like, in Kosovo. I have no desire to hump it all that way to the middle of nowhere just to hear this story again, how having a family stole her of whatever, these dreams she has. I have no interest in any of that anymore. I'm done. I'm officially done.'

Heath squints at this person who looks like his brother but sounds nothing like him. He goes to say something but instead rolls dice, spilling out a one and a three. He bears off his last checker, finishing the game. For a moment both men wordlessly consider this outcome. Then Parker fires his emptied beer bottle into the sink. Glass flies.

5

Roll call finishes and students scatter, assuming positions throughout the shop, starting in on jigsaws and belt grinders. In minutes the room is filled with noise: grinding, band sawing. With only a week before semester's end, a minor panic to get rivets set and edges sanded has set in. Blades are spinning, bits are drilling.

At the front of the room, George Carruthers, Industrial Arts department head, sits with arms folded in a casual slope on his desk's edge, his cream-coloured wool sweater tucked into his trousers, his scuffed steel-toed boots hugging enormous feet. He speaks with two students, Gwen Huang and Chara Reichmann, who react to whatever information he relays with nasal titters, exaggerated laughter that may be flattery or simply embarrassment on Carruthers's behalf. Undaunted either way, the teacher leans back and indulges in his success.

Owen Sweltham sits on a wooden stool at the back of the shop, biting the plastic lens of a pair of goggles, glaring at this scene: Carruthers, getting his rocks off checking out Gwen's white pleated tennis skirt, letting his perverted imagination go oh so fucking wild at what lies beneath. Owen does not blink.

From across the room Chuck Byng, working a band saw, calls out to Owen that these slats aren't going to slat themselves. Ignoring Chuck, Owen locks sights on Gwen Huang, at her hyper-straightened hair, at her bronzered skin, at the way her chin retreats into her neck as she laughs, sort of turtle-like.

The Byng comes over.

'Come on. We need to move on finishing this doghouse. Staying late Wednesday, not optional.'

Owen looks but does not speak.

Chuck: 'Yo, dipshit.'

'I thought it was a birdhouse.'

'It got bigger. What the hell, cock.'

'*You* cock. A tree fell on my house.'

Chuck gets up. 'I heard. I'm getting going on these slats.'

Exit Chuck. Owen sniffs, returning his attentions to the front of the room. Chara is rifling through her bag while Carruthers remains buoyant in conversation with Gwen. Watch, look: punctuating a word, some remark on her overdue dustpan perhaps, Carruthers reaches and, for at least one full second, holds Gwen's upper bicep. This hand is then retracted and hidden again in the pit of Carruthers's folded arm, but there is clearly an effect to this gesture, as Gwen's titter dies and her ever-flicking head relaxes; for at least two seconds she makes eye contact with her teacher before again tossing her hair and casting her eyes down at the sawdusty floor. Owen sees all this.

At lunch kids flock to the woods beyond the infield's fencing. The morning's downpour has ebbed. Down well-worn paths, bushes littered with chip bags and old bottles, they shed raincoats and unhood heads, curtained by the dripping limbs of junked firs and telephone poles. They spit and laugh and smoke hasty cigarettes before afternoon classes, joyful for the school year's coming end.

Owen sits on a fat coil of jutting tree roots away from them all, sucking a Belvedere, headphones on, his Discman playing DMX.

Then here is Ike, like nothing ever happened.

The house we stayed in in Germany was 400 years old, Ike says. *Older than Canada. It was like a mountain. Apparently some guy high up in the Gestapo lived there.*

Gestapo.

I might have seen a ghost one night. The backyard got seriously foggy and you'd think you could see things. Maybe it was the high-octane weed they have over there.

Owen spots Gwen Huang among a cluster of girls down by the centre yard line. Her outfit has changed over lunch, her cardigan replaced with a loose cowboy shirt. As usual, she flaunts her boredom, engaging something private and inaccessible.

My sister said one night she was taking out trash to the little wooden shack thing in the back. And she swore she felt something weird and cold. A smell, I guess, something meaty. Like brimstone. She came in crying, but nothing really happened. I don't believe in that stuff. But.

Owen thinks he knows what he means.

Getting an apartment with my cousin Abe next year, Ike says. *Then taking that road trip to Whistler. Going to be a big fucking year.*

Then The Calch and Lucky are there, both wearing irritating grins. And of course Ike is not there, not anymore.

'Sweltham,' Lucky says. 'Where have you been?'

Below the woods' slope, a referee's whistle echoes off brick and concrete, officiating cross-country drills. But Owen is now hearing Fultz's voice, that monotone soundtrack: *Honesty isn't a chore. It's a gateway. It's the only way you can earn any genuine trust.*

'You guys heard,' he says. 'The thing with Carruthers.'

'Industrial Arts Carruthers?' The Calch laughs. 'I don't have him.'

Lucky: 'He's a testicle.'

Owen shrugs, making a show of it. 'Testicle he may be. But Chara probably doesn't think so.'

A moment, a laugh, then they look to Owen, waiting for details. He has succeeded.

'So,' Fultz says, 'how's school turning out?'

The office's pale blue walls and muted lighting and cyan sofa, plus the enormous painting on the south wall of what appears to be a killer whale bursting through a seawall, conspire to create a strange sense of being underwater. Not, Owen thinks, the ideal therapeutic environment. They are submerged a thousand metres underwater, squirming among protoplasmic jellies and eyeless fish living in deep fissures, far from any soil or surface. Things don't have to be so brutal; they could stay here, protected in the bluishness. But, as always, discussions ruin everything.

'Fine,' Owen says.

'Soccer again this summer?'

'Trying out.'

'Good. And feeling okay about what lies ahead? University applications?'

'I'm on it.'

Fultz considers the slim file he keeps at the ready. 'Feeling okay, digestion-wise?'

'Except on Mom's Meatloaf Mondays. Ha ha.'

Only a testy blink. 'That's not the first time I've heard you make fun of your mother. She seems to me a pretty astute individual. Yet you portray her as some hapless buffoon. Why is that, do you think?'

The Paternal Unit is George Washington charging hopefully against the Hessians crossing the Rubicon, as honest as a cherry tree and *Guns Don't Kill People People Kill People* embroidered on his sash. The Maternal is Florence Nightingale Rosa Parks Nancy Reagan tending the wounds and reputations of civilizations of slaves before hopping the service elevator to the stars and all the penthouse joys reserved for the blessed. And Owen, burglar and trespasser, Problem Child, led a revolt in Heaven and sank like a turd into the yuck of Hell to tempt and sully juvenile delinquents into an infernal army of archfiends – and when he climbed up on that icy bridge's rail to assume the mantle and finally cast himself back down, deeper into Hell and everything that is not the world, he had only the most humble of plans. So when his assailants came surging with their sirens chirping, Dudley Do-Right and Dirty Harry pinning his arms behind his back, it became clear: this world is not an honest world. It is an orchestrated ordeal of disappointments, resulting in nothingness. Gymnasiums and sandwiches and acne: barely a life being lived.

He knows these streets so well, even by night: these winding crescents and arterial courts, these sleepy houses lit within by bluish TV radiations. Light rain has glazed the sidewalks, and now begins anew. Owen hikes up his jacket's collar, barely aware of the surrounding *shoosh*. He moves automatically.

Reaching the clearing, a single lamp humming overhead with yellowish sodium light, he stops to cup and light his only cigarette, stolen from Prendergast earlier that day. Beyond the wooden fence and the dark tree-enclosed pathway are a row of rear yards tiling identically down behind this segment of brick townhouses. She is in one of these basements. Ditching the cigarette, he kneels to the wet earth and peers under the fence's slats, muddying brand-new Buffalo jeans, trying to discern any sign of anything. But from here there is nothing.

As he hops over the fence to land in the damp grass, everything is weightless. The earth is a sponge, his legs are pipe cleaners. He'd felt this way on the bridge, then in the woods, then sleepless under crunchy bedsheets. Alone and invisible. With his back to the house's wall, he edges nearer to the undraped window, looking over his shoulder, down, as a light snaps to life in a basement window at the row's end, suggesting motion within.

Rain falls on everything but him. He is untouchable, sanctified. He finds himself knocking his knuckles together. That voice: *Don't worry – all's all right in the end.*

A single bedside lamp lights the bedroom. She sits at her desk, hunched over a computer keyboard at the room's furthest corner, wearing pyjamas, her hair up in an elastic. She types. The room is sparsely embellished: simple frames neatly arranged on the walls, mussed bedding, a full-length oval mirror leaned against a wall, a topple of magazines and textbooks bedside. A huge *Romeo + Juliet* poster, dry-mounted on the adjacent wall. Notice: her shoulders, bare, bonier than imagined. And whatever she types, she does so mostly using her ring fingers.

Owen places a cautious hand on the window, but doesn't knock – not yet. The rain meets the grass of the Huangs' backyard in a steady rush, just another noise. He watches as Gwen stretches her arms upward, rotates her wrists, yawns. Then she rises, heads toward the bed and snaps off the lamp. The room goes dark. Owen exhales, his terror a cloud on the window's cool glass.

6

'I remember something told to me by Steelers head coach Chuck Noll,' Deavers says, his eyes squarely aimed at the camera. 'This is during a tough-as-heck pre-season battle against the Redskins, and Chuck was a real mentor for me, not only in defensive strategies, developing the two-deep zone, but in personal matters as well. He told me, *Hal, there's the type of faith that brings you strength and the type of faith that makes you weak – the mark of a strong character is in being able to make the distinction between the two.* Hell of a thing to tell a young buck in the prime of his life. Hell of a thing.'

The storm is here: in the abattoir gait of workers shuffling through subway stations, in the flutter of junked wrapping and wet newspaper pasted to tiles, in a pre-solstice sky still looming ultraviolet and ominous. By 5:30 the downpour is in full assail, the trailing ellipses of a Caribbean hurricane: a battlefield overhead.

Patterns form: species evolve and go extinct, empires rise and fall. And yet, hurrying through the subwaying herds to initiate his pre-dinner ashtanga session, a sweat-soaked agony that makes his testicles ache, things have changed. Heath's new signpost is discipline. The only authority is command over one's self. Patterns will form, but these patterns have to be designed in steadfastness. Like Former Green Beret and Operation Just Cause veteran Bret Albo, focus interviewee and guest star on the first half of Tape 4, *Special-Ops Reboot*, who counts down the horrors witnessed in both overseas operations in the former Yugoslavia and a tenure with FEMA counter-terrorism response teams, mostly in prep field research after those Tokyo subway sarin attacks a few years back.

'You come to realize,' Albo tells the viewer, 'there's nothing more important than family and duty, and duty to family, and our duty to God. God bless America – but more importantly God bless us all.' Albo then demonstrates some effective abdominal crunches one can pump out even when stuck in traffic during the gruelling morning commute.

Heath can't help but consider his stomach's folds, this shapeless fluff so unlike Albo's chiselled midsection. His body is pale and pimpled, neglected in an un-vibrance of laze. And he considers his own credentials – an IT certificate and an unfinished Sociology BA – against Albo's glowing record of heroism. He is lesser in every way. So: from now on there must be limitations, yet no limitations. Greatness will be rooted in strategy, in defiance against a status quo, against mediocrity – his *Zero-G Life Trajectory*. That's Tape 5.

Worldwide hysteria erupts. Millions, unable to process such information, go catatonic. All kinds of nightmarish scenarios emerge. In the nightly news, on sidewalks and in malls, ordinary people fall to their knees in anguished outcries, overwhelmed by fear. Strangely, or pretty obviously if you think about it, suicide rates drop: such pre-ordainment means these deaths will simply not happen, so they don't: when you know for certain you'll die in one way, you don't bother pursuing another. Murder rates, however, persist unabated – knowing precisely how such killings will happen, victims offer little resistance and killers' plots go smoothly. Everyone's reaction to this thing is uniquely theirs, yet it's all the same. It's pretty confusing.

This affliction is fully established in the screenplay's first five or six pages. From this point forward, it serves only as an engine, a backdrop. Reference Weisgrau Section 3.6, citing examples of cinematic explorations of global events through microscopic, ground-level interpersonal dynamics; he suggests *Close Encounters of the Third Kind*, which Heath has mostly forgotten except the mashed-potato-mountain thing. What we need to get into is the fundamental stuff. The real story is about a group of friends at the cusp of adulthood and all the dynamics within such loosely defined networks, because story is essentially linked to character and such human truths. These are familiar types: two young parents; another cute dude and his girlfriend, currently in a state of relationship crisis; a pair of hotshots still cruising for chicks, one of whom grows increasingly depressed by such a frivolous life, the other a typical pussy baron who occasionally makes racist jokes. Plus a few other secondary characters to flesh out the ensemble and provide levity when necessary.

But then this phenomenon, this occurrence. Everyday concerns suddenly pale to this thing. In an intense scene of hushed conversation, maybe over coffee when the kids are with the sitter, the young wife demands to know of the young father how he's seen his own death. Tensions arise when he refuses to divulge, prompting her to also refrain when he demands the same of her; known only to us via cuts or fades, Young Dad is due to get crumpled in a car crash next winter, while Young Mom will live well toward centenarianism and die peacefully. He doesn't want to destroy their family's future hopes, and she doesn't want to ask too many questions, because her husband is conspicuously absent from her own hazy future-memory-vision, which frightens her. Similarly, the dude and girlfriend – this guy should probably, for structure's sake, be Young Dad's brother, maybe a bit more schmo-ish, and the girl is a model or actor or something that implies superficiality, distrust – are also challenged by this shift, but theirs is a more measured response. They discuss their own visions: his finds a slow decline through ALS in his early fifties, sustained by medical technology; hers is a sudden stroke, apparently in her mid-seventies, though the context is murky. It all casts an unbearable shadow of pointlessness on their love. So they have to deal with this.

Alongside these conflicts unfold the horrors of the two other male leads; call them Hotshot 1 and Hotshot 2. Best friends since days of T-ball and GI Joes, their crisis begins – and this will be the pivotal instance binding these characters in their pain – as Hotshot 2, the more carefree and party-loving of the two, sees that he will die in the same wintry car crash that kills his dear pal Young Dad, both thwacked into the great beyond, though of course their knowledge of this moment is private and exclusive, and only through a gradual piecing together of details is this shared moment fully understood. Dialogue here will be kind of tough to wrench out: the rule is *show don't tell*. Anyway, through a crushing revelation later on, we learn that Hotshot 1, by nature the more responsible of the two, was/will be in the driver's seat of that ill-fated ride. One ferociously depressing snowy night after a downtown pub jaunt, Hotshot 1, depressed and full of self-loathing, throws down/will throw down a gallon of J&BS and many ciders, then offers/will offer Hotshot 2 and Young Dad, also somewhat blotto, a drive back up the expressway to his apartment to explore an uncracked bottle of Maker's Mark and the first season of *Twin Peaks* on VHS. It's one of those sad snowy nights inspiring melancholic feelings about the past, or in their case, the future. And the full truth of their shared fates on that grim night comes to light only when each identifies some idiosyncratic detail about Hotshot 1's banged-up Accord in future recall, like a song on the radio maybe. This is the icy truth that really propels the movement from the first act to the second act, or what *Shear the Chaff* designates as *pulling the pin on the grenade*. Guy essentially killed his two best buds. The crunch being: they know it, but he doesn't, since in the accident, Hotshot 2 and Young Dad instantly die, but Hotshot 1 does not, so knows nothing of what they know. Since the Hyundai boasts/boasted/will boast a functioning airbag only on the driver's seat, Hotshot 1 walks/will walk away with only bruises and a court date. Despite the cavernous guilt that will haunt the rest of his years, Hotshot 1 simply lives on while they do not, and so the morbid ramifications of this incident are not provided to him; his death vision is as a wheezing seventy-something grandpa overseen by a gaggle of offspring he doesn't recognize, but eventually will. Therefore he is accused, affirmatively and without doubt, of a crime against his two best friends, of a murder of which he hasn't, and can't possibly have, any memory. The complex webs of distress between all of the above will have to be explored, but there's only so much you can squeeze into a standard-length ninety-to-hundred-page screenplay. Only so many words, and only so many hours.

Night after night, Heath sits in front of his ThinkPad, purchased on a financing plan, scratching at his chin's scars, trying to make it happen. Tape 3 of the LifeSystem 2000, *Hazy Equals Lazy*, insists, *Every day in which you fail to pursue your passion is one more day you wait in vain for what you hope to materialize.* And yet every night Heath spends without any real progress beyond a few scribbled notes and six pages of improbable character development is another night he longs to hop a cab down to Pizza Hut to kill a thick-crust pan and a couple pitchers of Keith's. The challenges are too huge, the work too lonely.

'It's just inspiring to see someone so delicate face this huge obstacle and not be at all afraid. Like they take their fear and just *destroy* it.'

On her weekends off from the Delahayes' store, Brunhilde teaches scuba lessons at an outdoor aquatics centre for disadvantaged pre-teens, including her niece Heidi, hindered in her own ways due to acro-cephalosyndactyly III.

'Everyone needs a reason to do what they do,' she says. 'Heidi's my reason.'

Heath nods. 'That's really ... clear.'

He fears for his life. They are speeding south on the 420 in Brun-hilde's tiny Golf, and she drives seemingly without awareness of any lanes or limits, weaving through traffic without a sideways glance. She's invited Heath to accompany her on this trip, the annual occasion of marking her father Herc's passing to prostate cancer with an after-noon indulging in his favourite activity: drinking cheap whisky and shooting rats in the labyrinth of piled junked cars behind LT's Auto Salvage & Parts, about ten kilometres west of Niagara-on-the-Lake, a yard founded by their great-uncle Lazlo and the site of Herc's first teenage employment. It is also, as the story goes, the site of his virgin-ity's shucking in the backseat of a crumbling Chevette, piled there in the rusted metal.

'Fucker,' Brunhilde spits, narrowly dodging a head-on collision with a Ryder truck.

Herc's spirit has been seen roaming this cluttered yard on certain nights, his spectral traces dancing over heaps of abandoned cars exud-ing this Jerry Bock whimsy, light on his feet over rusted hoods as he never was in his last days, somersaulting free from worries of a tetanus jab on an old wheel well or pried trunk. He's still there, she insists as she weaves through lanes of traffic, living beyond life.

Then they are there, passing through the chain-link gate. As they leave the car and head into the pried wreckage and steel carcasses,

Brunhilde cracks a bottle of Bushmills and hands Heath a .22. He reminds her he's never shot a gun, never even held the grip. Fret not, she assures. But the weapon, the weapon. It sits firmly in his palm.

'Feels strange to hold,' he says.

'Like a lover.'

No – not like a lover. The metal is cold in Heath's slick hands; when Brunhilde fires off several quick rounds from her own vintage Grizzly shotgun, he fears he'll lose hold. Ammunition barks all around; her jaw clenches before each shot, the muscles of her face rippling.

Heath raises the gun, trying to find something to shoot. Scanning the wreckage, he locates not vermin nor bull's-eyes for targets, but rather that JPEG Nicole had forwarded to everyone on her email list of herself stretched out on the beach at Boca Chica in a baby-blue bikini fitting her formerly wide hips, now miraculously narrowed, her stumps playfully sifting the chalk-like sand; the bikini, he surmised, must be new, perhaps a gift from this *Lukey*. He works the trigger – *squeeze, don't pull*, he'd been instructed – and the kick jolts his forearms up and back, yet not as violently as expected. A coldness travels from his feet to his eyes. His heart paradiddles.

Another shot. Another. With each he is more prepared for the recoil, more in control of the physics at play. He hunts no one but his doughy self, bulleting away his waste and squander, assassinating the lesserness of himself. When the magazine is expended, he sighs, wanting more. When he asks Brunhilde to reload it for him, she refills the chambers quickly, pleased at his enthusiasm. Her paleness is highlighted by the salvage yard's joyless arena of dead chrome.

Brunhilde takes a swig of whisky and points her shotgun at Heath's chest. 'I hold your life in my hands.'

'Um. Looks that way.'

'One good shot and your body is Hubba Bubba.'

She pokes his nipple with the barrel.

'The thrill of the kill would be enough.'

She lowers the barrel, releasing her target. In a momentary shift of the surrounding light, Heath notices a strange scar, barely detectable, etching a razor-thin line from her left ear to the point of her chin where that rash begins. He can smell the cherryish zing of her lipstick and hear the work of her escaping breath as she looks at her watch.

'Okay. The kids need to be in the water by seven.'

'Or they shrivel up and die?'

Her smile vanishes. 'You think that's *funny*? It's not. That's really not funny at all.'

Heath winces. 'Kidding. Seriously.'

'*You* shrivel up. *You* die.'

Though traffic back is light, she again pushes the Golf to its limits, a laboured 125 km/h. Other than her intermittent curses at the road, they barely speak. Heath gazes out the window at the highwayed world, the gridded chaos of lights and logos, billboards and boulevards. As he dozes off, his last thought is that his own driver's licence expired three years ago.

He is roused by Brunhilde's hand gripping his. They are parked at the corner outside his apartment. Their fingers intertwine and rest on the plastic drink holder separating the seats. Blinking away sleep, Heath smiles; she does not. Her face, glossed in the flicker of a nearby intersection's advance red, is impossible to read.

7

The Econoline van still sits parked halfway up the front lawn's slope, cocked at an almost hilariously errant angle and emblazoned with bold text: *ProFix 0% Hassle Repair & Removal*. Parker parks the Camry on the street and hurries over with his keys still in his fist.

Three skinny black men in matching blue T-shirts linger at the corner of the house. A half-unfurled blue tarp, toolboxes and a case of Laker Red sit at their feet.

'Hi guys,' he says.

They look at him in silence, then in a synchronized move each looks to the heavens. Parker follows: Adam, shirtless, is on the roof.

'Good morning,' he shouts down, saluting.

Parker calls back, or tries to. But his scratchy throat faults – it's been bugging him all day, despite sipping buckets of lemon-honey water – and the sound he emits is more of a pubescent squeak. The men stare at him, drinking beer.

'We walked.'

'You *walked*.'

'Many of us did.'

'That is … I don't know. I can't imagine.'

'It was necessary,' Daniel says. 'War was happening. We moved away from it. No need to make it sound like something. All of us have done interviews, these journalists from *The Fifth Estate*. They talk slowly, as if you don't understand. The world continues, no one cares, who cares. You own anything worth worrying about, then you worry. When you own nothing, you don't worry about anything except your own skin. Now we're here, so there you go. Fuck it all.'

Parker wipes his nose. 'But you just *walked*.'

'Five weeks. Get a map, man, I'll show you.'

'And you were just boys,' Parker says.

Daniel leans forward. 'I had sex with many girls, so young. I knew it was bad. I *knew*.'

'Easy,' Santino says.

There are four of them on Adam's team: Santino and James say little, while Daniel speaks in a snarl; apparently they all live together in a duplex in East Scarborough. Parker looks to Adam, who remains silent, engrossed in a half-empty pint glass. Smokey's Cookhouse, located next to the Home Depot in the industrial park off Terry Fox Way, squirms around them with busy light, yet feels dark. Screens in every sightline display TSN highlights: Sampras at Wimbledon.

'Ten years old, I was ready to rule,' Daniel says. 'You?'

'Me?'

'When you first had a woman.'

'I … I was young too. Pretty much.'

Adam leans in and finally speaks. 'The age of optimism. Every thought you think is unlike the one before.'

Daniel snaps his fingers at a passing waitress. Another round.

Adam: 'In a world of violence and death, you don't resist the tide. Unless you're a fool.'

Parker: 'I'm not certain what you mean.'

Adam smiles in a way Parker doesn't understand.

Daniel interrupts. 'He's talking about survival, man. You just keep going. You go miles with no destination. You eat dirt when a soldier is jabbing you over and over in the shoulders with his rifle. But you just keep fucking *going*.'

Daniel slams his empty glass on the table. 'When *you* apply for the low-interest business loan, they don't immediately write you off. Do they?'

Parker: 'Who, a bank?'

'They dismiss you, then throw you a handful of condescending, what you call, *brochures*. Then move to the next in line.'

'Yeah,' Parker says. 'But that's …'

He goes to say more, but doesn't. Daniel looks for the waitress.

'There are geopolitical concerns at play,' Adam says.

Daniel leans back in, saying something to Adam that Parker doesn't hear. Adam shrugs it off and turns back to Parker.

'You don't resist the tide in a place where blood flows freely,' Adam says. 'Your only hope is to see the setting sun. But here we're sitting in this restaurant, all these restaurants. And the hospitals and hardware stores. This country thinks about life in a different way. Here we have more to consider. Yet less.'

'You're saying we should appreciate our luxuries,' Parker says.

'I'm saying you have to ingratiate yourself,' Adam says.

Drinks arrive. Daniel downs most of his glass in one swift go, then glares at Parker with accusing eyes. Parker is uncertain what is happening. Things have changed – lately he is stuck on the impossibility of all his memories being anything but faded recall, rosy images. Everything exists only in the powerlessness of his mind. And the only purpose of these memories is toward maintaining the illusion of purpose. Pointlessness is the underlying joke of all things. He feels ill.

'Taking a piss,' Daniel says, and departs.

Parker sets his glass on the table.

'Adam, tell me. Tell me.'

'What.'

'Tell me.'

'Proceed with what you're asking, man.'

'Are you … *angry*? At all that's happened, or happening. At all this injustice. Your country, your, I don't know, family. Your people.'

Adam licks his lips. 'My *people*?'

'Just how do you rectify this …' Parker shakes his head, looking at his hands, struggling to assemble the words. 'It's just, to me it reminds me of the, the nothingness. Us on the earth with our brains and our lungs. All the things we try to do and be. And there are centuries and centuries. It's all … hollow. It makes no sense.'

'Are you mentally retarded, man? What are you talking about?'

'I don't know.'

Daniel returns from the washroom, sliding in close next to Parker.

'We're going to sit around picking our penises, or we're going to go meet some females? Mr. Parker?'

'I'm a married man.'

'Not my problem,' Daniel laughs.

In the Smokey's parking lot they hover, parting ways. There is so much not being said. Adam's detachment, his dismissal: like he's become lost in time's slipstream, living out a destiny he wasn't meant for. Parker's throat clenches again when he sees it: Adam looks like Owen.

While the others debate their next move, Adam approaches Parker, shepherding him away from the others.

'Next time, before you call Swaffe, call me directly first.'

'Swaffe's who answered the phone?'

Adam nods. 'But next time, cut out the middleman. I gave you the card. I think you see where I'm coming from. Financially.'

'I think so. Maybe.'

Adam grins. '*Ha*. Miscommunication like true allies. Like *Simon & Simon*. You know that one?'

'Yeah, with Major Dad and the other guy. You actually got that, out there?'

Adam gives him a look that says *you haven't heard a word I've said.*

Daniel returns. 'I have a small favour to ask,' he says to Parker. 'The possibility of an advance.'

Parker looks at Adam, who says nothing. 'An advance.'

Daniel: 'On the roof work. Swaffe said it was a common arrangement.'

Everyone here knows this is a lie. Nonetheless, Parker obliges. Fifty dollars.

'Tribal civilization thanks you,' Daniel says, pinning the bills between thumb and index, turning to hail a taxi.

Adam lingers for a second, extending a hand to Parker. They shake.

'You and I are going to talk,' Adam says. 'We'll have a long talk. I have some ideas.'

Then he heads off with the others. Parker watches the taxi peel across the Smokey's parking lot and disappear into the eddy of highway traffic.

8

12/20/79. Found out my AST206 prof D. DaBeryl died two days ago. He kept talking about seeing the Honda-Mrkos-Pajdušáková comet cruise by in a few years. Then, heading home for holidays, a bum ticker, zap. Meanwhile there's R. Last night he has a seizure when I demand a condom, twists away with his boner still twitching. He lies there, planking the timber, telling me I've failed in earning his love. Where do we stand? No idea. Saxons on their longships. Year Zero. I wouldn't even know where to start. And that's how it goes. No justice.

'Blood type.'

'Um. I forget. The most common one.'

'O?'

'At school, I presume. A mother worries.'

The nurse looks up. Trixie sees her flub.

'Oh. O. Right. Yes, that's it. Ha.'

'Allergies.'

'My eyes water when I eat apples.'

The nurse cocks her head. 'That's not on your chart.'

Trixie wonders if these prescriptions are shovelling away at her brain. You think about side effects. Where treatment ends and symptom begins is a hazy distinction.

'Still experiencing headaches and lethargy.'

'But that goes way back. Nothing new.'

The nurse goes to check off something on her chart, but her pen runs dry. She presses harder, then harder still, scratching at the form until the paper tears under her pressure. The report is destroyed.

12/31/79. End of Days. End of Decades. Goodbye seventies, hello misery and self-loathing. R, you say you want solitude but you just can't stand being alone. You say you love beyond love but you act like a conceited jerk-off. Love's made me lazy. Romanticizing our misery and the photo book with the Chernobyl vats and the stale bread and you're so irritable when the saq is closed. Who are you to weep? Someday all of this, the slushy sidewalks, the men smoking in front of the Old Brewery Mission, all this will be forgotten.

As Kapuściński wrote: *it used to be real, falling, sinking to the point of losing oneself, falling into dust into ashes into a shivering quivering fit on the ground, hands reaching out and beseeching mercy.* It was that book on Haile Selassie Trixie had digested in one difficult summer evening for a grad paper, way back when, at the seventies' end, and it now frames this supplementary editorial preface, a month overdue now, that has been a constant aggravation. A kingdom crumbling, the cold rattle of artillery and emptying courts – this was the beauty of defeat. *They fell, but it was such an unanimated falling, so sleepy as if imposed on them as if done only for the sake of peace, slow, lazy, simply negative.* It was something she sought but never found in her own nightly typewriter sessions and journal scribblings, the shattered earths and portals to greater significance. That desire evaporated, somewhere along the way: lost, even now, with her own empire in decline.

In the mall she passes countless shops and their begging gleams, her flow unerring, feeling anachronistic and alien. It is 12:15; she has a meeting at one and many files yet to check back at the office. But Eaton Centre's turbid world drifts away as she mentally replays today's Sierra Leone interview footage, thinking only of bodies bulldozed into heaps, tallied in columns and transferred to downloadable records. She places one foot before the other, unfurling motion with the same care she invests in explicating survivor accounts, witness testimonials, battlefield correspondence, the entire genre of murderer verse, a gore-drenched canon of atrocity. Corpses float in the food-court fountain and entrails bask in greasy counter heat lamps.

She rides an escalator to the department store's third floor, light-headed in its arena of cottony swaths, the mirrored pillars creating an unfun funhouse of angles and corners. Trixie inspects bins of thongs and frilly stretchables, squeezing a wad of underwear like an enemy. The store's racks abound with possibility even as her internal reality seems like a carjacking, a failed moon landing. Fewer days ahead than behind, wrinkles everlasting, the flirtatious grimaces of young bucks in office hallways vanquished for good. She is scarcely herself anymore. Yes: End of Days. In the dimness there is no one around to see her, to bear witness to these transgressions. She stuffs the underwear in her bag and hurries along.

01/06/80. Come to kiss him goodnight. There at his desk with his notebooks and that noisy electric typewriter. I lean in and he winces like I'm some chlamydic ghoul. He says, 'My writing is suffering.' I can't help but point out this statement could be taken more than one way. Just a joke, but he looks at me like I'm Nuon Chea or something. Asshole.

And then: hostile lights overhead, mounted in ceilinged panels. She peers up into sharp burrs of light, the security cams and networks of sensors spelling her doom.

The stubby floorwalker with the bashed-in nose crams his ID back in his pocket and pincers her forearm, leading her through the store, regulating stride without forcible movement. As they march past perfume displays of Lauder and Burberry and Dior, shopladies sneer and customers back away. She is led as a criminal; she is a criminal. Thumbing the lapel of a mannequin's velour jacket, a woman of about Trixie's age looks on with horror. When the guard whispers into his shoulder-velcroed radio, she thinks for an instant he's addressing her; when she turns out of politeness, he raises eyebrows and says, 'Dontcha squirm now or'll bust out the cuffs.' The way he says *bust* is more like *boost*.

The sick reality sets in as she is led to a small office shooting off from the store's back elevators. The bashed-nosed guard steers her with the same forearm grip to a plastic chair, then takes a seat at a small desk opposite. He finds a pen, gives Trixie a weary look, then produces a pad of forms.

'Name.'

Trixie Sweltham, a woman of esteem in both professional and domestic accomplishment, mother and wife and citizen of the twentieth century.

'Picture ID.'

A recently renewed licence, a flushed headshot, ponytailed.

'On here is your current address.'

She blinks. It is.

The bashed-nosed floorwalker splashes a spectrum of confiscated mid-budget panties across the desk, then spends a good ten minutes hunched in filling forms. A cashier appears to sum the value of the underwear, then vanishes. Trixie cranes her neck to see what is being entered into the record – the title reads D5: *Petition of Restraint* – but he catches her gawking and shields the form from view. Finally, he leans back and puts down his pen. 'Why, with a Mastercard Gold in your purse? Half a million cameras here, just *aching* for someone to take a chance.'

She doesn't respond.

'This your first offence? We're checking, so don't you lie. I know liars, and how they lie, and the last thing you want to be is a liar.'

No, the underwear alone was not worth this. But some crimes serve no purpose but for the act itself.

A policeman proper arrives, an imposing Trinidadian giant clutching his belt, just as the guard's walkie announces chaos in sporting goods, summoning him away. The cop glances at the guard's report and laughs out loud: a high-pitched giggle. For forty-nine seconds Trixie has a criminal record. Still she does not plead her innocence.

Only when hurrying across the echoing parkade does she fully register what has occurred. Finding the Volvo, she enters and sits, turns the ignition, then looses a gasp. Somewhere stacks of petrol-soaked corpses wait for incineration. But here, on an afternoon so quiet: only a tired hush.

9

This night breathes hope and sweat: a night of June bugs battering screens, heated cats yowling, a glossy haze trapping a luxurious moon above. Shadows converge, half-dimensional spectres in Gore-Tex and sweatshirts, beer bottles and mason jars of stolen liquor raised like muskets in defence of a shared threat, the curfews and expectations. They slouch on the house's doorstep and stumble in the backyard: a cacophony of tribes, drawn by rumour and gossip, kids from other schools crossing town in parents' vans and GO trains, alight with the school year's end. Chirruping laughter fights thundering bass from anguished woofers: Tupac, Mystikal.

The house's three-storey immensity befits its inhabitants' assets portfolio, its brick the hue of razed wheatfields, the adjunct garage's yardage storing two Audis and three Ski-Doos. The Squelces live here, Bill and Uriana, parents of Corrina and Oliver – 'Olie' – and proud partners in what Bill terms the Ultimate Timeshare Smackdown, a chalet-style bungalow and six-acre spread at Eagle Beach just outside of Oranjestad where you can not only, as Bill enjoys describing, whack eighteen holes amid the soothing whoosh of pines trembling in a cool ocean breeze with a jumbo mojito in hand, but also, seasonally depending, beat the piss out of between six and seven manmade rivers teeming with trout with zero lake patrol checking your ice chest. This is where Bill and Uriana are now, sunning and cocktailing, unaware as dozens of teenagers lay their family's home to waste.

Chuck Byng has been asking around about Corrina Squelce at least since Spring Fling, but hasn't really pursued it full steam. Now she probes him with eyelinered baby blues, explaining to him over the noise how she always thinks of herself as older than she actually is; she constantly has to remind herself she is only seventeen and not thirty. *Thirty*: she caresses the word lovingly, dreamily. Chuck is unable to respond with any coherence, occupied mainly with the distant sensation of his mind's collapse. He is presently under the total sway of mushrooms provided by Olie, a known juggernaut as far as his narcotic intake and also sort of malicious in his generosity.

'We think we're young, but we're not so young,' Corrina says.

But they are young, and they are beastly. The Bying begins to worry about the bite of something crawling up his neck, something leggy and tendrilled that may soon engulf his brain. He tries to tell Corrina how his cousin Vince, an astrophysics grad student, sent him this thing on his iStar account that explained how the rotation of the earth interacts with our galaxy's flux to fashion a pretty believable definition of the human soul, in all its manifestations and conceptions. It was pretty damn interesting. But when he tries to speak, all he manages is *Cuh-neer-ah.*

'*Co-reen-ah,*' she corrects.

'Yeah, yeah. Jus' fucked.'

Young and beastly: Lucky Chartrand and Owen Sweltham wobble through the living room, each with a six-pack of Schooner tucked under an arm. Lucks recognizes a biggish guy seated on the loveseat from the rival St. Pat's basketball squad, a curly-haired centre named Jamie Pinnick; he moves forward and pokes him in the nipple. The guy at first laughs it off good-naturedly, though clearly irked. Lucks also laughs, though more sinisterly. Then Owen throws a full foaming beer in the guy's lap. The guy leaps to his feet and chases the giggling two into the dining room, a spacious windowed solarium of sorts, where they face off around a ginormous circular oak table.

Lucky is not a pussy, but neither is this guy Pinnick. Words, barbs, are exchanged. As the two come almost nose to nose, Owen lights a cigarette. Olie now tumbles down the stairs into the front foyer, wild on Canadian Club and those mushrooms, scything through the still-gathering throng there, and upon signs of brewing conflict is immediately keen to amp things up. Onlookers groan and hoot, ready for the inevitable showdown.

In the kitchen Matt Calcaveccia is talking with two guys he's just met. The room smells like smoke and Drakkar Noir and french fries.

'Just twenty days basic,' the first guy says. 'Get a pamphlet.'

'And you do it full,' the other says. 'Drop and target. Field craft. Greasepaint. We need a shot.'

All three down a quick swallow of Wild Turkey.

The Calch is skeptical. 'But you could get shipped to like fucking Kosovo or Côte d'Ivoire or something, and next thing you know you're getting your scrotum shot off.'

'You wouldn't get cock. It's mostly just marches, ceremonial shit,' the first guy says.

'It's *all* ceremonial,' the second guy says. 'And then you're on Scholarship Boulevard. Plus there's that cheque every month. Grub's not even that bad.'

'Plus they gave me this kick-ass hat,' the first guy says.

It's an aqua-blue denim cap, fitted by an adjustable strap and fronted with a logo: *forces.ca*.

The Calch nods. 'That really is a killer hat.'

Chuck, still unable to move his neck, descends into the vision that is Corrina.

'I see dollar signs in your eyes,' he says.

'Full moon tonight,' Corrina says.

Inside the house a renewed mania of voices rises. Gwen Huang sits on a couch in the living room, embarrassed as this guy Joachim tries to force a tape of his band Drive Like Yahweh on the stereo, facing adversity from some fat kid from Secondary vying to dictate the night's soundtrack with a Hatebreed bootleg. The static between Joachim and the fat kid, built like a one-guy avalanche ready to engulf teams of heli-skiers, is accelerating into actual threats when Owen Sweltham emerges from the basement carrying Bill Squelce's old bag of golf clubs – recently replaced by killer new Titleists, an anniversary gift from Uriana, clubs he was just hours ago swinging gustily for his first-ever eagle at the Smackdown – slung over his shoulder. Owen marches toward the dining room, unswayable. As he passes, Gwen recognizes the look on his face: her brother Elroy often moved with such anger, storming through the kitchen late at night gripping his pager like a mace. Elroy is now serving six to ten in Millhaven.

'I want to take you upstream,' Chuck Byng says to Corrina over the surrounding din.

Horror in her face. 'I don't do that.'

'What? No, no ... I mean. S'go upstairs.'

Fingers, marching, miming footsteps: Up up up.

'Upstairs. Up … there.'

They go to the staircase, Corrina first and Chuck a step behind. She pauses at the landing and turns to face him. Her lips and eyes, caught in the stray light, invite him, and The Bying is suddenly overcome by something he'd detected but never really been awash in, knifing through the darkness to pummel him in the vicinity of his kidneys. Yes, the drugs are definitely a significant factor in this anguish. But the effect of the light and the lips and the languor is really something. He gulps.

Then: glass shattering. The whole plot is rocked as voices rise in shrill alarm. Bodies fill hallways, lights snap to life. An already tenuous order is crushed; everything's intensifying. Owen swings a nine iron at everything breakable within reach, glass and wood and ceramic, while Lucky, hurrying from the kitchen a second behind, does good work with an eight, clearing away the shreds of what O leaves behind. Pinnick tears off his sweatshirt, his face fire-truck-red, pledging to *exterminate these fucks*, calling for the forcible insertion of their genitals down their own throats. Some onlookers are on his side, others on the opposite, but most are simply amused by the escalating tension and the promise of an altercation, looking forward to where this craziness is going.

Olie Squelce, staggering from the basement cocking his Career 707 air rifle, looking forward to shooting someone, anyone, shouts against the bedlam: 'Burn this house *down*.' Referring to his own home.

It all ends up on the back deck. Pinnick fights to throttle Owen, but Sweltham bats away the attacking hands with a move of shoulders and a half-swing of the club. But the advantage gained by this defensive manoeuvre sets Owen off-balance, and Pinnick's responding lunge sends both toppling to the deck's weather-sealed pine. The deck's completion, just two summers ago, brought Bill Squelce such joy it unleashed a grilling binge that lasted a full two weeks before Uriana demanded sushi for the love of Christ. Pinnick and Sweltham end up in a multi-limbed wrestle, Pinnick managing to overpower Sweltham, pinning his arms to the ground and jamming his knees into Owen's windpipe. A girl whoops. Another girl demands, 'I wanna see some ball sack.'

Gwen Huang shoves through the surrounding mob, craning her neck to see the brawl play out just as Matt Calcaveccia suddenly drives gridiron-style through the crowd, taking Pinnick by the forehead and jaw as if palming a Spalding. Pinnick makes a sound like *gack*. Some of Pinnick's cronies make a move but are restrained by two guys from Calcaveccia's rugby squad. One guy, losing his Raiders cap in the process, delivers a robotic flurry of jabs to the solar plexus of one of Pinnick's buds, while one of his associates, astonishing all, delivers a reverse roundhouse to someone's temple. Meanwhile Owen tears back into Pinnick, now full nelsoned by The Calch, managing a slightly whiffed head-butt to the bridge of Pinnick's nose before the cronies haul him back by his arms. Blood flies.

Upstairs, in Olie's bedroom, Chuck and Corrina are shedding clothes.

'You should try and not cry,' she says.

'I'm trying. Son of a cock. I'm *trying*.' His left hand is on her inner thigh and his right hand is on his own wet face.

'Are you going to keep crying? Because if you are, I can't ...'

'Just give me a second. Serious. Pull myself together.'

With a *bloop* of siren and splashes of red and white light, the police cruiser barrels into the driveway behind Richie's Integra. With most attendees out back watching the fight, the closest to answer the doorbell's chime is Olie, still waving the air rifle in druggy delirium.

He opens the door to two officers waving flashlights like truncheons.

'Hi,' he says.

The cops pounce, disarming him of the rifle and sending him to the floor. Word of the cops' arrival spreads quickly. Partiers near the foyer make for the back door, the basement, closets. Out back everyone flees. Calcaveccia releases Pinnick, who appears ready to vomit, taking Owen's sleeve.

'O. Five-O on the freeway.'

Owen doesn't need to be told twice. He horks in Pinnick's panicked face, then vaults over the deck railing, The Calch and Lucky a second behind. They make for the woods bordering the back of the lawn, toward streetlights fractalled through branches, toward escape.

Slow as a gully eroded into existence, like a capstan reeling, these apparitions come to life in tempests, forecasts to come. The shades that struggle against the light are familiar and wiped, living here – ghosts behind gates, a continent-wide sprawl. Dream of volcanic valleys and solar storms, a world populated by berserker warriors and zombie hordes manning the wrecked shores from which nefarious gods are born. These incarnations converge in a plaid-skied valley set between chundering volcanoes, flanked by untold legions: bloodthirsty ogres, succubi of fangs and armoured shells, all slick with fluids and guck. Here battles stew between the dead and the living, and those trapped in between. Bear witness: The Calch and Lucky and The Bying, winged warriors, explode from a Valhalla of soccer shin pads and ChapStick sinking through stoned storm clouds. Behind them, Ike Seligman, eleven feet tall and draped in robes of human tissue, waves dripping hands against all shades of death, administerial monstrosities, plundered neighbourhoods, supreme annihilation. Lucky and The Calch strike first against the drooling ghouls, swinging bo staffs, Chuck on backup with zinging shuriken. Ike conjures barrages of hail and blindness and coma. But these infernal creatures wage their interminable war, summoning darknesses and magicks and weapons from abysses mortal souls can scarcely imagine.

And perched aloft an overlooking magma-spewing peak, a metamorphic Quiet Room temple of his own architecture, Owen Sweltham gazes down into this valley of bloody duels, frowning. Just as tides begin to shift, when the beasts have these heroes at their mercy, when all seems lost – he dives down. He is unstoppable, pummelling these pathetic yucks with haymakers, drop kicks, robotic pincers, laser vision, baths of skin-sautéing radiations. Protector of all, beacon of light, hope of hopes. Death comes to all who defy. Fallen bodies, warped and grotesque, litter the rocky ground. Battle won, the dreamer blesses this garden of carcasses in solitude. Rags flutter in the breath of left gases, death's wake brushing the hero's shins like a house cat. Herons yelp in unseen shallows, begging the morning. And yet skies remain unclear.

No dawn emerges. In this aftershock, the surrounding mountains only accelerate their volcanic violence. Gravy-sauce-like lava splatters over craggy rock, flowing down into the razed battlefield, its burbling creep cremating the valley. In the smoke rising from such ruination, the hero recognizes faces, caricatures: a father and a mother, the spirits from which all heroes spring. Timeless sphinxes.

But the vision lives only temporarily. Further shifts occur. Images fade and recede. He sees: one of his parents dies, the other lives. But which is which, he can't determine.

Owen opens his eyes. The bedside alarm clock reads 10:43. Soccer tryouts were at ten.

HELL

1

Satan prefers cool spaces. Patrol today is joyless, with hard sun pushing down through the usual filters of branches and eaves, leaving him to relish the brief arcs of shade in between. He executes a full scope, twice around the perimeter, down to the sidewalk and a check at the driveway wall's edge, a skip over the crevice puddle across the grassy way, then back toward home through the twiggy jungle near the big metal thing, aiming finally for the porch with a slight detour to sniff at something: a neighbour's Hibachi.

Satan is almost happy with this life. He recalls youth, a mother, siblings, though all only hazily. Laboratory jabs, noise, pleading yewls from all sides. Now each day passes the same as the last. No reason to dread the future or regret the past. There have been standoffs with sworn enemy Old Chartreux from down the street, but other than one swipe of claw and threatening rowls, nothing has ever made him fearful. Those who feed him have no idea how many lives he's taken, all the rodents and dragonflies. He doesn't do it for them, for anyone; he lounges in the gritty grasses and shampoos himself in the mud of death.

Returning to the deck, he waits with infernal patience to be admitted through the screen doors. When it happens he is grateful. It's cool inside, and there is food. Satan blinks, watching as the man follows him through the front foyer and into the kitchen. The man sets his bag at the foot of the stairs and heads upstairs. Satan creeps over to sniff at its aromatic leather. Usually it smells like safety. But today something is different; Satan backs off, crinkling nostrils, processing a change.

Then he begins his ascent, rising slowly and deliberately, batting at dust floating in captured light. On his way up the stairs, he slides his back against the wallpaper, claiming it again as his own. Memories of a traumatic run-in with the vacuum cleaner on these steps last year still haunt him – the whipping lash of that rubber cord like so many zones of obstacles and confrontations, below and inside everything.

Satan pokes his head into the bedroom to scan the way forward. The room is full of light and coolness. Moving to the bed, he discovers the source of the odd sound above: the man, bent at the edge of the bed, shoes still on. A quick hop up onto the mattress elicits no reaction. Feeling anxious, Satan digs his claws into the comforter, working its fibres in an effort to relieve his own confusion. He elongates his spine, stretches his legs. The man takes no notice. Satan pushes his luck, coiling up against him to assert his presence, his trace, on his surroundings. Still: this unfamiliar sound.

Satan hops into the man's lap, collapsing into his arms, his tail brushing the man's chin. As the man digs his fingers into the fat of Satan's lower spine, he stares up at the ceiling, at the windows and the colourless facade of afternoon beyond. The man's fingertips are smooth and unworn. As the man chokes on his tears, Satan settles into this heavenly place, and can't help but purr.

2

Knock knock.

Adam opens his eyes and leaps from the bed, still in his underwear. He reaches for the bedroom wall, steadying himself, then retrieves a pair of pants from a pile of laundry, hurrying in case Daniel responds first. But thankfully Daniel remains face-down on the living room pullout.

It's Tillie at the door, on behalf of Johnny Lou, her father.

'You,' she says. 'We need postdated cheques.'

Adam, still shirtless, rubs his nose. 'It's early.'

'There's a ninety-day policy. Get a shirt on and swing by the office. *Bring those cheques.* You guys are already on shaky ground.'

He shuts the door before she can say anything else. Last night he'd been up late fine-tuning his business plan, aiming for a month's-end submission deadline. Now is the time to strike; he's just about abandoned for good his shifts pushing a mop down at the Duracell centre, and soon will be free of the Swaffes and ProFix. And that Excel manual he requested at the Burnhamthorpe library should be in any day now. They stare at him, the teenagers who operate the basement computer lab, when he signs in for his half-hour internet sessions. Yesterday one of the ancient Pentiums crashed as he printed additions to the al-Durabi file; the kids sighed with unbridled condecension.

Yes, the other file, the plan – for this, he thinks of Parker Sweltham: tucked polo shirts, pleading eyes, a mortgage. The man and his obvious fear.

The line at the immigration office trails out past glass doors and into Dufferin Mall's lower concourse. Adam waits in line, foldered paperwork in hand. Ahead of him, Indonesian families push strollers, sharing space with glum-looking Arab students and older veiny-nosed men in walking shorts. He grinds his teeth and adjusts his Pistons cap, his empty guts whining. He considers abandoning these plans for a paper cup of New York Fries, but knows that in doing so he'd be sacrificing even this luckless place in the queue. So he stays.

Decades later he is ushered past a counter into a tiny office beyond. Adam removes his cap, folding it like an envelope.

'So let's get you sorted.'

The young Filipino rep behind the desk thumbs through the tattered purple folder containing Adam's documents: his certified business licence, immigration status, financials, photocopies of Adam's original IMM 1925B and Swaffe-signatured pay stubs.

'Looking to flow funds back home?' the rep asks.

Adam clears his throat and stares at this human, name-tagged Bernie K., at the gelled firmness of his hair's stalagmites, the near-invisibility of his glasses' frames, the incongruity of the emerald stubbed in his left earlobe. Bernie K. radiates a blended air of annoyance and frivolity. July marks the passing of the designated twelve months, he explains, leaving Adam ineligible for further funding from the Resettlement Assistance Program; by official accounts, his is considered a success story, though his access to such processes as credit approval still remains dicey. In the transition from resident to citizen, his status will regularly change. But this process, Adam knows, will be labyrinthine and interminable. So many battles lie ahead, so many fools yet to suffer.

At the refugee camp near Nyala, he was hurried from nobodiness to total systemic ingestion, processed and tented under clean canvas with a mattressed bunk. People tore apart plastic seals and swabbed his many cuts. Sympathetic eyes inspected him, and he was given gifts: a plastic toothbrush and a face cloth to keep.

One day a reporter arrived, bearded and wearing an impractical pocketed vest. The BBC, Adam was told, was part of England – he was shown a map of the world. Two people assisted the reporter: one man with a camera and a woman who claimed to be an interpreter, though Adam, then only fifteen, could barely understand most of what she said.

They asked: 'Do you miss your village?'

They asked: 'What was your journey like?'

They asked: 'Do you welcome your new life?'

One afternoon Adam and another boy found the reporter's vest left hung on a bench in the camp mess. The other kid was timid, but Adam felt no shame in rifling through. These pockets held notebooks and scraps, items useless for barter, but in one he found a clunky mobile phone. Adam had never owned one, or known anyone who had, but he'd seen such a thing in action enough at the camp to at least know what it did. He poked buttons, and soon heard the faint buzz of a ring. Holding the phone to his ear, he heard a woman's voice: 'Babe, oh god, is this really you? I miss you so much.' Adam tossed the phone into a nearby ditch.

The first time you ride in an airplane is the moment when you dismiss the mysticality of the skies. This is both a revelation and a verdict. You agonize with warnings of its impossibility, rumbling down the runway, accelerating, then tons of plastic and aluminum bid the earth farewell, thrust and climb, and the terrain you know with your toes is transformed into novelty, miniaturized, a faked world shielded by an airy gush. Airborne, you join zones previously reserved for myths. But this dream exists, made possible by vouchers and sympathy and the pressurization of air.

He spent time in transport: Nairobi first, then north to UNHCR processing sites. At each stage came questionings and layovers and certifications. He grew to loathe these waits almost as much as the sound of distant gunfire. From windows at transport gates he studied a world ruled by mechanisms: everywhere in Europe people wheeled the same Travelpro luggage, and everything smelled like chemicals and coffee.

Buckled into an aisle seat on a sparsely occupied 747 en route to Düsseldorf, he caught something slinking ahead, low and long. He went to rise from his seat, but a flight attendant insisted he stay put. The seat-belt light was on; there would be turbulence. But something moved in the aisles ahead, a shadow: it was the lion, following him, even there. The creature prowled, sifting through seats, its growl a murmur. His scent had been caught, and would be kept.

Smokey's is bustling tonight with not one but two stag parties underway, and some tension rising between these blocs. At one cluster of tables completely ripped engineering students order pitchers and giggle among themselves, while at another group beefy dudes in matching sweatshirts – ironed-on text screaming I LICK BALLS FOR TERRI CALLAGHAN GARY POOR SUMBITCH BACHELOR DESTRUXXXION – are killing Jack Daniel's with suicide wings for chaser, occasionally tossing balled-up sauce-soiled napkins at the other table. Hostility between these factions is definitely broiling.

At a booth across the bar, Daniel is being pissy at Santino for something involving a pair of girls they'd met earlier this afternoon downtown. All day Daniel has been taunting him, saying *special traditions bad manners special traditions bad manners*. And Santino has been submissive, even more so than usual.

'This one, *this one*,' Daniel says, indicating Santino. 'An inspiration to us all.'

Adam picks at a scab on his knuckles. His mind is elsewhere. Hours ahead sit like hills to be conquered, desolate tracts to be tackled, sweaty pre-invoiced hours of putty and gypsum board to be endured.

Daniel continues harassing Santino. *Special traditions.* These girls, it comes out, responded favourably to the two's offers of cigarettes. One girl accepted a swig from Daniel's flask. Things appeared promising. Then, according to Daniel, Santino started in about *back home* they have *special traditions.* The whole scenario was immediately decimated: they looked like idiots, Daniel says, finishing another whisky soda. Because of this guy. Santino says maybe Daniel overestimated their chances. Daniel tells him to shut the fuck up.

Adam tries to read Daniel's eyes as they scan this room of men. Daniel, he knows, has recently begun carrying a switchblade.

Slumped in his seat, James is only worsening the tension, having already polished off four cans of Bavaria 8.6 before even leaving the apartment, now casting bleary eyes around the room, captivated by the smoke of a neighbouring table's fajitas. James is the only one of the three not presently working for ProFix – he'd been fired by the Swaffes for kicking Ronnie in the shins on one of his irregular work-site visits. James first pleaded his innocence, claiming he was only protecting the van and mistook Ronnie for a burglar. But his later drunken cries of *rich son of a bitch* worked against his defence. Since then he's been returning cans to the Beer Store and hustling stolen TTC tickets, bumming off the others while claiming to be waiting on a cheque from a cousin who ended up out west in Similkameen. He's always around, but is never really anywhere.

The adjacent table of engineers erupts into hollers, prompting barks from the other stag party: 'Shut it, fuck.'

'James,' Daniel says.

James looks up from his glass.

'That one, with the glasses. Nose. He's looking at you.'

All look: a guy with thick spectacles framing a wide beak laughs among the engineers. Adam says he doesn't see anything there. Daniel grins.

'You're just not seeing what I'm seeing.'

James sips from his glass, squinting past two tables of drinkers and the din of voices and music, his focus obviously failing.

Adam has long absorbed the assurances of tutors and advisors and case workers, read pamphlets and scoured government websites. He has thrown himself at the mercy of suffocation over and over, only to be met by the same condescending sniff Doug Swaffe throws at him: a peeved look, as if he'd been offered flaming feces as an appetizer. But his response will not be hasty, or ineffectual, like so many of his brethren. He will reply on their own terms. The violence they have staked.

'You have to see how they look at you,' Daniel says, edging closer to James. 'They're provoking you.'

Santino rises. 'Toilet.'

Daniel: 'Special traditions.'

'We should leave,' Adam says. 'Due 9 a.m. on-site. The house with the tree.'

Daniel finishes his glass and tops it up from one of the two pitchers they have on the go.

'That man? Racist hog.'

In the men's room, members of the Gary Callaghan stag contingent engage in minor vandalism: two brick-bodied dudes work the towel dispenser from its wall bracket while another guy tries to urinate into the sink, drenching the entire counter. A fourth guy, squat and spiky-haired, giggles so enthusiastically he spills rum and Coke on his crotch. Their attentions turn to Santino as he enters. He tries to sidestep the action, making for an empty stall, but the spiky one comes lurching forward, slurring something about *knew this guy since college six fucking years.* The dudes demand that Santino join them back at their table, come have a shot with the groom-to-be, the *poor detesticled sonofabitch.*

Santino recognizes the wildness in their eyes. Taking flight through burning grasslands, teethy men, brutish with drink and bloodlust, at his heels, their shadows rising in flames – he's seen many such men in such states, beyond reason. His English is still lacking, so after rinsing his hands he tries to escape the restroom without inviting conversation. But the dudes follow close behind, back into the bar.

'Bro. Bro. Come have a frigging shot.'

'Gary's saying his vows in like twenty, thirty-something hours, man. Come have a shot, fuck.'

'It's important, bro. Have a shot.'

Santino doesn't speak. One dude grips his arm, an uncertain gesture that could be an attack or an embrace, but Santino flaps it away, saying, 'Fuck off.'

And then Daniel is there, James a step behind, both baring fangs. The dudes still insist: 'Have a frigging shot, Jay friggin' Dee.' Daniel moves forward, unafraid, actually overjoyed at the rising fires. He reaches for his back pocket, cornering the dudes against a Golden Tee console.

Adam can't be bothered to follow the violence that ensues; he's seen how this will go. He remains at the table, thumbing his phone. These are only minor wars, empty bravado, all small things, unfocused. He has calls to make and plans to consider.

Mornings in the school meant English lessons with Deirdre, a giraffey woman with freckles so vivid the first time Adam saw her he feared for her life. Her skin's translucence seemed wrong and cruel; she could wisp away on a breeze. Weeks upon weeks. Lessons, impenetrable meanings. So many assumptions. One day Deirdre produced a cardboard box, another donation. Old junked comic books, maybe a bit more fun than the dreary Farley Mowat and Bobbsey Twins stuff, she supposed. And some interesting vocab and non-rule-book structure. Adam dragged the carton off to a private corner and began rifling through.

These yellowing pages of coloured compartments showed humans, but more than that: muscular and unblemished, they were capable of incredible feats. They weren't shitting in roadside ditches and wringing blood from birds. They lived in impossible cities and fought battles in Arctic plains, in volcanic craters, in locations beyond the sky: places like dreams. Deirdre confirmed that some of these realities actually existed, though in less exotic forms. Adam grew anxious about not under-standing the text in these pages' sections, demanding definitions. This man, this hero, who? The common thing being they all came from the same place as Deirdre: across the ocean. Superheroes weren't born along the White Nile. Superman could deflect bullets and fly. Angel from the Uncanny X-Men bore horrific wings, like a vulture's. Hawkeye, a steel-toed archer, made a lot more sense. But why shoot an arrow when you can shoot a rifle? He read of weird beings like Firestorm the Nuclear Man and Rom Spaceknight and J'onn J'onzz the Martian Manhunter. Deirdre translated: *nuclear* meant a powerful fire; a *spaceknight* was nothing; *Mars* was a planet, a star. The Flash was faster than anything: that seemed something to envy. The Flash belonged to the Justice League of America – *America*, a land more like a well from which came basketballs, computers, syringes – it all seemed so unreachable, worth-less to even waste time dreaming about. But this notion of justice – this was something he thought he understood.

At the bottom of this box he picked out a nearly liquefied issue of *Action Comics* no. 531 of May 1982. Superman's adventure – *The Devil ... and the Daily Planet!* – was uninteresting, but it was backed up by another episode featuring a less-celebrated hero dubbed The Atom. Titled *No Time Off for Heroes*, the story found The Atom in his alter ego Ray Palmer, mild-mannered physicist – a physicist was a special type of doctor, Deirdre explained – away with his wife, Jean, in a place called Curaçao. The story was brisk: The Atom discovered an odd high-powered device requiring immediate deactivation, but meanwhile his body was doing weird worrying things, stretching and shifting, that might have something to do with all this strangeness. Who was the villain behind this? How would The Atom save the day? Find out next issue.

To Adam, The Atom's superpower of becoming small, invisibly small, seemed the best power of all. No, you couldn't clobber enemies to a paste or somersault untouchably. But you could be invisible to those who would do you and your family harm. Even if you could pummel them with giant conjured sledgehammers like The Green Lantern, you still wouldn't really change anything. If you were The Atom – like *Adam*, his Christian name – you could lie hidden when they came knocking, and see them as they really were. And in the morning you would be someone else, a secret identity. No one would ever suspect.

ProFix Reno & Removal is a partnership between Ronnie and Swaffe, originally from Michigan, where they operated a small and unsuccessful chain of office furniture discount warehouses. Lately, with Ronnie occupied by a messy, litigious divorce, Doug has been the more hands-on of the two. Violating the detox cleanse he agreed to in solidarity with his daughter, he's enjoyed a couple laps of Dewar's this morning while poring through time sheets and employee records in the ProFix office in Aurora, again experiencing mixed feelings regarding these immigrants who now comprise most of his workforce. These kids generally don't give him shit, but they can be unpredictable. That one kid James or Jamie or whatever, he and Ronnie got into it a while ago. Had to let him go. But for the most part they're pretty docile. As long as the job gets done, they're just names on a list.

The door's bell jingles. Doug slides the bottle behind some papers; Ronnie would gripe.

A face appears in the doorway. One of these kids. Adam.

'Hey,' Doug says. 'I was just thinking about you guys.'

Minutes later they are pouring a second glass.

'If you have a Discover Card and a social insurance number, this country's a buffet,' Adam says.

'You gotta watch it there, though. Check your susceptibility. Read the fine print, watch the service fees. Solid credit history's ultimately worth more than staying liquid.'

This Adam is thin, edgy. He shifts in his seat and drinks without enthusiasm.

'I'd like to consult you on a matter, if I may,' he says.

Doug sighs. 'Let 'er rip.'

'It's been two years,' Adam says. More, seven seasons, since Adam first filled out Swaffe's employment form and opened his Scotiabank Value chequing account. Many sundowns. A quick signature on flimsy paper and he was existent in the eyes of the state. But little progress has been made since, despite his ambitions.

'Tell me about how you got started,' Adam says. 'The story of it.'

'Ronnie would be better at this sort of thing. But okay. Well, as you probably know, we had our stores in Dearborn and Lansing, these enormous showrooms we picked up from this old guy, this …'

Adam raises a hand. 'No no no. What I'm asking is how do I go from the paper and the idea to the thing. This office here, for example. I presume you have a lease.'

'Yep.'

'And some sort of security.'

Doug reaches for the bottle to top up his glass. 'This isn't exactly downtown Africa. I keep a firearm tucked away, but I hope to never have to use it.'

'I see. And when do I have to register with the business bureau?'

ProFix used to have an operations assistant named Vance who supervised new trainees. Ronnie loved to say how Vance was super-qualified to teach the art of general maintenance; he possessed the *patience of Job*. A hundred times he said it: *patience of Job*, shaking his head in wonder. Adam went to the library to seek out the meaning behind the reference. Job suffered scourge, boils, loss. So the Swaffes saw their staff, these skittish young African men marvelling at hoists and cranes, as the whim of God's punishing ire. When Adam explained the allusion to his co-workers over their dismal cheese-sandwich lunch, how the Swaffes considered them mere nuisances to be tolerated, Santino told Adam he was misinterpreting the implication, and making a big deal out of things, and they should just appreciate having a job at all. Everything wasn't as serious as he took it. Adam spat back: *don't speak about what you don't understand, village boy.*

Returning late from his final shift at the convention centre, stiff from battling the aged bucket wringer and its rusted wheels, he finds the building's elevator's button panel ravaged, clearly worked at with a crowbar. He recognizes this handiwork. Though it's past midnight, he finds Daniel still up, watching television in his boxers and working on a large plastic bottle of Rockaberry Cooler. Adam's entry prompts only a raised eyebrow.

Daniel described a recurring dream, based on a true memory of the desert. In reality Daniel once went six days across the northern desert through a sandstorm with a group of boys who were attacked by chiggers. Boys sobbed, burying their legs in cool lower sand to alleviate the itch; in doing so, several were bitten by cobras and boomslangs. But the memory reappearing in Daniel's dreams is always of an F-16 swooping overhead out of a rising sun. The fighter flew low, groaning a downward Doppler groan and trailing bluish smoke. The boys looked up, awed by the aerial machinery as it sank toward nearby hills. A moment later a sound like torn thunder echoed across the plain.

Hours later they came upon the wreck. There was little but gnarled metal and glints of cinders. Several of the boys suggested investigating; most were too spooked. Daniel dove in, hoping to find valuables he might barter at the next junction. It was like junk, he said, the plane's entire body compressed into half. Picking through the debris proved impossible, but he did discover a metal case containing binoculars and ammunition, though no pistol. The bodies of the pilot and passenger were barely discernible as bodies. A jaw and a uniform and a pair of leather boots.

In Daniel's dream he is always shading his vision with a raised hand and staring up at that plane, still soaring backlit by sun in its doomed downward trajectory, its engine trying and failing, its underbelly briefly blocking out a cloudless sky. Night after night, metal and sky. The dream only the descent, the pained screech, the imminence of it.

Adam joins Daniel in front of a *Saturday Night Live* rerun. Daniel stares across the neck of his bottle, barely watching a caricatured onscreen Bill Clinton: *Hillary has heard from countless others who go to sleep fearing that the next time they drink a Pepsi they'll swallow a syringe.* Neither of them laugh: you hate to admit you don't get it, even when knowing what's going on seems not worth knowing.

'The elevator,' Adam says. 'Why?'

Daniel drinks, dozing. 'They came and knocked. There's a time and a place. The time was then and the place was there. It's been a bad week.'

Quasi-Clinton smiles to the camera: *Say you buy a major body organ for a transplant and while in the hospital the organ is lost or stolen. If you put it on your Gold Card, we will replace it within ninety days.*

Daniel begins to snore. Too many like Daniel succumb to these temptations, Adam thinks, forgetting the thieveries of the past. They become what they dread most. But Adam will not be digested into this hell, this failure of flab and neon and ignominy. This flaccid empire offers nothing. Africa was an idyll: tough, yes, but unpaved and free, until you suck up NBC and porno and you think systems analysis is somehow superior to your home, your people.

Adam takes the remote from the couch's arm and flips channels.

And, as if summoned from other realms, there it is, via newscast: the sparkling plate of teeth beaming from Abdel al-Durabi's jaws. This is the mouth that ordered a blockade of jeeps to block the village south road, to set afire the half-built vaccination centre, to abduct dozens of street children to be used as human shields. *Today the controversial African president arrived at Pearson airport accompanied by an entourage of Dinka musicians as part of his upcoming Eleventh Hour Trade Summit* – he nods, eyes shielded as always by Oakley sunglasses – *the flamboyant and outspoken President al-Durabi kicks off a tour quite unlike the typical diplomatic rounds* – *the former militia commander – a controversial figure who has recently reached out to the international community.*

There were years, when he was younger, in which the sun's setting meant rest and release, not dread of what headlights might stutter through branches, what gunfire might come bellowing, years that never foresaw such sourness. Those days are gone. He turns the television off.

Adam drops onto on the lumpy twin mattress that came with this miserable apartment and snaps on the bedside lamp. He sits back to sift through the sheaf of printouts culled from dailies and magazines, the amassed al-Durabi file. Though familiar with their contents, he reads and rereads these accounts until powerless against the pull of sleep. He clicks off the lamp. In his resistance he is true.

3

Lights hummed, hallways clanged with adjustable beds, kids buried themselves in hopelessness and punched their chairs. An entire hidden life of specialized turmoil passed, led by wardens and anaesthetists and cooks. A season went by, snow fell.

It was at St. Dismas where he first glimpsed mankind's destiny. It was another day mired in Fultz's office, watching the second hand lap the minute, looking forward to lunch: it was grilled-cheese day. Fultz was pushing him to articulate this sweeping world view upon which he'd seemed to have concluded, having spent all week with the encyclopedias.

'I don't know,' Owen said.

'Doesn't that deflate your belief that there's nothing left worth knowing?'

'I don't know.'

And yet Owen then almost involuntarily began to disclose details about the end of this world. The day when Allah permits al-Qiyāmah and the shofar blows and the last of the virgin birth Saoshyant descendents of the prophet emerge to rescue us from Kali Yuga alongside the final Frashokereti and the world's renovation. Fultz politely asked him what he was talking about exactly. Owen explained he just got his computer-lab internet privileges back, and it had been a long morning.

'My impression is you're looking for something to which you can attach belief,' Fultz said.

'I don't know.'

'Maybe because of the year, and the tenor of the times?'

'I don't know.'

'But you do agree this isn't a ridiculous thing to ask?'

Pause. 'Maybe.'

Fultz said to himself: 'Except a man be born of water. And of the Spirit ...'

Owen perked up. 'What?'

In St. Dismas's closet-sized library, Owen had discovered an old King James edition, bound in worn leather; on its inside cover a shaky pen had inscribed *Dearest Agatha, For eternal happiness, Your love, 'Hank.'* 1964. Finding the origins of Fultz's quote in John 3:5, he tore the page out and stuffed it into the mail slot he knew to be Fultz's, the page markered in red: *pushing religious propaganda – yr sooo FIRED!!!*

The only one who seemed to understand anything was J.F., the skinny older guy from Trois-Rivières who arrived at St. Dismas during the third week of Owen's incarceration. J.F. smoked unfiltered Camels and saturated his hair with Dax and spoke to no one except Daley the janitor. One night Owen, located back in general dormitories, awoke from his usual nightmares and rose to do laps of the upper hallway, trying to wear himself out so he could maybe sleep. He found J.F. in the smoking room hunched over an overflowing ashtray and a paperback. Owen said hey; J.F. nodded. Owen asked for a cigarette, diverting J.F. from his book, which he saw was called *Dichtung und Wahrheit*. They ended up talking for hours, J.F. cupping his hands together while damning the evils of the Ontario Court of Justice, punctuating every word with a sneer. No one had ever spoken to Owen with this sort of conspiracy, not even Ike, the only friend he actually liked.

'They said you stole a Bible,' J.F. said.

'Maybe.'

'I went through that,' J.F. said. 'It's the family, the farmhouse, the what-you-call ... pews. You get thinking about it. Unfair gods. Like in the Pentateuch, this older brother breathes on his chosen people as they tramp down into the desert with the Kingdom of Og and Ten Plagues or whatever. It's man's self-reckoning.'

'Um.'

'It's what's easier to sacrifice. Flesh or the ... It isn't about repent*ance*, just repent*ing*. The people were chosen, like those guys at Rancho Santa Fe with the Nikes.'

'Yeah. With the comet. That was pretty gonzo.'

'It's all happening now, at the end. The millennium.'

J.F. continued this way for over an hour, rambling unfocused in distinctive Anglo-Quebecois inflections, until Murphy the guard came by, asking them what the fuck they thought they were doing there after lights-out, and sent them back to their bunks. Over the next few days Owen spent more and more time with J.F. between classes and work details, watching *Home Improvement* with other culprits in the West Common Room or talking theology, or what J.F. weirdly called his *two-car garage* version. Though he never divulged exactly what he was in St. Dismas for, and Owen never asked, J.F. was blasé about his incarceration, scoffing at the all-abiding woefulness, the staff's judgemental scowls, the interminable boredom. J.F. never laughed, but seemed forever amused by everything. During a back courtyard cigarette on an uncommonly sunny day, while J.F. rambled about the Brahma Kumaris and mining unions, Owen noticed that his skeletal upper forearms were barnacled with phantom dots, unmistakable scars of injections.

One night he taught Owen about the genius of murder. All power structures, he tried to explain, were based on representations of the human body. Metaphorically. And all human ailments could be reduced to bottlenecks of power. Not metaphorically. Electrical, ergonomic. Owen fought to follow J.F.'s thinking: Biblical dietics, chemistry of feasts, pulmonology of famine, the causality of drought and divine embrace.

One stormy evening after another Hamburger Helper dinner, they sat chain-smoking while J.F. tried to teach Owen chess.

'This is pawn capturing *en passant*. That's French.'

'Okay.'

The game seemed as maddening as algebra. J.F. gushed about the *surgical elegance* here, demonstrating the *zwischenzug*. But he seemed troubled, tired.

'There's so much arrogance,' he said, sniffing. 'Assuming the significance of … *humanity*. Everything. We all know it's ending anyway. Nothing you or I do means anything to anyone in a thousand years. A hundred. Why bother. Why plant a tree. So fucking arrogant.'

Owen picked up a rook, rolled the wooden piece between his thumb and index.

'But you have to take the longer view, right,' J.F. said. 'What's your option? Go ballistic. Next you're howling you're the reincarnation of

Sirhan Sirhan or something. No guy wants to be that guy. In the end you just have to establish your own, you know, standard of how you choose to operate. You guide your own path. Against everything, you have to keep pushing. Odds are against you, always.'

Something new shaded J.F.'s face then, an expression that for the first time showed he wasn't fully assured of his own truth. He smoked quietly, staring at the board, then stubbed out the fuming end of his cigarette and rose, saying he was *hitting the haystack*. It was his move, with a knight left vulnerable. Owen asked if they could finish the game in the morning. J.F. only nodded, sniffing again. He raised a palm, splaying fingers, looking at this appendage like it was a parasite.

'I had it all,' he said, then left.

That night Owen dreamed of chessmen, a kingdom mapped with pillar pawns and skyscraper queens, cathedral bishops and stallion knights galloping across foaming waterways, all of it suspended above a tiled board of alternating dust and fire and under a sky swarming with these weird soldier moths and beetles manning hang-gliders. The dream culminated in the city's nuking. He woke at six and lay shivering in his bunk until breakfast, which meant another line, another ritual. He looked for J.F. in the queue, with no luck. Then he signed his check-in clipboard and accepted his Dixie cup of pills, cramming them down still thinking of horses' blood and wondering who Sirhan Sirhan was.

The night's thunderstorm left everything freshened and slick. At the rear entrance, Owen found Daley on his way out, pushing a mop cart. Owen asked if he'd seen J.F., but Daley only nodded blankly. After a hurried tour of the ward and yard, Owen went through Security 1 to the med clinic, finding it unusually vacant.

By noon he still hadn't found J.F. Sticking to schedule, he headed downstairs for morning mess duty. Elevator doors parted to reveal Fat Brian, still eye-patched, still nervous and fat. He tried to manoeuvre his way past, but Owen blocked him, asking if he'd seen J.F. Fat Brian gave him a strange look.

Lower-level admittance brought its usual officiation and ripe coffee atmospheres, the assembly-line flow at its typical rate. Chaerim, the doughnut-faced girl who manned the desk, barked at Owen as he entered, asking what he thought he was doing there. Before he could respond, Owen saw a trio of EMTs rolling a stretcher from the reception bay to a waiting ambulance. The horizontal shape being hauled was unmistakable.

He had it all – he even said so. But now all J.F. had was a neck purpled with bruises and a heartbeat beaconing through springtime fog. J.F.'s honourable days were complete. He had it all.

Time passed. Winter gave way to springtime's loll. Free to re-enter the world, Owen was advised by his protectors to not be scared to succumb, to not fear lack of control, to admit powerlessness. Seek solace in others, in family. Things don't have to be impossible. Owen knew he couldn't legally be held beyond his decreed sentencing unless he posed a threat to himself or others. There was a system of justice, and it was in his best interest to believe in its virtues. Best to hobble back out of the netherworld chained only with an envelope outlining scars no one would ever see – or so it was hoped. Plus prescriptions and sessions with Fultz in weeks to come. On his way out he received a few nods from fellow inmates and a hug from this nurse whose name he kept forgetting.

He walked a bridge between life and death, a bridge built on beams of light, or lava maybe. Populations hurled weapons for belief in stranger things – Owen Sweltham: Vindicator of Ages, Swordsman of Apocalypses, 110% Fearless Motherfucker. The only one who dared to walk the bridge and spit into the blackness below. The only one to lunge headfirst and dive deeper down into Hell and everything there, finally.

4

'Holy wow,' the radiologist says. 'Today's been a real fuckdown.' Motors whir as Trixie is eased back, sliding headfirst into the scanner's bullet-like cylinder; the attendants tell her they nickname it Big Pig. They speak into her headphones. Is she comfortable. Is she experiencing any discomfort. Lights dim, everything turns a jaundiced yellow. Is she feeling any pain. Then there is darkness, pressure, dislocation.

'Okay,' the radiologist says via intercom. 'Just try to relax.'

Once the foundations had been laid, the dream had become real. It was just a frame, then there were shower heads, then they were barbecuing chops in the backyard. The sizzle of kebabs in late May, the solemn gush of sinks, cement still fresh at the front door – with Heath headlocked at left, a tallboy clutched at right, Brother Bo declared *this patio is a triumph.*

Ernie looks tired. Greyish-purple sacks drag down his eyes.

'Here's a question,' she says. 'Do you have friends?'

'Pardon me?'

'Just you see, men, when they slide into the middle years, they stop having friends. They lose touch.'

'I have my colleagues. And my brother, we're pretty close.'

'But not like when you're young, when friendship is that way. There's that *force.* You know what I mean.'

Ernie looks annoyed. She doesn't mind.

'So, middle-aged men … we're, what? Empty?'

'You tell me.'

Inside the MRI she lies in cryptal isolation, with only the hum and knock of machinery. Her neck and skull rest secured in foam, preventing any twitches that might affect readings. At regular intervals the pads sleeving her bicep squeeze to gauge blood pressure while a heart-rate monitor squeezes her index finger, which she fears might slip off: she is sweating. Her shoulders itch. Strange processes are occurring. Some data is invisibly, phantasmally, being swabbed from the meat of her brain. She feels her neck's cords tensing and worries this could bias the results. Time dissolves.

They'd married in autumn on the beach by the A-frame cottage her parents rented near Oxtongue Lake; Allie sought tranquillity there for her watercolours. It was an occasion of enveloped invites, oak seatage, a lobster supper with custom-quilted bibs. Heath struck a bonfire; Bo wiped out in it. The beach's shoreline shooshed as she and Parker kissed for the cameras; the dress's strategic fit cloaked her already swelling midsection. Vows were exchanged and flashes flashed. The lake lay flat as a tray. Centrepieces were white orchids, Asiatic lilies, lavender lisianthus and bluebird roses – Allie's neighbour was a retired florist. The groom declined on delivering a toast, but after dinner individually thanked every guest with a handshake and a personally poured flute of Pol Roger.

And you, Beatrix, sign right here – and here. Now you, Parker. Here.

When she signs her husband's birthday cards *Love XOX*, she doesn't wince. And on those rare occasions when she fellates him, she does so willingly. But nothing in this marriage is as it was meant to be. Initial discussions with her lawyer about current options have left her soured and wary. She urged: regardless of any conclusion, the house will not be sold.

'You okay in there?' the radiologist asks via intercom. Trixie says yes, even as she slips through years.

Allie and Trixie clinked tumblers of cheap spumante, seated on the half-built deck's raw pine. 'You know what, kiddo?' Allie said. 'You're young.

This house, you see only a big place to fuck. You and the champ. You're fucking on the kitchen floor, on the lawn, on the roof. All over the place. But trust me, after twenty years of marriage you'll look back and see the shape of things to come. Don't take it lightly. Lay roots. Lay them deep. Here's where you'll make it happen. It's a home. Not just a place to fuck.'

01/15/80. *Let us speak now of worthwhile endings. R tells me he wants to be gutted. I'm sooooo sick of his routine, so self-satisfied and overjoyed at ruining everything. R – you're chained with so much freedom. The rest of us have Nicaragua and Afghanistan proxy wars, but you keep barking about truths beyond truths. My head pounds. Bleed all over this floor, the dusty sills. Fear of death, fear of everything. I wish you'd just die already and we could live forever. Too many clichés and too late, too much, too long.*

Then she is nine years old, and Lloyd is explaining how what makes your teeth's gums so pink is the blood pumping throughout you, the redness – *Your body's just a machine*, his sleepy ghost mutters in absentia. But eventually these wells run dry. No more blood, no more pump.

'Just a few more cycles,' the intercom says, 'and we'll get you out of there. Don't worry.'

There are no hot fudge sundaes, no cheesecakes, no drippling syrups or gooey whorls of goodness; there is no sweetness, no rainbow sprinkles, no fields of crème fraiche or oceans of meringue. No culmination or caramelization – only an interior brokenness. It surges in unwarm warmth and ungushing flows and static floods, uncollapsing. And there is no parting of clouds, no drawing back of curtains, no avalanche. Straddling this strange man who is not her husband in a condominium that is not her home, all that exists is anticlimax – no cinnamon heart, no pink frostings or trimmings. Nothing beyond this terminal instant, unflooding heat and unshuddering jolts. Even in imaginary escapes: only disappointment.

Oof, he says. Trixie eases herself up and off, collapsing to one side. Ernie's chest and forehead are glazed with exertion. Rustles of hair *bunch* at his freckled shoulders and at the base of his spine. Again: Oof.

Against half-shed tears, her eyes achieve something like focus. The room is silent and dim, only a desk lamp burning. Their clothes lie puddled on the floor: the waistbands of crumpled boxer shorts, Ernie's loafers, her own underthings drooping over a sock. The various props outfitting this farce. Then Ernie props himself up on one arm, wiping his face with his hands. The blood flees his face. She asks what. He leaps for the door, and a moment later pukey heaves echo from the bathroom.

Trixie sits up and rehooks her bra, then reaches to the nightstand to pluck a Kleenex. She wipes herself, then tosses the wadded tissue into a trash can beside the bed. The bedroom betrays little insight into its occupant's soul; the only photo on the bedside table shows Ernie and another man of similar age and build, both in life preservers and sunglasses, on a lakeside dock, fishing poles over shoulders, faces crackling with sunburns. This is presumably the older brother he claims to worship.

Ernie re-enters the bedroom, his face drained, still naked; his spent penis, shucked of condom, droops between thick hairy thighs. For a moment he stands apprehensively, back of wrist to chin.

Trixie feels a need to say something. 'You … okay?'

He comes forward, smelling like Colgate. 'I wish you could stay,' Ernie says.

'We'll need you to stay,' Bokeria says.

Trixie, dressed again, considers a plea for sympathy from those with whom she shares these limited days. But she can't, and doesn't; she is, she knows, a good liar. Even as she is led to her assigned bed and handed her cloth hospital gown, even in such defeat, she contacts no one. Fear is her primary nutrient now, the carbohydrate fuelling her excavation. Only a fool would not be frightened in these dwindling evenings. All remains weighed in disposable commodities: condoms and wetted tissues and fleeting sensations. Nothing stays, nothing lasts.

Night in the ward is quiet. The examination rooms lie mostly in darkness, only a few residents on night shifts. A custodian in coveralls and plastic gloves works an enormous growling buffer down the hallway, then disappears into a service elevator.

Too anxious to sleep and too unfocused to concentrate on the sheaf of copy edits deadlined for Monday, she shuffles uncertainly through the halls. The few souls she encounters pay her no attention. Wrapped in a coarse housecoat over paper pyjamas, Trixie knows she looks worse than she feels. She is barely here; husband and child believe she's at her sister Bethany's in Ottawa. They know nothing of this awfulness. And no one, not even her irritating Georgian neurologist, even fully understands what *this* actually is.

Down the ward she encounters a team of nurses shoving a stretcher down the hallway. A small body is strapped in, stained red; only eyes wide with panic and a mouth in mid-wail indicate any persisting life. As EMTs guide the stretcher through swinging doors into an operating room beyond, two attendants remain in the hallway. To her surprise, Trixie recognizes one of them: Sadie Calcaveccia, RN and mother of O's friend Matt and, Trixie knows from Sadie's annual doorbell ring, key fundraiser for a downtown women's shelter called Stop the Cycle or something along those lines.

Trixie moves forward, saying hello. Sadie's reaction is slow, multi-staged: a turn, confusion, then recognition, concern, finally regained composure.

'Trixie. How about that.'

'If I'd known,' Trixie says, 'I'd have worn my Sunday best.'

Meaning the housecoat. Sadie smiles.

Moments later they are seated in the M Ward's food court, vacant tonight except for a Chinese family grouped silently in the corner, a wheelchaired grandmother as epicentre to their subdued gathering.

Trixie sips her iced tea. Sadie fiddles with a cup of vending-machine coffee, but doesn't bring it to her lips. They briefly discuss their sons: both are, they say, fine.

Trixie pre-empts the obvious question. 'Just some tests. Lubov Bokeria. Do you know him?'

'Is he kinesiology?'

'Neurology.'

'Well, that's something.'

'They just need to do some tests.'

'So you said.'

Sadie looks to her left, at nothing.

'I was having blackouts,' Trixie says. 'So I was referred by my GP, and now…'

Trixie feels her face begin to flush.

'They're telling me all these things, about metastatic this and that, and they do the CT scans and everything. But no one seems to know anything. They can't even tell me what … I keep coming in here and filling out the same forms of consent over and over, and they say not to worry, that everything's still preventative measures. But then they tell me it's all over. Forty-one. This is how I die. In this fucking housecoat, in this miserable place.'

Against her best attempts, for the first time in weeks she begins to weep: quiet, tepid tears. A moment passes. Her sniffs echo throughout the cafeteria.

'I'm sorry,' she manages.

Sadie taps her cup. 'You know what I think?'

Trixie shakes her head, pinching the bridge of her nose.

'I think it's revolting. How you feel so entitled. With the dream life, that you deserve the fairytale ending. The women I work with downtown endure real pain every day. Horror stories you wouldn't believe. Crack pipes in their vaginas. In our safe little pockets, we just don't know. And life, to people like you … it's just a barbecue.'

Tap tap. Sadie rises to leave.

'Anyway, onward and upward, cupcake. There are greater things than us. Don't drink the coffee here, by the way. They reuse the paper filters.'

5

The idea is heroism, and heroics, and the possibility of redemption. In this unprecedented case, there exists an encyclopedia's worth of sins the sinners aren't even aware of committing. There should be interesting ironies. But the problem, it comes to light during a particularly difficult scene set in the backyard of the beta protagonist, is that everything in this story wheels 100 percent around premise and zero percent chance of redemption. Zero, on two levels: 1) all there is is global anxiety, with no hope of the type of escape motivating a satisfying conclusion, no transcendence of pain, or, to cite Weisgrau's pet reference in *Shear the Chaff*, the climactic moment when tornado hunters Helen Hunt and Bill Paxton venture into the titular storm in *Twister*; plus, 2) with no escape possible on any level, no convincing way exists of wrapping up that is both logically satisfying or providing the slightest insight into the human condition, no way of approaching such an emotionally wrenching quandary in a larger sense that, as they say, *speaks* to us all – a requirement, as is vaguely articulated in Weisgrau's and all of the screenplay how-tos stacked on Heath's kitchen table, that still remains a nagging requisite for anything that's going to get beyond ticking time bombs and exploding buses. Too many questions emerge that don't make sense. Too many twists writhe out of this story's set-up, dead ends like vines crawling into sewers.

And then there are the messages Nicole leaves: *Yeah, it's me. Wondering if you actually have a plan yet for the loveseat. Elysia's in next week for our next round of training, so we're hoping to move the rest of it all into the condo. Anyway, call me back – but not at my work line this time. All right. Bye.*

Two in the morning, Wednesday, and his intercom buzzes. There was a time in his life when an unexpected visitor at such an hour was a good thing, maybe the best thing. But that was long ago, and he has one of those punishing orientation sessions at the office at eight tomorrow and the requisite C++ binder has barely been cracked. Plus, heeding one of the regimen's key recommendations, he's been struggling to establish some semblance of a structured sleep schedule, albeit unsuccessfully.

But the buzz buzzes, and he can smell her even before the door opens: turmeric, gin, Salon Selectives. Then she's hunting out the bottle of Baileys he says might still be around, tapping her shellacked nails on the counters, unbelting her jean skirt. When he asks if something's wrong, Brunhilde begins cursing Alston, the Sri Lankan reggae DJ she'd described as her *last-most boyfriend*. As she describes his enormous penis, its improbable girth, his massive testicles, Heath locates the Baileys in a cupboard above the fridge. Brunhilde pours out a mug, chugs it and is immediately stricken with convulsive hiccups. Moving toward the bedroom, she tells Heath that if he really respected her he'd be man enough to sleep on the loveseat. Before he can respond, she is in his bedroom, locking the door, taking the bottle with her.

The month has drowsed in pre-emptive measures anticipating the Y2K system shutdown. Yet, along with this panic about dates and digital turnovers, an almost festive mood has overtaken the office, as remedy to absurdity: managing directors touring from Ottawa and Gurgaon have been delivering gift baskets; brainstorming lunches among grunts and on-the-clockers have been expensed. There is tension alongside a prevailing feeling that, against all logic, the entire department is somehow complicit in this almost cosmic crime of programming oversight, one laid decades before. At one point, Drew Stickings from Head Tech – a guy notoriously feared for showy firings – held a late-night powwow dressed only in his Concordia sweatshirt and Dockers walking shorts; rumours suggested the Thermos he always wielded contained home-brewed ouzo. Many late-night testings, fuelled by huge Thai Express orders, ended in paranoiac imaginings and doomsday scenarios conjured around board tables. Like the trading of ghost stories – except these scenarios described the future, their own future.

Now it's almost seven and Heath is still hunched at his cubicle, hoping to split before the systems analysis crew elevators back up from their downstairs check-in, when a new email pops up in his Netscape inbox, an unrecognized sender.

Hey sweetie!! Sorry sorry for last nite. I'll make it up to ya. Biiiig news about Nairobi so call me? Xs & Os!!!! B.

As Heath struggles to decode this – the mention of Nairobi is a complete mystery – Brittle Dave from downstairs pokes his head over the cubicle barrier, asking if he's in on this next tandoori-chicken group deal. Heath breathes deeply and looks up.

'Yowch,' Brittle Dave says. 'You look like you just shit out a ghost.'

In one crucial sequence of scenes, pinpointed on an index card marked *scene b5.1-5.7* tacked to the bulletin board next to his makeshift office at the kitchen table, the Young Dad guy, knowing of his imminent undoing, strikes a shaky deal with this sketchy Portuguese guy who mans the underground parking lot of the tower where Young Dad suffers a crappy job at a brokerage firm or something. It's a preposterous set-up: a scheme to sneak into the firm's vaults after hours before their weekly emptying, looking to make out with a few fat envelopes of cash and the presumed thousands in trading bonds. It's a plot this Portuguese weirdo has been hatching for a while – foreshadowed, as it were, in earlier scenes – and he's decided he needs Young Dad's participation to get past building security unchecked. This storyline is inspired by a failed caper Heath read about in the *Sun* last winter, a news-wire item buried between dealership ads – Weisgrau says *a storyteller is forever listening always with pen hovering above the page*. The Young Dad sees the plot for what it is: totally bogus. But looking at his young daughter over morning granola, then at the mounting stacks of bills, considering his wife's increasing unreasonableness and, of course, the recently acquired knowledge that he's not long for this world anyway, he figures what the heck. He's in.

The Young Dad wants only the best for a future he knows he won't see, thanks to the cosmic premonition at the heart of the story, so we as audience sympathize. Yet watching as he participates in this inevitable train wreck makes our pulses race, or so is the hope. We're torn. According to McKee and Field and Weisgrau and Goldman and all these screenwriting sages, such is the stuff of engaging drama and suspense. But the plan, it turns out, is a shitstorm: they'd planned to evade detection by building security by having Young Dad fake working late, caught by cameras as leaving about sevenish, when in fact he'd actually hide out in the second-floor cafeteria, dodging detection down to a service entrance where he could then let the Portuguese guy in. The service stairwell takes them to the targeted sixteenth floor, but when they try the door it's locked; they're trapped in the stairwell and alarms are immediately triggered. The Portuguese guy makes a futile run for it back down to the basement, only to encounter shut doors and eventually cops, but the Young Dad simply slumps onto the stairs and tries to figure out what this failure means for the future, which is now for him, and us, a convoluted murk: the immediate and imagined future. Sirens scream in the distance. Fade out.

Of course Nicole's changed the locks; that he'd anticipated. But he hadn't expected she'd have already changed the name on their mail slot: gone is the handwritten *H & Nic*, replaced by a label in bold letters: *N. Chaisson*. There are no lights inside the apartment and the curtains are drawn. He checks under the mat, but the backup key is gone.

The last time he'd seen Nicole was the day he helped her move the table. That fucking table: a sickeningly massive oak beast she'd boosted from an estate sale only weeks previous. Already late for work, he'd hauled that desk by himself down the treacherous fire escape, dragging it on sleeping bags to protect it against scratches from the concrete walkway, down to the sidewalk to wait for movers almost an hour late. This was certainly not the sort of undertaking Bret Albo envisioned on *Special-Ops Reboot*, scowling into the camera and describing how one finds one's true inner self by learning to *gear up and reach for the raw*. Heath sat on the stoop as a limp rain began to fall, waiting with the table protected under sleeping bags. When the young Russian mover and his mummified father finally showed up with their cargo van, Heath did his best to advertise displeasure, but in the end still levered the table into the van pretty much by himself. Nicole, when she arrived, only blathered incessantly about the difficulties of consolidating equity toward this condo she'd bought downtown. She spoke the word caressingly, as if by repetition it became more viable and true: *condo condo condo*.

The course of history is shaped by tactics, missions. Nicole left him to pursue a *purpose-driven life*: a wider existence than McCain Superfries and overdue videotapes, minimum wage, loathsome co-workers and their lakeside cottages. And now this Global Adventure Challenge: a mission of self-delineation and determination. But how she plans to mountain bike the Welsh mountains of Coed-y-Brenin without the use of handlebars is a mystery he thinks best not explored.

Yes, the courtship they'd founded was strained and strange. Co-dependence, trust and suspicion, an unswooning slowness. He helped her with her prosthetics; she scored wicked weed from her friends at the bar. And they lived together; that apartment was theirs. Grim as it was, with its weathered paint and crumbling grout and fruit flies in the summer, it was theirs. They'd been hemming and hawing about asking the super to install this vintage claw-foot tub from her grandmother's attic.

Gear up and reach for the raw. His neck's cords tighten and his teeth gnash as he revisits past bickerings, unwinnable feuds. Cutting his losses, he splits before being recognized by the neighbours, jogging back to the TTC stop. They had plans, a life. Now, mere weeks later, he flees their home like an intruder.

It's almost ten by the time he finally returns to his building. Approaching the entrance, he sights a familiar shadow on the front steps, a bidi's smoke, the bulge of headphones. He almost retreats, wondering if he has the keys to the back entrance on him, and if the alley is clear. But it's too late: she sees, rises.

'You kept me waiting *so long*,' Brunhilde says, taking his arm with both hands. 'Where *were* you?'

'Work. I didn't know we had plans ...'

'Tell me where you were.'

'Brun. I ... You know, it's work. It's the glitch, the end of the year. Continuity. Everything has to be recoded.'

She glares at him, crinkles her brow.

'Fuck you. I know exactly what you've been doing.'

Later they are in bed. Heath stares into the crook of his own elbow, listening to the wet sounds of Brunhilde removing her contact lenses and flushing them with solution.

'I wish I was blind,' she says. 'In another life I was an oracle.'

He is so tired. 'What's this Nairobi thing, in your email?'

'My trip to visit the Kipsigis. Last year, I was scheduling a circumcision safari for my thirty-second birthday. Appositioning the labia minora. But then woo woo *woo*, my mother's giving so much grief. So the plan fell through. Now it turns out things might be ... Oh, forget it. Let's cuddle.'

She settles in, draping an arm around him, breathing heavily, contentedly. Heath remains quiet.

'Thank god things are now becoming simpler,' she says.

What we really have in Young Dad, character-wise, is an ordinary guy. Not exactly a total sad sack, but definitely a dude anyone could, or should, relate to. Working with a pretty unrealistically over-the-top thing here, plot-wise, all bets are off. This is a tough world for normal guys, no matter when or where.

But really – the prospect of seeing, really *seeing*, through one's own eyes in that final tick, the last thing ever, would of course make a guy go shithouse crazy. So can we really relate? So many questions remain, so many ways this story can go wrong, that after only a couple dozen pages he's totally lost as how to piece it all together. He types FADE IN: and waits. But nothing comes. Every night he sweats through his T-shirt in his apartment's brutal un-air-conditioned heat, cracking bottle after bottle of Nestea and wishing it were strong beer. It shouldn't require heroic leaps just to prove a point, to make things up. Wars shouldn't have to be waged. Awfulness happens, people realize what they realize, kablooey. The story of a life lived: that should be a story. But it's not enough. Success never lasts.

This is a tough world for ordinary guys.

6

Administrative Assistant Raekwona has already occupied twenty-two of the thirty minutes requisitioned for this Monday morning's general meeting. In her first three weeks she's already laid to waste the office's backup systems, reformatted the inventory access management structures, digitized the contents of the adjunct file room, and brought in these gnarly cacti that may have led to an epidemic of spider mites. She even took great pains last month to aggressively introduce her fiancé Kaelan – newly testicular-cancer-free, grinning – to her entire department.

Now she is pitching a new vision for sales-staff expenses submission and processing – that is, methods for streamlining travelling costs not requiring actual personnel transport. Denise Movenpick, DynaFlex Senior VP, daughter of founder and CEO Boswick 'Blue' Movenpick, nods encouragingly at the completion of each of Raekwona's bulleted points, as listed in the hard copies of the PowerPoint presentation she'd prepared but was unable to screen since the projector had seemingly gone tits-up. With the conclusion, Denise leans elbows-down on the table, hunched oddly; her chiropractic rigours have been much discussed. At the tick of 10:20 the meeting is adjourned.

Forty-eight minutes later, Parker is looking at the wrinkles of his knuckles, the pads and his fingertips, an ancient scar on his palm, when Deryk Cheung and his assistant Michaela from Smithson International appear at his office door.

Parker jumps to his feet. 'Deryk. Michaela. It's still raining?'

Cheung is a stiff man, but today his reticence is almost android-like, while Michaela, as usual, displays the preparatory lean of a linebacker. Parker finds them chairs, but even seated they convey zero ease. Parker intercoms Raekwona to bring two bottles of water. Better make it three. Raekwona suggests licorice tea as an interesting alternative.

Parker says, 'Water, please.'

This is the moment when he is to be his most reassuring professional self, to wield his expertise, to do what Parker does best. Deals are to be dealt with, reassurances provided, problems resolved. But all he senses are the filtered wash of windowed sunlight and tinges of someone's fishy lunch.

Parker: 'We really appreciate you stopping by. Trust flights and everything were fine.'

'Actually,' Michaela says, 'conveniently, Deryk had to be out this way for Dicky's judo tournament.'

'Dicky's the blond flat-top with the Mustang?' Parker asks.

'Dick is my son,' Cheung says. 'You're thinking of Harlowe in Client Services.'

'Of course. We made plans for a Braves game a while back, but it fell through.'

'Actually, I let him go last week. He was bleeding cash through Hospitality. I pulled a rice-bag reversal throw on that rodent, clear across the lobby. When I want something done, I use my hands.'

'That's why you're in Athletics,' Parker says.

Michaela interjects, annoyed: 'Can we stick to anything but this?'

The two are in town to talk wide leasing, pricing for national-continental. The numbers work, but right now it's a matter of confidence. Smithson International's need to re-establish itself as a legacy corp, Cheung says, is more crucial than negotiating advantage or expansion. Prestige is involved. Names get tossed around. Loyalties are fickle, unpredictable. But legacy – that's the jogging hamster, the wheel. Smithson needs to define its legacy even as it augments its branding strategies. So what they're currently doing, Michaela says, is assessing and taking stock of all external partnerships and stakeholders. This includes their relationship with DynaFlex.

'Let me be frank,' Michaela says. 'Ever since our last meeting, we've detected a slight … dip in your enthusiasm for this project.'

'I'm genuinely shocked to hear that,' Parker says.

Deryk looks away, huffing.

'All right,' Parker says. 'Deryk. Let me appeal to you as a human being.'

'I'd rather you didn't.'

There is a knock at the door. Administrative Assistant Raekwona is there, a packeted bundle in hand.

'Sort of in a meeting,' Parker says. 'And that water?'

'So so sorry,' Raekwona says. 'Just wanted to drop off the numbers. Hot off the presses.'

Parker asks her to just leave it on his desk. Raekwona obliges. But Parker sees: something in the narrowing of her eyes, something accusatory. He makes a mental note.

At East Side Mario's, Adam starts with the Sizzling Calamari Al Diavolo, then goes with an New York Calzone with Caesar Salad, plus a Sprite. Parker opts for the Soho Chicken Salad and an Amstel Light. He hands his menu to the waitress, a redhead with an outrage of rosacea spotting her cheeks. As she departs, Adam makes a gesture of disgust, a wave across his face.

'Did you see.'

'Young people, the skin. My brother had acne. My boy's getting it.' Adam shakes his head. 'Terrible.'

It's unclear whether he's expressing sympathy or censure; when the waitress returns with their drinks, he cocks his head to lock sight on her face, a move that clearly makes her uncomfortable.

Adam had pledged he'd call with more info by tomorrow morning. But he also said last week his crew would have the damage repaired by yesterday. Parker has considered ringing the ProFix office, but recalls Daniel's exhortations: that Doug Swaffe is complete scum – pays less than Canadian Tire and treats us like mules. Parker leans forward to say something about this, but Adam speaks first.

'You saw the *Globe* today?'

'Mm. Front page maybe.'

'He was cozying up to this German ambassador in Helsinki for the trade summit. I'm getting calls from overseas. It's evil business, man. Evil. Old mothers, dead in the roads. And these corporations, these multinationals, the trucks and the crates of hand grenades. There's a whole invisible economy. You couldn't possibly understand.'

Adam explains further: to mark the fourth anniversary of his seizing power from the previous administration, President al-Durabi is celebrating his trampling of international law with a continent-crossing diplomatic tour, his own heroic revue of sorts. Of which next week's Toronto appearance at this trade summit to be held at the Smithson downtown is part.

'On CNN they called him, let me get this right … a developing-world fashionisto. So they malign a hundred thousand souls in one swoop. Makes me ill. This man and his lickspittle cronies are sending my country back into the sixteenth century. We used to have fucking dignity. Now we have land mines in the chicken coops and Land Rovers in flames on the roadsides. These men are swine. Worse.'

Parker: 'He killed people.'

Adam glares at him, low-lidded and certain. 'He did everything and worse. But now there's us. There's you.'

The tree still sits imprisoned in its own branches, secured for now with a hammock of tightened duct tape yet still posing a threat. Parker sits on his bed's edge, considering this gape that defines the ceiling's southeastern quadrant. Wearing no shirt, he sweats, though the room bears a chill.

For exactly thirty-six seconds he considers possibilities of burning this house to the ground, knowing a half-drained container of kerosene sits shelved in the garage. But that meagre spill would never be enough to consume this place. And its brick skeleton would certainly persist. Such fires would accomplish nothing.

There is a moment of panic as he slides back the bedroom closet door to discover its contents have shifted. The laundry basket has been moved and a cardboard box spills folders of photos, stationery, historical junk: it seems Trixie has been rummaging. Parker drops to his knees and claws through the clutter. Old notebooks, her university journals, lie fanned across dirty sweatsocks. Parker slides this stuff aside and feels around for the wad of old blankets he'd stashed at the back, hoping Trixie hadn't looked deeper. But the blankets are still there, untampered, still hugging the package Adam left in the car. Parker rests the bundle on the bedroom carpet, peeling back layers to reveal the thing inside.

At first Parker had objected to Adam's choice of implement. But practicality is the abiding principle here. You can't just wade into a roomful of delegates waving a hacksaw. Adam explicitly stressed stealth, inconspicuousness. It was Adam's way or no way at all.

Once, as Adam recounted, President al-Durabi, touring the site of a military raid with sanctioned photographers in tow, had reached down to haul up the crumpled corpse of a young soldier, one of dozens slain in recent combat now lying in ash-raked grasses, and, mugging for cameras, peeled the corpse's mouth into a wide grin to puppetize the man's face, making him say, *Oh bless me as I fly up to Heaven! I'm so sad now!* The incident, Adam said, was reported differently by regime-sponsored newspapers, the administration's propagandists, but Adam claimed to have learned the truth from others who had actually seen it happen.

The fury with which Adam recounted this story was so palpable, so just, it made Parker sweat to hear it. It was unfathomable, yet somehow so clear. Adam was seeking a path of righteousness. He can and will not be swayed. But the moment, and the action to be taken, would have to be Parker's. Only he has access, by both birthright and profession. The decision, to acquiesce or to resist, is his. He slides the gun back into its hiding place.

Trixie enters the bedroom, bathrobed, shadowed in the bedside reading lamp's dim orangeish light. Barely acknowledging him, she moves to the bedside table and turns on the CD player to something lazy, low: Chet Baker, a compilation someone gave them last Christmas.

By the bed he sees her day bag, a crumpled pile of clothes next to the hamper, signs of this overnight visit to her sister's, of which she has spoken little. He approaches and places his hands around her neck. She stiffens against his touch.

'You're like concrete,' he says.

'Been skipping yoga class.'

He begins to massage these tendons. Trixie breathes deeply, moving into the pressure. This could be another time, another era: he'd return from his old office in Don Mills, tearing off his tie and toeing off his loafers, and hurry over to her tiny alcove – her hair, then down to mid-spine, swept back, glasses on her nose as she waged war against pages and pages of thesis research – taking her shoulders and kneading ready muscles, knowing her sorenesses and stiffnesses like a map. His breath would brush her ear, and she'd reach to pat his cheek with appreciation. And with a finishing squeeze, he'd hurry off to put in a 10k run before dinner. Just the two of them, exhausted and in love.

Tonight his hands work similar motions on the same sectors, but everything is different. She doesn't reach to bring him closer, and his touches are procedural, probing but not tender. Trixie notices she has stupidly neglected to snip the hospital band from her wrist and pulls down the sleeves of her robe. She keeps so many secrets from him now.

Parker releases his grip and she begins sorting clothes from the bag, expecting him to make his exit – after work he typically unwinds before *SportsCentre*. But he remains at the edge of the bed, shoulders hunched unfamiliarly. Then he abruptly moves to the floor, to the hand-knotted New Zealand rug they'd bought for their anniversary eight years ago. He lies there in silence, chest down, working his shoulder blades as directed by his chiropractor. Seizing the moment, Trixie nabs the fingernail scissors from the bedside table's drawer and nicks off the bracelet, shoving both back into the drawer.

Hail Satan, prowler of doors, saunterer of rooms. Always a slut for affection, he enters and collapses onto the rug next to Parker, rolling onto his back with paws splayed. Parker gets back up on his knees and focuses on the cat – Satan in his wrath rolls over to fully extend his spine, claws mangling the rug.

'There's three massive strip loins defrosting downstairs,' Trixie says. 'Plus some Early Girl tomatoes. I can make a salad.'

She waits for a response, but receives none. Parker, she thinks, might be drunk.

'If you're not interested, tell me now,' she says. 'I'll throw it all back in the freezer.'

'Trix,' he finally says.

'Yes?'

Another excruciating pause. Even if tipsy, this is not the Parker Sweltham she knows. But it is. She is about to give up and leave him to brood. Then he speaks.

'Trixie.'

'Jesus. What?'

'Do you think people can die from … from their thoughts?'

She almost snorts a laugh, then catches herself; he's doing an impersonation, she assumes, of their son.

'I'll get those strip loins happening.'

Parker's eyes are half-closed. 'I really want you to know how much I appreciate everything.'

'Okay,' she says, not entirely following.

'I want to be certain you understand that. Fully.'

'I guess.'

Pause. 'These tech IPOS we went into, all that stuff is performing.'

This is news to her. 'Really? Can I see the statements?'

'It's long-run. But we stand to do well.'

Then, to Satan's disappointment, Parker rises from the floor. 'Please tell me if there is anything, anything, possibly preventing you from knowing and believing how much I've appreciated you. I feel … I need some reassurance.'

'This is turning into a rather macabre line of talk. Are you hammered?'

His eyes express nothing, but his intensity is clear. She finds it hard to not be embarrassed.

'What do you want me to say? I appreciate. We do. O and me, everyone. And we are all extremely grateful for your appreciation. Does that make you feel better?'

'I can't tell if you're being sincere.'

She nudges aside the bag of clothes and takes his wrists in her hands. 'Sincerely.'

She lets go of him, noticing his throat's quiver. He steps away, saying he'll get busy on a salad. We have those tomatoes. Satan trails closely behind.

Trixie sits back on the bed, rubbing her temples. She might explode, actually spontaneously combust, giving in to this enduring imbalance of internal and external pressures. And when it happens, her insides will paint the walls of the house in a beautiful splattered spectrum of every humanly hue.

THE SECURITY PERIMETER

1

The security perimeter around the hotel is severe and comprehensive. Security personnel, bored-looking brickheads, man the revolving doors, circulating in a casual sort of officiation that could almost be mistaken simply for dudes hanging out, if not for their intermittent whispers into lapel mics and adjustments of earpieces. Authority through display of thoroughness is evidently the strategy.

Parker stands under a hackberry tree kitty-corner to the parking lot. July has arrived; it is another gruesomely hot day.

He should have worn the blue shirt. Bo told him again and again: heading cross-border from Maine with a trunk full of cheap Winstons, *Always wear a blue shirt. White shirt freaks them out, black shirt you're a bad guy, stripes plaid polka dots you're a fifty-fifty – anything else you're a clown.* And always unbutton the top button, even under a necktie. Bo's logic went that a guy with his shirt buttoned all the way up carried an agenda – *never have an agenda*, he insisted. An agenda harvested disappointment, and masked a deficit in a guy's ability to *knock it down*, whatever that meant. Bo loved those regular cross-border shopping trips, hitting TJ Maxx and low-tax liquor marts, stopping at Dysart's in Bangor for a Paul Bunyan Platter. He'd cross at Lewiston in an undershirt and return two days later wearing six layers under a swollen XXL raincoat, impatiently drumming the steering wheel.

Yes, amid today's atmospheric broil and downtown Toronto's July sewer stink, Parker thinks only of his father. In his broadcast career – at first only occasional guest stints on 610 CFGL-FM's *The Big Show with the Nut Crackas!* – he'd always attested to that personal belief: *The winner is the biggest guy in the room.* Another cryptic claim Parker never understood – did it mean one should aspire to get big, or that by being a winner one would then be considered big? He should have paid more attention. But like all the many questions he still had for his father, the explanation he sought would never be found.

The cylindrical guard manning the revolving entranceway appears to be the primary filter for entry. Risking a test stroll past, Parker sees the plan will have to be both more precise and more loose to succeed: beyond lie checkpoints, cameras, agents. Doing his best to remain inconspicuous – checking his watch, thumbing his cell, nodding at a bellhop pushing a cart laden with plastic chairs in stacks – Parker sneaks glances at their belts, the bulk of their jackets. Tough to tell if they're armed.

Touting the sweeping lowering of cross-Atlantic trade barriers, friendship across territorial and cultural barriers, the *new age of global consensus* established on foundations of *trust* and *love*, al-Durabi has been attracting a surprising level of media attention; according to Adam, he's hired an illustrious stateside PR firm to pump up next week's Eleventh Hour Summit, portraying him as a debutant coming out to the flashbulb glare of the mainstream news. His teeth beam in photographs, on *The National*. Apparently a UN envoy will be arriving, accompanied by certain affiliates of the Silicon Valley elite. Security is suitably amped.

Sixty, seventy thousand dead or uprooted. Schoolhouses littered with collarbones. Beds fashioned out of cardboard to accommodate the paralytic and diseased. Thousands drifting across flaming deserts and kilometre-long trenches of rusted mud and ash, once baobab and flowers.

He is chancing a third pass by the main hall entrance when a large man in a light blue suit bearing a Smithson crest approaches. Parker strafes to the left, phone at one ear and finger in the other, feigning annoyance. The man follows. Parker picks up his pace.

'You'll have to speak up,' Parker says to no one.

The man taps him on the shoulder. Parker turns, waggles eyebrows, raises a hang-on finger.

To the phone: 'Look, I'll give you a shout when I'm back at the office. Cheers.' He snaps the phone shut and smiles to the blue-suited man. 'Hi.'

'Sir. You have a laminate.'

'I do?'

'That's a question. Do you have.'

Parker looks at his phone.

'Sir.'

'Yeah.'

'I'm really hoping to see your laminate.'

'My laminate.'

The man sighs, reaching for his belt. 'Okay.'

'It's in the car,' Parker says, edging away. 'I just hate those things, with the ribbon and everything. Gets caught in my tie. You know.'

Back outside he makes it as far as the sidewalk before hazarding a backward glance: the guard appears from the revolving door, a taller, identically attired man a pace behind. Parker lifts his phone to his ear, hurrying, the keys in his trouser pocket jingling. He realizes he isn't wearing a tie.

Adam sits at a booth in the Subway on King Street, picking at a foot-long Cold Cut Combo, marvelling at the sandwich's complexity while considering the *Star* left on the table. *Milošević accepts* NATO *proposal – agrees to troop withdrawal.* Next page, a story on expanding call-centre opportunities. *Seeking young, ambitious fast-trackers.* Adam tears out the ad and folds it into his wallet. He is tired.

Back home the concept of *ambition* was more refined. Or, he thinks, it was perhaps more abstract. He remembers as a boy, in a time just before his village's ruin but knowing things had turned quite bad, sitting by the main road, trying to fix the zipper of a Patagonia jacket picked from a delivery truck on the village's outskirts – besides this score, it was a gloomy week made gloomier by the death of a family goat. While fiddling with the jacket's zip, he sensed the rising roar of coming engines. A convoy of soldiers sped past, pairs of mud-spattered lorries. Adam looked to find sweaty faces at windows, weary eyes scanning passing terrain, rifles propped on the knees of slumped men. One of the soldiers, a boy not much older than Adam, looked him squarely in the face. His fatigues hung loose around his wasted frame; a red-stained bandage wreathed his neck. And as they locked eyes, the soldier hoisted his Kalashnikov and pumped it once into the air, a gesture meaning something unknowable. The trucks shrank into the distance.

Parker enters, looking wild-eyed. He is sweating through his shirt, his cotton jacket draped over his shoulder. Adam beckons him over, wiping his mouth with a paper napkin.

'Sweet Betsy, she's a hot one,' Parker says, sliding into his seat.

'Betsy?'

Parker looks at him funny, and Adam realizes once again he's gaffed, played the fool. Like Arsenio Hall as Eddie Murphy's lackey in *Coming to America*, from late-night TV – this is how these men chuckle about him, his homeland. Simple, insignificant, grinning: *they come together to celebrate cultural traditions* and such shit. Even other men, black as him – like Pete, the department lead down at the Duracell, who was always complaining about his thyroid gland, showing scissored clippings of record-sized goiters – are like one-season veterans laughing at rookies. It's all a tournament of who's on top, wretched and flailing, united in the sludge. But even the victors in this battle – like the Swaffes, with their Eddie Bauer relaxed slacks – enjoy only illusions of security. This is something Adam learned in his first weeks here, inside these borders. They expected him to befit his demographic: awed and eager to please, another mouse in a laboratory, thankful just to be acknowledged. Merely another file, a participant in systems from which he'll never demand answers. This is what they expected, but not what they will find.

Adam pushes the last stub of sandwich aside. 'So. How does it look over there?'

'All right. Organized.'

'Metal detectors.'

'Didn't see any. It was a bustling scene,' Parker says. 'There were people arriving and departing. I just weaved in and out. Security was pretty tight. I think I drew attention.'

'You "drew attention"?'

'I got stopped. But it was fine. Don't worry.'

Adam grunts, processing this. He eyes a pair of construction workers at the counter and sips on the straw of his Coke.

'Stinks of onions in here,' Parker says. 'Kind of peckish myself. What's that you're having there?'

Adam ignores this. His eyes are again serious, murderous. 'If we're actually going to talk about anything here, then let's cut to the chase. He's exiting by those front entrances?'

'Mm. Uncertain.'

'If there's media, I would imagine front. The flamboyant nature. Soulless whelp.'

The way Adam glares out the window, the way he slurps on his straw: Parker again perceives that fury sizzling, that vicious fire driving him, creating him. For a moment Parker fears he can actually *smell* that fire, but then realizes it's just the toasting of subs.

'The plan is compromised,' Adam says.

'No,' Parker says. 'It's fine. We're fine. You can trust me.'

Adam picks a shred of mustard-dabbed cucumber from his sandwich's wrapper. He throws it on the floor and belches.

'The scales of justice,' Parker says.

Adam nods, touches a serviette to his face, then nods again. 'Hmph. Justice. Of course.'

There was such a fear of the precipice in the Palace that everyone tried to hold on to His Majesty, still not knowing that the whole court – though slowly and with dignity – was sliding toward the edge of the cliff.

Trixie closes the Kapuściński paperback and returns her attention to her computer monitor, which remains frozen on the Windows 98 start-up screen. She taps keys, grunts a sigh, then searches her drawers for ibuprofen. There is none. She closes her eyes.

The way she'd imagined her life's final act was, she supposes, the same way most did, and do: a gentle cascade into grandmotherly greyedness, batty and gushing, – an old crow complaining of the cold on a springtime afternoon. Cartography of varicose veins would shape her legs and liver spots would glove her hands, just like her grandmother Annabelle in her sunset years. Trixie remembers Allie repeating this cliché – *sunset years* – one evening, maybe two years ago now, as the family loosely ganged in the kitchen for Bombay Pantry takeout, tubs of curries and satays. A life as a day, exuberant dawn, workmanlike afternoon, twilight twisting into nightfall: this was how her mother described it, though her own behaviour bore nothing of such dreaminess. Allie prattled spookily about Annabelle's foggy spells, which Trixie vaguely worried might manifest generations later in her own son, sitting with his face buried in a TV *Guide*, the stink of marijuana on his jacket.

But these final days are, apparently, now. The End Is Nigh. She's been to Bokeria's office so often it almost feels like her own secret time-share. She sits in the same dreary exam room, waiting for who knows how long – sometimes an instant, a terrifying half-hour. Giving the same sample of the same blood, subjected to the same analysis. At this point, it is impossible to determine where the sickness ends and she begins. Her moods, her movements – everything's dictated by her internal decrepitude, or at least its projections. Last night a show on the Discovery Channel featured these gory diagrams illustrating the human nervous system, how it works like a railway of signals transmitted from skull to skin. This is how Alzheimer's transforms encyclopedians into vegetables, how Parkinson's immobilizes triatheletes. But this is not her. Bokeria initially said he knew what to look for, and rigorous testing followed. And yet he continually comes back with the same inconclusions: her thing is undiagnosable, obscure. It's *in* her, they say, so she is somehow in it. Yet until now the only real misery she's experienced from her condition, aside from the blackouts that seem to have at least temporarily subsided, has been this endless cataloguing and probing. Mere months to live, she is nonetheless told.

There is still much that could happen. Her days are not quite yet done. But the belief in some dreamy pasture of unbounded possibility – this has been yanked out from under her. It happens to everyone. But she never imagined so soon.

Debbie the intern knocks on the door with a box of gold-wrapped chocolates in hand.

'Ferrero Rocher?'

Stars and damnation. Trixie takes three and says thanks.

There was the year her parents flew the entire tribe to Key Biscayne for a March break of poolside lounging, Tampa, piña coladas, togetherness. An unseasonal tropical depression sequestered all to their villas, and close proximity brought out hints of secrets before suppressed by distance: Allie and Lloyd still upheld appearances of vitality, flaunting their Pik 4 loot – though this was just as much a delusion as Lloyd's denial of those increasingly frequent spells of forgetfulness that later meant his sad damnation, yet then came the reveal that Allie had sunk an enormous chunk of her winnings into financing an ill-fated independent film about Anne Sexton tentatively titled *This Ragged Apparition*. Also, Lloyd clearly wasn't what he used to be. Once a tank of a man, he now had to be told to zip his fly. One morning over brunch Trixie offered him a wedge of grapefruit, and her father looked at her without a trace of recognition. Then he coughed and said, 'Okey doke.' This was the true onset of decline, and it would be gruelling and undignified.

Not even quite noon, but the day is already sadistically humid. Dazed following another morning of tests and bloodletting, Trixie waves away a taxi; the nurses won't let her drive herself home after appointments, but she isn't yet ready to return to work. So she walks, heading west by the University of Toronto campus. The sidewalk hauls her forward, tile after tile, through an anonymous sequence of bodies. She needs a drink.

The first place she finds is an empty brew pub, where she slides into a window booth and fights to not weep. A young bartender wearing a leather tie adorned with a picture of Sylvester the Cat comes over.

'She's gonna reign,' Trixie hears. She takes a second to decode this statement, then only nods. Ominous clouds indeed loom outside. She orders a gin and tonic.

Gazing out the window, she is struck by three realizations: one: she will not see the publication of the Spring 2000 *Record of Truth* for which she's just spent the entire morning formulating a workback schedule; two: she may have wasted considerable funds on legal consultation on matters now entirely moot; and three: for the first time, she now worries more for her own soul than her son's.

There are so many things remaining in this life. The foreboding smell of the Atlantic Ocean. The grief of bladder infection. An easy Gewürztraminer in a thin glass, plus knowing more was cooling in the fridge. Solitude, when needed. Orgasm, when possible. Uninterrupted sleep. The stress and narrow joys of work. Reimaginings of the past, and her failure as an artist. Rare pleasures and endorphin glimmerings. Then, terminus. This life isn't just another dream, one she can simply shudder about, then move on. It ends, all of it.

She wipes her eyes with the meat of her palm, quickly drains her glass and hurries back outside. Against forecasts, the rain holds off.

02/23/80. Called him last night but he doesn't pick up anymore.
Wednesday confirmed what I suspected: bolting out to B.C. to work

for Forestry and be a fire lookout like J. Kerouac in that stupid book about the mountain. No plans to return. Will I cry when he tosses off his goodbyes? Blessed are the childish for they shall inherit the armpits of a slutty world. Blessed are the young and drunken for they shall carbonate the seas. I fight to understand what Rimbaud means by a paroxysm of caesars. I have no idea who I am anymore. I sound like an idiot. Goddamn him.

Huddled together beneath the cosmos they were nobodies. Splayed on damp concrete, clutching hands, they were nothing, mere specks in the hugeness. Asteroidal interference, possible spokes in Saturn's B Ring – she pointed out constellations while Rory gulped at the impossibility of it – meaning, once again, the unknowable sprawl of time, the vastness of the universe, the cold waste bin of death, the infinity of uncertainties encircling them. *The saddest thing is the failure of memory*, he said – a line that sounded very prepared. In a dim combo of moonlight and streetlight she was annoyed by the tremble of tears hanging on her boyfriend's eyelashes, the choke in his throat – he was prone to weepy gushes when drunk, which he always was – and her adoration sunk again from affection to concern and ultimately into the bowel of pity. There, in the dark, vows dwelled. His quavering mother's piety taught him *the trillions of stars in the universe are all the souls in heaven.* Imagining her own soul as a star, supernovaing in the frozen depths of space, supervising gases and orbits, only made Trixie queasy. She'd just been hired full-time at a patisserie on Beaubien and dreaded the coming morning. The roof was wet with the residue of evening rain, yet they lay on their backs, the surrounding city hushed in a haze, passing back and forth a twig of a joint and a large can of Black Label. Here they could have attempted anything, tussled or fucked, performed calisthenics, sang to the spirits. But they were stumped by stars; overhead swung baffling views. A woeful Adventist upbringing taught him *in the end all that we have is our obligation to our God, against all decree of eternal torment*; Rory took this as ammo in his own dreary metaphysics. In a frenzied pastiche of blank verse, a testament of scratches and absurd leaps of prosody: *bathing every veine in swich licour with open yë and dank Corinthian chambers and fizz slumped on Persian floes suckling lovelace of Gynecia and fields of Thrasimene stats flanged in Ceres's bosom of steeples to swim Reddi-Wip currents of Tiresean foci in luschbaldic lakehouses fatigated dreamy in flexes and sulks with heroes turned maintenance men and cogs within cogs* – and on and on. It was terrible, and in endless quantities.

And yet her prince would rise, shirtless and puffy and flushed, tripping over his feet, driven by his own longing to melt all resistance. *The saddest thing is the failure of memory.* Picture Rory, braying like a brain-damaged donkey, hugging his Hilroy notebook as an armament against loss, constantly scribbling, a beer at hand. All was record-keeping, getting it down. Everything was important, no moment unmiraculous. But that was long ago.

At a stoplight, she freezes: walking blindly, she's lost her bearings. The sidewalk ahead veers up an on-ramp. From some distant location, church bells chime. For the first time in weeks, she succumbs to her longing for a cigarette. A pack of Benson & Hedges 100s has been rattling in her purse for days, a totem both of desire and discipline. She digs out a book of matches and lights up. Her mother would scold, but Trixie immediately feels calmer, less atomized by panic. She looks for a cab.

Perhaps Rory was the love of her life. Maybe it was her husband, to whom she has now been unfaithful. But this life is now ending. Now the years, the days, of deep feelings and wishes, are concluding: her love and hope have abandoned her. At one time she vowed Owen's birth was the best moment of her life, but now she can scarcely even remember it, her mind is so clouded by fear. In this end she finds proof of how correct Rory was: yes – the saddest thing really is the failure of memory.

3

In these subterranean recesses, Satan lords over laundry. Creviced next to the new Inglis front-load dryer, true sanctuary can be found. Here he can lie in preparation, reserving powers for coming tactical movement. He dozes in a plastic bin on a flop of unsorted socks, burrowing into forgiving cotton. His enthusiasm for surveillance, the rounds, is waning of late. Maybe it's the fluctuating temperature, the rotten humidity and rains certain to come. Maybe it's this new collar, which is killing him. But this daily routine, this perimeter circuit defining his duties as upholder and defender of this place – today it only bores him. A day rises and sinks without any unique blip. This does not dissuade him from waking; no, but nor does it provide comfort. Monarchic pride sends him to the back door, which has been parted for his exit. His day must be as his day must be.

Under the back porch suspicious activity simmers. Light shifts, tilting through the porch's slats in slim angles. Asteroids of dust plummet before his eyes. Over a pile of spare timber and extra fence posts a whirlwind of yellow jackets circulates in a feverish cloud of work, constructing their nest. Satan knows these strange bugs and their behaviours, but doesn't understand their plan, their underworld conspiracy. They operate on principles of equity and togetherness, effacing the individual. The colony is all. All is the colony.

But patrol is Satan's objective. Sniffing along the base of the house's southern foundation, he follows a trace of something vegetative and wet. At the corner where slab meets brick he pauses. He can see: in this stone is weakness and decay, mould atop anemic soil. The house is not set to endure. Constructed in haste, these foundations were never meant to survive generations, only meet quotas. Soon warping will be evident and innards will groan. The soil will not sustain these walls. The whole thing will wince in discontent and eventually dissolve, like a snowbank in the sun.

Across the street he weaves through shrubbery with caution – his vowed enemy Old Chartreux also frequents this route. Satan slides through the brambles, blinking against thorns, remaining alert. Reaching the rear lawn of the house opposite his own, he defecates, then follows the puddled brook demarcating the border of two subdivisions. Satan peers into the water's flow, at particles of soil and pebble dragged along with the current, at something wormlike floating past. He bats at it with a paw, but it's nothing: something latex and human. He lets it drift away.

A skip across the brook leaves his paws wet. He shakes them, irritated, then heads up toward the weedy patch and the boulevard beyond. But at the incline's crest, he pauses. Something eerie looms in the untamed grasses and discarded trash ahead, something orangeish, furry, stationary, curled in the grass. Drawing closer, he sees: a young Siberian, its eyes pressed shut. A sash of blood dries in her tabby fur from throat to tailbone. Treading cautiously forward, Satan lowers his posture in respect. By any guess she is a casualty of nearby traffic, sideswiped while dashing across, then pressing as far as she could endure into unruly grasses to die alone, hidden. This is their way.

But Satan and the Siberian aren't alone. Haunching up he sights a pair of calicos across the weedy patch by the road's guardrail, both gawking at the fallen. And behind them, by the gravelled wayside, a scrawny black collarless stray approaches apprehensively. Satan steps back from the corpse, then senses something to his rear. He spins to discover the auburnish kitten from the house at the end of the street has been trailing him through the long grasses. The kitten comes to his side to stare at the body, rowling mournfully. The cats by the road draw closer. They come to honour and to gape, to congregate around the killed. They come to see themselves in this expiry, to bask in their own vitality, to understand it all. The reek of death saturates the air, here in bottomless perdition, in penal fire.

Old Chartreux steps forward through the littered grasses, unblinking with his copper eyes. He is old but ageless, thin but somehow vast. The other cats shrink back, tensing; they know. Satan does his best to hold ground, lowering himself even further. But as Old Chartreux comes to where the young Siberian lies still, all enmity dies. With the others, even this creature bends to honour a casualty. The cats are silent.

Back across the street, Satan aims for home, bracing at wind rustling in leaves. Returning to the back porch, the expected rain finally comes. Satan skips up the steps and finds shelter under a plastic patio chair. Shivering, he meows and watches the screen door for any action within the house. He hopes for a light, a sign of a way in. None appears.

4

Parker enters the house dripping wet. With the ProFix crew's pails and apparatus still piled in the driveway, he was left to park on the street, and the rain is absolutely pissing down. For the next hour he retreats to the basement, working the StepMaster and executing flexes with the new Total*Contour Alpha prototype. Contrary to the assurances of the model launch's promo brochure and accompanying QuickTime video CD-ROM, after twenty minutes his pecs and lats are aching with an almost nuclear burn. Nonetheless, he drops to the floor and fires off quick crunches. Then back on the StepMaster, this time in Alpine Trekker mode, his knees pumping through a steady quasi-march, conquering a dream terrain, upward to nowhere.

Half an hour later he is on his knees, ass up and face buried in the carpet. His forehead gushes sweat and tears well in his eyes. Despite his best efforts, he can't absolve himself of this fear: soon he will stare down death.

He hears Adam's voice: *Are you completely mentally retarded, man?*

Parker rolls over onto his back. So, with death as his sidekick, best to stick with the plan. The only pinprick of clarity he's discerned in weeks has been in the bloodshot veins of Adam's eyes, eyes that have borne witness. Yes, the plan.

You're either all hustle and no strategy or no hustle and all strategy. Bo the Bro cupped a mug in the kitchen doorway, the yellow 610 CFGL-FM *Sound of Summer* mug he rinsed and refilled over and over all day, constantly drifting throughout the house's rooms without fully committing to any; it's a thing Trixie has also identified in Parker. But Parker is young again, lying on the living room couch in his volleyball shorts, elevating his swollen tape-wrapped ankle. The pain was dull – a flubbed volley during the afternoon's match versus Queen Elizabeth High: a decisive victory. Bo told Parker to stay off the ankle for at least two weeks. Parker said the doctor suggested more like one. But Bo loomed over him, considering this ankle like some uninvited guest stinking up their home, stabbing a finger so pointedly Parker actually flinched, Bo telling his eldest son that if he doesn't treat these injuries seriously now he'll suffer for the rest of his life. 'The rest of your life,' Bo said. 'Think about it. You get so damn distracted. Get your ass in gear. Stay in the moment.' Then he loafs back into the kitchen, still barking critiques. Parker dreamed of finally saying it: *Fuck you, Dad.* But he didn't say it. Never to him.

Parker doesn't want to relive former days. Nostalgia is not in the playbook. But he tries to recall his body when it would effortlessly sail over crossbars, never creaking or whining dissent in its joints and fibres – and simply can't. That medal-earning forearm spike simply doesn't exist anymore. He isn't the same person.

Noise upstairs announces the return of his son and wife: the clomp of sneakers on tiles and words scarcely said. Then Owen is at the head of the stairs.

'Those guys still haven't fixed the roof?'

Parker sits up and mops his brow with his forearm. 'Not quite.'

'It's because you hire immigrants instead of real carpenters.'

'O. Come on.'

'It's like Lou Dobbs says on *Moneyline*.'

'Okay. Cut that out. Let's get some nosh.'

They both prefer to eat their Stouffer's out of the package, direct from the microwave, rather than fancying up the presentation with flatware or seasonings. Parker assumes his chair, a relic from his mother's old house, while Owen takes the couch. A rerun of *Friends* is on, the one where Monica makes endless supplies of jam until four in the morning. And when Ross and Rachel enter, Ross asks, *Where'd you get fruit at four in the morning?* Monica, manic: *Went down to the docks – bet you didn't know you can get it wholesale.* Rachel confesses: *I didn't know there were docks.* Laughter.

Owen and Parker watch wordlessly. The only sound other than the TV is their forks excavating the plastic of their meals.

'Stuffy in here,' Parker says. 'Did your mother shut down the AC?'

Owen slurps clean his sauce-drenched fork. 'She said she was going upstairs to lie down. Think she's sick.'

'Sick?'

Parker is intimate with Trixie's menstrual cycles, her migraine patterns, her pre-Paxil leanings, her epidermal drynesses. If she is sick, he should know.

Owen: 'Do we still have any of that Breyers?'

'Not unless someone took the initiative.'

Pause. 'Darn.'

Owen plops his emptied stroganoff container on the carpet and sits back. *Friends* cascades to *Roseanne*. Parker sits up. Somewhere, Parker thinks, men are being beheaded, judged for the piety of their ancestors, damned for the bad luck of being born on the wrong side of a river, a valley.

'O. Don't put that there. Come on. Think.'

Parker finds the bedroom already dark, only a hint of light from the bedside alarm clock casting a greenish reflection over the covers' topography. Trixie never goes to bed without at least a half-hour or so of reading and nose-blowing and minimum two bathroom trips. But tonight she's already nestled in.

He packs his shaving kit for the next day's trip to Montana with Heath, shivers with dread at the prospect, then peels off his T-shirt and slides under the covers. There is silence. Here he is smothered by a downy duvet and cooled by kindly ductwork, stomach full of chicken parts and light beer. Parker punches his pillow and huffs a baritone huff, unaware of his wife's held breath, how she lies in her own paralysis of overwhelm. She is neither rueful nor angry. Medication meant to purpose her salvation is weakening her, cell by cell, wreaking havoc on her sleep patterns. She dreads possible afterlives, none she ever really wanted or expected. And most of all she is sleepless over the decision about how hard to fight the fights looming ahead. The answer should be obvious, but it isn't. She turns over onto her right side, tucking her arms under her. Parker lies flat on his back, also very not asleep. Something is different: it takes her a moment to figure it out, but then she realizes he has been exercising, yet hasn't showered afterward. He stinks of effort.

A moment, more, passes before she is even aware of her hand resting on his chest. He first flinches, then relaxes. Here is his heart, his lungs, the breakability of his body; Parker is naturally an almost hairless man. Even now, in all that he has accomplished, invoiced – so much still just a boy. There have been so many nights in shared discovery: the azure sunsets in Nassau, the winter skewers Hibachi-ed on the fire escape of their first two-bedroom, the nights tending to their newborn son, wild even then.

She moves on top of him and pulls down her underwear, brushing away covers. Even in the scarce light his concern is evident. But she continues: she hikes down his boxer briefs and smushes herself down on him, and his response is quick. Then he is inside her, and she buries her face in the sheet. Their lips don't meet; their breath is unshared.

After another thousand years, this world will be a cadaver of boiling methane and steam, if anything at all. Mere months from now, less, she herself will be shrouded and cremated. And every day, thousands perish in memos and charts. Every day: infinities of whatevers, gasps, anticlimaxes. Work and worry, the ardour of all that is done. She reminds herself to double-check the exhumation of actual billable costs for her corpse's processing. Parker spoke of an expected quarter-end pay bump.

Her husband's abdomen moves underneath her, working against her motion. Oh, to strip back all this skin and tear away these organs, to squish them in her fingers like kneading ground beef. To surgery out the strings and tendons binding this body and watch them spill over the mattress and the carpet, the foundations, the earth in total. To be doused in his blood and together be carcasses alone in the cold.

His hands move from her shoulders to her lower hips, squeezing. She removes them, but they immediately return, reaffirming their grip. Again she peels away these hands.

Oh, to rend this person, limb from limb.

Her nails rake his chest, digging in, and he fights back, seizing her wrists and pinning them to her chest. She struggles to resist, but fails; he is a strong man. Yet even as they struggle she feels him twitch inside her. Like rival crocodiles, they wobble in standoff. She shifts her hips and moves back down, coaxing a grunt. There is no sweetness here. No purpose, no meaning. Her hair spills over her face, free as water. And just as unfree.

She heaves a nostrilled sigh as Parker unbinds her wrists, his palms returning to her shoulder blades. To fuck seriously, athletically – for the first time in countless seasons, they share a purpose. *Blessed be this holy union.* But Parker squints hard; just as he senses the first tingle of conclusion stirring within, he opens his eyes to see his wife's fist coming down hard onto his sternum.

Buckling, Parker gasps for wind. More fists hammer his shoulders, his collarbone. He lurches, batting away these blows and dismantling Trixie from her straddle, pulling at the bedsheets' corners. He tries to restrain his wife, but her attacks are relentless. Neither cries out or speaks. Finally he winds up and wallops her – not a full-on punch, but a decisive whack with both hands and forearms. She is moved back, striking the bathroom door cranium-first with a loud *duj.*

Parker, unclothed, kneels and reaches to help her up, muttering something. And she rises, first to knees with hair in her face, face in her shoulder. Her hands move up his arms, seeking his face, his skull. As her fingers crawl to his scalp, Parker waits in silence. Then she grapples him by the head and brow, trying to wrestle him into a twisted kind of head-lock, still fighting – a last gesture of revolt. Both stand vulnerable in their nudity. Years have passed since they've stood in opposition this way. His penis droops.

He spins her, shoves her back face first onto the mattress and storms from the room, a pair of his running shorts in hand. She lies there, breath held, until a moment later she hears that distinctive whirr and squeak: the StepMaster downstairs, working overtime.

SHOCKED QUARTZ

1

Day dawns again over this continent, another sun of gold hems over stretches of clouds: systemically and ambitiously, it creeps beyond the contemporary, beyond the sensible.

The weather forecast, as outlined in both the complimentary *USA Today* provided by the gate attendants at Minneapolis–St. Paul en route to Billings and the in-flight newscast filed by CNN, assures approaching low-pressure zones and 100 percent possibility of precipitation. But as Parker and Heath lug their bags from the arrivals gate out into this afternoon's brawny heat, the authority of these reports is thrown into doubt. Heath instantly breaks into a sweat, grimacing under the assault of heat and the burden of his overstuffed duffle, while Parker scans signage for the Hertz booth.

Later, as Parker steers the rented Cavalier through the parking concourse, Heath eyes his brother with suspicion. Throughout this hectic day of travel and connections, embarkings and disembarkings, Parker appears suspiciously faded: the squad captain and sales dynamo, now commander of nada. For both flights he'd sat nearly motionless, wide awake, not even an eye to the window's spectral wash, only gaping at the flap of fabric backing the seat before him. Now, even as they rush through twisting on-ramps and off-ramps and cables of concrete, he sits tightly drawn, stilted. Like some crazy person. Ossified. Zombified.

It's about 200 miles, four hours give or take, northeast from Billings – The City Beneath the Rimrocks – to Jordan. Fat clouds lie low in the breezelessness. But here, in the rental, air conditioning amply separates the outside. Parker and Heath sit cooled – Heath with a two-litre bottle of Aquafina between his knees, Parker with a gas-station coffee set in the dashboard's cup holder – as an almost mystic Montana landscape rolls past, so unlike the chained ramps of the continent's laked and expresswayed chest plate. Rocky buttes rise in ribboned layers next to wide plateaus of lichen and brush. Petroleum County – weird paleontology here.

The fifth track of Led Zeppelin's *Led Zeppelin III*, 'Out on the Tiles,' starts on the stereo, Heath's cassette dub. As its opening riff launches, Heath reaches to jack up the volume.

'Easy,' Parker says.

'What?'

'Can you not porcupine me with the volume?'

'It's Zeppelin. It feeds the soul.'

Parker: 'I prefer their early stuff. "Stairway to Heaven."'

'Are you serious? This is *III*, that's ... agh. Forget it. You're useless.'

The road ahead introduces peeling road signs and stern notices of off-ramps, contradicting the AAA map they've been sticking to. There has still been zero discussion of this trip's purposes or implications.

'I actually gave Owen this on CD,' Heath says.

No response.

'I found a second copy with this clutter. I've been clearing house.'

Pause. A clearing of throat.

'I was able to pare down the shelves and ditch a lot of stuff. The abandoning of childish things. There was a Nintendo 64 and a bunch of games. I dropped it off to him last week.'

Parker reaches for his coffee and sips, eyes undeviating from the road. 'O already has a Nintendo.'

'It was just stuff I thought he might like,' Heath says. 'Not like it's biological weapons. Jeez. Plus he doesn't have the N64.'

'Okay, but. We're just trying to stay on top as best we can. Doctor's recommendations. So let's just think about what you expose him to. You know what I'm talking about.'

Heath crunches his water bottle. 'Don't look at me. I'm detoxing. Smell my shirt.'

'I'm not going to smell your shirt.'

The highway peels below them. To the east: pale bluffs. West: swooping flatlands, cattle grazing in the distance.

They stop in Winnett for dinner, just as the sun is sinking. The town's silence and sparseness, the streets lined with wild brush and pickups parked outside sleepy two-storey shops, stills them to a knowing silence. The first restaurant in sight is a diner welcoming with the overpowering smell of sautéing onions, but the only patron is an old man gazing into a small glass of beer at the counter. A faded T-shirt is displayed for sale behind the counter, its ironed-on text reading: *Winnett, MT: Not the End of the World – But You Can See It from Here.*

A tiny teenaged girl appears from the back kitchen and guides them to a small booth by the window, its plastic cushions cracked and its Formica table etched with ancient coffee rings. The aged menus are two laminated printouts with stickers correcting most of the prices.

Parker, to Heath: 'Doubt you'll have much luck scoring organic lettuce here.'

The window looks out at the town centre, a single row of sun-faded storefronts and sloping yards. A rusted Chevy rolls past with some oldster in a mesh cap behind the wheel; as Heath and the guy make eye contact, each raises a hand of salutation.

The waitress returns. 'Decided?'

Heath asks if the tap water is filtered. Parker concentrates on the menu. Both finally order chicken burgers.

Locating a pay phone on his way to the men's room, Heath uses the last nine minutes on an old calling card to check his messages. There are two. One is a pre-recorded solicitation from a local carpet cleaner, the other beginning with a gush, traffic in the background.

Hi. It's me. Really need to know about that loveseat. You really gotta call me.

So her master plan has panned out: the lady assumes her manor. The mortgage, the condominium replete with doorman and acrylic breakfast bar and amenities in surplus. The on-site pool and concierge. And dear Lukey. Lukey who solves crises. Lukey who effortlessly moves furniture. Into her *condo.*

Heath erases the message and hangs up.

Orlando. They were just boys, wild and energized, but still they knew not to complain about the tininess of their shared room. Two mini-beds

and a Jacuzzi the size of a bidet, the sharp peroxide whiff of overclean-
ing, and tomorrow Mickey and Frontierland and untold stimulations;
the park had opened only a year previous – to the boys, the anticipation
was pure strappado. The parents were less electrified; the first day
Valerica spent almost three hours locked in the bathroom running her
Braunmaster hairdryer while Brother Bo watched competition water-
skiing on the colour TV, transfixed. The week followed in a strangled
whirr of euphoria and tension: endless queues at gift shops, demented
animatronics, It's a Small World – Valerica carted the boys around,
appeasing ice cream demands and basting them in Coppertone, while
Bo clocked hours on the deck pool lounger, a Len Deighton novel in his
lap and a sixer of Coors at his feet, nodding with an odd possession as
the young brothers, upon return, breathlessly recounted the day's
wonders. It would be the last place they went anywhere as a family.

That was almost thirty years ago now, '72ish. Yet here they are
tonight, in the Garfield County Motor Inn off Highway 200 and Heath
is plopping his duffle on the carpet and kicking off his shoes. Nothing
has changed, but everything has changed. Parker sits on the other bed
with his leather day planner beside him. He sits motionless, eyes on
his hands.

'I'm going to give her a call,' Heath says. 'Just to let her know we'll
be there bright and early.'

Parker: 'You'll have to confirm we can call out.'

'I confirmed when I reserved.'

'Make sure you get a receipt. That's on my company AmEx,
remember.'

'Park. Seriously.'

Heath thumbs on the TV, and they sit in silence watching the last
few minutes of a 60 Minutes segment eulogizing John-John: his princely
demise haunts all news, the scattering of ashes to the sea to the lamen-
tations of pundits. Neither brother comments on this.

'Think I'll get in a quick run,' Heath says.

Pause. 'What?'

'Just down the road and back,' he says, pulling Reeboks from his
duffle bag.

Parker is confused. 'You're going *running*?'

'Sustained anaerobic activity is the cornerstone of any impactful regimen.'

Straight out of the literature. Heath is clearly onto Tape 5, *Zero-G Life Trajectory*, in which Deavers employs the same roping tone found in previous years' DynaFlex campaigns, with other pro athletes or model slash actors pushing *PosiCtivity NOW!* or *The 0% Apology Free Zone*. This last entry turned out to be a disaster for communications – was it a total of zero apologies in a 'free zone'? Or exhibiting zero percent of an 'apology-free' zone, which would, presumably, contradict the program's very concept? In the end they just rolled with it despite consequences, to profitable returns. The launch was over three seasons ago, and though it has since been backburnered, its success still resonates in the trending of DynaFlex's marketing lean. CEO 'Blue' Movenpick was proud as punch.

In the swell of this third installment, Deavers truly gets to business, shoving his all into the system: procedure, the sacrifice. No beer or Sunny Delight, no bleached flours, only next-stage extensions and crunches. Deavers sneers at dietary fads and banishes spas to hell. As is seen interspersed between clips of Deavers with the legendary Steelers, Deavers buys his loaves straight from the baker and his flounder still dripping from the fishmonger's tank. Guys smile. In *Burn the Couch!*, effort trumps all. Strain and pull.

Parker watches Heath lace on spotless new Reeboks. It's strange: these mid-thigh shorts, Floradix bottles, shirking beer for seltzer on the plane. He's even starting to *smell* like Hal Deavers: Noxzema and a whiff of coconut. Parker watches his younger brother perform preparatory lunges and stretches, adjusting his sweatshirt's cuffs, looking winded before he even gets out the door. His joints creak audibly – ligaments, pot-sautéed brain, all out of whack. But then he's hupping it out into the night, sneakers agleam.

The pay phone in the motel lobby seems to be dead. 'It'll work,' the impatient clerk at the desk assures. 'Just keep sliding your card.'

She answers on the second ring. 'You're in Montana now.'

'Got in this afternoon. Where are you?'

'You called me.'

'Right.'

'So you're just checking in.'

'Thought I should. I ... Maybe put him on?'

'He's not here.'

'Right, he has soccer on Tuesday.'

'He quit it.'

'No, he goes.'

'*No*. He quit.'

Pause.

'I'm back on Friday,' Parker says. 'Probably late. We'll talk then.'

After, Parker sits cradling his planner. A distinct fear of unclenching has overtaken his jaw and is now working down his spine, a tension severe enough to prevent him from buckling under the pressure of his thoughts. He eases back into pillows, trying to relax, but fails. Echoes trail down the pipeline, criss-crossing continents, responsibilities still to be fulfilled. He is in some American nowhere where he doesn't belong.

Misery Gulch sits embedded in the foot of a chalky mountain range several miles off the main highway, a desolate landscape of brackish mudstone and tawny sandstone, its craggy patchwork like the marbling of a steak.

Valerica is there to greet Parker and Heath as they pull up. She tramps up from the dig site with arms stretched greedily, slimmer and more sunned than in her card two Christmases ago.

'It's like the universe unfolds before my very eyes,' she beams.

Her tour of the site lasts all afternoon. Throughout, the wind is unrelenting. The site thrives in dryness, dust and tatty plastic, perimeters of rope.

'It's one of the most bountiful formations of the Cretaceous period, very rich in samples,' Valerica explains. 'The history of the world literally lies under our feet.'

Parker: 'Well. Not *literally*.'

Valerica looks at him with an impatience he recognizes. 'We can only grasp the enormity, how it's come to be what it is, and what it is *not*, by probing the phases and shifts. When you're just, I don't know, changing a light bulb, it's easy to lose sight of the overall … '

Valerica stops herself, looking at them both in turn. Despite all that has changed, she is still small, her bony collarbone still juts forth and her biceps, though muscled, are still slight. Her hair is shorter, a yellowing-grey, at her ears. They are knowing one another all over again.

'It's been what, five years? And I'm lecturing. It's just that … this is my way, lately. Trying to finish editing this book, it's been years in the works.'

Heath says that sounds interesting. Parker tells her Trixie and O pass on their hellos: not entirely true. And she of course passes on her love to them.

'He's … sixteen now?'

'Bingo. Well done.'

She smiles.

This is how the day passes: measured chit-chat between Valerica's extended catalogues of staggering geologic history, why she is where she is. But there now seems a greater purpose behind such expostulation. She waggles an index against the sky, praising the sections of torn earth and describing its booty: triceratops jawbones and shark teeth and crocodilian osteoderm sections. These divisions, these hauls of earth, represent times when more than half the world died. Dinosaurs, trolling the earth like freighters, evaporated in a flash.

'Relatively speaking, that is,' she says. 'In the grander perspective of things.'

'It was an asteroid,' Heath says. 'In first year I took Astronomy. Total bird course.'

She smiles. Back at her makeshift office she shows them samples. The expressions of the rock, shocked quartz, tell the story: a meteor impact binding the Cretaceous and Paleogene periods, kicked up from the Chicxulub crater in a blanket of dust drifting north on stratospheric winds. Death was delivered to the dinosaurs, reptile kings in their heyday.

'So we approach that cataclysm. There's a record; just as astronomers see the universe's history in the stars, I see it under a microscope. I'm luckier. I hold it in my hand.'

A student hurries up and asks Valerica a panicked question about EDM calibration. But she sends the kid back on his way, telling him not to worry. They'll get to it in good time.

Parker loses track of all these introductions and so much exposition. He can't tear his eyes from these layers of rock, hauled by wheelbarrows and exposed to the sky. Generations, years beyond years: in every pebble the footfalls of a thousand souls reside, creatures, weird vertebrates in anonymous gasping deaths. What dreams a fossil might dream. He checks his cellphone: still no reception out here.

'You look so darn *trim*,' Valerica says.

'I'm on this program,' Heath says with pride. 'Not just day-to-day. It's hour-to-hour. It's about deflating what was once inflated, and constructing what was once just, um, desire.'

Directly channelling the litanies of Deavers again, this time Tape 3: *Hazy Equals Lazy.* Valerica's shifty reaction tells Parker the compliment was actually meant for him; he's now an easy ten pounds lighter than his stable 175, while Heath really hasn't changed at all.

The dig team is international, some from Bristol and Melbourne, a young couple from Hong Kong, mostly grad students from Idaho and El Paso plus a few hourly workers. Working under Valerica and her associates, they wear fleece vests and dirt-worn work gloves and tennis visors, smudged spectacles, knee-length shorts, treaded rubber soles. They chug canteens of burnt coffee; many are sunburnt. In total the crew numbers a couple dozen, thirty tops, though the total number appears fluid.

It's the birthday of one of the students, a beaky Midwestern under-grad named Franz. As dusk nears, some of the team heads for quarters off-site, but most converge at the site's north ridge for an impromptu party around a coffee carafe and a forty of Captain Morgan. Someone crafts a campfire in a discarded sample sieve and all gather on logs and stones around flames crackling with woody smoke. There is a comfort here, that rare and specific human intimacy found under unfiltered stars.

Heath watches Valerica, seated in a lawn chair at the other end of the busy gathering, gazing into the fire, making quiet conversation with a pair of students. He tries to read her expression: judiciousness, maybe. Thoughtfulness, doubt at some accrued data, maybe. Or only consideration of another day's work done, and nothing more. With probably fifteen years on the next youngest, hers here appears to be a maternal role.

Parker, it seems, has disappeared.

Picking at a pile of kindling, Heath finds himself joined by a freckled guy and a chunky stoned girl tossing around an enormous head of black coils. Both had been hastily introduced during the afternoon's tour – the guy is named Pavel, Heath thinks, and is from either Boston or Austin; the girl's name is lost. She pinches a scrappily assembled joint and stands, rolling her shoulders back, eyes flickering in the fire.

'Canada,' she says.

'You bet.'

'Calmer there. Winter.'

'I was in Canada once,' Pavel pipes in. 'Went to Vancouver for AbstinenceQuest 2 through my Covenant: Ezekiel 36:27 Youth Group. We rented this bus and headed up to protest that stupid same-sex-union crap they're planning. It was a blast. We had these foot-long Bavarian sausages, then got our faces painted and ran down the street getting cars to honk for the Lord. Went to the Hard Rock Café too. Really great day.'

Valerica rises from her seat, bidding goodbyes to all. In between air-kisses and waves, she and her son inadvertently lock eyes across the fire. *Goodnight.*

Later, someone pulls up in a pickup with a case of Miller and a huge box of red wine to a chorus of *whoos*. Heath and the girl with the hair – he gleans her name is Amber – sit at the far edge of an incision at a corner quadrant of the dig, looking down at the gathering. Though she grew up in Garfield County, Amber explains she's only been working at the site for a week.

'Did my B.Sci. in Environmental Sciences at UCLA, which was a bit of a boner. I couldn't do the calculations and chemistry. Stuck around on the coast for a while. Now here I am, back on my home turf.'

Poking her eye into the mouth of a Nalgene bottle filled with rum, she says she's celebrating the anniversary of her older sister's death – while overseas, she'd contracted mad cow after eating a cheeseburger off an unclean Hibachi. As her sister's brain devolved into a useless slaw, the rest simply shut down.

'She lost all the things that made her her,' Amber says.

She produces another joint, wrapped in some sort of brown-green leaf, sparks it and passes. Heath accepts without any of the hesitation he knows he should have.

'This is the earth, right,' she says, her eyes glassy. 'This is our *planet*. And you start to realize that everything within it is as, what's the word ... *malleable* as warm clay. There's beauty between the soul and the soil. And the sky and the stratosphere. And *everything*. It's tobacco fields and sustainable economies and kissing glaciers. I think it's all so very beautiful.'

Heath nods, not quite following. In the upstage backdrop of this moment, he is calculating the caloric impact of the beer in his hand, his third, plus the two Dixie cups of rum, and weighing it all against his pledge to Do It Dynamic! And now there is this weed, which is kicking so much ass, and looking out at the landscape, the purplish glaze of mountains by nightfall, all this. It's almost idiotic how easily this landscape grapples you into meaningfulness: layers of earth and heavens, not a Popeye's in sight. No Kit Kats. No Monday office tech check-ins, subway battles. No stifling basement, no cryptic calls from Brunhilde.

It all seems so perfect, so inarguable, packaged in a material he just doesn't know, but wants to.

'I love it here,' Amber says. 'We're lost in time. It's mystical.'

Heath smiles. 'Forty-eight hours ago I was in a Shoppers Drug Mart buying sunscreen.'

She sniffs. 'That's cool. In America, drug markets are illegal.'

Her brownish thighs, revealed by baggy cargo shorts, resemble oddly shaped casseroles of skin lustrous with an oily varnish. She spreads out a sleeping bag, which he hadn't even noticed she'd brought. Down by the fire a hairless young man juggles flaming devil sticks to the applause of a few drunken onlookers. The dancing flames stutter through the darkness until he fumbles and drops one of his sticks, instantly setting fire to someone's burlap knapsack. Laughter cackles.

The party breaks before midnight. Most will be back at dawn, meticulously panning soil. Tipsy and tired, all salute the residual soul of the sky.

Motel ceiling, veiny wallpaper, purring mini-fridge. Shooshing highway outside.

Parker couldn't sleep there at the site, in the fly-net tents amid dreadlocks and geology lessons, exposed to all that dust and history. So he stole off with the Cavalier, back to the motel. But even this asylum brings restless hours. He sits in his socks watching a *Cheers* rerun – another classic rivalry between the gang and Gary's Old Towne Tavern – and then a thing on CNN about the conflict in Kashmir, until he can't stand another second and pulls an early lights out.

Yet the silence keeps him awake. Headlighted slats train from the windows' blinds to the yellowed ceiling. The sheets smell wrong, reeking of corrosive cleaning agents, grating with others' DNA. In the emptiness, there's just so much. The wrung blood of omitted lives and a well-vacuumed office. An office, a mortgage, a son's life. Even lying still under blankets, he is overpowered by motion sickness. His bones might be sweating. His neck sinks into the pillow's unforgiving foam, lower, down through concrete and plaster, into the soil and the sculpted crust and stewing lower mantle. Here will be found a small pile of teeth and shampooed hair that once was a man.

In the lobby, two dollars fetches a humiliatingly small baggie of pretzels and a Diet Coke. Trying the phone, he suffers four rings before a percussive click. Then a click and some sort of rustle.

'Yes.'

'Adam? It's Parker.'

Pause. 'Repeat, please.'

'Parker Sweltham. I'm away, in the States. In Montana.'

'Montana?'

Voices compete in the background, plus a roar of music.

'You're asking about the roof and the debris,' Adam says. 'We'll be renewing construction on ... Thursday at the latest. Thousand percent guaranteed.'

'Actually, I'm calling about ... the other thing.'

Adamadamadam, someone calls through the hubbub.

Parker: 'Can you hear me?'

'What are you asking?'

'Just checking on the status, where things stand, with everything.'

Adam coughs. 'Things are not going well.'

'I didn't ... Are they, your family ... ?'

More strange background noises. The irritable clerk from the previous night returns to his desk from a cigarette break and stabs Parker with a look of irritation, as if he's the only person who's ever used this telephone.

'I looked at the photocopies you gave me. I think I understand.'

Adam, back on the line: 'It's fucking civil war, man. Boys in combat zones, wearing bootleg Diesel jeans with the chains and things dangling, boys with Kalashnikovs, smoking Marlboros. Fucking *civil war*. And meanwhile there's your white armbands and your bottled water, these school builders and bulldozers and pharmaceuticals with their ... their bulletin boards about condoms. What do we do? Tell me. You. You're either fully on board with the plan, or step aside.'

More background noise. Adam sounds drunk.

Parker: 'Adam, I ... '

'Your roof will be rebuilt. The plan continues as planned. Sleep tonight with your concerns eased in the United States of America.'

'That's great, but ... '

But the *click* has already clicked.

It is late, but he knows he won't sleep. He heads down the road, away from the motel. A Chevron station waits at the closest junction; Parker extracts a six-pack of Michelob from the cooler at its rear, then slides a twenty through a metal slot to the kid dozing behind a wall of bullet-proof glass. Only once outside does he realize how much he's overpaid. He considers going back in, but doesn't. Parker instead takes a seat on a guardrail near the parking lot, cracking the first beer and draining it, then another. He listens to roadside brush rustling, cicadas chirping. This place is all hidden menace and expanses of sky, wiring and steel flowing up and out, huge desolate stretches of flattened land and little else. Girders and fencing, acres of weedy growth, transport trucks on roads leading nowhere. It makes no sense; it's too American, too big.

Grandfather clock. Grandfather clock.

Someday he too will be forgotten, merely another granule of quartz under plastic for some student to catalogue and file – or never to be found at all. *It is foolish to imagine the human body as a planet, worse still to compare a family to, or with, a human body*: so insisted his wife, locked over dinner at Magic Thai with some of her bookish friends in a shiraz-fuelled argument about French poets; Trixie always went to poetry after a few glasses. Foolish, perhaps, this line of thinking – but not wholly wrong, he'd thought at the time, though he hadn't said anything. He openly admits his own capacity for metaphor is kind of laughable. But now his body is the world; North Dakota is a nauseated gut. Perhaps he is experiencing what one of his mother's minions had described as a *magnetic polar reversal*. The total, natural upheaval of our earth's magnetism, ass over elbows. But it will happen: a meteorite in the sky's eastern quadrant, plunging down through the mesosphere, a rogue slab scattering clouds and steaming with the heat of re-entry, fifteen kilometeres wide, led by mass to touchdown. Impact in a valley somewhere near the lower Andes, and in a shudder or a flinch a dust storm engulfs half the world. Zebras choke, Eiffel Towers topple, cities are chewed. Arrogance and insignificance roast everything to bones. A tough concept to grasp: a metaphor. The world is its own metaphor.

Once Parker might have been chilled by these visions, just as he once might have worried about these recent messages from the brokerage hyperventilating about the fed's zooming interest rates, how these tech stocks surely can't reap such dividends forever. But things have changed. Rally, set, match. Blood on a sun-soaked pool deck, rain on a windshield. The flow of overpasses, the posts of power cables: all of this was once just potential, a walkable wilderness. Now it is desolation. All will soon be forgotten. Parker can only be a patsy to this process. All he has been will be, maybe already has been, nullified. His whole era, all this work and money and effort of the twentieth century, is but a capricious drift of fatal dust blown north, settling wherever it chooses. The only power is in endings; everything else is merely upkeep. It can be conquered only through revolt – as Adam said: *fucking civil war*. Which leads him to decisions, how to proceed. Stars and damnation.

The beer fails to calm him, but he continues plowing through the six-pack. Neon flickers ahead: ATM. COLD BEER. 24 HRS. He is so tired, but fears sleep will never come again. It gets cold here at night.

He is roused by the squeal of brakes and something dinging him in the jaw: a Sprite can.

'Hey,' someone shouts.

A red Civic idles before him. The driver is a stocky gel-haired guy with an intricate goatee and a bruise under his left eye. In the passenger's seat is a skinnier, more needle-ish version of the same.

The driver spits out the window. 'Give us your credit card.'

The skinny guy puts out his hand, demanding. Parker looks at him, then the other.

'What are you asking?' Parker says.

The biggish driver makes a thumb-and-index pistol and shoots him. '*Pshoo*. You're dead, faggot.'

The car squeals away.

Stan Jr.'s Sports Hideaway is more spacious inside than its exterior would indicate, more subtly sinister in its sweaty innards: deep-frying, ceiling fans awhirl, stale splashes of draught. Entering, Parker is stunned by the decor: NASCAR posters coating all walls, exploding beer logos, screens of ESPN2 mounted in corner brackets. But two pints of Heineken later he thinks only of Guus Goorts, who once claimed people who enjoy the movies of Tom Hanks represent *the lowest rank on Western civilization's intellectual totem pole*. Parker took this in stride at the time, but now he burns with resentment at this memory. He likes and even admires Hanks, at least the flicks he's seen. One snowy evening Trixie returned home post-work with a tape of *Saving Private Ryan*, but then bowed out of viewing to catch up on a muddled manuscript for a deadline; Parker was feeling restless due to lingering heartburn from a Buffalo sales trip, so he'd stayed up with the movie, expecting to conk out after a few minutes. But soon he was assaulting an Omaha beachhead with the hero, Captain John H. Miller, as played by Hanks, leading a ragtag platoon of GIs inward toward the Merderet River in a rush of honour and soldierly duty, witnessing young chests geysering blood. Yes, Parker stayed up later than he had in months, watching the movie all the way to end, truly captivated. It was solid. It was *authentic*. And even though the movie ran you through the wringer, you knew things would sort of work out. Yes, there were far-fetched moments, and he was asked to accept that butter-cheeked Matt Damon would make it through when other, tougher infantry like that Vin Diesel had to make the ultimate sacrifice. But the main guy had to live. Who would want to sit all the way through the story of these ordinary guys, in the midst of all this hellfire, enduring all this awfulness, to have them just *die*?

Parker orders another beer. Goddamn Goorts.

Down the bar a red-haired red-eyed guy in a yellowing cable-knit sweater has been loudly talking at their barmaid. As she heads off to the kitchen, he shifts a stool down and leers at Parker.

'*Salut*,' Cable-Knit says, raising his glass.

Parker only nods sullenly as his drink arrives. This is all just a dream, a forgotten realm where the kegs' pipes haven't been cleaned since the Future Spa pinball game in the corner was installed, where kids in undershirts translucent with deep-fryer spatters hurry from swinging doors carting plastic buckets.

Cable-Knit edges forward, waving a Winston Light. Beery and bloated, he's got a progress of patchiness overtaking what once must have been a dense shrubbery of curls. His huge face is centred by a nose webbed with burst vessels.

'You're just in time,' he says in a strange accent, offering a cigarette. 'These are weird nights. For the weather here.'

Parker declines. 'Know what you mean. My back was sweating when I drove in. But now I'm dry as a bone.'

'I tell you. Glands switch biases. I used to sop. Now I'm a crocodile. Comes and goes.'

The woman behind the bar returns. 'My boyfriend's forehead sweats like crazy. Especially when he's on the beer.'

Cable-Knit nods. 'It's my highland blood. All we do is sweat and eat and toss cabres. Still all we're good for.'

Parker: 'Scotland.'

'Crossed the ocean for a woman and ended up staying in the States for six years now. This place reminds me of home. Must be the cattle.'

'You know, Jakby,' the bartender says, 'I completely forgot about Scotland. It's not really in the news much.'

Cable-Knit/Jakby turns to Parker. 'And you find home port where?'

Parker tells him: Nova Scotia's north shore, birthed in the wake of a boom that never held its light through the storm. He and his brother steered bikes through headland towns primed on steel and coal, through lobster coves, past Daughters of the Empire crafts sales, auburn leaf insignias, towns of church bingo socials and whipping winds. Now it's usurped by call centres and shopping compounds, sleek facades slipped over heritage homes like porcelain bathtubs installed over old moulds. He left it all for an education, then a career; marriage took him further. Since Bo died, he hasn't been back.

'Work keeps me in the city now,' Parker says. 'Toronto.'

Jakby sniffs. 'Bah, fucking hell. I'd rather be unsuccessful and free.'

Parker considers this irritating red-nosed puke. No, he wouldn't rather, because he's not free. He conjures freedom in the middle of nowhere, shirking contemporary trials, the daily smog index. But he isn't there, checking in on the boy, the syrup bottles in the trash. He isn't walking for weeks across the scalded desert with threats everywhere.

'Bo used to say … ' Parker tries, but gives up.

Jakby leans in, interested. 'What's that?'

'My father would say this is a tough world for ordinary guys, no matter when or where. But he's gone now. So who knows.'

'I think of life as energy,' Jakby says. 'It's a system of pulses and thrusts. Or I guess you say blips. Bleeps.'

He wipes a hand over his big face, stretching the flab.

'It's an explosion, right? That forms this galactic production out of a single force. To go from just gas and pressure to us, sitting here drinking another drink – which I'm dying for, thanks, Marcie – that's the accelerating force that creates the universe. We should all be fucking humbled. It's huge and unstoppable.'

He pauses, apparently amazed by his own words. The bartender arrives, and the soused Scot reiterates his order.

'Actually,' Parker says, 'I've heard the universe is slowing down.'

Outside there is still the moon, still the night. Still this strange territory. Something in the air smells vaguely chemical, a peculiar sweetness. It evades him until, after a minute, he nails it: Clearasil Daily Acne Control, the cologne of Heath's adolescence in a distinct sluice of time. The bathroom always smelled like the stuff.

When he was young his heart was strong. But now everything has changed.

Tomorrow he'll need to get the rental back to Billings by late afternoon, then endure the airport and its torrent of headaches until getting back home late, if they make it at all. Maybe Trix will pick them up at the terminal, though she dreads the airport more than she dreads

Christmas. But getting out of Montana is imperative. He craves his Step-Master and his morning Tropicana. And fewer ghosts in the atmosphere. Footfall on pavement and strained respiration behind tells him he's being followed. Parker hurries, unsteady on useless legs.

'Hey hey,' comes the call.

With a resting heart rate of 67 and a 19 percent body-fat index, Parker knows he can handle this stocky son of a bee, this dishwasher of a guy. At the very least outrun him, if need be. But: these drinks, this crippling fatigue.

'If I take death into my life, acknowledge it and face it squarely, I will free myself from the anxiety of death,' Jakby slurs, gaining on him. 'Only then will I be free to battle myself.'

Parker spins and casts himself skull-first at his shadow. It's a clumsy and unplanned move, lowering his head too far, driving forward line-backer-style into Jakby's midsection. Sharp pain is instantly telegraphed from Parker's cranium to coccyx. He rebounds, backing away as Jakby reaches for his arm.

'Idiots,' a woman's voice, the bartender's, calls out. 'Come on with this.'

A few stray gawkers poke their heads from Stan Jr.'s, curious to watch these two beeros tear one another apart. This Jakby coughs; Parker read-ies fists.

'Easy there, friend,' Jakby says. 'Best to live in peace.'

The distaste Parker feels for this man at this moment is practically nuclear. But yet the sweaty Scot comes forward with arms wide, look-ing, it seems, for a hug. Parker spreads his legs to shoulders' width and brings his hands together, locking fingers in a bump set, readying for any coming spike. But instead of delivering a volleyball back over a net, his hands thrust into Jakby's ribs. The sound is much like the sound of Trixie's nightly punching of her pillows, desperately trying to coax sleep out of sleeplessness – an emotionless thump. Stunned, Jakby falls, gasping for breath. His eyes widen and he raises a hand in defence, croaking something. Parker looms over this man, forcing his own knees to not buckle.

Then stone grips take hold: a bouncer goon binds his arms in a submission hold and walks him face first into a nearby brick wall. Parker bites his tongue, squirming against this grip.

Jakby rises to his feet, an apostrophe of blood at his mouth's margin. 'Let him go, Eric. We're just hotheaded tonight.'

Parker is released.

'This fuck is *not* getting back in the bar,' the bouncer says, lumbering away.

Parker's mouth fills with the taste of blood. Cable-Knit/Jakby clears his throat, holding a fist to his chest, then gestures for him to follow.

'Let's go to my car.'

Jakby has a bottle of Cutty Sark in his Tempo's glove compartment. Parker is unsure of what's happening, but he feels unable to resist. They pass the bottle back and forth, huddling in the freezing car. 'Heater's on the fritz,' Jakby explains. Then he begins telling a story: 'Bear with me,' he says.

'There was this kingdom. And in this kingdom, after a long period of insurrection and war and madness, there came stability and peace, though the kingdom itself lay in tatters. At the end of this long war, the king had died. A long-reigning king, an unglamorous, ordinary death, leaving debate over titleship. The military's got its head up its rectum, coffers are spent and the monarchy's in disarray. Infighting has left it unclear who's actually in charge. So someone amid all this hoo-ha decides the only solution is to reboot the whole system. Establish a new royal lineage fresh. They survey the populace and court. Debate rages regarding kingly virtues and credentials. Eventually some agreement emerges on the basics: logic, perspicacity, athleticism, the ability to inspire. Resolve, with an open ear to counsel.

'After a season, findings are announced to the populace. One young guy stands out. Not only does he fit the criteria, but he radiates an almost unearthly trustworthiness, an inner glow. Destiny has prevailed. It's announced: he's the new king, and honoured to serve. And decades of prosperity follow. Joyful toil of industry, boars and harvests. Waters run clear, wombs deliver healthfully. All praise to the king. The kingdom enjoys an era of unparalleled glory.

'Then one morning, the king wakes up in his royal bed, stretches his arms, heads to the balcony for a huff of air, looks down upon his botanical gardens and keels over. Barely fifty, no heir. Many kingly concubines, but no wife – this lineage begins and ends with him. Panicked palace officials meet to dig up old scrolls defining royal decrees and processes. The kingdom's zest for a new, equally cherishable leader is rabid. It's all they have to believe in. So there's another vote, another lengthy selection process. And the miraculous occurs: a guy emerges, just as prime, seemingly just as divinely gifted as the previous king. He even *looks* like him. The people pray with delight. In his coronation speech the new monarch delivers an oratory that uncannily echoes his predecessor's. The kingdom breathes easy. All will be restored.

'But hailstorms and drought and, you know, crickets consume the kingdom. Hostilities with neighbouring territories flare. The court's full of suspicion. The new king pledges to pluck every citizen from disaster's brink. Clerics entreat for divine mercy. Territorial skirmishes in northern villages report barbarian hordes moving in. It's all getting very very bad.

'Finally the king, the disappointing king, assembles his court. He looks terrible, hasn't slept in days. He tells everyone he's failed to achieve the destiny they'd foreseen. He rises, thanks them all for their faith, then unsheathes a sword and falls on it, hara-kiri style. Plans are made for a memorial. The king's aides entomb the body. A rudderless citizenry lies in shock. But the next day begins to a hushed rainfall. Even as the council converges to discuss next moves, in grief there are whispered hopes for a shift in fortunes. For the first time in years, spirits are almost high.

'That night the barbarians arrive. They lay everything in their path to waste. They rape women and girls and boys, decapitate men, saw thousands in half. The army is unprepared and ill-equipped for the carnage. Streets flow with blood. Overnight the palace's been sacked. Its steps are littered with corpses. The kingdom falls in a day. Come morning, clouds part and sun streams through. Gentle rain falls on outlying fields, now vacant. Blossoms of dandelions and buttercups soon appear. The razed villages begin to disappear under the growth of weeds and vines and brush. Untended farmlands go untilled, degrading to sogged marshes. And the palace, once opulent and grand, buzzes with flies. Raided for its riches, it begins to crumble. The former kingdom is forgotten, dried up, *kaputski.*'

Jakby hands Parker the bottle. Only a last dribble left. The Tempo is a refrigerator, a crypt in polyester upholstery.

He thumps the steering wheel. 'You see what I'm saying, friend.'

'No.'

Jakby belches another swallowy belch, falling asleep. Parker widens his eyes and yawns; he'd nodded off. Something ugly stirs in his ribcage as the day restarts, dawn reviving the world. Reaching for his chest, he finds this agitation isn't a seizure but rather his cellular phone, set on vibrate, buzzing at his breast pocket. The incoming number displayed is unfamiliar, and at first he fears it's Glen Mucks at Western Distro. Reckoning with Mucks here, in the front seat of this ash-stinking Ford at the end of the world, is a fearful prospect. But it's not Mucks: it's a Toronto area code. Parker thumbs the keypad and answers Adam's call. In a moment, Parker has crystallized a future of murder. Power only in destruction. Stars and damnation.

Heath rolls over and buries a cheek in pebbled sand. He opens his eyes and sees nothing. The morning sky is an unspoiled pane of electric violet. The girl is gone, but a crotchy tickle remains: hopefully nothing of concern. Amber.

Back down at the main dig site, coffee is already pouring and beards are being scratched. There are earth-stained pails of charcoal and legal pads tracking numbers. Under the crew's supervision, Heath manages to make himself semi-useful, hauling and sifting, up and down rocky slopes. Noon arrives and passes, the sun waging its full assault; he sweats until his shirt is more a glaze than a garment. Valerica arrives with SPF-50 sunscreen, watching vigilantly as he smears a generous ploop on his neck and nose. She knows how he burns; they share the same pale complexion. The sun shines directly here, cruelly.

Through work Heath forgets himself in total. For months his only considerations have been his own woes and confusions, tumult and self-pity, avalanches of Nicole, the relentless pursuit of turning things around. With knees in the grainy soil, watching a trowel sculpt a protrusion, such wars dwindle into the past. This is the ground in which Valerica has invested her life. This beaten soil, these silt samples, the alkalinity and magnetic susceptibility, pH and salination. All the quotients she references, a chewed pen between her fingers in lieu of the cigarettes she always fights. They are, Valerica said, *excavating the planet's soul.* And he finds the oddest thing: concern for this past and future soul.

At lunch Heath sits at a picnic table with Pavel, a master's candidate named Kev, and Tiger, a skinny tattooed Puerto Rican guy from Oregon. Tiger's cousin, currently in Pensacola for illegal firearm discharge, has been sending books: Jungian types tests, oneirocritical analyses, neuropharmacology, probings of the dorsolateral prefrontal cortex. This cousin says his lucid dreams have been providing clues to his own eventual death, which will be drowning in open seas.

'That voodoo wigs me right out,' Pavel says. 'It's witchcraft. It's godless and contradictory to Christ's message.'

'I don't know,' Tiger says. 'Read Jung and tell me you don't doubt that unshakability.'

'Not when I have the Almighty in my heart. I don't go for … *things*, just in the brain. I go for spiritual rejuvenation.'

'But Christianity's founded on visions and prophecy, right. Paul jogging to Damascus and Nabataea. And John of Patmos, and the whole handshake, the covenant. These are experiences taking place in the higher consciousness.'

Pavel is getting irritated. 'I would say only sensory. Not much else. That's relativistic thinking.'

'What you Bible bonkers don't understand,' Kev says, 'is how chaotic things are. It would seriously take *nothing* to spark mayhem in this country. It's just so huge and weird. Ask Amber.'

Heath hadn't even noticed Amber was there. Standing nearby in a grey raincoat, she lights an American Spirit. Everyone looks in her direction.

'So my father was one of the Freemen. Whatever.'

'Those insaniacs,' Kev says, 'were churchy freaks who build septic tanks on land pinched from the Blackfoot.'

'You guys just make fun 'cause I'm from ranchers, not academics. And my Dad's not churchy. He's in anger management now.'

Tiger laughs. 'Right. The tinder lies ready.'

'The point is the militia refused to wallow in complacency,' Kev says. 'Anyone with half a brain can see history's rooted in acts of defiance against the status quo.'

'Don't be ridiculous. Every five years someone talks Second Civil War. John Birchers and guys in El Paso with their binoculars. No sane human would really entertain that. It'd decimate the economy.'

'My pap says the only true difference a human can make against the depot of an unjust universe is through inner tranquillity,' Amber says.

'*Despot*,' Kev corrects. 'Despotism. Tranquillity is a luxury of the ruling elite. But if you're just one person within a corruptive system ... I'm just saying there's a reason for your Kaczynskis and those dudes.'

'You sound like a frigging terrorist,' Pavel says. 'My cousin was killed in Desert Shield, so watch it.'

Kev sneers. 'So, Heath. Have you found your own path?'

Heath: 'Me?'

Tiger puts down his fork. 'Don't harass our guest.'

Kev shrugs. 'We're just jamming here. Heath's a smart guy.'

In his *Fuel for Thought* daily workbook, Heath transcribed an axiom attributed to Wayne Gretzky: *You always miss 100 percent of the shots you don't take.* Not so intellectually deep. But part of the program's approach involved clearing away the cobwebs of ambiguity, focusing on gritty truths and how false gestures of civility and decorum have diluted the human spirit – how the flaccid nature of the contemporary psyche results from a deficiency of *push* and *fuel* and *vision*. Meaning that the disordered mind is the one most prone to terror and trauma. Sanity equals purity.

'If you ask me ... ' Heath says.

They wait, listening. But Heath can't finish the thought.

Valerica pours out two cups of tea, her special stock of Mei Jia Wu Longjing, imported in from Zhejiang. Costs a mint to get it shipped, she says. In such isolation, you prioritize your wants and determine what really constitutes luxury. So once a month she gets her shipment of organic produce and teas, and Simon, the technology guy from her office back in Stanford, burns her interesting CDs. Lately it's Suraphol Sombatcharoen, who she's been told is the King of Luk Thung: Thai twang.

They sit at a card table in her trailer. Heath is due back at the motel within the hour, where he assumes Parker is waiting. But he doesn't know, hasn't heard from him. Valerica pushes a cup forward.

'So now we can finally talk,' she says.

'Sure.'

The window looks out on flatlands of mosses and ferns, stretching into horizon's infinity. Heath inhales sharply. Recalling the second half of Tape 4, *Focus the Freeze-Frame*, he meets his mother's eyes as firmly as he can muster.

'Now would be the time to talk about whatever it is we're talking about.'

Valerica downs her tea. 'Did I ever tell you how your father and I got together?'

He knows the mythology. Valerica – arriving in Nova Scotia on a research exchange from Bucharest by way of Oxford, towing an ESL certificate and a Master's in Earth Sciences, seeking emancipation from Soviet stifle, daydreaming of the West Village – was wooed and hounded by local boy Bo Sweltham, at the time cascading into the late phases of a once-promising hockey career, even ice time with the Bruins. And something occurred, and she ended up staying in the coastal province. Heath always found this attraction baffling: the grizzled rink rat and the stone-faced nerdette. But then again, the pattern endured: his jock brother also ended up with a bookish wife. Heath has heard from his mother all about how the divide between the two became clear early on, too early. A story was once told of a lobster-and-champagne dinner hosted by Valerica's uncle Paul, whose story was well-known family lore, his dramatic escape from Nazi-occupied Netherlands posing as an electrician down the French Atlantic coast to La Roche-sur-Yon, where he waited out the war; there he met Cristina, Valerica's aunt. At dinner Bo made an incredibly tactless joke about Dehomag punch cards. Before Valerica defused the situation, she thought her geriatric uncle might actually take a swing at her new husband.

'Mom. I *really* don't want to hear any more stories about Bo.'

She blinks at the ceiling. 'You can't allow an old woman to reflect on the past?'

'Mom. We came all this way. Come on.'

She nods, takes a preparative pause. 'I've always been diligent about examinations. More than most. But I guess I just never really … I get migraines. Shortness in the lungs. But what you need to know is that there is no fear. Absolutely. It's been how long now since we've sat like this?'

'A while.'

'Probably four summers ago now.'

Heath grinds his jaw. 'Seems right. You're killing me with the suspense here, Mom.'

She rises, crosses the kitchenette and pours another splash of tea. 'They caught a malignant tumour in my left breast.'

'Jeez, Mom.'

'So I pounced on treatment. The system was thorough. I can tell you this was a whole new level of exhaustion. And vomiting, quite a lot of vomiting.'

'Mom …'

'Relax. I'm fine. They told me dedicating my time to the field instead of the lecture hall has made me robust, for my age. A hardy constitution was the key. *Hardy.* I laughed out loud.'

Heath shakes his head. 'Wait wait wait. What are you telling me, exactly?'

Valerica kneels before him, takes his right hand in both of hers. Her hands are rough, worked.

'Through the treatments, through the agony, I've come to see, despite, despite all we know …'

Indicating the whole scene, the dig, herself.

'… there is no body. The body is only evidence. It crumbles, Heath. It's temporary.'

She releases her grip, leaving his palm to sweat. She has, he notices, regained touches of the Romanian accent she'd previously fought to repress.

'I now believe in the soul.'

Their drive back to the motel brings little further discussion. The highway and this glaciated landscape chase by; Valerica revels in description and explanation: *Here's the west southwest depression where colleagues from Stanford first something something – and here, the patch where they'd unearthed what was initially thought to be unusual chrysoprase traces, but it turned out to be some boring calcite.*

But Heath is barely listening. He spaces out, exhausted, feeling the short-lived bliss of Misery Gulch already dissolving. He just wants to get back to Toronto and to the gym, to sweat out these American toxins, get back on the regimen. He'd told Brunhilde he'd check in; he hasn't checked in. And there is this Lukey, and the pestering computer glitch threatening to destroy the world.

Returning to the motel, both Heath and Valerica are relieved to find the rented Cavalier parked in front of 321A. They enter to find Parker seated at the edge of the bed, posture perfectly stiff, combed and shaved, golf shirt tucked into khakis and braided belt tight, staring at a cranked television, an episode of *Dawson's Creek*.

'Oh,' Heath says.

Seeing them, Parker rises to his feet and moves to the bathroom, mumbling something as apology. Heath finds the remote on the bed and quiets the TV. Valerica goes outside to receive a call on her cellphone. Parker's DynaFlex project binder lies open on the dresser, next to his valise. Heath goes to shut it, hoping to pack up quickly and get a headstart on the long haul ahead.

Then he pauses. The exposed page is a calendar in sections: here are Parker's meeting plans for last week – *conf Jennings 8:30 quarterly GG bricklayerz* – and this week too, a detailed transcript of flight details, car-rental confirmations, addresses. But Heath also notices fierce pen marks slashed across today's and yesterday's dates. The only real entry for upcoming appointments is for the coming week: *Summit PM*. The scribbles are Park's, but not in his disciplined hand. Heath reads closer.

grandfather clock clockem sockem
thrill of the kill
life = barbecue
kingdom falls in a day

Parker reappears from the bathroom; Heath backs away from the dresser. Luggage is gathered. Cordial hugs are exchanged. There is brief talk of Christmas. But there is no talk of chemotherapy or diagnoses, only a wrenched series of well-wishings. She slips Parker an envelope to pass on to her grandson. 'Sure he'll really appreciate it,' Parker says.

At the airport, they barely speak while checking in and queuing at the departures gate. Even when squeezed tight into adjacent middle-row seats on the stuffy United flight home, they remain distant.

'Crap,' Heath says.

Parker: 'What.'

'Left my notebook in the car. Now I have to start my caloric tracking chart all over.'

The in-flight entertainment is the romantic comedy *Notting Hill*. Heath and Parker both tear apart plastic wrap and settle complimentary headphones around their ears, just in time to hear Hugh Grant narrate *And so it was just another hopeless Wednesday as I walked the 1,000 yards through the market to work, never suspecting that this was the day that would change my life forever*, while all around human lungs respire and, miles below, the world braces for the coming end.

This morning, as Trixie rechecked the other Kapuściński quote that concluded the *Record* preface, now apparently done, she felt a wave of complete exhaustion: *We could feel the temperature falling, life becoming more and more precisely framed by ritual but more cut-and-dried, banal, negative.* With this she was blasted by overpowering weariness, realizing just how universal, how crushing, this banality really is, how dry and long it all feels until it's over, and how disappointment more than anything has thematized her days, doing the things she's done and not the things she'd wished she had.

But all defeats and victories are only temporary, and small relief goes a long way. Traffic on the 403 was mercifully thin, the roads almost eerily free. Q107 flowed a full side of *Beggar's Banquet*. The pastry she'd wolfed down sat comfortably in digestion. The urgent, slightly manic-sounding phone messages from Ernie Baxter seemed to have abated. So even if the sky harbouring toxic pollutants assumes the same ashy shade as the stubs left in the Volvo's ashtray, even if she's still told no one about her affliction, this non-diagnosis, and even if all she has been told will happen is actually happening – despite it all, she is still here, still mostly herself for now. There's that.

The last time she'd seen Niagara Falls was when she was – what? eight, nine? – as part of a mostly forgotten family vacation, memorable only for the practically tubercular sinus cold her father developed, with the sucking and retraction of his nasal cavities a constant gush that now lay entrenched in her memory more deeply than the roar of the great falls themselves. Now, here on the banks at dusk, clutching a rail, looking down at that rushing water and a gory sunset, pressures skirmish in her chest: nerves versus a strange calm. All around is jubilation, clusters of families, tourists, more genuine joy than she'd anticipated. It's not an elegant scene: tacky carts shilling felt pennants and hologram bumper decals and polyester sweatshirts, minimum-wage girls at soda stands bearing a season's misery until autumn's frosh rushes and freedoms, sweatpanted mothers scolding lippy brats – but any abject despondency is mostly defeated by the allure of sizzling colours, the happy *cheep* of arcade bells, air saturated with floral fragrances and rotisserie chicken steam.

For a moment Trixie considers renting a room at the Radisson and killing a bottle or three of rosé by herself instead of continuing on. Or she could abandon this project entirely, surrender her parking stub and be home in time for *Nightline* and a jasmine soak, unlaced with regret. But to do so would only delay strange but necessary occurrences ahead – duties to uphold. She keeps expecting her chronic lightheadedness to send her face first to the ground, but all remains clear. Typhoons could touch down, time's fabric folding upon itself Möbius-style. But no: she continues.

Bokeria, her neurologist, whom she does not trust, told her *You can use this experience as an opportunity to reach out to the special people in your life*. Trixie heads down along the walkway, killing time, then stops in her tracks: on the path ahead a small family clusters around a spread map, all wearing Maple Leafs toques and jerseys. Tallest of the group is a teenaged boy, and Trixie's eyes widen: the boy is unmistakably Hood Head, for whom she'd illegally procured booze, looking impossibly young. Trixie hastens past, securing her sunglasses, but in the periphery of her vision she senses him glancing her way. The boy's parents and sister, however, pay her no notice, and only stare out into the falls' enduring spray.

Passing through the automated silver doors of the Meteoric Grill, broad double doors wheezing in their hinges with a simulated vacuum action, is less like entering another world, as its decor apparently intends, than like phasing into an alternate reality in which customer service has become the prime directive motoring future civilization.

A robot with blipping LED eyes greets her as she enters.

'Welcome to the Year 2046.'

With its cylindrical shape and scoop-like appendages, the robot uncannily resembles the citrus press now tucked away in a lower kitchen cupboard back in the Swelthams' home: a Christmas gift from her brother-in-law, used only once with sloppy, pulpy results. The robot runs down a menu of options, suggesting *the universe's most*

exhilarating gaming experience in the Kosmic Kasino and the service of the
replicator to fashion your ultimate culinary excursion – including the
Supernova Sundae Saloon. The robot speaks in an affected whirr and
stutter; Trixie wonders why in fifty years computers would talk even
more shittily than they do now.

'I'm here for an appointment,' she says to the robot, then realizes
how wrong this sounds.

In the Interplanetary Waystation Pub, she's handed a cryptic drinks
list by a server in a silver jumpsuit. Bombastic synthesizers swell,
embellished by robotic *skronks*. Polished faux chrome and corded
rubber adorns walls while a governing ceiling opens to a universe
dappled with purple dust and impossible comets. Entirely inaccurate,
she laments: a parody of the NGC 604 nebula disproportionate to the
Orion, all clearly cropped from a junior textbook. It is a future of
utopian optimism, a freeze-dried oversized universe, not the raptures
of hellfire being chalked out for the millennial future.

The server catches her gaping at the ceiling. 'Pretty cool, huh.'

Instantly, Trixie sees this was much more foolish an idea than she'd
even imagined. It seemed ideal: to meet on another planet entirely, or
the closest available thing to it. And it was just about a median spot
between her office and his place south in Dunnville. But it was clearly
an idiotic plan, to expect the rest of the world might cherish what she
cherishes, that her longing might bear some meaning in light of what
is to come. It's time travel again – fudging with past happenings,
inevitably storming the present. She knows this. Last night she'd
finished reading the journals, her overwrought chronicle of those long-
gone years. The final entry, in the early spring of 1980, hadn't stirred
in her the melancholy she'd expected to find: these spirals of idiotic lines
headed nowhere could have been written by anyone. She returned the
notebook to its storage, leaving it forgotten, a time capsule to be redis-
covered by archivists from another age to come.

The saddest thing is the failure of memory. No, it isn't. The saddest
thing is realizing such failures are all we can expect. Two sips of her
Cybernetic Caesar later and dashing from this scenario is still possible.
To be away. *Savasana.* Corpse, sky.

And then: a light tap on her shoulder, and she turns to a face that is initially unrecognizable, a human she might easily have brushed past anywhere else without taking notice. But then it is clear.

'Well well well,' he says.

'Wow,' she says. 'Holy. Yeah.'

Despite the strobing interference of stellar light, he is, remarkably, the same person, inhabiting the same skin stored in the stifling lobby of her reminiscence. Some added chub to his jawline, more grain to his forehead's creases, hair tinged with advancing grey. His shirt, loosely collared, tells of a doughing form. Just like her: softening where there once was sharpness. But otherwise, this appears to be him, Rory. She rises, and as they hug she is shocked by the broadness of his back; it doesn't seem possible – she can't remember if he was always so large. In so few years they have – she doesn't want to say it, but they have *transformed*.

They move to the quieter realm of the mostly empty TimeLapse Lounge, quickly downing nervous cocktails and ordering more. Smiles, sighs, conversation follows about the location's weirdness. Nods, details – he sustains a detectable hesitation when beginning to speak that she doesn't recall. He was surprised to get her call; she'd actually found him easily in the phone book.

She describes her family and work with as much brevity as she can summon. He knew she'd gotten married, was unsure about kids.

'You don't fantasize about yapping on and stressing about property taxes,' she says. 'But you have to, so you do.'

'Of course.'

A weird female Robo-Cockney voice makes intermittent announcements from unseen speakers: *Martian lander ps-x1 now arriving at Gate Epsilon 5 – Central Hub reads intergalactic travel conditions normal – Have a wonderful day at Base Meteoric.*

Rory explains that after leaving Montreal and spending those several seasons out west working as a terrain ranger at Grouse Mountain, he'd followed a girl down to California.

'You don't want to hear about her,' he says.

She doesn't, but she does. Rory wears no ring, but the past clearly weighs heavily. In between these drifting years and his eventual return to Canada, he lived in California, working with this family of Mexican illegal immigrants in Vallejo setting up a scuba-diving school on San Pablo Bay. Easy days, Rory says, but it was a dicey operation: the Apodacases' eldest son, Alejandro, was back hanging out with his Sureños cronies even after finishing two years for a B&E and the admonition of his parole officer to stay away from his old *cuates*. The father Hector was an idealistic, gentle man, an environmentalist and yet a self-dooming believer in the ability of the universe to sort itself out with minimal fuss. His other sons – four in total, plus the daughter, Zapopa – were almost hilariously well-behaved and level-headed. Only Alejandro messed with the *hierba*, and kept dropping in and out of school. Still, Hector refused to take drastic measures, and forbade his other sons from getting on their older bro's case; they all feared him anyway. Rory tried to stay out of it, concentrating on the school's business registration, fudging the paperwork as best he could to avoid any sniffing from U.S. Immigration. But one night he was late at the office, finishing some spreadsheets before kicking off to the taverna down the bay, when Alejandro came tearing in, his shirt caked with blood. Not his own, he explained through a panicked blubber. The culmination of a feud with some older Norteños, a territorial skirmish that had, until then, been just posturing, pistol waving. Then Alejandro and some of his posse had finished off a bottle of Bacardi 151 and gone raiding near Springs and Tuolumne, chucking lit cigarettes at kids on bicycles. Attention was drawn, brakes were slammed, and soon guns and blades were drawn. Alejandro had gutted one with a machete and ran, top-speed through roadside brush all the way back east to the freeway and the marina.

'He just stood there, bleeding all over the brochures, expecting me to do something,' Rory says. 'I dropped him off a block away from his house, then went straight to my crappy basement bachelor apartment, packed and left that night. Didn't even leave rent. I'm a bastard.'

Trixie: 'Why'd you go?'

There's that wince. 'I was just … I knew it was going to go so wrong. The Apocadases were obviously about to sink into this darkness they could never resolve. You know?'

236

Sadie in the hospital: *In our safe little pockets, we just don't know.*

'The kid had fucked up his life,' she says. 'And you didn't want to see it go to shit.'

'Yes. No. Maybe it was just an excuse to get out of California. All the sun and saltwater was ruining my skin. Turning me into a triceratops.'

Laughs, drinks.

Trixie: 'And then you came here?'

'No. I was in Glasgow for a while, managing a bar, living with Gabe. You remember him?'

She doesn't.

'But eventually Mom had her liver resection, so I hauled it back to Dunnville and helped her out. And I never left, for the most part. Moved around a few times for work, but I always come back. Our family has that house. It's been fine, I suppose. I get by. But you blink and you're forty-*fucking*-three. Doesn't seem possible.'

'Still writing?'

By his pained smile, she can tell this is the worst question she could have asked.

'There are frustrations, but such is how it is. You know me.'

No, she doesn't. He's not the same summed mass anymore, and neither is she. They wear recognizable masks, but the truth remains: their cellular compositions have decomposed and regenerated a thousand times over; they have shed hair and bled blood and scrubbed skin into new incarnations. Who was the guy she knew? A hand in hers. A soft kiss and a chest of patchy hair. A scribbled stanza on a crumbling page. Always unsettled in the present, yet comfortably cataloguable into past scenes. Now he stares into his glass, apologetic.

'This is a bit of a nostalgic ... or not nostalgic, just a strange experience,' she says. 'Just being able to be here and talk about ... where we are, what we've done.'

He smiles weakly. 'Yeah,' he says. 'I guess it is.'

And the currents coursing in their brains are no longer powered by school-night rainfall trickling on bedroom sills or the endless agonies of young heartache. No: it's the remorse of recalling precious days you can't quite remember, but spend forever retreading. It's Rory's shudder of discomfort when swiping his debit card to pick up the tab, the dread from which modern adults suffer and the young do not.

'How's your mother now?'

'Actually,' Rory says, 'soon after I came back we learned she'd contracted necrotizing fasciitis. Actually, she's buried not that far from where you guys live.'

Out in front, back on earth, she tells him she doesn't need an escort back to her car, doesn't need to borrow his phone to call ahead to the fictional colleague she'd be fictionally dining with later, saying they shouldn't let these renewed connections go neglected. He clearly detects her insincerity, and several drinks in, Rory looks unfocused; his forehead is sweaty and his words trail off. With another hasty hug they part ways, closing parentheses on their shared time on this planet – on the two of them as a twosome. Now it was certain, guaranteed: she truly would never again be there, in those old days of torture and joy. This was a foolish venture, but this is how things happen. Anticlimax. The only real truth is in endings.

03/25/80. Hurting all day in the library killing myself on the Willa Cather paper, pretty miserable about entire semester. Probably lose scholarship unless I tough it out for summer classes. Ugh. Then went to Marie-Claude's new opening. Pretty sedate, had a few wines. R used to say sculpture was a dead medium but M-C does some pretty wild things in fake amethyst. This jocky guy asked me what I thought. Said something idiotic, so tired. He said he worked with Liam, guess that's M-C's new beau. Ended up talking to the guy all night, neither of us knew anyone there. He asked for my number. I said no, asked for his instead. Might call when I finish the paper.

2

The only real truth is in endings, Adam thinks as he mops James's blood from the kitchen floor with a wad of paper towel. Even when things seem to be functioning smoothly, at the end of the night they inevitably decay. Careful to avoid the remaining shards of shattered glass, Adam tosses the wadded towel into the trash. The apartment is warm; Johnny Lou had said he'd stop by to rouse the ailing air conditioner, but still hasn't shown. Relations with their landlord have soured. Adam pleaded with Swaffe to get their cheques advanced a week; Swaffe said he'd get back to him, and hasn't.

James lies on the carpet, his fists sloppily wrapped in bloody gauze, snoring in a sort of semi-coma. Plastic 200mL bottles of rye whisky anoint the scene. Adam sees that in storming out, Daniel has again left his house keys on the shelf by the door. Another late buzzer and storm of indignation lies ahead, wrecking any hope of a peaceful night.

Adam heads to the bathroom, drops his cargo shorts and sits on the toilet. The roar of the bathroom's fan drives away his thoughts, the memories and predictions he works to shake away. He rubs his temples, scrapes fingernails across his forehead, trying to focus.

As dusk fell on his last day at the international school in Düsseldorf, hours before his delivery overseas courtesy of Boulder Church International Compassion, Adam sat on the concrete steps looking out on the school's back parking lot, a can of lemonade between his knees. Overhead came the moon, the same moon he'd seen every night back home. It was clearer back then. But like everything of the past, the moon grew more indistinct with every passing day; perhaps Europe's pollution was toxifying his brains. Or maybe things were finally being opened to him. His education had become so focused, so comprehensive, he'd even begun to dream in English, in conjugation, in homonyms: *there* and *their* and *they're*.

He spotted Deirdre, his teacher, crossing the lot on her bicycle. He waved; she saw him and headed over. Deirdre wore a grey kerchief bridling her curls in a way that made her look poorer, older. She locked her bicycle and joined Adam on the steps, smoothing her skirt and tightening her bootlaces.

'Cold tonight,' she said.

'Really not so bad,' he said.

Together they faced the nearly empty parking lot, glistered flickers of towers and the autobahn's hurtle generating the horizon. Tomorrow he would be staring down at another impossible ocean, teleported again. Though they'd spent many hours together in lessons over the previous two years, rarely had they discussed their lives, their pasts. He knew she was a strange but patient woman, originally from Massachusetts, attended school in Hamburg and was twenty-eight years old, unmarried; she knew he'd come to the school as part of the experimental UNHCR program for child soldiers. In classes she'd inquired about his age, and he sometimes said eighteen, sometimes twenty-one: his birthdate had never been recorded.

'You must be looking forward to getting out of here,' she said in her strange bi-continental accent.

'Possibly. I don't know.'

He'd read and reread the welcoming letter from the church, arriving several weeks ago: *Greetings! We are here to welcome you to our ministry, our community and our country. There may be moments of confusion along the way. But one thing our cultures share is the importance of family. And we invite you into our family. The family of Christ. Amen.* Then just days ago he and a number of his classmates – Santino and Daniel, plus others they would come to know – had been posted confirmed tickets for a flight to Heathrow, then connections to Pearson, along with notification they would be met by host families. Their new lives would begin.

'Can I ask you a question?' Deirdre asked.

He said of course.

'You seem very … That scar seems to continually bother you.'

He reflexively touched finger to lip. 'A soldier tried to cut out my tongue. But he failed.'

'Oh.'

'I'm still here, and he's not. I still speak. As you know.'

And the moon was still just a moon, and no matter what the future introduced, or how fuzzy his recollection of the past might become, he would still know what had happened. He would still know on whom to lay blame, and he would still be ready to set right the scales. Of justice.

After a night of dreamless sleep he wakes to television: the snickers of Katie Couric on *The Today Show*, coupled with the pained sound of James dry-heaving into the toilet. Adam rises, slides on track pants and heads to the living room.

Daniel is on the couch, scraping a cereal bowl with a spoon. 'Another happy morning,' he says, eyes on the TV.

The electric kettle is on the floor, tipped into a brown puddle.

'What's this?' Adam says.

Daniel shrugs. 'He was looking for Advil.'

Adam heaves a weary sigh. This is how they live and how they fail. He bends, returns the kettle to the counter, sliding aside empty beer cans.

Katie Couric is interviewing the singer Mariah Carey. Mariah's bare midriff is a perfect stripe of caramel.

'God,' Daniel says. 'What I could do with that.'

Back at the international school, Daniel ruled unchallenged. Physically imposing, fearless, with an uncanny knack for his lessons, he was almost preordained as departmental chieftain, lording over other boys, even some girls. While many were still wrestling with basic sentence construction he was already dropping esoteric slang and teasing new students with insults they couldn't understand. During a grammar session with the Kenyan teacher Saiyoto, a younger boy from Kaberamaido threw up his hands in frustration, crying, *It's too long and too hard!*; to this, Daniel said, *That's what your mother told me.* The younger boy, confused, exploded into tears, while the other boys gaped at Daniel, baffled. Adam was fairly certain he understood what was meant by the quip, but kept his mouth shut. No one else got it.

'Give me half an hour with Mariah,' Daniel says, 'Then kill me a happy man.'

'Don't say that. You sound like an idiot. And stop forgetting your keys.'

There are so many tasks, so many items to secure, so many tracks to cover for keeping the plan in place. Cancelling the bank application, confirming the Greyhound schedule outgoing from the Dundas terminal, picking up his last mail from the Boulder Church service. He finds his phone and dials Parker's cellphone. It rings and rings, but there is no answer. Good, he thinks, somewhat relieved.

James appears in the hallway, wearing only baggy Joe Boxers. He rubs his neck with his left hand while raising the right, still a mess of ragged gauze and masking tape.

'And here's our gentle prince,' Daniel says.

James quietly nods hello to Adam, then drops onto the couch next to Daniel, who shifts a cushion away.

'What time are we on today?' James manages.

Adam shakes wetness from the kettle and wipes it with a washcloth, then refills it and plugs it back in.

'Not today,' Adam says.

Daniel scowls. 'You said we were on all day. The one in Erin Mills, then wrapping up with your racist friend with the tree. I need the hours.'

'We all need the hours,' James says.

Adam looks at these two, then shakes the electric kettle, which hasn't warmed and seems to be irrevocably debilitated. He'd purchased this kettle the first day they'd moved into independent housing; a hot cup of tea, even if not brewed in the close warmth of a morning fire, reminded him of his mother, and the undesecrated life he might have possibly lived.

'Fuck you both and your hours,' he says. 'I'm taking a shower.'

The plan as it exists represents a leap of faith, one he dislikes even considering. It's the work of great ambition – he knows this. But he also knows this is the only way things can happen.

For a second he worries his key to the ProFix office isn't going to work, but with a bit of oomph and a sharp fiddle it gives and unlatches. Squinting against nighttime's dark, he enters the entry code into the keypad: Ronnie's daughter's birthday, March fifth, 0305. Another moment of concern passes, then relief comes with the *dootdootdoot* of its disarming.

He snaps on a light and moves to the desk – no point in squandering time in needless caution. Swaffe keeps the petty cash in a lower desk drawer, locked in a metal box that will take time to destroy and infiltrate; Adam jams it in his backpack. The wall safe behind the aluminum pane, with its combination lock, is another matter. Adam stares at it, momentarily stymied. It could be worth speculating a few further formulae here, based on what he's learned of the Swaffes and their sentimentality. More realistically, it would be an arbitrarily assigned sequence. But when he delivers the safe a tap of sneakered toe, its door simply swings open – a gift, then, or an invitation of fate. Or more likely: Doug has been tipping the Dewar's again and carelessly left it open.

Adam bends to look. Inside is as expected: manila envelopes and tabbed folders adorned with the company's standard oval labels. He withdraws the safe's entire contents and piles it all on the desk. It amounts to little in terms of immediately redeemable gains: deeds, bonds, ledgers. A small stack of German marks and some Canadian cash, about 400 dollars' worth. He feels disappointment creeping up. Then: he notices a small envelope, unsealed, amid the stack of papers. He turns it upside down, and about a dozen large diamonds tumble out.

Adam sits in Doug Swaffe's swivel chair, staring at these shimmering fractals, quieting his thoughts. For the first time in a long time, he doubts his actions. A former version of himself had harboured faith in conquering this world, in triumphing over the larger forces shaping its course, in showing these fattened fools he would never be a jellyfish powerless against their tides. Instead of smiling agreeably for their brochures, he would learn from, interrogate and eventually purchase them. He'd had his paperwork in, his credit application pending, and he'd acquired an internet domain: maintenance123.ca. As Swaffe would say, he had *all his ducks in a row*.

But there was a greater opportunity that couldn't be denied. It began at the Duracell centre with the fragile tremor in Sweltham's eyes. Then the summit at the hotel, and the access Parker could provide there, the pistol from the glovebox of Swaffe's truck, and the evil tyrant's lax sense of spectacle – in all of this came a convergence, a larger arena of justice. And so he had to entertain the possibility of a perfect, inarguable path he was meant to take. It almost made him believe in God.

Now, with steps in place, he is trapped, yet completely free. He could head west, try to assimilate himself there. Work in these new oil sands, where they say money spews from the clay. He dreams of returning home, to the rubbled savannah, the crush of parched soil underfoot, the rustle of dik-diks on trails, the heat of equatorial solar noon – but that would mean presenting his passport, acquiring a travel visa, seeking approval with questions he couldn't answer. He'd be asked to justify his presence on the planet, when once, when he was young, that was all he knew. Soon he'll be alone again, with unknowable distances ahead, violence left behind. Maybe he'll ride a train: that would be something new.

Adam rises from the desk, stuffing the gems and wadded papers into his backpack. He gathers the remaining documents and slides them back into the safe. He eases it shut, then backs away, squaring his backpack on his shoulders.

Then: from near the doorway, a familiar growl.

The lion hunches in the doorway. Its sleepy breath's ventilation stills the room. Years have passed, and much has been modified, but nothing has changed. The lion only watches, fixed on the boy as he tries to escape into the past's nighttime roads, even as light from the parking lot crosses the room – Ronnie Swaffe pulling up in his Chevy, here to fetch a file of receipts requested by his divorce lawyer. When Ronnie's key clicks into the lock, he emits a surprised *huh* at finding it unlocked. The lion rises, flexing its shoulders. Locking eyes with the terrified boy with the scarred lip, the lion twitches his head and suppresses the roar that would betray them both. The door opens; the creature slinks back into the shadows.

3

Video footage: the camera moves in a jerky lateral sweep across the set of *Rockin' Sockin' Jock Talk*, across vacant guest couches and a scuffed stage, finding host Brother Bo Sweltham stuffed deep into his vast tanned leather chair, almost squirming away from the training lights. His face, shunning the lens, is peppered with broken blood vessels; his eyes fail to achieve the incisive glare for which he's known. And when he speaks, it's in a subdued tone irreconcilable with his usual bluster.

'So. This brings us to the end. I'm gonna say thanks to Brick Denson from the station and Kylie, um, the blonde. So that's it. Brother Bo signing off, I guess for good now. These zookeepers are telling me to lie down and die. Make way for more basket weavers and spastics. Yeah, Tommy, I see you waving. You can cut whenever we hit time, I don't give a … I just want it entered in the record. I really wish I could say it's been swell. Wish I could, but I won't. Eleven years on the *Jock Talk*, more than my days on the ice, and barely made a rusty nickel. Now I got a divorce and rotting insides. The cancer's in me, and it's not slowing down. But that's that. One of the guys here in the studio asked what I've learned from life in the sports game. Okay, no one really asked. But, truth is I haven't learned squat. A bunch of yobs whack a puck around a rink beating the piss out of each other, year after year. All you ever get is heartbreak and disappointment. Hell, you barely get that. Okay, Tommy. I'll wrap up. There was a time when I was young. Young, dumb, full of cum. Yes, Tommy. But, okay. Just grant me the dignity of a tidy wrap-up.'

He coughs a cough, not exactly a healthy cough. Production credits begin to roll.

'There was a time when I was pretty confident that competition was the main thing in life. Kill or be killed. Take the shot or you take a hit. Not a lot of MVPs in the unemployment line. Each of us has a responsibility. Uneasy lies the head that wears a crown. But now, coming to the end, you see that's all just kitty litter. There aren't any real victories, sports fans. Hard to get jazzed about the Leafs when you've got a pipe up your pisshole. And these Semites tell you you have a year, then six months, two months, then six weeks. They tell you to count every day as a blessing. Bless this, Mordecai. Okay, Tommy, hold it. Sports fans, in the end I never even –'

Fade and out.

Just this morning, over grapefruit and blackberry yogourt – a breakfast that has replaced three fried eggs with Tabasco and raisin toast doused in marmite, sided by a travel mug of Pepsi – he completed his viewing of Tape 6 of Do It Dynamic!, the series' close, titled *The Next Now Is Now*. In this final segment, the series' occasional co-host Lynn Goel is found seated on a bamboo bench in a light-suffused room, cheerily decorated, she explains, in a Californian spin on traditional Nyingma shrine designs. Addressing the camera directly, she smiles and remindfully recaps the program's varied phases, the six-stage process toward improved body-spirit-societal situationing. But then there is an abrupt cut to an unprecedented three-quarter angle where Lynn resettles herself, thanking the viewer for *embarking on this brave journey* and making the decision to *burn the couch*. She cocks her head and says, *But as we all know, life is an ongoing struggle – a never-ending tug and pull, in which there can never be any true victory, only our own satisfaction at living our lives to the utmost and being at peace with that satisfaction – that's the only true goal in this life.* Then credits over a cut to Hal Deavers waving from his own Hatteras 72 Motor Yacht, speeding along the coast of Costa Rica in the glittering Gulf of Nicoya.

Heath was stunned by this quasi-conclusion. The essence of the program in all its components and key messaging rests on the very concept of victory. Indolence and the inability to commit to rigorous discipline are inherently set in opposition to the current culture's lust for ambiguity, wishy-washiness – the withering of toughness as a virtue. Tape 3 even spells it out: *Hazy Equals Lazy*. But if there's no chance of ultimate victory, then what could be the point of aiming for – to cite Deavers at the Empowerment Expo – *vanquishment in the fourth quarter* and *going for the long bomb with those gorillas gnashing their teeth to blitz your butt?*

Why bother, Lynn?

Amid the lunacy, some cool heads prevail. Voices rise to quell widespread panic, hoping to reinstate composure. A cabal selected from the international scientific community analyzes the incident – again, some research will have to be done here to fill in the blanks for purposes of realism – and in a fretful press conference, a spokesperson announces that the enveloping phenomenon, the shroud or wave prompting this effect, is not stationary, and will continue its drift toward the sun, presumably to then be snuffed out. Hypotheses still abound as to the true nature of this effect, and what it could mean for mankind's future, but the present politicos and their lab-coated advisors testify with total confidence: everything will soon be copacetic. The next thing is crucial, and would be perhaps emphasized by a zoom and/or soundtrack cue: a sharp-looking reporter poses the unavoidable question: *So when it goes away, what happens to us?* This chief scientist character, a well-groomed analytical type, clears his throat. A general hush falls. It goes something like: he can provide only reasoned speculation, given that this thing is without precedent, and any theoretical connections reside within unexplored areas of research. Based on the scant details accessible, there is the strong possibility that the effect will be reversed. Reporter: *Reversed? Can you elaborate?* A weighty pause. This scientist will adjust his spectacles, dashing and determined at the boldest frontiers of science, yet clearly conflicted with the burden. Conflict being the natural essence of narrative: page 16 of *Shear the Chaff*. His hypothesis is all these memories of moments yet to happen will retreat just as powerfully and instantaneously as they arrived. Reporter: *You mean we'll forget everything we've seen?* Scientist: more awkwardness, a succession of coughs and throat-clearings. This is precisely what he surmises. MEG readings et cetera – still more technical research needed here – indicate the implantation or installation of such brain activity within the short-term, or maybe future-term, memory zones of the brain can, effectively, diminish. But nothing is certain. Nonetheless, the idea is disseminated by the media: in mere days this pseudo-precognition will no longer be a part of the collective experience.

Heaps of dramatic irony naturally emerge. Not only has mortal fear stricken our primary characters to their core, their friendships have been tested to the limits. Yet they learn that all this horror and dismay and catharsis will, in a matter of days, be rendered moot. And so, as the moment of the phenomenon's dispersal approaches, everything becomes poignant in voided autumnal tones, sun-flare effects to indicate moments of revelation.

But there are still so many gaping plot holes kicking around here, thinking about it all makes Heath's head hurt. For instance: assuming this story is to be swallowed, with the effect's passing, will everyone have their knowledge simultaneously drained, even their memories of events occurring *during*, and of course shaped by, this spell? And if so, what will the nature of these memories be? Do folks awake totally agog, amnesiacs rubbing temples, out of the blue? Are there neurological consequences? If someone, say, falls in love, or gives birth, or goes to jail, during this confused period – how does *that* function? And what's to prevent someone from actually transcribing or recording the visions imparted in days' strangenesses, and thus defying any temporariness of the effect? To the last note, an argument could be built that any record of something as harrowing as one's own death would never resonate as deeply as the actual thing implanted into one's consciousness. Yes. But this only prompts further questions: how well do our minds capture *anything*? Are future 'memories' any less subject to doubt than those of the past? If we remember, do we *know*? There has to be a point at which suspension of disbelief overpowers inconsistent details. And then there is the whole matter of time zones and the bigness of the earth. How that works is a whole other thing.

Heath stares into the mirror. A pair of Nicole's cotton Hanes underwear droops through his fingers. This trance consumes him, the bathroom's new starkness, stripped of the coral shower curtain and dingy bath mat, the shelves bared of de-frizzing conditioners and B12 supplements and panty liners. He drifts through time. Then he hears a door slam.

He freezes and drops the panties. For a moment he assumes it's the movers fetching last items for Nicole's move into her condo – a fourteen-foot U-Haul was parked across the street. Or, worse: it might be Brunhilde, who he really hopes remains waiting at the Coffee Time at the end of the block as he'd begged. She's been unpredictable since his return to Montana, detecting his obvious desire to break things up, not letting him out of her sight. There is terror there.

But the husky sniffs detected are clearly that of a solo dude. Heath weighs his options, seeing no other way out. *Zombified.*

In the emptied kitchen a biggish guy with thick glasses and a Goo Goo Dolls T-shirt is lifting a sack of cleaning supplies from the floor, eyes on the wedged kitchen window. Only the usual detritus remains after the move: phone books, dust clusters, fridge magnets, a few empty picture frames and torn catalogues. The apartment echoes strangely, like a skeleton shaved of its fat.

As Heath enters the room, the guy spins and points a bottle of Windex like a weapon.

Heath raises his hands. 'I live here. Lived.'

Pause.

'Oh,' the guy says. '*Heath.*'

'I came by to see about a thing. I spoke to Nicole. Seriously.'

Heath makes for the door, but the guy moves to block him. 'How'd you get in?'

Heath looks at the Windex bottle pointed at his chest. 'Like I said. I used to live here.'

'Yeah, but Nic changed the locks,' the guy says. 'And yet here you are.'

The guy gets close; he smells like deep-frying and Speed Stick.

'Hey,' Heath tries. 'No need to get hostile.'

But the guy edges closer. 'It's dudes like you that traumatize people. Preying on the vulnerable. It's fucking psychological torture.'

Heath is about to object when there is a clunk on the front stoop and a familiar voice calls out: '*Lukey, call me a total ditz, but I forgot that Mondays is when.*' Nicole enters, backing against the parted door. Seeing Heath, she doesn't seem entirely surprised. Disappointed, maybe. 'Heath. What.'

Lukey: 'I can frisk him.'

'Look,' Heath says, 'I just need to get my brother's glue gun.'

Nicole cocks her head. 'Are you *serious*? What about my loveseat?'

'Nic. Come on.'

Nicole crosses the kitchen, her face flushing. Heath moves to her semi-instinctively. Lukey intervenes with an attempted block that is more of a forearmed knife-hand strike, hitting Heath square in the larynx. Instantly Heath is back in the emergency room, tight-chested, the divide between mind and body rendered nil. His first impulse is to cower in retreat – he hasn't been in a fight since schoolyard brawls, not even threats of altercation – but Bret Albo whispers in his ear: *Gear up. Execute the mission. Reach for the raw, you goddamn pantywaist.* Proficient in seven disciplines of Eastern martial arts, from Qixingquan kung fu to Shuai jiao grappling to Dravidian Silambam staff combat, Bret punctuates the end of each of his scenes with a signature move on a dummy in desert fatigues: a rapid-fire roundhouse in which his immaculately shined boot shatters this plasticized torso. Which then, inexplicably, explodes.

Heath attempts an Albo-inspired similar move but stumbles on the turn, tripping over his own legs, accidentally delivering Lukey a sharp knee to the scrotum. Lukey falls back against the counter, swearing. Nicole shouts and waves her stumps, but Heath hears nothing. Lukey regathers and connects a ridiculously hard jab to Heath's left shoulder: not a deadly blow, but enough to make him dizzy. The next thing Heath registers is a fat Jamaican man in a sweat-soaked T-shirt pressing him against the refrigerator. A similar, skinnier guy is working a telephone, fighting for a signal, saying *fookin fook*, then whacking the phone against a table. The fat man tells Heath to chill out. Before Heath can respond, Brunhilde storms in, wielding a bag of muffins and a large coffee. Heath winces.

'You said you were going to wait,' Heath says.

Brunhilde's eyes are turning wild at the scene. 'You said *ten minutes*.'

All eyes are on her, then Heath. The Jamaican dude backs off.

Lukey: 'What the fuck, bud?'

Brunhilde's hand becomes a claw, snapping at air. 'It's 1:16.'

'Brun ...' Heath tries.

Nicole is pacing. 'Can you all please *get out of here*? I needed everything out and gone hours ago. And how has it been four hours and all that shit's still in the driveway?'

Heath notes how Brunhilde scows at Nicole. Some strange transference is happening here, something ominous. Not good.

'This is *her*?' she says to him.

The movers exchange murmurs. Heath feels a weighty globule of sweat trickle down his spine.

Lukey, again: 'What the fuck?'

'This is *her*?' Brunhilde's volume increases; her upper lip tightens in a way he's never seen before.

'Just tell me where the glue gun is,' Heath says, 'and I'm out of here.'

Brunhilde does that wrenched clawing move again, staring at Nicole with something resembling awe.

'She's a freak.'

Heath's heart stops. 'Oh jeez, Brun. Okay, let's go. Let's all just go our separate ways.'

'A *freak*. How can you even look at her? You actually *fucked* that ... thing?'

The fat mover snorts a laugh. Lukey again moves forward, looking ready to sock someone. Heath himself is lost, trying to mentally scan all he's processed, the Total LifeSystem and the *Zero-G Life Trajectory*, everything. But nothing useful comes. He can't even look at Nicole; all he hears is Brunhilde saying *freak*. *Freak freak*. And Lukey shouting back, telling her to shut it. To his astonishment, Brunhilde whaps Lukey's temple with the side of her palm, as if chopping into his skull.

One good shot and your body is Hubba Bubba.

The thinner mover crosses the kitchen, still thumbing the malfunctioning phone. With his other fist, he winds up and clocks Brunhilde in the nose, hard.

Silence.

Nic – everything's changing. You're looking for a purpose. I know, I see. But let me show you the sunsets of Misery Gulch, the terrifying bones. Let me explain that there's nothing to seek and everything to find. It's not squaring yourself with badness. Let me prove to you that everything really does matter, if we make it that way. Let me share with you what I think I'm onto. Even if it's completely purposeless.

'I'm *bleeding*,' Brunhilde shrieks. Then, quieter: 'I'm bleeding.'

Fade and out.

It passes easily, like a fever. The world gradually gathers its senses, shaking away this weirdness just like battling a mid-morning hangover to finish testing SQL standards. What has been accomplished or gained through this psycho-celestial phenomenon is unclear – and that's the problem with this story. So there is a concluding scene where the main characters together ride a vintage convertible past some iridescent harbour in a way that is, or should be, conclusive and meaningful. But still, throughout this thing, conflict swells and deflates but never achieves any resolution. Scenes taper off, half-written. Nothing convinces or redeems. The story goes nowhere, and he lacks the power to prevent it from derailing. Characters struggle, but their efforts go squandered, because true conflicts never end. Even if today's horror passes, others lie ahead. They fight fruitlessly to situate an afternoon in the context of a continuum. They throw luggage. They drain magnums of sparkling wine. They starve themselves in fear. But it changes nothing. The story is ultimately about failure.

4

At summer's dusk the parking lot outside the Community Hockey Club is crammed with parents picking up the exiting roster of PeeWee B West-Central Junior Off-Season Intramurals. Small helmeted bodies, burdened under padding, step shaky on blade guards from the exit to the lot. At the lot's edge a trio of confused gulls raid a dumpster, wrenching some sort of stringy semi-decomposed thing from the bin's pried lip. Dean and Chuck watch this, seated on a curb, sharing a cigarette.

'Do you think Corrina expects me to buy things for her?' Chuck asks.

Dean: 'Make her a T-shirt. *The Bying squeezed my boobies.*'

'I did squeeze her boobies. And she squeezed mine. It was rad.'

'Thank you, Marv Albert. So where's O?'

But then he's there, across the lot: a figure in grey and green, hoodie and army pants, his head lowered, tramping past the arena with some sort of box stuffed under an arm.

Dean stands. 'Do you think O would ever …'

Chuck follows his move in rising. 'Do I think O will what?'

Dean shakes his head and spits. 'I think I'm kind of starting to hate him.'

Buzzer. Then Owen and Chuck and Dean are entering the overheated belly of Sad Tony's apartment building. Close hallways reek of carpet cleaner and porkish stinks. Shrill chatter hides behind every door. At 602, Tony's place for years, this shirtless guy in a Dalmatian-print ball cap opens and steers them in. Chuck and Deanerz remove their shoes, but Owen leaves his on; they all wear Jordan IVs in different colours.

As always, Sad Tony lies horizontal on the couch, dressed in only a hacked-up pair of denim cut-offs, exposing his bony torso and hairy legs. Tony is not looking good; his Duchenne dystrophy makes him look ageless. His scoliotic ankles are noticeably warped and his chest is a wasteland of pimpled sunkenness.

The air conditioner rages. Wall-mounted speakers blare an arena of laughter: Eddie Murphy, *Delirious*, on CD.

'Tony,' Owen says.

'Hang on. I love this,' Sad Tony says. 'This one's about how Mr. T's a faggot. Oh god. We're lowly.'

A sick, sour aroma hangs heavily and mysteriously, until the source identifies itself: six or seven gerbils are housed in an enormous wire cage at the room's farthest reach.

Owen, louder: '*Antonio*.'

Sad Tony raises a hand, fast-forwarding. 'Hang on. When he does that thing, Elvis and lemonade, the cool refreshing drink. That's the funniest.'

Krissy, thought by most to be Tony's ex, appears from the kitchen with some pinkish drink in a plastic jug bearing a Brockville Speedway logo. No offer to the others is made.

The Bying drums fingers on his legs. 'So how're things these days, Tone?'

'You'd split in half if you knew.'

Krissy and Tony each drink from the jug in turn.

'So I'll not keep you,' Owen says. 'I have this Nintendo 64. You could get a hundred easy for the thing.'

He produces the box. Sad Tony raises an eyebrow.

'That better not be pinched,' he says. 'Here, only victimless crimes.'

'No such thing,' Krissy says.

'No no no,' Owen says. 'My uncle gave it to me.'

Tony turns to Krissy. 'Can you believe this? The child trades his birthday presents for drugs. Fucking degenerate. And this is what the twenty-first century holds in store.'

Krissy: 'A long downward slide.'

'Comes with FIFA,' Owen says. 'This, plus nineteen dollars. And Mortal Kombat.'

Sad Tony budges forward in a clearly difficult reach, sitting up halfway. Catching a floor lamp's light, his emaciation is striking. Deanerz suppresses a gasp. Sad Tony: like the tides, like the stars, he's always just *been there*, in this hovel, doling out pinched baggies and crackling tinfoil, one eye on the TV. But now he's degrading into a new incarnation, even more transparent than the previous. A thing like death.

Sad Tony sighs. 'All right, all right. What were you juvenile delinquents imagining, exactly?'

No moon here, on the newly sodded soccer field still smelling of fertilizer, the grid feeding an ashen sky. A synthetic haze haunts the thermosphere's lens. Post-dusk, this space is transformed from the whistling rigour of laps and drills into a refuge of adultlessness, the crush of curfews the only harness. In uncommon quietness, summer's submersion and a prevailing mood of preparation, they sit near the south goal line, loosely circled around an open two-four and mason jars of rum swiped from liquor cabinets. Lighters light, girls speak in secret dialects and ciphers. Intermittent whoops echo across the field. The grass is cool, dew-ready; it could rain.

'What? I could totally eat a hundred,' Chuck says.

'A *hundred*?' Dean says. 'Fuck off.'

'The regular ones. Not like a Filet-o-Fish or that shit.'

Calcaveccia is absent, which is strange. Dudes have been getting the impression he might have plans in the works that don't include hanging with the usuals. Chuck has brought Corrina and some of her troops, and it appears Dean might be developing some sort of project with Marianne Battillana, which would be dicey because last year she went out with that insaniac Olie Squelce, and word is he still holds a torch.

'Ten, maybe, and you'd yak.'

'I'm serious. When I hit McDo I get like six and I'm not even close to stuffed. It's like eating Kleenex. You buy, I'll eat. Let's do this.'

Marianne laughs. '*We* buy? What's in it for us?'

'Fuck you all,' Chuck says. He puffs on his cigarette like it's a sport. 'I'll eat that shit and you chumps will bow down.'

He scans the field, sucking his cheeks. A familiar figure moves in the distance, jogging in a circle and punching invisible opponents with heavyweight huffs. One of the girls calls out – sound travels freely on the flat field. Everyone sort of laughs.

But downfield Owen continues tracing bleached goal lines as the loose-leaf sky above screams murder, everything craning up and back and out of sight. Continents are sliding into reefs of foam. Gravity reverses, suns supernova, everything turns to fizz. That whispered voice of reassurance – *All's all right in the end* – is nowhere to be heard. There is only the void and the filtered distant cackle of girls' laughter. Owen tears off his shirt and runs bare-chested toward the trees, stumbling forth into the waiting dark and a shadowy crust of clawing roots and devouring firs. Shouts follow him into these nethers, but he ignores, he runs, he *defies*, then trips over an unexpected dip and wipes out in the mud.

Along with the hash, Sad Tony had also slipped Owen a baggie of powder that went unidentified. Tony did this under the radar, didn't announce it to Deanerz or The Bying, nor to Krissy. This was a one-on-one pact, or assignment, established between O and Sad Tony alone. It felt intimate, brotherly. Owen, He Himself, never had a brother. He snorted half the shit as soon as he had a moment alone. Now his hammering heart's pulse resonates to his temples, his jaw, his knuckles. He sits up and cups his left pec in a palm, working to taper the flow there, pacifying the warring factions between his ears. A skid of cool mud stripes his hip up to his collarbone like a gash of blood; he tries to laugh at this, can't.

They're all dead now: He Himself and all these others, skeletons strewn across this burial field, Paternal and Maternal Units, his crew and co-conspirators, stop-motion gods, Princess Di funeral processions, all this concern and landscaping – all dead now. At this he can only laugh. Every day this stupid soccer field is cleated to bits and raped by bugs, then John Deeres and pesticides renew it all for another season of doom.

He works to remember: Knight takes Pawn. Bishop takes Knight. Forks and skewers. Combinations and fate. *En passant.* Zugzwang.

Chuck appears. 'O, serious. You need any first aid?'

Owen finds his eyelids fluttering. 'Comes in waves. I'm really high. No, I'm *really* high. You don't know.'

Chuck crouches and grips his arm. Chuck Fuck Snuck Fuck. Knows nothing.

'Just don't think about it. Come have a brew-dawg and decompress.'

But he has no choice: Owen rises and allows himself to be led back to the group. A beer is fetched, and he drinks. Someone, Marianne, is talking about a ghost seen in the school basement, appearing every

Monday morning, scampering around the girls' lockers, moaning in a subsonic baritone.

'Right,' Dean says. 'Probably just Carruthers looking for a panty sniff.'

Laughs all around. Meanwhile, Owen fights to command every molecule or whatever of his body to not blow sky-high. Jackie Bentley, with whom Owen shared a chemistry lab workstation last year, moves over next to him.

'I want to ask you something,' Jackie says.

Owen, cross-legged, rubs his face, still working with and against what's happening. Jackie's glossy mascara makes her eyes shine like a dying dog's.

'This thing about Chara and Mr. Carruthers.'

He swallows as much beer as he can manage in one gulp, spilling some into his lap. 'Mm.'

'Because we all know it's bullshit. And they called Chara in to talk to Worthe and everything. She's losing it. Lucky said everyone heard it from you. What did you *say*?'

'I've got my own shit to worry about.'

Jackie glares at him. 'That's really insensitive. Honestly, I'm losing respect for you.'

'Yeah, well.'

'My dreams are always about sniper missions and manhunts,' Chuck is saying. 'Last night there was, I was in this weird warehouse chasing this kind of enemy guy, and it turns out this guy was me, myself. It was intense.'

Marianne: 'But dreams have deeper meanings.'

Dean: 'Ask Owen. He understands psychology.'

Owen is cracking one of the last remaining beers when he realizes all eyes are on him. These, his friends. Seated on a field. He says nothing.

Chris McGough's goal right now is to get these kids vamoosed by closing, signalling the loitering shitheads still at the plaza McDonald's to wrap things up with a rotate of gloved finger and jangling of keys, up and down the aisles. But they're just not getting it, still crowded at booths with empty wrappers crunched before them. One punk even has an unlit cigarette in his lips, which if he sparks up will mean a serious heave-ho.

McGough doesn't need this grief. Shifts here are a nightly drudgery of annoyances, a race of frustration trying to get back to Nancy, now six months' pregnant and convulsing in crying jags if left alone for more than a couple of hours. McGough checks his watch; her fury will now be at its apex. At twenty-six, he feels he is losing an already enervating tenancy within his own life. Kid on the way, bills stacked, and all he can think of is rocking those VLTs up at the Copper Penny. Royal Spins. Hexbreaker.

But then something's happening at the east entrance, so he double-times it back there. Assistant Night Manager Meredith at the cash points at the door: some turd, backed by his hammered pals, is beating fists against the door, trying to get in: classic Friday-night yo-yos for whom a badge means nothing. In the Security Services Procedures Manual there is a general, insistent directive: barring an emergency, The Locks Stay Locked. And right now, for this wild-eyed kid, the locks are definitely staying locked.

McGough knuckles the glass, shakes his head: nope. The kid's yelling something about getting the grill ready. *A hundred burgers now.* His knocks increase in intensity, drawing stares.

With a quick scan back at the lingering customers, McGough frees the bolt from its lock and opens the door, just a C-hair. He tells the kid and the whole Babysitters Club behind him to ease off statim, or the call will go in. But this one kid is spastic, trying to push past. *Fire up the grill, fire it up.* Meredith is nervous, saying they need to put the call in. McGough assures her this is an easy take-care-of.

But a few minutes later he's out in the parking lot with the kid in a shaky full nelson, and the kid won't submit. Amazingly, sadly, McGough recognizes him: it's Sammy Prendergast's younger brother. Chris and Sammy did rugby together in eleventh grade, like five years ago. And now he has to transition into a chokehold to restrain the grunting kid. Passing headlights stripe the sloppy scene.

McGough's just loosening the kid's legs to work him to the ground when something goes bananzo at his skull's base. Everything lightens and he loses hold. Something is actually being *inserted* into the back of his neck, just above the top vertebra. He turns to see a spread of blood gluing his shirt to his skin, a shirt for which he will totally get docked if a replacement is required. As Assistant Night Manager Meredith rushes forward, waving a cordless phone, McGough bellows, 'Call it in, call it in.'

They scatter and flee, some toward traffic lights and sanctity beyond, others darting southward to a construction site abutting the sunken plot at the other end, a half-accomplished mallscape set to open in the new year. They are shadows by streetlight, gold and green, disappearing into plastic and gravel. Behind, a pair of police cruisers pull into the plaza entrance, blaring halogens, then both shift and burn away, their hunt heading elsewhere.

The grocery store, a Loblaws, is still only a frame of girders and lumber draped in protective polyethylene. The southern face is barricaded by fencing, but the rear is open to anyone dexterous and persistent enough to tackle its brief perimeter of tape and rope. Owen is the first to attack the barriers.

'Alarms,' Deanerz warns, but Owen heads in anyway.

Floodlights bring forth uneven earth, crude fractures of light in a maze of scaffolding and a webwork of wiring and tubing. Owen and Dean move through the aspirational building, cautious at first, but finding no resistance, they continue with destructive bravado, tearing away plastic and diving into crates, seeking anything worth pilfering. Here is the skeleton of a familiar idea, a future of aisles and shelves springing forth from bare creation, a temple of delicatessenry, racks of cans and packets, housewives pushing carts of cat food and mayonnaise-type dressing.

Leaving Dean behind, Owen climbs half-built stairs to find a metal desk littered with scraps. He rifles the drawers, hoping for anything: petty cash, titty mags, a blank chequebook. But there's nothing, only plaster dust and meaningless papers. A rotary hammer drill, no AC cable attached; he tosses it aside. Reaching to his pocket for cigarettes, he finds the wad of foil containing the last crumbled ruins of Sad Tony's foul gift. He snuffs it up in a few quick moves, then biffs the foil into a garbage-stuffed corner. He wobbles – his brain is about to squirt out of his ears, like Gillette shaving gel.

Back on the floor Dean extends a sip of beer. Owen accepts.

'Did you actually *stab* that guy?'

Owen ignores this, looking past him. 'Where'd Jackie go?'

Dean picks up a cinder block and throws it at nothing, a pile of blunt planks at the edge of a derelict shelving unit. Then another, and another.

'Jackie's a racist pig,' Dean says. 'She told Natasha she'd never date a black guy because African nations can't establish technological civilizations. Bitch.'

Owen, still trippy, is distracted by the arc of the thrown block. 'Yeah.'

In the Quiet Room there was nothing more fascinating than your own hands. How they sign a name, how they light a cigarette – how lightly they move. How, humbled and defeated, they help you masturbate into a bedsheet. And then you begin to detect numbness, then doubt whether this numbness is real or just another product of the imagination. Then everything is imaginary: the pulse of your lungs, sunlight in your pupils, patterns of waking and catatonia. It's all in your mind, in the clench of your fists.

Deanerz: 'How do people even fucking stand themselves?'

Answer: the *spaks* of his missiles, echoing on untiled surfaces, unstalked floors.

As they cut through the woods past the drained reservoir, having bunkered down in the store for what seemed like an hour, and now heading for their homes, Dean dreads the hours to come. He knows his parents will be tucked away upstairs in bed, dreaming about whatever they dream following their monthly viewing of their *Schindler's List* tape, peaceful in post-atrocity cool-down no matter any clatter or sickness.

And he wants to be presentable for breakfast tomorrow, given his father's Wittmaack-Ekbom's syndrome and the lecture Dean was given by his mother about how he is now part of a support system. Returning home this drunk would be in bad form. Plus Owen isn't doing so well: one step ahead of Dean, he wobbles wildly, his face glossed with sweat even though a cooling low-pressure system now banks in.

Suddenly Owen wheels around. 'You hear that?'

He points up, toward the nearest embankment. Dean looks: nothing, just headlights and flashes from the road, signposts and steel. But Owen flattens to the ground, readying himself. Dean, unsurely following his lead, also ducks. And yes: over the nearby crest a crew of silhouettes appears, ranking five, backlit by headlights, on their way.

By O's eyes, he's pushing DEFCON 1. Dean asks who.

'Vengeful scum.'

Dean has witnessed O's ferocity, like last November at Square One when he chucked a Coke bottle stuffed with flaming paper towels into that guy Dwayne Bixby's car – Bixby's alleged crime was calling Sweltham a *demented shitstain* in the caf – doing serious damage to the upholstery of Dwayne's dad's S-Series coupe. A fight ensued, ending with O throwing several fistfuls of rough gravel into the air, laughing as it rained over everyone. This was even before the thing with Ike.

Dean is getting scared. 'The golfing party. Let's go.'

'No way. Can we get anyone?'

But they have no one, and not a pay phone anywhere close. One of these approaching shadows emits a sound like a hippo's roar. It's coming: tonight they will harvest the fallout of the chaos wreaked at the Squelces'.

'So we bolt,' Owen says to Dean.

They bolt. They descend into a clearing at the reservoir's sunken base, tumbling into grasses near the surrounding fence, finding a bunker in the wet leaves and pebbled mush. There they breathe heavily and wait.

'Total Passchendaele styles,' Owen says.

Backyard lights from nearby houses cast scarecrow shadows through fencing and branches. From the street an engine revs, then fades into a Doppler wane.

'Motherfuck,' Owen says. 'They're circling.'

Owen heads up the slope in the direction of the sidewalk. Dean, unsure, follows. For a moment their safety seems secure. Then they encounter doom.

From the facing darkness: 'Yo, cocksnot.'

Five columns approach. This seeming commander leads the advance, slapping together motocross gloves and chewing on a rum-tipped Colt. Flanking him are two beefy sergeants-at-arms, and another guy feeding on a bag of McNuggets. A larger ginger crewcut guy brings up the rear, quietly menacing.

'We know you guys,' The Commander says.

'Whatever you're talking about,' Dean says, 'it's no.'

The guy with the McNuggets snorts. 'Fuck this guy.'

Owen: 'No need for the potty mouth.'

The Commander sort of brightens as he lumbers down into the clearing. 'Suck my ball. Our boy Olie's on probation now. You're paying for that window.'

Dean looks and, wow, apt: The Commander even handles a four-iron for a weapon. Other invaders follow his advance down the slope. The guy and his cronies are unfamiliar, but the consequences of that night's chaos are becoming clearer. Owen digs a heel into the ground. Dean sees his eyes working – this is the refashioned O, post-institutional, who simply doesn't care. Dean doesn't want anything to do with this, not tonight, and he books it back down into the woods. One of the two sergeant-type guys moves to follow, but Dean, a wind-sprint champ, has already disappeared into the dark. All attention is on Owen.

'Retribution,' The Commander says, coming forward.

The McNuggets guy burps and tosses aside his bag, joining his advance. 'Pound of flesh.'

Against everything, you have to keep pushing. Odds are against you, always. Owen leads with his right fist and, as anticipated, McNuggets flinches and moves to block. With only a peripheral look to his right, Owen drives an elbow hard into The Commander's chin. There is a sound like a lock catching. As The Commander recoils, Owen butts his brow on McNuggets's nose, transforming his face into a blotchy volcano.

As O's own eyes well with tears, arms seize him, the sergeants grappling as McNuggets stumbles blinded through the trees, holding the bridge of his nose, saying *fucka fuck*. Punches come to Owen's midsection, but he is immune to pain now. He is phasing through dimensions. These thugs constrain him, but they don't *have* him; he casts himself forward, face first to the ground, unsettling their supremacy. Instinct kicks in, and he manages to wedge free, for a moment, before The Commander's golf club comes down on his back like a crashing wave.

But now Owen is a windmill, deflecting all attackers. One of the sergeants takes hold of one his legs, but O levitates and drives the other into the dude's testicles. Then this shadow, the mysterious ginger creature he'd almost forgotten about, charges. Now is End of Days, when all deities and demons converge to wage battle for dominion of this human plane. The membrane dividing Heaven and Hell has been breached. If an ounce of his young blood falls on this unholy terrain, armadas will sink; if a millennial second goes wasted, generations' dreams of victory will be crushed. Owen bounds over treetops, his fists swelling to mighty sledgehammers and his brow a helmet of bristling flames. His ginger foe launches in an opposite arc, pinwheeling, fangs gnashed and claws extended. They collide mid-air with an explosive *voom*, each ricocheting downward. The earth buckles with impact, Richter-scaling at unprecedented magnitude. The freckled fiend howls victory.

Owen Sweltham – foe of goodness, breaker of vows, subject for clinicians, partaker of Robitussin, convicted felon and witness to suspicious deaths – springs to his feet. Slapping his palms together, he issues forth a mighty clap of thunder, an energy pulse that flattens grasslands and ignites a darkened forest's cabaret in an ultraviolet flash. Eyes aflame, his attackers prepare as Owen, shielded with exoskeletal armour, issues a howl that is grave and incantatory, like the theme song to JAG.

But this compass of solemn enemies re-encircles the hero. Commander and sergeants, McNuggets and ginger crewcut, rogue hostiles of future and past, the shadows of a thousand enemies reflected in the flashes of their Bic lighters: Fat Brian, Principal Worthe, Carruthers, Parental Units – all these *people*, lumberjacks seeking to hack him to timber. They circle him like wolves, sniffing at his sweat. He is alone here, as always, defeated from the start. Stars and damnation.

'I had it all,' he says, or does not say.

They pounce.

Lamplight and television glare and the stereo's LEDs colour this room in orange and blue, like a courtyarded evening of fires and ambulances. She sits penning lists in her saddle-stitched notebook, a gift from the Russian boy. Only months ago in the vacuumed hope of a Sheraton lobby she'd unwrapped it from purplish tissue; kissing his oily cheeks in gratitude was sweeter than she'd ever imagined kissing could be. Now he is kibbutzed in Israel and her heart is in purgatory. Lately her only pleasures are dew fall, long morning showers, the laboratory scent of artificial pine.

Gwen blinks, contact lenses sitting sorely on her corneas. Her drifting mind reconstructs today and past days, channelling lists and stocking them like dried flowers between scrapbook pages. Blurriness of vision means fears of decay; her Nana went blind from untreated glaucoma, then descended further to dementia – if she saw Elroy now, jailed and scarred with brands, she would howl. In late years she stumbled around her house mistaking brooms for grandchildren and singing Chinese children's songs to the television: *Two tigers run fast – one has no eyes – one has no tail – how strange.* Gwen vows she'll never be that lost. So she makes lists and designs itineraries, and one day she'll read back and reminisce about it all.

Then: punctuated knuckles at the window.

Peeling back the translucent curtains, this hooded phantom kneels in the dark.

'Come on out.'

'Quiet,' she whispers. 'My parents. What are you doing?'

He bids her to come outside for a cigarette. She declines. 'Come on. Just one smoke.'

Out in the cool night they sit curbside several houses down, she in her flannel pyjamas under a windbreaker, he hiding his face under his hoodie. She shivers, but doesn't seek his warmth.

'So you guys were out ripping it up.'

'Nothing too major. Friday night.'

She notices his hands' tremor. Then the blood on his knuckles. 'Shit,' she says.

She takes a hand to see, then pulls back his hood to reveal an eye purpled and gruesome, blood on his lip. She looks him over with the intimacy of a bed nurse. He shudders away.

'Yeck. And your shirt is shredded. What happened?'

'N-fair guz ...' he slurs.

'What?'

'Un ... fair. Unfair gods.'

'Okay. You're weirding me out.'

She stands, flicking away her cigarette's butt. Sweltham is clearly demolished, and she worries if she leaves him here he'll pass out with his chin on the curb. Meanwhile her true love cuddles up to bellybutton-pierced bar managers in Israel, gaining muscle tone and arguing with Zionists, steadily forgetting about her, day by day, as she snores through Physics B, doing her darnedest to get decent enough averages to enable escape to UC Santa Cruz Marine Biology next year. Away from all this exhaustion, these dull nights.

When they return to the backyard and her window, Gwen tells Owen goodnight and moves for the bedroom window. He takes her hand in his bloodied own, a move so disarming she doesn't initially resist.

'Gwen,' he says. 'I had it all.'

He brings her hand upward to his face.

And some in dreams assured were of the Spirit that plagued us so.

'You're impossible,' she says.

He presses the back of her palm against his heated skin, smushing her knuckles into his cheek. For a moment he has her. Then she takes her hand away. She bends to crawl back into her bedroom, but Owen grabs her by the waist and pulls her back, spinning her around; she is light, lighter than she appears. He backs her against the house's brick, his weight pressed hard against hers, chest forward, thighs shoving thighs, his lips attacking her neck and cheeks. Her hands are on his chest efforting him away as he tells her *I love you*, and he really really does love her and she is all that is beautiful in this ugly world and he moves his hands to the waistband of her pyjamas and tries to tug them down but she resists, not yet grasping that this is actually happening, and with one hand he slams her wrist back against the wall and with the other moves his hand down her thigh as the night's cool air fills her pyjamas and his fingers rise as he tells her again that he loves her *he loves her and Gwen you just don't know none of you know what I really actually mean when I say what I'm saying and where and when I actually am because I mean it even if no one even believes me or if I actually even exist.*

J.F. once blathered about Four Noble Truths. *Birth suffering aging suffering illness suffering death suffering.* Origin, cessation: suffering. The remainderless fading away. And then J.F. himself was nothing, self-generated nothing. There was much he could fire off by memory; maybe he was making it all up.

Mornings found the veins of Fultz's fat nose throbbing and his shrubbish eyebrows in disarray, his eyelids sleepy and thumb pads stained with newsprint. On one of these suffocated mornings Fultz proposed an exercise. He asked Owen: 'Choose five words to describe yourself. No qualifiers, only affirmative, descriptive words. Take a moment to think about it. Not an exam. Just a way of considering your *self*, the individual. Go ahead.'

'*Owen. Sweltham. Waste. Of. Fucking. Skin.* Wait, that's six. Cut *Owen.*'

Fultz sighed. 'The perennial comic master. A rare wit.'

'Whatever, Hiram.'

'I take it you're not going to even try and address with any seriousness these things we need to discuss.'

'I just did.'

'Owen,' Fultz said, overemphasizing that usual brow lift, 'I have a legal obligation to report on our progress. These cutesy dialogues are getting tired.'

'Okay.'

'Then answer me this, since you are such an expert. On yourself, that is.'

The pause, for effect.

'What do you *want*?'

Demonic energies fuel his movement as he hurries through lamped crescents and wooded paths, shirking attention, heading south in the direction of the expressway. With the knife now released from his boot, his feet move lightly. At this hour, only desperation and occasional taxis inhabit these dead lanes. He hops barbed wire and finds himself in the rear lot of a car dealership. Crossing past this Dixie Honda showroom, he catches his own face reflected against a pair of Civic GXs in pigeon-shitted glass. Moving through the lot he loses track of time, then finds himself in a cemetery abutting an expressway on-ramp, its grasses dotted with stones and bronze markers, a wilted flag overhead. His feet tramp along the path, gravestones and devotions at all sides. Dozens of putrefying bodies claw forth from graves to glare at him, pointing accusations: *Boy – you are unworthy. Come swallow this rancid pedosphere*, they caw, *and dream with us in the universe's bowel.* None of this makes sense, but Owen is not afraid. Grains of dust become cosmic wars. The world chews you up like a chicken burger. They used to have those public service announcements on Saturday's NBC cartoons, *One to Grow On*, with Punky Brewster or whoever talking about what to do if you lose your mother in a department store so as to avoid being raped in the accessories section. And in five seconds you, a child, understand that with investment in this world comes responsibility and darkness. This was his life, and Ike's life. He's always wanted to lose himself, to get away from this shitty world and this shitty time. The gentleness of a morning's Robitussin and a quick crumble of hash to turn your mind to 7Up, to dew fall. To not think about things, to not grieve about what might lie beyond life's plastic shrinkwrap. Yes, his mind has been possessed with flares of waistbands and the destruction of enemies. But now is the time to spill it all, let it spew. When they wanted him to say anything, he said nothing. Now he wants to say it all, but there is no one to say it to.

He punches buttons at the GO station phone booth. Tones pulse, then: *You've reached the Etobicoke offices of St. Dismas Health Services. Our offices are currently closed. Please call back between the hours of.* Quarter No. 2. At Fultz's private line, another plea goes unanswered. His knees loosen. He drifts, breaching protocol, seduced by badness. Owen presses his forehead into the booth's Plexiglas. Then he breathes and goes.

Last night of winter holidays, early January, a world pelted with freezing rain. After most of a 1750 mL Jose Cuervo pinched from the Byngs' and a ton of cough syrup, Ike and O were out of their heads and on the move. They bounded across the 427, woofing and yowling as Ike lobbed the drained bottle at the moon; it landed and exploded on the median strip, as perfect and instant as a scud. The glass sparkled like crystals in the dim.

The next thing Owen remembers is automatic doors parting as they stumbled into the roadside Mac's, slapped with the store's brightness. Owen drifted toward the freezers, his stomach rolling with desire for Twizzlers, Jos Louis, microwave taquitos. Adrift through aisles, he was powered simply by his own wastedness and freedom from all concerns of the world. There were no other customers. It took a lot to feel good, yet he actually felt good, though also sort of sick, lazily opening a freezer, breathing its metallic coolness, gaping at Creamsicles.

Then something was happening at the front counter: Ike was yelling and the old Iranian man behind the counter was yelling back. A stack of Winstons spilled over the counter as Ike tore open bags of Munchos, loosing a rain of chips. Owen hurried over, still laughing as Ike spun, and they looked into each other's wet eyes, exchanging something under the deadness of fluorescent lights and advertisements and stained mirrors and security cameras.

Ike then transformed into a version of himself never before known, punching gum displays, cursing racks of pistachios and Certs, unloading an elbow drop on a Caramilk display, growling in tongues. The tiny counterperson shrank in fear, only furthering Ike's guttural freak-out. Everything was escalating too quickly, and as Owen chucked aside his earphones and tried to talk Ike down, clutching him by his K-Way sleeves, there was a moment when everything hung at a balance, a trembling second where this could all be just a joke. But Ike shook his head and shrugged away these moves, saying, *Don't worry – all's all right in the end.* Owen backed off, confused. Then the clerk picked up a cordless phone, thumbing the keypad, and Ike lunged forward. Owen said *no*, but there was no stopping it: Ike vaulted over the counter, his knees slipping on the glass of scratch-ticket displays, seeking vengeance for crimes only he could envision. Before the man knew what was happening, Ike was upon him.

Owen backed away, bracing himself against the ice-cream freezer. His head woozed. The kaleidoscope of racks, the wet thump of Ike stomping with his Doc Marten shitkickers, the flings of blood spackling a cardboard Energizer battery display and register spools – this should have been just a sick dream. But he was awake, and it was no dream.

As he would later testify to his accusers, the next he knew he and Ike were flying again over wet-slick asphalt, scaling fences and tearing through leafless trees in darkened backyards. As they ran they were transported into lost years, childhoods, summery times of waterslides and lawn mowers, seeking a fire that was not a flame but a voice.

And then they were at the bridge, the river surging on rocky shores below. Ike, speeding ahead, leapt up to hang on the iron rail in a slo-mo pirouette, sashaying into the darkness to shoot back at the searchlights of imaginary SWAT team choppers. In the deepening night and persistent icy rain, he abandoned everything, even Owen. Everything was slippery: metal, time. As Ike shuffled along the rail, Owen fought to remember where they were, where things were or should be headed. He lit his last cigarette, palming its heater against the rain, and scanned the dark road for imagined pursuers. None were coming, yet. Climbing up the rail, he watched Ike slipping, fighting unseen spectres, gnashing his teeth. *You crazy motherfuck*, Owen shouted to him. *Let's get got.* Then something happened he didn't see, and Ike was not there anymore. Rushing over, Owen arrived just in time to see Ike disappear into the deep, into nothingness.

Soon came sirens, ambulances, mayhem. And later, when they questioned him, asking whether Ike had jumped or slipped, Owen said nothing. When they wanted him to say anything he said nothing. But he was tried for his crimes, and crimes then yet to be committed, and he of course denied nothing.

It is somehow and somewhere in the twentieth century. First week, sanguine September. Grade 3 or 3 million. Ms. Eisenhower, homeroom teacher. Children at desks, blushing, dirty laces. There is this kid; there was this kid. Freckles, bowl cut, no front teeth. Remember, forget. Kid, Eisenhower, Milk Day – if your parents ordered whole milk for you, you got called *Homo*. Freckle Face knew his cursive, four times four, sealed his own velcro KangaROOs. But on the third or fourth day of classes, there, among everyone in the morning hubbub, he began to mumble to himself non-stop. Chatter died down as Eisenhower, tolerant but reptilian, called the roll – bright voices, one after another: *Here.* But Freckle Face kept mumbling. Heads turned, girls tittered. Quietly, over and over in a chugging rhythm: *grandfather clock grandfather clock grandfather clock.* And then a few kids at the back, giggling, picked it up: *grandfather clock.* Insurrectionary chanting, a spontaneous call to arms: *grandfather clock grandfather clock.* Singsong. Soon they were all saying it together, even Owen. But Freckle Face never raised his pitch above that persistent register. He was lost in it; he'd found something in the words beyond himself. It meant something to him that no one else could have.

Across the Credit River dawn rises, the sun a puked-up purple. Owen says it aloud: *grandfather clock.* And below, only the stucco-ish chaos of frothing waters. With a look around at the trickle of weekend morning traffic, he hops up onto the steel railing and manoeuvres over the ledge. He can't recall what happened next that morning, with all the kids intoning their mantra. It must have at some point come to an end, but how exactly is lost to the dimming corridors of his memory. Perhaps Freckle Face is still saying it, somewhere. *Grandfather clock.* He tries not to cry, but fails at that too.

Owen died and lived for all these sins, rose again, rolled entrails and smoked them in wrinkled Zig-Zags, then crawled back into the polluted mud and decomposed honestly, like an old dog. And when he finally fell to the wind, dislodged from these steel fences and gushing lanes, he would be absolved of all cruel justice. He would murder these tides and rise awake, aware of everything. Gone evermore.

Owen steps down from the ledge. Odds are against you, always always. Against everything, you have to keep pushing. They will try to knock you down, defeat you, make you less. But against everything, you keep pushing.

5

The Eleventh Hour Trade Summit brings together an unlikely collective of international trade ministries, multinationals and venture capitalists, all under the supervisory sponsorship of various pharmaceutical supplier/developers. The incautiously worded press copy describes it as an *era-defining opportunity for worldwide economic awakening*, but according to Adam Abot it represents only a way for a cabal of, in his words, *third-tier corporate slavemasters* to wheel deals and draft contracts – the kinds of deals that renovate valleys and rewrite borders.

And Abdel al-Durabi, co-chair of the summit's founding committee, has made himself the most vocal and visible of its delegates, making time with local news outlets and undertaking frenzied PR campaigns. The World section of today's *Toronto Star* offers a flattering shot of al-Durabi – *still an enigmatic and controversial figure* – engaging the Colombian ambassador in a crippling headlock, both in matching sunglasses. An accompanying caption quipped: *The New Global Etiquette?*

This afternoon, in two hours give or take, both leaders will be among those participating in a moderated panel on comprehensive trade regulation and tariff policies between transnational co-operations and transitional developing economies. But media coverage is light, mostly city reporters interviewing straggling diplomats and lackeys. Parker edges through the automatic doors amid a hastening throng of squat women – an order of Bengali nuns, a flyer handed to him by an ecstatic pantsuited coordinator receiving them explains – and stakes his position in view of the parking receiving area, monitoring all ins and outs as per the plan. A regiment of uniformed humans enters the lobby, followed closely behind by bellhops hauling bags. Parker drifts toward the coffee kiosk at the lobby's south quadrant. Surveying the scene, he notices a trio of identical black minivans pulling up at the main entrance, no apparent indication of their cargo or purpose. Jingling change in his pockets, he edges past a line of Swedes crowding a pamphlet display. There is a swell of noise, then battalions of guys storming in. Parker is urged back, losing his sightline of those minivans.

As he follows the crowd's stream, a tiny woman throws herself into his path; her over-pierced ears oddly remind him of his sister-in-law Bethany. She asks for his clearance.

'I'm here for the panel,' he says.

Her walkie crackles and she waves him along, vanishing back into the mob to field some other rising crisis. The event sculpts itself into hurried process, and at 10:45 a woman in a red windbreaker appears to bellow against the dullish din, directing all to assigned seating. There is a program at play here, herding all into participation. Journalists at the rear, delegates at the fore. He can't stop jangling his pockets. Three bucks of dimes. He slips his hand into his jacket, touches what's there.

You can't just wade into a roomful of delegates waving a hacksaw.

A life of projecting an air of staid competency has served Parker well. Professionality and leadership, he's learned, demand a controlled, unflamboyant manner. Order has been his ally: *quid pro quo, ipso facto.* Every joule of effort expended guarantees a reciprocal return, somehow, in some way. Every passing second means a new future. And so he believes this: amid the supremacy of confusion in recent days, there have also arisen opportunities and coincidences, intersections both familiar and uncanny.

This is his only explanation for what happens next, as he moves forward through the crowd, bumping into strangers. For to examine circumstance too closely, to scrutinize too deeply the processes that have led him to where he is and what is to occur, would be to lend credibility to higher ideas about fate or something. Or at least to deny the cadences of contemporary truth. But Parker, his eyes pried wide and lower lip bitten bloody, feels more tapped in to his raw existence than ever before. There are opportunities, he sees. Everything happens according to plan.

And when she cocks her head with a certain withdrawal, he thinks she sees it too. The way she blurts out his name confirms it: *Park ... er.*

'Funny seeing you here,' he says.

Michaela, Deryk Cheung's assistant, wears an expression of both guilt and annoyance – clearly, she'd spoken before deciding whether she wanted to engage him or not. Unlike her usual power suits and terse blazers, she now wears baggy sweats, her hair bunned in an elastic. Greyish valleys tray her unlinered eyes. He moves to reach, to shake, then abandons the gesture.

'How have you been?' she asks.

He smiles. 'Amazing.'

Then he sees Michaela's companion knelt behind her, fighting a suitcase latch. As she rises, her forehead weirdly sweaty, he almost doesn't recognize her.

'Babe, I can't get this shut,' Raekwona says.

Michaela turns, tensed. 'Hey, look who.'

Parker spreads his hands as if to corroborate something, but remains quiet. At the last DynaFlex biweekly staff meeting, Administrative Assistant Raekwona had purposefully and uninhibitedly enumerated sixteen areas in which costs could be cut by reducing field expenditures; i.e., fewer executive reps logging actual miles and greater concentration on liaising via telecommunications. Her proposal was lengthy and determined. Parker had spent the entire meeting absently pondering the state of her groom-to-be Kaelan's rallying testicles.

The woman in the red windbreaker approaches, wrangling those continuing on to the panel: *Let's go let's go.* Raekwona looks like she's going to punch someone.

'You're here … why?' Michaela asks.

'The, um, panel,' Parker says. 'But security's tight.'

A moment passes, frozen in uncertainty and awkwardness. And when this security guard comes over to move them along, Michaela flashes some sort of credentials, an ID badge. Nodding with understanding, the guard turns to Parker, who indicates he's with the women. Raekwona looks at her feet.

'Escort Mr. Sweltham to his destination,' Michaela tells the guard. 'Please.'

This is the moment where we fulfill our destiny.

We now possess a unique opportunity to usher in a new era in global relations. The networking capabilities available to us now are unparalleled throughout history, and should be embraced beyond restrictions of eras past. A new spirit of co-operation: in technology, in innovation, in community. We have reached the Eleventh Hour. So we move the clocks forward and usher in a new promise. Brotherhood across oceans, traversing meridians. A new millennium. A new world.

Al-Durabi's associates work the hall's entrance, all in matching green cotton suits with grey silk ties, handing out the prepared leaflet: *At the Precipice: New Directions* outlines his administration's alleged achievements since his assumption of command, bannered with a watercolour portrait of the man himself in his trademark sunglasses and a beige Nehru jacket. As a representative for Denmark's Directorate of Fisheries takes the podium to expound on the viability of biodiesel extraction from the Afghani opium papaver, Parker scans this document, reading *73 percent increase in deployment of support troops to U.S. efforts in security-oppositional regions*, gaining nothing useful from this.

The reedy Dane wraps up to indifferent applause. Next up on the itinerary, as introduced by Joanna Cruxiom of Gopal & Dodd Pharmanetics, is the summit's hosting sponsor: Abdel al-Durabi, he himself.

'A rare and promising opportunity,' Cruxiom says. 'Real conversations and real change.'

Parker slides past a bored-looking cameraman toward the exit. Back in the lobby, he tries to recall the precise mechanics of today's plan. Right now it's an unnavigable haze. He concentrates, metering his breath, looking around for Adam, who was supposed to be here by now.

Then something twists in the room, a scent jabbing him with an unexpected memory: seven years ago, maybe, in a post-Christmas languor. Keystone Kelly's, snow curtaining down, erasing a crammed parking lot. They were safely boothed, aromatic with jalapeño poppers and scarred coffee, yet the general mood was tense, with Trixie engaged in a jaw-gritting argument with Allie over her convulsive overspending. Yes, it's someone nearby wearing Allie's perfume that revives this scene: floral, close. And the youngest, the son, stared out at the snow with severe eyes, just like his mother's, not deliberating over optioning extra sour cream or ice with his Pepsi, but something presumably bigger, stonier. Son and grandson, father and husband. This was Owen at nine years old, asking the question clearly troubling him on the heels of Brother Bo's passing – Owen had barely even known his Paps beyond a few strained visits to that stuffy duplex in Lower Sackville, but the aura of death, the rituals of funeral and phone calls and solemnity, had stimulated the kid's wonderings; and just when the argument between mother and daughter grew really heated over the minutiae of Allie's failed film production and its botched accounting, Owen turned and asked, 'Dad, what happens when we die?' Before Parker could respond, he went further: 'What happens when I die?' The only answer his father could provide was: 'Whatever you want.' Obviously, this answer was incorrect. But those livid, querying eyes scoured him, begging for explanations, until Owen seemed to accept this half-assed answer.

Now it's too late. As the boy's father, he had an obligation to lie. He was supposed to steer his son toward honesty. In this, he fell short.

His phone vibrates. He waits, then checks the voice-mail message: it's Trixie, asking when he'll be making it for dinner up at Allie's place. He considers a reply, but tucks the phone away. That's all behind him now.

In the laze of the post-panel melee, journalists and junior delegates shuffle back toward the lobby. As expected, al-Durabi and his team circulate, shaking hands and grinning for photos. The Oakleys, as always, stay on. A platoon of African dignitaries poses for a group shot, arms in a brotherly link. Flashes flash.

Parker waves the cheap Pentax 35mm Adam recommended as a prop, squeezing through the bottleneck at the conference hall's doorway. It appears the entourage won't, as Adam projected, convene in the lobby. There is little sense of order, only an influx from an arriving shuttle bus and an unprepared staff. And those worrying minivans. Under his jacket and cotton sweatshirt, the sweat in Parker's pits collects into a hopeless swamp.

But: al-Durabi shakes hands with a procession of suits, delegates from Tokyo and Dubai, radiating the same effortless cool he does for dignitaries and press alike. This is it, Parker's moment to extinguish the flames, to crush against the pressure. This light of awareness came to him late in life, but now he sees: a predetermined trajectory has been there all along. It came late but hard, like a cross-court spike to the nose. He is here, but could be anywhere, tapping toes on ancient bones in the riled Montana dust.

The handlers surrounding the man stand equally enchanted by his swagger, providing Parker ample room to slither through. The man is two, maybe three arms' lengths away.

'Mr. President,' Parker tries.

His throat is dry, caked.

Again: 'Sir. *Hello.*'

Eyes on him now. Parker hoists the Pentax like a badge, as if it means something. Security refocuses; the man turns.

'Do we ever get to see those gleaming eyes,' Parker asks, 'without the shades?'

Al-Durabi sniffs, then grins, mugging for onlookers. Slowly, he lifts his Oakleys to his brow, showing faultless sclera and bronzeish pupils, eyes boyishly bright.

'Ta-da.'

There are titters and snorts. Parker too laughs; it actually is funny. Then he reaches into his jacket's inner lining.

'You have what you need?' al-Durabi asks.

It does not happen in slow motion, as cinema has led him to expect. It is quick and instinctive. In a sequence of indistinguishable simultaneous occurrences, he has the weapon out, he points and clenches, and in a thunderclap the idea becomes material. They are on him instantly. He is spun and slammed face first into the carpet with arms pinned at his back. Parker offers no resistance when his body strikes the floor, only an involuntary *gak*; he is lost, deafened by the ammunition's retort and the cracking of his own clavicle. Tears come as knees dig into his shoulder blades, but not from pain – the untouchable has been touched, the inescapable dodged, and there is only this: almost unbearable joy.

6

In its austere appliances and clutterless surfaces, the kitchen, redone this past spring, feels heavy with Lloyd's lingering presence: efficacy, function over form, tactility. Allie runs her fingers along the engineered stone countertops; to her joy, the contractors tracked down porous quartz slabs pigmented the precise shade of the new palette. Oil-rubbed bronze fixtures and refitted piping, slate tiling: her husband quietly insisted on sturdiness over sloppy craftsmanship. Diligence, dignity – early on, he instilled in his daughters the virtue of vigilance, never allowing things to be steered awry. His authority was gentle but inarguable. He laughed easily, though giddiness lay outside his repertoire. And there had been much laughter. Wintry afternoons were spent entangled together on the chesterfield at their first duplex's front window, man and wife palming teacup saucers, Bethany and Beatrix's hallway arguments at a distance and the beagle Echo Jr. on the rug. They stared out at neighbours' sedans trapped in snowbanks and a street disappearing into white. The snow seemed heavier then. But this was life before the Pik 4. After, she couriered ice packs of Icelandic graflax and hovmästarsås and boxes of expensive Japanese kozo paper, mailed off silver foil photos of her and Lloyd whale-watching in Alert Bay and slurping oysters in Abu Dhabi. At the time she thought it a crime how he refused to abandon his humdrum career, civil engineering for an obscure department with the province, rather than luxuriate in this newfound wealth. They were, after all, millionaires. In her fifties she could retire from teaching and lounge like an heiress. Yet Lloyd was not interested in doing so, and still put in his weekly forty-two hours. Though he indulged her dreams of grandeur and propulsion, and willingly unpacked boxes, whirlpool to whirlpool, the prospect of waking without a tidy shave and not matching shirt to necktie would, for him, be to participate in his own demise. So with the money, and all the idiocy that followed, came a gradual separation. This is her life's regret.

One supposes his finish was a regression, though Allie fought to think of it more like a retraction, a backward spooling of his acuity: a reply, not a loss. And yet he maintained beauty, even in his gradual vanishing. Yes, her husband was a beautiful man, as righteous and staid as engineered stone.

When you are bent over a hospital bed, dabbing froth from the lip of the man you once desired most, finding yourself tallying his funeral expenses and smelling his involuntary bowel movements, this is when you are most alive.

His death unleashed a dreaminess – suddenly it was auctions and Tuscany tours, the palatial home in Miami now belonging to that humourless Finnish couple, the promising investment in a chunk of land outside of Managua. So many foolhardy whims, so many days of dislocation. She patroned and executive produced like a fool. Played the ponies in Naples and drank expensive frizzante. The Anne Sexton biopic, once so plump with possibility, became just a woeful file and a stack of broken contracts, millions squandered. She went to Park City as a silly old lady, slapping her purse at premieres toward young directors with severe goatees. She drank iced gin in a hotel bar in Manhattan with an Israeli producer who proposed anal sex; she excused herself and fled to a taxi. Then she returned home, shamed with loss and litigation, unable to fathom how things went so poorly so quickly. Yes, it was practically criminal, and her present guilt is her penance. No one knew how bad it had gotten. No one but perhaps her lawyer, with whom she'd sought counsel after the production company had truly, finally, sunk the fleet. They'd met last week at a Coffee Time in a squally afternoon, and she'd supplied her battered stack of records documenting the outcome of this extended season of delusion and loss. He looked at Allie like her hair was on fire. *Not a financial analyst*, he said, but in his estimation the only person she should be suing was herself.

Perhaps the florists on Eglinton bear pity for her standing order, those same gerberas and irises, week after week. Surely they disdain a devoted widow's grief, a tortured life of mournful Sundays. The lanky kid with the nose ring likely scoffs as he snips stems and bundles her bouquet, inwardly amused at her obedient march past graves, hands folded, irrelevant in her sadness. Twenty-nine dollars plus tax every week, prepaid, capitalized on her monthly statements, only to be rinsed away by rain or broomed off by some custodian. So she is indeed cruel and unworthy in cancelling the account, as she did in efforts to exercise some fiscal discipline, further offending the marital contract in its harbours of duty and honour, breaching a pact staked in wind and kisses, way back when. Years resculpt futures and everything goes to soot. Under the sun-ruined grass and soil lies the body of the man she loves, loved. He disappears, and there is nothing sadder than that, nothing.

Field greens in the glass bowl, wooden tongs submerged into the base. Chicken thighs, roasting. San Pellegrino, a chilled rosé, warmed baguettes, all at the ready. Cool air and soft light seeping. Cutlery divided and shining. Despite a spatula misfire, oil spilled on the new hardwood, all remains calmish. An atmosphere of garlic and oveny heat and Raid: this summer has found the veranda besieged by blackflies, so the dining room becomes central, screens screening and fans fanning. Stereo seeping alto saxes and timbales. Place settings set. Upstairs to fetch the A535 for the pesky bursitis. A glance in the mirror, a delinquent blotch irritating the glass. Water dabbed under her eyes to clear eyeliner destablilized by tears.

Allie is restocking toilet rolls and hand soap in the second-floor bathroom when she hears her daughter's car pull up; with this, her anxiety is renewed. Beatrix wobbles under the weight of the crate cradled in her forearms: the new crank bearing and parts for the CoreRigour2LE Home-ConFig that has had such a fretted history. She's almost lost track of the whole hoo-ha. Initially Parker had suggested to Allie she simply test-run a demo, but she expressed reluctance; to her, these strange machines were too remindful of archaic torture devices – things meant to break, not to build. Then, spurred by an *Oprah* exploration into the long-term digestive and pulmonary benefits of spinal realignment, she'd wincingly resigned to accept some sort of toning apparatus; unfortunately, by that time the window for Parker to easily slide her a comp model had closed. And yet, even with it not being any big deal, Parker, being Parker, couldn't just refuse, and kept promising it could be done, despite her repeated retractions. If she really wanted the thing, she'd just write a cheque. But Parker seemed so deflated by any suggestion of his inability to provide on his promise. All of this had remained mostly undiscussed and kind of touchy until May, when he'd left Allie a message, reporting from the echoing warehouse itself, that he'd finally been able to locate an unshipped CR2LE, and was himself watching it being loaded on the skids, and he or whoever would lug it over. Weeks passed. Then one morning a Purolator truck backed into her driveway to dump the five-foot box on her welcome mat. Yet even then the DynaFlex set missed a necessary joint bearing, so the thing in its complication was sentenced to forgettability in the spare bedroom downstairs. Another failed ambition. All that remains is only circuits and plasma; everything else is just bank notices and camera flashes and patience. And then you go, and those you love mourn your passing as their own. And that's all it is. No reason to shed any more tears than have already been shed. Fix your mascara, move on.

Allie opens the door as Beatrix humps the replacement thing onto the front doorstep. Unlike most women in their lineage, she is gifted with considerable upper-body strength.

Trixie touches the sleeve of her mother's blouse. 'I like this. Frills.'

Allie laughs. 'This fucking thing? Whatever.'

Trixie heads into the kitchen. Something troubles her daughter, but Allie doesn't let it become a matter of concern; if something needs to be said, it will be said. As Lloyd decreed: all in due time. For now things continue truly, ordinarily, shaped only by simple function and desire, by want and need, the usual systems. This is how it goes. In the end, it's all kind of pointless, nothing.

Acknowledgements

This book was written and revised in Toronto and Montreal and Nairobi and Delhi and Chicago and Halifax. Many friends, foes, bandmates and barkeeps deserve my gratitude for laughs, support and needed distractions. Endless thanks to Alana Wilcox for her patience, talent and kindness. Likewise to the esteemed Evan Munday and everyone at Coach House for making things happen. Kudos to Bill Kennedy for getting it. Thanks to the Canada Council for the Arts for money; please send more. Thanks to Janet Benvie for everything. Thanks to Stephanie Stonehewer Southmayd for love. 'Pay to Cum' is a song by Bad Brains. Lyrics by H.R.; reprinted as an epigraph with the generous permission of Bad Brains Publishing. Quotations by Arthur Rimbaud come from *Rimbaud Complete* (The Modern Library, 2003, translated by Wyatt Mason); your edition may vary. Excerpts by Ryszard Kapuściński are from *The Emperor*, the 1989 Vintage edition translated by William R. Brand and Katarzyna Mroczkowska-Brand. Lines from Federico García Lorca are sloppily lifted from *Sonetos del Amor Oscuro*, an edition now vacuumed into somewhereness. Samuel Coleridge quotations are from an old banged-up *Norton Anthology*. The quote from William 'Refrigerator' Perry is something I heard a few years ago. My deepest appreciation to all these geniuses, and to you.

About the Author

Rob Benvie was born and raised in Halifax, Nova Scotia, and has since split his time between Toronto and Montreal. His writing has appeared in many print and online publications, including *McSweeney's*, *Joyland*, *Matrix* and *Broken Pencil*. In his musical life he has recorded and toured internationally with such endeavours as Thrush Hermit, The Dears, Camouflage Nights and Tigre Benvie. He is the author of *Safety of War*, also with Coach House Books.

Typeset in Whitman and Franklin Gothic
Printed and bound at the Coach House on bpNichol Lane, 2011

Edited and designed by Alana Wilcox
Cover design by Bill Kennedy

Coach House Books
80 bpNichol Lane
Toronto, ON M5S 3J4
Canada

416 979 2217
800 367 6360

mail@chbooks.com
www.chbooks.com